Ebook ISBN: B0BQ53X14F

Paperback ISBN: 9781916521148

Publisher: Dirty Talk Publishing

Editing: Mom Loves Books Editing and Proofreading

Cover Design: Maddison Cole

Formatting: Emma Luna at Moonlight Author Services

CONTENTS

Deprived beings bonded by the Eternal flame make the trickiest captives.

Divided.

Disconnected.

Yet stronger than ever.

I don't need to see my men to feel them; the hum of their raw power simmering beneath the cuffs clamped around my wrists. Christopher may have us trapped once more, his mocking laughter echoing around the walls of the asylum, but he's overlooked one simple fact. With my harem, I am fierce. Without them, I'm feral.

Dying is no longer an option. Hiding in Hell is a distant memory. A war has been waged upon the Mutes, and it's not just Christopher in my sights now. It's the entire human race. Whatever it takes, whatever I have to do, I will be free of these stone walls and the world of poverty beyond. If an uprising is needed to gain the Mutes equal rights, then I'm prepared to fight. For love has found me in the most unlikely of places, and Hell hath no fury like a mutant scorned.

AUTHOR NOTE

TRIGGER WARNING

This novel is the third and final in a dark paranormal RH trilogy. Certain themes such as sex, self-harm, death and controversial beliefs are featured. However, those who always fall for the twisted, deranged villain and never question their own sanity about it, then come on in. The Afterlife Asylum is the place for you.

If you enjoy the All My Pretty Psychos series, please consider leaving a review on Amazon and Goodreads.

Reviews help authors get more recognition and promotion, and it's also helpful to get your feedback.

If you find any spelling or grammatical issues in this book, please don't report them using Amazon's new feature.

Instead, contact me using the details at the back of this book, and I will ensure they get fixed straight away. Contacting me directly ensures it gets fixed quicker.

Please also remember that despite being a UK based author, this book is based in the US, and uses US English spellings.

Thank you for reading and supporting me!

DEDICATION

For Stephanie Linn.
Thank you for your support and
enthusiasm for my work!

REIGN OF CHAOS

ALL MY PRETTY PSYCHOS BOOK THREE

MADDISON COLE

A scream reverberates through the hallway.

Another slice of agony flays my soul bare of any strength I may have mustered since the last round of testing.

As much as I know I should clamber to the hatch in the door and shout back to answer Ghost's bellows and let him know I'm okay, I can't. Instead, I take the pussy option and shrink back further into the corner of my prison, clamping my hands over my ears.

It doesn't help.

There's no hiding from the suffering of my men. They're too busy roaring inside my skull.

Who knows how long has passed since the day we watched Christopher's mirage of a labyrinth dissolve and reveal we'd never left that damn asylum. Scratch that - Pyro and Hoax never left. Ghost and I were actually free.

That's the most damn frustrating part of this entire situation.

We were walking the streets, hunting for a purpose. And the only one we found brought us right back, instead of working on a legit plan to rescue those we love. We took for granted those precious moments of freedom we weren't even truly sure we had.

So yeah. Instead of continuing to scream, resist and lash out - I'm working on understanding the heat continuously erupting inside of me, despite the freezing cold cell. Every once in a while, plumes of frigid air leak from an overhead vent, intensifying the juddering of my jaw. Yet the state of my physical body pales against what's happening on the inside.

Fires rage against the confinements of my chest, threatening to combust from my skeletal body. There are four distinctive strands, each bringing a different flavor to the back of my tongue. Sweet to spicy, light-hearted to dangerous. Although, at the moment, everything has faded away, leaving only terror in its wake. Tainted by guilt for so many reasons, I've come to recognize my individual flame as the one coated in bitter ash.

A light flashes at the door's hatch, a torch searing my retinas as I hiss and curl further into myself. Satisfied I'm still alive, despite the lack of food I've been given, it disappears, leaving me to my reprieve.

The shadows have become my friends, the damp stone surrounding me a welcome balm to my burning hot flesh. Steam passes my lips, clouding the dimmed area before me. If I squint and block out the screams and my thoughts, I could easily imagine I'm in a sauna. I hold onto that sweet, fleeting fantasy until Ghost's next roar of anguish, my name sinking through the walls. All the while, beyond the ability-subduing cuffs tightened around my wrists, my fingers tingle with the need to expel fire.

Sinking my head onto my raised knees, a tear leaks from my eye. The comfort of a hand stroking the tear away warms my cheek, yet I know he's not really here. Fuck knows where any of them are, but Pyro always knows how to find me. His spirit won't leave me to succumb to my own pity, won't allow me to give in when all hope seems lost. My constant companion, the foundation of my very soul since he first laid eyes on me. To do anything but fight for us all would be an insult to the life he's given me. As soon as I've figured out how to stand upright without the pain of their suffering threatening to slice me open at the seams.

The deadbolt shoots open, like a bullet in the dark making me wince. Before I can see who's invading my privacy, a shock of electricity bursts from the cuffs, sending my body into overdrive.

Writing on the floor, I refuse to let a single sound leave my lips in case my men are able to hear me. Adding to their suffering won't help any of us. Yet the resounding roar from down the hall echoes around my skull and I know it's pointless. They can feel me as easily as their own anguish poisoning the purity of our eternal flame, coating it with smoke so black, that its only purpose is to snuff us out.

Gloved hands grab my upper arms, dragging me from the solitude of my darkened hole. Not that I wanted to remain alone and forgotten, but I needed more time. I need to understand the cues, to learn how to communicate with more than flares of longing. Our souls are bound, and that has to equate to more than playing into Christopher fucking Gordon's hand.

Cracking my eyelids against the sporadic lanterns lining the dank hallway, the rough stone scraping against the skin on my dragged feet glistens with a trickle of water between the cracks. Giant doors of chain and metal sit side by side, only one threatening to burst from its hinges.

"Ghost!" I shout, a flare of energy banishing the electric volts sparking at my wrists. Not even the hands on my arms can hold me as I break free with surprising strength, and throw myself against the small hatch.

"Mania," a pained growl sounds in return. A slip of light casts over Ghost's hunched frame, the clinking chains hindering his movements attached to the very door I'm pressed against, sending another shudder through the damn door. "Don't let them take it! It's ours!" he roars, struggling against the binds in an effort to get closer to me.

Pressing my hand over where the rusted chains seem to attach to the inner wall, a bolt of energy races through my palm, despite the cuffs. Ghost's left side falls free, giving him enough freedom to rip free of the others. I've never seen him like this. A feral glint in his milky white eyes, a snarl etched into the blood coating his lips. More crimson coats his tattooed chest which slams into the door and his fingers latch around mine on the hatch.

"It's ours," he repeats in a whisper this time, his face inches away, yet too far. I need to feel his mouth on mine, to reassure him I'll be okay. I don't need any context to know what *it* is, since Christopher has been vying for our eternal flame since Pyro created it as a lovesick boy at an MRA orphanage. Ghost's anger subsides for a fleeting second, revealing the depths of his distress concealed underneath.

"They'll never take what's ours," I vow with a brief nod when a baton slinks around my neck and tears me backwards. My cries are nothing compared to Ghost's bellows of fury, the whole wall shaking as he throws his weight against it again and again. When I catch one last glimpse of his face through the hatch, blood pours from his temple, leaking into his beautiful white eyes that hold so many words he can't bring himself to voice right now.

Instead of continuing to struggle against the broad chest at my back and baton at my throat, I let myself relax and focus on what I can control. Sending a pulse of love directly into Ghost's chest, he draws a single, sharp inhale from the hatch now fading into the background. *Received safe and sound*, I muse to myself instead of resisting the pull on my throat at being dragged along the hall towards a steel door at the far end.

Now I'm more in tune with my senses, the coppery tang of blood and desperation surrounds me. I breathe in deeply, fueling the bloodlust that's going to see me out of this asylum with all of my men by my side. Even Hoax, regardless of whatever brainwashed perception of Mutes he has now. Christopher may have warped his mind, but his soul aided our bonding. He's in there, somewhere.

The steel door opens automatically, released by a guard on the other side hovering over a surveillance screen. Fluorescent lights blare overhead, drawing my attention upwards to the stubbled chin jutted out overhead. A badge scrapes the back of my head as I twist, spying the deep royal fatigues of an MRA agent. He doesn't meet my gaze or loosen the grip of the baton until I'm pushed into a room bathed in a clinical smell.

A hospital bed takes up most of the room, the shackles in all four corners drawing a growl from my blackened lips. Trollies have been pushed against the walls, giving the illusion this isn't the room's usual purpose but they're rolling with it. Thinking of illusions, I grit my teeth, remembering that the Mirage twins are firmly on the top of my shit list, just below Christopher and Camo. Fuck it, and the

Blacksmith. To be fair, it's not so much a list as it is a pile of signed death warrants.

The shift of a white lab coat draws my attention to a frail figure bent over one of the trollies, preparing a tray of vials hosting different colored liquids. The brightest oranges to the most vibrant blues. Beside them, a row of needles sitting along the edge makes me feel sick, until the woman straightens and doubles that nausea into a full-on retch.

A ponytail of lilac hair tumbles down her back, her purple eyes peering out from the swollen welt of bruising. White straps band over her nose, her jaw a similar black and blue with a hiss being pulled from her split lips as she fully rights herself.

"Please, don't fight," Tate begs of me. The guard removes the baton from my neck, shoving me a step into the room to close the door.

"Or do fight," he sneers. "Either would be just as entertaining." I ignore him. My glare directed towards Tate as she gestures for me to willingly hop onto the hospital bed. No fucking chance.

"What the fuck are you doing? Ran straight back to your master?" I spit but the venom soon runs dry. It only takes one look at the misery in her lowered gaze, the defeated hang to her head, the limp in her step, to know Tate hasn't broken by choice. Christopher has got to her, and not even the lack of cuffs banded around her wrists is enough to find the strength to fight back.

"Just give him what he wants, and he'll let you all go free," her small voice drifts across the room and I snort.

"You know that's not true. He'll never let his prized Mutes stroll out of here." Not without his white hair clutched in my fist, a jagged tear along the seam of his throat. An image assaults my mind, one so real I can hear the drip, drip of blood hitting my boot. Arms band around the lace corset clinging to my body, a husky whisper of freedom drifting into my ear. I shake my head, knocking Ghost's vision aside to concentrate on the scenery on Tate's face.

"He will if you're not Mutes anymore," she whispers. My heart freezes over, dread coursing through me as the guard behind has enough of waiting. Slamming his elbow into my head, he is swift as a lion, catching his prey when I topple aside and before I know it, I'm strapped to the bed with my limbs extended in all directions. It's times like this I really wish my bite was as fierce as my bark.

A mix of conflicting emotions clamor around my being, all fighting for my sole attention. Ghost's desire to rip apart every being here, human, Mute or other. Pyro's soothing caress, easing the toxic taste of my rising panic, and somewhere in the background is a confused and stoic Hoax. He may not be as comforting as the others, but he's there and that's all that counts. Simply by breathing, he soothes me in his own kind of way.

Releasing the tension from my body when the inner strength I'd managed to find at Ghost's cell fails me, I watch Tate keenly. Her eyes are glazed with tears, which isn't ideal when she's strapping a cord around my forearm and lifting the first needle of many.

"You're not going to struggle?" she cocks a brow, pausing mid-motion.

"What's the point? You have your ability to debilitate mine and take what you want anyway." I attempt a shrug, noting the guard's watchful glare. He doesn't blink in favor of drinking in every movement, and after a beat, it's not just me he's watching. It's Tate.

"Mania, I know this isn't ideal," I give Tate pause with a bitter laugh, "but trust me, it's better than the alternative. You don't want to see Pyro right now."

"Wait, what? What the fuck is-"

"Enough talking. Get on with it," the guard kicks the bed and I wobble beneath Tate's already shaky needle. Steadying my breath, I flutter my eyes closed.

Ghost is pacing around my subconscious like a bull in a China shop, threatening to pierce me with his horns if I don't ease his psyche. Flashbacks to the mechanic monster in the maze rise a shudder from my otherwise limp limbs. Been there, died by that. Stroking him with my inner flames, I push my attention towards Pyro. He's there, as always. A wall of comfort, a cape of solace I can escape to. But delving deeper, I hint a twinge of pollution in the water. A drop of oil in his ocean of purity.

A sharp scratch against my left forearm draws my gaze back to the present, and the horrified twist to Tate's features. Given my dulled senses and lack of humanity, I know why I should be alarmed at the fact I could feel that but her concern is what worries me.

Following her eyeline, I spot the needle pressed against my vein, or rather - the stubby remains of what was a needle. The rest of it has splintered off to lay on the sheet by my head. Before I can contemplate the lack of hole in my skin or how the guard rushes forward in equal shock, Tate speaks. Low, dread-filled words that will play on repeat long after I'm discarded back in the cell.

"This is bad. Really fucking bad, for us all."

Murmuring voices combine, my head too heavy to lift. Beneath my closed lids, shadows dance like tumbleweed in the wind. I don't know where I am. Hell, I struggle to remember who I am, but the small smile that pulls at my lips leads me to think the gentle breeze on my blazing skin isn't a notion I've felt for a long time. Light spears my face and with enough imagination, I could pretend it's the rays of an unforgiving sun until a shadow looms overhead and breaks the illusion.

A rubbery mask presses down on my face when the voices become loud enough for me to murmur back. My memories swim and I spiral back into the dazed clutches that have me so tightly in their grip.

There was pain at first. An excruciating agony I thought I wouldn't survive, but just as quickly as it started, it ended. Or my body gave up fueling the energy it took to scream into the dark abyss I can't escape. Now, there's only silence. The quiet of my spirit tethering on the edge, choosing to focus on something else. I'm not sure what it is, but it saves me from wasting away all together.

Safe beneath the surface, a golden light coaxes me into its warm embrace. Like a hug from a long-lost love, and despite not being able to make sense of anything else, I know I must protect it with my life.

To coat it with the fires battling inside me for control, to shield it from the voices. If they take my light, the one thing I'm holding onto, there won't be any point in continuing on.

Time passes in both a single second and an endless eternity as I cradle the golden glow, a sharp stab at my forearm drawing me back to the operation table I'm stretched across.

Gasping, my eyes shoot open, panicked pants raking through my chest. Yet there's no one currently by my side and definitely nothing stabbing at my left forearm. Taking in the room for what feels like the first time, despite a twinge of familiarity niggling at my gut that I've done this before, I desperately try to commit the sights to memory. They might help me to remember where I am.

A white cover hangs from metal poles, blocking the view of my chest downwards. Those lurking shadows pass instruments behind, like a puppet show for my personal amusement. Just in view, screens flicker with numbers and a heartbeat monitor confirms I'm alive if nothing else. In a hellish purgatory, but alive.

The lights are too bright, the smell too offensive to my rousing senses. I'm careful not to break my mental hold on the golden glow, using it as an anchor in case I don't like what I see and need a place to retreat to. The walls are powdered blue, matching the scrubs of a woman at the far station.

She's washing utensils, her brunette hair stuffed into a net and her hands also gloved in blue. As if feeling my gaze on her, she twists a straight nose and pair of doe eyes over her hunched shoulder. Familiarity flares there, mixed with sheer panic. Did she not want me to see her? Should I know who she is?

Breaking our connection and turning away, I consider the gentle hitches to her shoulders and conclude she's quietly sobbing. Why would a nurse feel the need to cry? Not for me I hope, because that just leads to more questions.

Twisting to place the cleaned forceps on a trolley at her side, the outline of handprints become visible on her slender neck. My vision bleeds red. The agony I woke to is a distant memory, and in its place, unhindered rage brews. Whoever this woman is, whatever she's aiding to be done to me, I know I care. My response to her being harmed is too visceral to ignore.

"He's crashing again!" a voice shouts, and the nurse in question whips her head around. Ignoring the sea of attendants in scrubs who appear from the other side of the white cover, rushing for trollies and a defibrillator, her widened gaze holds mine.

Don't, she mouths, slowly shaking her head. I try to ease the hatred burning through my veins, but the closer she steps and the more defined the bruised hands around her throat become, that decision is no longer in my control. My body knows what it wants, and apparently it's revenge.

Binds try to hold my wrists down but I snap them with a rough yank. Heat explodes in my palms and as I reach up to rip the curtain away, it simply sets alight and disintegrates. I keep my hands raised, staring at the orange flames licking my skin without a trace of pain. Blue tendrils sway amongst them, and lost in the trance of their beauty, a fuse snaps in my mind and it all comes rushing back. Mania, my boys, the asylum. Christopher fucking Gordon.

"Call Brainwave!" a shocked man half-hidden behind a surgeon mask shouts. I shake my head, forcing the lasting effects of whatever hypnotic bullshit so recently possessed me. There's nothing my fires can't fix, and even less they can't destroy. Moving to sit upright, I find my torso hindered but there's not a strap in sight. Instead, as the attendants rightfully flee for their lives, I peer down at the state of my body and hesitate. Is that...no, wait...where are my...organs?

From the base of my collarbone to below where my navel was, my skin has been sliced open and peeled back. I stutter over a gurgling sound in my open throat, the awkward angle of my head causing my breathing to shallow. I can tell because my lungs are right there, filling like a pair of whoopie cushions after each exhale. Unprotected and exposed, thanks to the lack of a rib cage protecting where my heart *should* be.

Its actual location is in a jar on the far countertop, a single tube penetrating the aortic valve connecting my heart to a machine that's running diagnostics like I'm a fucking car engine or some shit. In my chest, a small...for lack of a better word, machine...pulsates to keep the blood flowing through the visible network of veins running through me.

If my stomach were still present, I've have vomited then and there. As it stands, a wave of dizziness has my head rolling backwards just as a broad asshole in a suit enters the room.

"What's going on in here?" Christopher's voice booms around the theater. The nurses and surgeon shrink away from my peripheral vision and in no time, his sneering smirk commands my vision. "You know what I like about you Pyro, you're a fighter. I always thought you'd be the first to break, but here you are – thriving amongst them all."

My nostrils flare, my subconscious ordering me not to take his bait. I still have my mental hold on that glow and now I have the memories to understand what it is. My light in the dark, my escape at the end of the tunnel. The love I hold for Mania and my brothers that's seen me through, although admittedly I don't think it gets much worse than this.

Clicking his fingers, an army of MRA agents storm the room, grave scowls fixed onto their faces. Careful of the dimmed flames still crackling in my palms, despite the state of shock preventing me from doing much more, two agents take my forearms and clamp a pair of cuffs onto my wrists. The external flames die instantly, but not the ones that continue to rage on the inside. They roar within my skull, taking on an entity of their own.

The brunette from earlier, who I can now put a name to, steps forward with an oxygen mask in her hand. Claire is reluctant to place it over my mouth, until Christopher's glare makes her visibly flinch without him having to raise a finger. Three guesses where her bruises came from.

An apology glistens from her eyes and fuck it all, I force my lips to slant upwards. It's not her fault, and look at me. I'm not going anywhere until Christopher deems it so and has my body frankensteined back together again. All I can hope is for my mind to be intact when he does.

As if conjured by that thought, the doors slam open once more, filling the room like a circus ring. An audience fit to watch my reappearing act from death's doorstep. This time, a Mute with pale pink shaggy hair and freckles across his nose, and an MRA agent push inside, shoving to be first. The agent wins, rushing over with determination in his long strides.

The oxygen mask hovers an inch from my face, the sleeping gas just in touching distance to give me a gentle high. My body prepares to levitate me into a dreamland, my focus shifting in and out as Christopher listens to the agent whispering into his ear.

A cruel smile graces his face. Knocking the mask from Clare's hand, he swiftly slaps me across the face to bring my attention back to the present.

"You must think yourself real clever," his lip curls back in both humor and disgust. I can't even find it in me to quirk my eyebrow, my face numbed by the gas' paralysis. "Protecting your girlfriend from my experiments. As if we haven't got everything we need from you already. She was just a bit of fun," he chuckles and the MRA agents in the room join him.

Images I've never wanted to see or think about assault me then. Triggered by the mocking laughter, I can picture exactly what 'bit of fun' these uniformed assholes could have had with my soul mate and I'm lost. Spiraling with the cyclone etched into my being, letting it find every scrap of fire I possess and erupt within. Inside, the inferno blazes so hot, I temporarily lose my vision and hearing, aside from the roar of twisting flame inside my ear canals. Yet, despite all of that, the cuffs prevent any of the effects bursting free to flay Christopher where he stands.

"Fascinating," a voice cuts through my turmoil. Blinking some clarity through the red and yellow haze flickering in my irises, I find only Claire is still at my side. Reaching a hand out, she strokes the sweat-coated hair from my brow and looks towards the group huddled across the room. Light shines through the gaps in the crowd, urging me to hold my grip on reality. The MRA in front steps aside, giving a full view of the heart that should be in my chest cavity.

Gold. It's sheer gold, beating too quickly to track. The shimmering draws a tear to my eye, either from the beauty of it or the strain against the sleeping gas to keep my head cocked upwards. Like molten lava beginning to cool, my heart crusts over with a coat of black, just about allowing the golden singe to shine through as it eases back to a steady rhythm. The connected computer monitor is a chaotic mess of numbers and code, collecting every trace of data I just unknowingly gave them. My emotions, my love, my secrets.

And Christopher is in the thick of it, slowly turning to grace me with that malicious smile. He's right - he's now got everything he wanted and all I can do is lie here, hoping he'll have the good grace to put my heart back into my body. To let me return to Mania a somewhat complete man while he destroys whatever bond we've finally created. That's the goal right? Take everything I have and make me suffer as an onlooker.

"You know, I wasn't going to bother dragging this on any longer than necessary," he retraces his steps. Pressing his hands onto the table either side of my head, I can't help but notice the lack of wrinkles or blemishes apparent on his youthful face. The man staring down at me, with his refined jaw and glistening teeth free from whiskey stains, could be a younger clone of the man I first met.

"But the four of you are proving too entertaining to deny myself the pleasure. We've got everything we needed anyway. Why would I bother destroying the fine specimen you are myself, when I can let your own downfalls do it for me?"

Shoving away from the table, Christopher barks a series of orders as my mind reels. He whips from the room like a tsunami, leaving nothing but the wreckage behind. Even the MRA agents are swept up in his orbit, tumbling from the double doors that swing back into place. All except the Mute I can only guess is Brainwave.

A white sheet replaces the last and the oxygen mask lowered by a regretful Claire. No, not yet. I can't forget this. I can't forget my reason for fighting in fear I may just give in. Shaking my head, Claire places a hand on my cheek, muttering soothing words I don't want to hear.

The lights begin to fade, the room drifting into non-existence. Opening my mouth to protest, no sound follows and it's only then I realize my voice box is amongst the vital organs I've unknowingly had removed. Just fucking perfect.

Crumpled in the corner of my cell, silent tears fall in the dark. My weakness leaks between the cracks in my lips and fills my mouth with its saltiness. Drawing my knees up to my chest, a tender discomfort spikes in my chest and a sob becomes locked in my throat. Something's wrong. My heart is too tight to beat, too heavy to carry on. The air in my lungs escapes in short pants and nothing I do can calm the nerves racking across my skin. My thumb rubs absentmindedly over the crook of my forearm, where the needle should have pierced my skin.

None of Tate's tactics worked, not even with the cuffs temporarily disabled and her ability washing through me to quell Pyro's fire. My pale skin visibly glowed from the flames shifting beneath it, creating an impenetrable wall. So after quickly stepping out, the guard returned with the genius idea to use a more invasive method, and lingered to watch the entire time. A shudder rolls along my back - not from the cold. From shame.

I can't be this weak. I can't break this easily. Not when my men are suffering physically, hurting emotionally and being traumatized spiritually. There's no blissful reprieve of death awaiting any of us, so we have to make this life count.

I need to figure out how to tap into the old version of Mania that never used to give a shit and took torment in her stride. The one who'd have sussed out how to access the flames powering my being, despite the cuffs preventing me from them. Or maybe she's just a bullshit figment of my imagination. An over-inflated ego, boosted by Pyro's strength. But then again...why the fuck does it matter anymore? I'm here now. I have to do *something*.

Dragging myself up onto my knees, I drag myself back from the chasm of self-pity I can no longer drown in. With my hands placed palm up on my thighs, I inhale and exhale long and deep. My motives tumble from my lips in a mantra that I'll hold at the forefront of my mind.

Unite with my men. Escape Afterlife Asylum. Kill Christopher Gordon.

The tests I can handle, even if they become ten times as intrusive in Christopher's desperation to understand our eternal flame, his urgency growing each day. But the knowledge I'm the weak link in our group – that shit hurts more than the flames bouncing against the cuffs on my wrist and shooting back into my being with a bitter shock. Even they're telling me to get the fuck up and fight. Stop moping and channel the badass bitch you know is in there somewhere.

Unite with my men. Escape Afterlife Asylum. Kill Christopher Gordon.

Over and over, I repeat them back. My daily affirmation. My reason to carry on. Cool air gusts from the vents, enveloping the room in thick cloud. No doubt a tactic to beat me down. I feel the eyes on me, lingering in the shadows. I feel the hatred for my kind and draw on it for strength. I've died enough times to not fear my demons. I've risen enough times to know I'm never out of options.

Somewhere in the midst of my chanting, just as my body is filling with the willpower to believe I'm truly invincible, an alarm sounds. Red flashes outside the hatch in the door and a shock is sent through the power-binding cuffs. Dropping back onto my ass, I yank at them in turn, the searing of electrocution burning my wrists as the dead bolt to my door is thrown aside.

The shadowed figure responsible waits until spots prickle in my vision before storming in. Untied laces whip about his army boots, close to smacking me in the face when he stops short of trampling on my head. Heaving me upwards, I'm powerless. We've done this dance before. Hands clench my biceps, a firm chest bumps my back. Except this time, we're not the only ones in the dimmed corridor.

"Mania!" Ghost flies out of his guard's hold, sending the MRA agent crumpling into the opposite wall, only to be hit with another jolt of electricity through the cuffs. The only difference is, like before, a similar restraint has been hooked around his neck. Coated in blood from his broken nose and busted lips, the shackle sparks from the weight of voltage being shocked into his system, yet his steps barely falter. Ghost stumbles towards me like a man possessed, a crazed, hungry look in his white eyes.

"Please-" my words are swallowed in the trap of Ghost's lips, his tongue urgently seeking mine. I don't know what I was going to say anyway. Something stupid along the lines of run, save yourself, but we're well past that. I know with the same certainty that his hair is white that Ghost will never leave me behind.

Strong sweeps of desperation coil around my senses, all tension draining as I slump back and surrender. Held in the tightened grip of a guard, I give myself to the beautiful male coated in blood and a craving that can't be quelled by me alone.

We all need to be together.

As soon as the thought passes through my skull, I know Ghost heard it. Maybe not in words, but he breaks away as the agent beyond his shoulder rights himself, briefly resting our foreheads together.

"I can't fucking wait Spitfire." Milky eyes glow back at me, solidifying our silent vow just as he's ripped away. It takes a monster of a man to make Ghost appear small, and the scars highlighted along the agent's jaw, neck and arms suggest he's not all man after all. They brought in the big guns to deal with Ghost. Yet the agent doesn't bother trying to subdue him. Instead, the tell-tale click of a safety latch being knocked off sounds just before a firm, cold instrument is jammed into my side.

"Obey, or we'll shoot," the agent growls. Whipping a pistol from his hip, he also levels the gun in line with my forehead and Ghost growls in submission. Tension ripples through the air, sliced apart by the door in between the four of us opening of its own accord.

A slender figure strolls out, his eyes unfocused. Without raising his head, he wanders through the center of the hallway and starts to make his way towards the steel door at the far end. As if we're not even here…

"Hoax," Ghost whispers, pulling on our internal bond to get his attention. I join him, intensifying the fires and directing them into the broad back walking away. Hoax pauses mid-stride and my heart is fit to burst.

He felt us.

Peering back over his shoulder, the nearest lantern permits me a real look at his handsome face. Indigo hair pushed back from his pale face, contoured by the gauntness of his cheeks. There's no fight held in his relaxed stance, nor a single blemish upon his tattooed torso. Wires inked into his skin illuminate with the flames tucked beneath, zipping to and fro like a living circuit board controlled by the mechanics of his being. Endless purple eyes rise to ensnare with mine, stealing the breath from my lungs.

My heart cramps as I barely resist throwing myself at Hoax. Screw the guard holding me in place or the two guns threatening to end me once and for all. Whether he's the spirit I fell in love with or a solitary drone of Christopher's amusement, Hoax is finally here, within arm's reach, after months of yearning. And helpfully not hell-bent on killing me at the present moment.

Regarding me with no recognition, Hoax's eyes slide to the flashing light of a surveillance camera above the steel door. The lock releases, the door opens itself and the figment of my heart's desire strides straight through. It's only as he steps into the elevator shaft and leans against the railing I realize Hoax hasn't been imprisoned in cuffs and a dirty jumpsuit like Ghost and I.

Not mentioning how the lengthy hallway I was dragged down either is no longer there, the guards shove me forward and Ghost is forced to follow of his own accord. Well, if he doesn't want twin bullets tearing through my flesh. My bare feet shuffle against the stone ground, reaching the open door's threshold where the guard at my back abruptly shoves me inside.

Flailing through the air, the purple carpet imprinted with a CG logo comes closer while I reach out for a gold rail running around the length of the elevator. Instead, my cheek slams into Hoax's chest, my hands latching on his hips for stability. Staring up, swirling eyes regard me with the same boredom as the opulent elevator.

"Help her then, asshole," Ghost grinds out, swooping me up in his arms. He checks me over while I peer over his shoulder, noting the guards have remained on the other side of the door sliding closed. Good riddance.

Ghost crushes me into the steel band of his biceps, cementing me into a cage that stokes the fires between us. We could easily drop to the dank floor and take back the love that needs rekindling, but it will seem hollow in comparison. We need Pyro to bind us with his warmth. Setting me down, Ghost stumbles back against the railing, clutching his chest. I get my first real look at him beneath the artificial lighting and scramble forward to grab his face.

Tilting his chin up, the light spears the blood dried around his mouth, presenting a series of scarred holes around the edge of his lip line. Did they sew his mouth together? Fury pulls a growl from me, a guttural sound full of promised vengeance. More scars hide beneath the skull tattoos and red splashed over his chest, which continues to heave between pained grunts.

"What's happening?!" I call out, feeling the shift of the elevator's movements. Wherever we're being shipped off to, we don't have long. My fingers hover just over Ghost's torso, his brow beading with sweat.

"Shit, I-I don't know what to do. Tell me how I can help," I beg of him. All the while, under Hoax's watchful gaze. Not a twitch of a finger. Not an ounce of concern in his stoic expression.

"I'm fine, it's not..." Ghost cries out, showing it's not fucking okay, his nails digging into his flesh. "Not my pain."

"What the fuck is that supposed to mean? Who's pain is it?!" I half-scream but the answer is written all over his face. Motherfucker. Twisting, I grab Hoax by the hair and yank him down to my height.

He might as well still be a freaking spirit for all the reaction he gives, his steady and black stare unwavering.

"Do your voodoo shit and find Pyro. Now," I order. When he doesn't move, I release him in favor of grabbing his wrist. Slamming his palm against the elevator keypad, Ghost's next cry has my panic reaching fever pitch.

"Find him!" Not a word is uttered, not a hint of understanding dawning behind his gorgeous face. My own heart cracks at the thought of holding Hoax, having his skin connect with mine and breath fanning my face, but it's not him. Not really.

Taking a step back, Hoax's gaze follows his arm falling limply at his side. Standing between the two men I love, yearning to save the third, I'm at a total loss of what to do. Empty vows are useless if I'm not presented with the opportunity to see them through.

The door pings, sliding open to expel us into a setting I recognize all too well. An empty canteen spanning the center of a concrete building, the shutters of the kitchen hatch closed. The rear exit is open, displaying the manicured lawn and gym bleachers in front of a reinforced barbed wire fence. Hello Afterlife.

Jamming my finger on the keypad, I will the doors to close long enough for me to see Ghost through whatever has him screaming and writhing on the ground. The door begins to close and I drop to my knees, pressing feather light kisses along his jaw. Not how I envisioned our big reunion would go.

"I'm here my love, hold on for me." My words may have been muttered to Ghost, but the intended recipient was the other part of our soul who's currently channeling him. Pyro. That selfless, compassionate bastard who is somehow shielding me from his pain through it all. Ghost's back arches and a crack sounds from deep within, all as a heavy boot stomps in the way of the elevator door fully closing. I didn't even see Hoax move, but he can bet his ass the full force of my daggers are being glared at his back.

Dressed in the same fatigues as an MRA agent, Hoax strides into Afterlife without a care in the world. That's the cue, apparently, for guards to rush inside and haul Ghost and I out, kicking and screaming. My foot connects with a ribcage, my fingers clenched in two fistfuls of oily hair before I'm subdued on the ground. A knee holds me there. The concrete ground is a terrible cushion for my smushed cheek and in my eyeline, I watch Hoax stroll and plant himself on a bench seat, his back is straighter than a spike as he braces his hands on the table in front, palms down.

I know it's not his fault. I know he's been killed, resurrected and reprogrammed. But I'm finding it extremely difficult to remember how his spirit looked at me. Protected me. Understood me. That man's a distant memory and one of these days, I need to properly mourn that loss before it creeps up to destroy me.

Quelling my misery, I turn my attention to the Mute who needs my help more urgently. Ghost hasn't stopped bellowing, making him easy to locate splayed across another table. A guard holds each of his wrists and ankles, another primed with a baton. And worst of all, the thing that really strikes me that this a dire situation, is that he's not even trying to fight back. Ghost can't give up, he's the strongest of us all. Physically at least.

That's when I stop struggling too. Wrangling my arms beneath myself, I place my forehead gently on the ground. The coolness is a welcome balm, sinking further down as I close my eyes and breathe. Breathe and remember my mantra.

Unite with my men. Escape Afterlife Asylum. Kill Christopher Gordon.

It takes no time to tap into the eternal flame, to see it sway behind my eyelids. Four individual strands intertwined, moving to an invisible tune. Unsurprisingly, the purple thread from Hoax is dulled but present, like he was in spirit form. A white tendril sparks and shifts, constantly circling. Always spiraling and I smile to myself. Typical that Ghost's contribution to our Eternal Flame would be so erratic.

The core of the flame blazes in the center, as red and passionate as Pyro always is. The constant warmth of his love wraps around me like a blanket, the strength of his passion pulling me from one moment to the next. And in the mix of it all, the thinnest black thread that occasionally curls in on itself and glints with gold before straightening back out. Me.

Around me, mutters catch on the edge of my subconscious but I refuse to let them deter me. I'm too close, too focused on knotting my strand into that gold knot that could tie us all together. Somewhere, at some point, I realize Ghost has stopped roaring with the force of a lion, just before his consciousness jumps into our bond. Not to aid me though.

His whitened flame breaks apart from the top half of the eternal flame, only connected at the base to flare before me, creating a barricade from the pain simmering underneath.

"Stop protecting me from the pain. I can take my share. We're an equal team, you stubborn asshole," I grunt, pushing my hands onto my chest with more force. Ghost doesn't waver in his attempts but I manage to smash through his reservations regardless, instantly consumed by Pyro's agony.

Bitter enough to make me gag, thick smoke appears to coil around the precious flame alight within. It may only be a single wisp created by our bond, but it's hotter than the whole of hell. Purer than water, rarer than diamonds, and it's all ours.

Through the blackened smoke in my mind's eye, I peer closer to spy the golden cluster in the center. Somehow, I managed to tighten my hold and anchor us down. Don't ask me how, and I probably couldn't repeat it, but the pleasured shiver racing through me couldn't care less.

Waddling through the smoke, the weight dragging against my spirit like a boggy swamp, Ghost's heat is right there alongside me. We stretch out, trying to pull Pyro free but he remains just out of reach. Our souls hindered, we stumble, stuck in place no matter how hard we push. We're not enough.

My physical form is hoisted from the ground, tossed around like a salad until another hard surface slams against my front. A groan is forced from my lips, my eyes cracking despite my desperation to remain in the bubble Ghost and I created. Purple, swirling eyes await the other side of my narrowed gaze, the inked circuit in Hoax's neck pulsing with underlying fires. *Fuck it.*

Pressing my eyes closed once more, my mind thoroughly hell-bent on protecting Pyro's flame, my hand pats around the table until it connects with Hoax's. Gripping his fingers in a punishing grip, I thrust his fires into our hold, giving us the last shove through the smoke to connect with Pyro. Wherever he is, whatever they're doing to him, he'll be able to feel us there. To know we're here and waiting, so no matter how bad it gets, he needs to pull through. He has to come back to us.

A blunt object connects with my side, my name being shouted by a graveled tone I don't recognize. Therefore, I don't give a shit. The weight hits me again, but I barely feel it. Nothing matters as I permit a portion of the agonizing smoke tormenting Pyro to seep into my soul and temporarily relieve him of the burden. Ghost does the same, and Hoax – although I doubt he even realized it.

Remaining there for too long, long enough for at least one of my ribs to be broken by the impatient guard, the tornado of smoke begins to dissipate around us. It refuses to fully disappear, but simmers down until Pyro's desperation for aid isn't so fierce. My limbs grow heavy and my eyes cemented closed for a whole other reason as the energy seeps out of me.

Shifting, an unexpected smoothness graces my cheek. Twitching, an unwanted absence greets my fingers. I force my eyes to crack open to take in my surroundings, just about making out the features of my old asylum room before I'm tossed back into my imagination. I didn't feel my body being moved, but that only goes to show how deep in our psyche this bond can take us. To a place where we're untouchable to the outside world.

MANÍA

I wake first.

I know that as surely as I can feel the eerie calm within my being. Rolling on the thin mattress, a sharp burst of pain flares at my ribs but I quickly quash it down. Not a single sound passes my black lips. Sleep is a blissful reprieve from the reality that's crashing down on me, and it's the least I can allow my men.

Coldness prickles at my skin, notifying me Pyro is resting, wherever he is. Hopefully resting for him means he's also healing, because I can't think of the alternative. The faint spark that is Hoax hasn't risen either. A snore rumbles through my skull and I find it in myself to smirk. Ghost's presence is practically non-existent when he's asleep but when he wakes, I will fucking know about it. He's an energetic inferno that cannonballs against my subconscious, consuming all of my energy.

Remaining still, I peer around the cell. If I'm not mistaken, and Christopher's sick sense of humor says I'm not, it's the same room I was given upon my first visit at Afterlife. A metal desk sits against the opposite wall, a tiny single bed in fresh linen pushed against the other. But it's not all the same.

The blend of decor between a mental hospital and a fancy hotel has swayed more in favor of the latter. What used to be a railing of gray tracksuits has been upgraded to a locker, the door ajar to reveal a mixture of clothing inside. Candles litter the back of the desk, the wicks mocking me with no chance of lighting them. A fur rug spans the floor and the sight of cushions in matching fur makes me feel nauseous at the chance to taunt me. All of us, in fact.

But my eyes keep returning to the blossoming indoor plant springing free of a wicker basket base. Green leaves curl back, hanging towards the carpeted floor while pure white flowers break free of their confines. Curved at the back and hosting a singular yellow stem stands proudly in the middle. Peace lilies, ironically.

I inhale, drawing the sweet yet pungent smell towards me and feel my shoulders ease. Is the scent somehow drugged? Probably. Do I care in this moment? Not particularly. I merely appreciate the touch of greenery in my vicinity. The hint of humanity amongst the chaos that speaks of anything but.

Carefully and ever so slowly, I draw myself up without jarring the ribs on my right side. Still in the orange one-piece outfit from yesterday, I peel up the hem and withhold my gasp at the blue and purple bruising coating my side. When Pyro wakes, he'll send his flame to heal me, much like he has been after each round of experiments. But not yet. I can manage for now.

My toes touch the carpet, my legs shaky as I stand and hobble towards the bathroom. Chrome sparkles beneath the artificial light I switch on, a walk-in shower presenting itself to the last of my resolve.

Pointedly ignoring the mirror spanning the back wall, I ease myself out of the grubby jumpsuit. Across the counter at the back of the basin, a range of tiny bottles are presented in rainbow order. Not recognizing them, I inspect one closer, finding the name and logo for 'Gordon hospitality'.

It'd be safe to assume these are leftovers from the hotel chains Christopher set up to house his precious bidders during the Mute games. So, with all due respect, I kick my foot on the small pedal bin and scoot them all in. Except for a mango shower gel, toothbrush, toothpaste and the hairbrush on a glass shelf; those can stay.

Waiting for the water to warm, I step beneath the spray and a moan accidentally passes my lips. Instantly, a heated spike in my being responds. I gasp at the rush of emotion tumbling into my bloodstream, my vision briefly turning hazy. Like a being trapped inside, a beast paces around my chest, roused by the pleasure seeping into my skin. I thought it was Ghost at first, but something gives me pause. The underlying tug of hatred, the pull of deceit that gives the impression this being doesn't really want to be here.

I don't attempt to push him out though.

Squeezing a dollop of shower gel into my palm, I rub my body. I usually shy away from touching myself, hating the feel of bones protruding from my skin. Despising the lack of sensation at my fingertips that reminds me of everything I've been robbed of each time I died. But now, confliction flares. It's Pyro's flame that kept pulling me back from Hell, but it's also because of that I lost all traces of humanity, such as being able to feel my men in all their muscled glory. I can imagine though.

Skating my palms over my nipples, they resound instantly. Dipping my fingers into the indent in my waist above my hip bones, I picture the three of them standing around me. Caging me beneath the spray of steaming water. I crank it hotter, needing to test if the temperature could equal the fires burning internally.

The presence inside responds too. His flame flares, his interest piqued. He can pretend all he likes, but he can't change the bond we share. A smile pulls at my lips, a wicked flaring in my mind. Eager to test the strength of our connection, I slip my fingers between my legs, circling my clit. I feel the reverberation of his groan deep down in my core, mixed with the butterflies flittering around my stomach.

Mania. The husky voice echoes around my mind, a plea and a curse. I part my lips to breathe his name, to pick apart his barriers and unravel the truth hidden underneath, when the fire inside erupts.

White eyes explode behind my closed eyes, staring at me intensely. I welcome Ghost in, searching beneath his overwhelming presence for the other that's fading away. I reach out, trying to grasp for him but it's too late. That strand of the eternal flame ducks his head and bows out before we can finish what I started.

Heat travels the length of my arm, halting at the power cuff at my wrist. Ghost pushes his willpower against the cuff, attempting to take over control of my fingers. His brutally handsome face in my mind strains, the impatient tick in his jaw and hunger in his gaze only driving me to give him what he wants.

Pushing my hand back between my legs, I gasp at the spark of intensity sitting behind my clit. Ghost smirks then, his flame controlling my reactions from the inside. Stroking myself, my pussy clenches instantly. He works me into a frenzy without barely trying, working my body like his puppet. Rolling my fingers in even circles, I lean back against the tiles, relishing their coolness at my back. The heat of the water never does equal the inferno raging inside my core, my fingers are doused in heat with how slick I am.

A thud sounds at my door. Once, twice, and then it flies inwards. I scream, covering myself as a suited Christopher Gordon strides inside. Sharp, powdered blue suit. Crisp white collar, navy tie and dress shoes. The whole facade is firmly in place.

Through the misted glass separator, his icy blue eyes land on me instantly, refusing to give me any privacy. In fact, he stands frozen in place, his gaze scraping over the forearm clenched over my tits to the hand covering my lower region and everywhere in between.

Whatever he's looking for, he finds it. Evident by the cocky smirk that splits his face in two. If I weren't already naked, that cruel grin would strip me bare. Expose my secrets, bleed me dry and gut my confidence all at once.

"Get dressed. I want to show you something," he says coolly. Knocking off the water, I peer around for an escape route, but there's nowhere to go. Nothing I can do. Ghost's in my mind, asking questions, wanting to know what's happening but I block him out for now. I need to keep my wits about me for an approaching ambush at all times. Gesturing for the towel, neither Christopher nor the two guards that step in to flank him budge. Not that I expected a trace of chivalry from any of them.

I have to slip out from the protection of the glass divider and whip a warmed towel from the rack. Luckily, it's huge and comfortably covers me from breast to shin. Only once my tattoos, scars and bruises are all covered does Christopher turn away, striding back into my room. I hunt for something to stab him in the back with, my eyes rising to the mirror wall.

"Don't even think about it," Christopher's half sings without looking back. Huffing, I release the fist I'd made and follow. A set of folded clothing has been laid out on the bed, which Christopher sits on the edge of. A guard steps in between me and the bathroom as I reach for them, preventing me from retreating.

I get what's happening here - the whole beat down your prisoner's will tactic. What Christopher didn't bank on is my sheer stubbornness, and the fact I now have four willpowers beating around my chest.

Dropping the towel, I dress at my own pace. My body isn't anything Christopher hasn't seen before and the guard softly chuckling at my back is the same one that watched Tate examine me internally. I'm surrounded by perverts and fuck knows, they won't see me break. Due to this, I ignore the tight jeans and crop top provided and opt for the most unflattering outfit in my locker.

Once the tracksuit, which is about two sizes too big, is hanging from my slender frame, Christopher slowly stands. I notice the lack of his cane and the smoothness of his movements, years away from the frail man I was first introduced to. He towers over me, a permanent and unbeatable smile presenting his straightened, white teeth. Now I'm looking past the trap of his icy eyes, his hair strikes me as the biggest change. Cropped short and dark, not a whisper of gray in sight.

Shifting towards me, I fight against the flinch that tries to make me look weak. Christopher extends his arm, expecting me to take it and I scoff.

"You may appear to own me currently," I raise the wrist cuffs, "but I'm not yours. You want to play God, buy yourself a doll." Jutting out my chin, I walk past him to the guard at the door. Reaching beyond the wall of muscle, I twist the handle as Christopher chuckles. I feel him close the distance between us, feel him too close to my back as his mouth moves beside my ear.

"Why would I buy a doll when I could create one?" My blood runs cold at his statement and Ghost pipes up in my head again.

'Mania, what the fuck is going on?!' Placating him with a lie that everything's fine, Christopher scoops my arm up in his and we exit the somewhat safety of my room. Noise hits me the instant I step onto the metal platform overlooking the cafeteria below. The shouts of MRA agents, the grumbled protests of their captives. Hair colors of every shade and intensity fill the area, huddled together where the tables and benches are supposed to be. Like cattle being herded for the slaughter. Like Mutes being marched towards their execution.

"Where..." I shake my head in confusion. "How-"

"It's a beautiful sight to behold, isn't it?" Christopher beams, tugging me along the platform. I stutter, failing to understand, much to his amusement. "What? You didn't think I'd reopen my best testing facility with no Mutes to fill it, did you?"

Clanging of the guard's boots ring down, drawing everyone's attention from below directly to me. The Mute woman walking arm in arm with their evil captor, directly towards the set of stairs leading to the guard's headquarters. I swallow thickly, ducking away from the sea of narrowed gazes.

The shouting commences again, prisoner numbers being called out to step forward and receive their room allocation and a bundle of folded sheets. Keeping my head downcast, I'm able to watch through the holes in the ground without being too obvious. From the main security doors, two lines have been formed with plastic tape down the center.

Mutes are prodded along the right side via electric baton, edged into the growing crowd. Their ability-canceling cuffs are already in place. Most on wrists, some on ankles and the odd couple around their necks like Ghost.

An agent appears at the left side of the entrance, his hands wrapped around a rope. I slow my walking to watch and Christopher permits it. A round of bleating breaks through the muffled panic rising from the Mutes as the guard heaves a sheep reluctantly forward. Its white coat is massively overgrown, making it appear much larger than I'd expected. Two fierce horns protrude from its head, thick and coiled back on themselves. I shudder, my hand rising to my stomach. I'd happily never see a horn again in my life after what the mechanical bull in the labyrinth did to me.

Kicking out and bleating like mad, the guard manages to drag the beast into the elevator shaft below and keeps it inside until the door slides closed between them. Then he turns and shouts that's the last of the farmyard creatures and to bring in the wolves. Wolves?! I balk, tugged along once more by Christopher and nearly tripping up the stairs to the headquarters.

"What the hell is going on around here?!" I finally find my voice. "What's with the animals, and where is Pyro?" Typing in the buttons on the keypad, the guard permits Christopher and I entry as the electricity on my cuffs sparks to life. I scream, trying to remain on my feet but it's useless. The voltage races through my body, debilitating me from asking anymore questions.

"I'm taking back charge, that's what," I distantly hear Christopher reply. He steps over me and leaves then, no mention of Pyro's whereabouts coming from his sealed lips. I did learn one thing though. If the end game was just another round of testing, then this whole parade was just a show of power. A reason for the new Mutes to instantly hate me.

When the electricity rakes through me once more, it's enough to silence Ghost's screaming in my head. Instead, the agony blinding my soul is halved as he takes as much from me as he's able. I love him for that all over again. Luckily, there's a hospital bed on hand for a guard to heave me onto and a pair of nurses to wheel me away from the display of surveillance screens before I can get a good look. I said luckily, but I didn't mean for me.

GHOST

I f I thought I knew what the longest day had felt like before, it paled in comparison to this. Stomping around my cell, my stomach growling and anger simmering. It'll do no good to act out. The brief release of my knuckles pounding against the walls will go to waste when Mania's agony settles back in, worse than before because my attention was divided.

I convince myself that, by remaining behind and calm, I'm helping by taking the brunt of her anguish. This is different to last time, and I can only guess because Pyro isn't awake to protect her. And then there's Hoax. He's a useless piece of shit at the best of times but right now, I'm readying myself to beat some empathy into him. Force him to take his share of the pain we're all enduring while he wanders around, not a scratch on him.

The last cell door down the hallway is secured shut, the tread of a MRA agent's boots thundering across the metal platform to the staircase when my door finally flashes red and releases. I shoot out, hunting for...well, anything. Whatever was happening out here, whatever sounds were drifting beneath my door that made me question if I was residing in a fucking zoo, has gone.

None of the agents milling around downstairs give a shit about me thundering down the steps, sensing I'm no threat in these damn cuffs. They manage to lock the grate behind them as I reach the bottom step, and who should I find there but the indigo shell of a Mute who was once my brother. Sitting at a bench shoved against the fair side, his back is to me, a plastic fork in his hand.

Closing the distance between us in the provided navy, canvas shoes, I raise my fist and reel my arm back from the center point at the back of his head.

"Ghost!" Mania's voice rings through the asylum. Directly above, I spot her three stories up, being deposited at the top of the staircase by a guard who doesn't give a shit if she falls down or not. Judging by her grip on the railing and the sway in her legs visible from here, I'd bet my life on her falling. *Not a fucking chance.*

My feet thunder against metal, my thighs pumping to get to her in time. All the while, inside my chest, I boost Mania with the strength to hold on. To remain upright and conscious. Fists pound against the inside of the cells as I reach the second level, hollers yelling to be released. A voice breaks through the rest, deep and graveled yet distinctly familiar.

"Ghost! Is that you? Help me – I can't take it again!" I skid momentarily to a halt and that distraction proves enough to draw my strength away from Mania. Leaning over the railing above my head, she reaches out to me as her red eyes drift closed and her body sinks over the edge. I'm certain the guard disappearing into the safety of the headquarters has everything to do with her not crumpling to her feet instead, but there's no time to question it now.

Skeletal limbs free fall through the air. Black and red hair whips around her porcelain and bruised face. Like a weighted feather, she drops into my arms as if she was created just to be there. That's selfish as hell considering she's fated to be with Pyro alone but I can't help myself. I need to believe there's some divine power driving Mania and I together, or I'm just that asshole who wants whatever his brothers have.

"I've got you, Spitfire. You're okay," I mutter into her ear, pressing kisses along her neck. Through our bond, I feel her hunger gnawing deeper than my own. In the safety net of my arms, I leave the voice and chorus of hollering behind as I descend the stairs once more.

My canvas shoe connects with the kitchen door, helpfully swinging open instead of snapping my ankle. Whipping a picnic blanket out of a wicker hamper, which is totally out of place in the industrial kitchen, I spread it across a counter and place Mania on top. She hisses in pain and I hate the shame rising within. How is it Pyro can protect her so much easier than me, even when being tortured himself. Sure, it's his whole flame gig, but still...I'm twice as tough and a million times hotter.

First thing to hunt for – ice. Whole kilogram bags which I slowly lower onto Mania's body where the blood seeps through her t-shirt. I probably should look, inspect her wounds, but damn it. I know I can't see a single fucking blemish on her skin and not tear myself apart with the guilt shredding at my soul. Like a mini cheese grater preparing my innards to top a bolognese. Not the legacy I planned on leaving behind.

Ripping open a shitload of boxes containing new supplies, I grab several packets of cookies and rush back to Mania. A thin line of blood has trailed from her mouth, pooling on the silver countertop.

"Ahh fuck. Cookies need dipping milk, not blood," I mutter, dropping the packets. Turning away towards the refrigerator, Mania's hand brushes my arm in a weak attempt to stop me. It's then I realize what I'm really doing. Stalling. Linking my fingers in hers, I stretch just far enough to grab a stool and sit before her.

Dazed red eyes fix on me, a feeble attempt at a smile pulling at her lips. Brushing back the hair from her clammy forehead, my thumb runs the length of the crack to her furrowed eyebrows. My voice betrays me, rasping out in no more than a croak.

"What did they do to you, baby?"

"Nothing that can't be fixed." Despite the sweat beaded at her head, she shivers violently. Wrapping her arms around herself, I shrug off the sweater I picked from the locker in my room without looking. Jokes on me that it's baby pink with a unicorn in the center but I'm comfortable enough in my masculinity to pull off anything. Especially items of clothing the guards no doubt chose to ridicule me.

Using the corner of the blanket to wipe away the blood lining her cheek, I carefully slide the sweater over Mania's head. She looks way better in the offensive garment, even if it's not her style either. Leaning in, I press a light kiss to her mouth, using the connection to boost our flames. Once coined as an emotionless male, I'm surprised how easily these feelings of affection flood to the forefront.

Her lips quiver under the weight of love I pass into her, her breath hitching. My chest expands, the glow beneath us brightening. Mania's eyes peel open, twin flames trapped in her irises as I use my fingers on her chin to open her up to me. Sweep my tongue inside and remove the coppery taste of blood.

My cuff knocks against the counter, the threat of an electric shock sparking inside the rim. They can shock me all they like; nothing will stop our eternal flame from burning. A scuffle sounds nearby and I blink away the daze Mania has lulled me into, realizing we're not alone anymore. Not by a long shot.

"Ghost," Mania whispers, giving me a gentle shove. She slowly rises on the table like the dead coming back to life, while my white eyes roll across our audience. A stream of strangers with an assortment of hair and eye colors stand in the doorway, each chained to the one behind like the prisoners of Hell I saw in Mania's vision once.

The Mutes edge inside, watching us too carefully. Seven of them in total, snaking around the outside of the kitchen and heading to the refrigerator. Scooping up Mania, the blanket and the cookies, I make a move for the door the second it's clear, not once turning my back on these new Mutes. Distrust thickens the air until I'm out in the canteen, and that notice only gets worse.

Every cell door on the upper level has been released. Bodies swarm the metal platform, looking over their surroundings and the competition. I see it in their scowls, the way power radiates from a select few who have others banded around them with their heads bowed. First rule of dominating a new space, hit the ground running. A fight will break out any minute, I can taste it in the air. A fight I'll win, as soon as I see Mania to safety. She's in no fit state to stand up for herself right now.

A few Mutes take the lead, shoving through those crowding up the stairs. Mostly men with a single female leading their ranks. Short and stocky, hair the color of the sun on its brightest day. Her golden eyes set on Mania. Hell no.

Sensing my stress, Mania's arms hook around my neck and her face buries in my chest. Sounds bubble from her lips, none of them forming actual words and I swallow hard. She's fading out again, and with bodies barring me from shutting her in her cell and standing guard, my only option is to run out the open rear doors. I peer across the lawn, spying the sky-high electric fence. There's no use running when there's nowhere to go.

Floundering with the urge to fight in her honor, the Mute sitting at the bench catches my eye - his back still ramrod straight in my direction. He hasn't moved a damn muscle this whole time. Striding over with long, measured steps, I ease Mania into Hoax's arms.

"Any harm comes to her, I'll hold you personally responsible," I threaten. Hoax's head tilts ever so slightly, our connection still strong enough for me to sense his interest is piqued. Returning to the center of the space cleared of benches, I find myself soon surrounded. The ray of sunshine takes center stage, her arms crossed and lips pouted bitchily. Whatever remark she was about to make is cut short by an unadulterated laugh rumbling through the entire asylum.

"And you thought the games were at an end," Christopher chortles like a fat little shit hoarding the last lollipop in the store. I hunt for the source, finding a speaker mounted beneath the metal walkway. Directly beside a camera which adjusts its lens to capture the show in full HD.

"Whoever said work and fun couldn't be mixed didn't have the power I currently hold. Are you sure you're ready to take on the entirety of the remaining Mutated population to save your side piece, Ghost? Just so we're clear - they've all been thoroughly briefed on how Mania single-handedly tried to bring the end of your species in order to win a pathetic game."

My hackles rise, the sheer audacity of that asshole spinning our test of survival in his favor only being overshadowed by a sea of furrowed brows and snarls set in stone angled our way. I see how it is.

Round up the remaining Mutes and pitch us against each other. Males fan out, the veins in their biceps pulsing with the need to punch me. I smirk in the face of them all, taking my cocky attitude to the death.

"I'll do whatever it takes to keep my soulmate safe," I grind out, not being coaxed into acting irrationally by Christopher referring to Mania as my side piece. She's the epitome of what a male wants, needs and craves. A rare jewel; solid in substance, feisty by nature. So much so, she's enough for three of us.

Movement shifts behind me, a figure moving in my peripheral as I turn and swing in the same motion. A hand catches my fist, simmering red eyes melting away the remainder of my reservations.

"We both will," Pyro nods, taking his place by my side. Knees slightly bent, arms raised, not even the bruising covering his exposed skin holds him back from protecting what's ours. The first male that runs at us receives the full force of my rage and I chuckle as he hits the ground like a sack of shit.

You know what, *for once*, Christopher is right. He does 'currently' hold the power, but with Py back as my right-hand man and Hoax peering at Mania with a curious glint in his eyes, he won't hold it for much longer. The flaws in his plan are beginning to show, and every Mute added to my death toll only cracks the foundation that little bit more.

PYRO

My feet falter as I dodge another oncoming attack, the slice up the center of my torso tugging painfully. After the downstairs elevator spewed me out, I tried to heal myself fully before showing my face, but I couldn't stand and watch Ghost take on the entire asylum by himself.

A fist cracks against my cheek from a Mute with endless black eyes and wavey honey-brown hair. Stumbling aside, Ghost tackles him to the ground as I catch the amused smirk of the apparent leader to the three circling us. A female with golden hair and glimmering eyes. She knows I can't keep going. She knows Ghost can't take on the entire entourage at her back waiting for their pound of flesh.

But surrender isn't an option. We're the only two Mutes standing between Mania and a mob who believe she's the reason most of our kind are dead.

Grounding myself with an open stance, I lift my trembling fists once more, preparing for the next Mute to step forward. He barges through the crowd, pushing those around him aside with the sheer size of his frame. Even the cocky female at the front isn't saved from his bicep knocking her in the back of the head.

"Hey, what the fuck?!" she shouts, attempting to shove him

back. He doesn't falter in his strides, and it's only then I focus enough on the male crossing through our fight circle. The sheen of metal beneath his skin is mirrored by the inked chains spiraling his forearms. Eyes of molten lava ignore us completely. Ghost rises from the ground, about to pounce when I weakly hold him back.

"Ghost, look," I urge. Ghost freezes for a split second before shrugging me off.

"What the fuck is he doing here?"

The Blacksmith doesn't care to hang around. He cuts a path through those that surround us, only stopping when he reaches the closed kitchen shutter to tape a piece of paper on the front.

Wanted.

Kitchen staff to start immediately.

Duties include preparing food for all inmates and cleaning maintenance.

The Little Miss Sunshine smiles, raising a single hand to halt those circling us, hunting for blood.

"We call a truce. You keep your girl, we get the food." Clicking her fingers, the three bulky males forget all about us and storm towards the kitchen door.

"It's an employment position. You have to feed everyone or they won't survive the experiments you've all got coming your way." I try speaking to the entire crowd, trying to warn them of what to expect. But not a single one seems to heed my advice.

"Don't worry Sparky, we'll feed you," Sunshine smirks. I can only imagine what's cooking up in her brain right now. She may appear sweet and innocent, but looks are deceiving. The Blacksmith heads into the yard, more pieces of paper in hand and a roll of tape on his non-cuffed wrist. That bastard has full use of his ability and he's still choosing to aid Christopher.

Grabbing Ghost by the collar, I pull him back a step to stand by my side.

"Fine, take the job. But if one hand touches Mania, we're burning the entire kitchen to the ground with you in it."

A false promise, but something in my fiery gaze must convince them, despite these cuffs, I could find a way to do it. Sunshine inclines her hand, snapping her risen fist shut and making her grand exit to the kitchen's side door. The three males are waiting there to open the door for us, each pair of black eyes intently following her every move. There's a commotion inside and within seconds, a band of Mutes all chained together are tossed out on their asses.

"And what are we going to do?" Ghost hisses in my ear once the remaining crowd starts to dissipate. "Starve to death and be no use to Mania anyway?"

"I'll think of something," I growl back. Heading over to the bench where Hoax is still cradling Mania, I brush my hand over her cheek. Red eyes blink open, a wide smile greeting me without a blemish or trace of injury in sight. I stroke a thumb over her bottom lip, sure I saw bruises lining her face when Ghost carried her across the room. My eyes flick up to Hoax.

He doesn't move, his purple eyes fixed on the opposite wall. His arms, though, remain curled around Mania's body, cradling her to his chest. That bastard's in there somewhere. And he's completely cuffless.

"Well, since you're being so generous," I half shrug. Mania wriggles upwards to sit on the table, watching the three of us as I lift Hoax's hand and my t-shirt simultaneously. Mania sucks in a deep breath at the state of my torso, the puckered scar failing to hide the horrors that have taken place.

Pressing Hoax's hand to my abdomen, a rush of heat flares along the length of the line. Searing flesh tingles my nose, the sound of my skin sizzling causing me to squirm. His purple flame winds in and out of my skin, stitching our bond into the lining and repairing the internal damage. Ghost marvels at the fading of my injuries, grabbing Hoax's other hand.

"Oh yeah, I want some of that." Ghost rubs Hoax's fingers over his cheek, massaging away the rising welts from the fight. "Fuck, how do you get your hands to be soft Hoaxie? Is it moisturizer? I bet it is, the coconut kind." Hoax doesn't move, blink or even breathe. Not a flicker of a reaction in his deadened gaze. "You've been holding out Hoaxie, this is some magical healing shit you've got stored in here."

Separating his index finger from the rest, Ghost rubs it along his lips to heal the split and scarred circles there. Spreading Hoax's hand open again, Ghost runs it down the length of his shirtless body, rolling his hips and beginning to open his sweatpants waistband.

"Do you think he could give me a bigger-"

"Stop that!" Mania jumps forward, her tits crashing into Hoax's stoic face. She slaps his hand free from Ghost's hold and lets it fall heavily to his side. "Just because he's not reacting doesn't mean somewhere deep, *deep* inside, he's not curling up into a ball and crying for the help of a therapist. You will not force Hoax to sexually assault you, got it?!" Mania jabs a finger in Ghost's chest and then turns to point that index in my direction too.

"Hey," I hold my hands up, "The thought never even closed my mind." A smile starts to lift the corner of my lips and Mania melts, shifting to throw herself at me. Thanks to the boost in strength and healing I just received, I catch her with ease. "Fuck I've missed you, my love."

Yearning beats against my chest like a bollard, desperate to burst free. Now the adrenaline of fighting has waned, my passion reignites as I crash my lips against hers, not giving a shit who's watching. Ghost can jerk off for all I care. In this moment, Mania is mine.

Pulling her impossibly closer, my fingers trail her body, committing her to memory. Since the day she entered my life, I've ached for one simple day to enjoy her. Relish the feel of our bodies connecting, revel in the bond we're barely begun to understand. Mania's ankles lock at my back, her mouth open and willing. Our tongues shift between the need to devour and the want to savor what precious time we have.

"I tried looking for you," Mania breaks away, her head dipping into my neck. "Like in the maze when I could see through your eyes. I really did try," a hitch catches her breath.

"It was better you didn't see." I whisper, rolling my lips over her ear. There's not one part of her I don't want to mark. Lifting her head, I fall into the trap of her large, red eyes.

"What did they do to you?" Placing Mania back on the table top, I take her face in my hands and stroke away her concern with her thumbs. Even if I had an answer to give, I would withhold it. As it stands, I woke in a wheelchair not long ago, with a sore chest and killer headache. A guard pushed me into the elevator and as I twisted back, I just made out Christopher's suited frame standing beside an army of surgeons and nurses. Everything else is a blur. Whatever happened to me, I can't shake the knowledge that it was horrific.

"It's also better you don't know. Come on, I need some air." Linking my hand over her fingers, I hoist Hoax up by the back of the collar on his navy long-sleeved top. Similar color cargos cover his legs before a pair of clunky black boots. Why is he dressed like an MRA new recruit? Ghost doesn't seem to notice, too busy grabbing the packets of cookies and picnic blanket that have more than a few Mutes lingering nearby.

Eyes follow our every step. As do the cameras mounted in each corner. The sun has broken free of a morning mist, beating against my face when I step into the light. Mania peers back at the notice board beneath the canopy, spying the other job vacancies the Blacksmith has postered up. I don't bother looking too hard. The only job I need is to remain at Mania's side.

I walk her towards a lush patch of green grass far away from the burn marks left over from our time in the labyrinth. Racing to our side, Ghost's hand lands heavily on my shoulder as he pushes the checked picnic blanket into my chest. I nod my thanks, fanning it out for the three of us.

"This is super sweet but I don't think-"

"Perfect. Don't think." I interrupt Mania. Gripping her chin and tilting it upwards, I capture her lips again for a brief, yet passionate kiss filled with need. A need that's going to have to wait.

"He's right. Acting on instinct is the answer to everything," Ghost rounds us to interject. Mania pulls away from me, her lips still puckered and upturned in the simplest, yet most beautiful smile I've ever seen. Serene and for once, genuinely happy. "By the way, I've missed you too bro so it's my turn!" Ghost barges between us to toss us onto the ground. He clings to me like a gorilla and starts flipping our bodies around, rolling us across the grass.

"What the...fuck, Ghost - stop moving!" He does, with me on the ground and him straddling my hips. Mutes radiate towards us, curious eyes watching our every move. Hungry gazes hunting for weak spots.

"For one of us to just lay on top of the other would be gay otherwise. There's no tops and bottoms here. We're all Mania's side pieces," Ghost shrugs, an innocence in his manly face that reminds me of the playful child he once was.

A petite foot connects with his chest, dismantling him from my waist. Mania drops to her knees by our side, a 'come-hither' look in her eyes. The figures around us create brief shadows as they circle like vultures, not relenting for one moment to remind us threats linger close. Regardless, the two of us prowl on her like caged animals. Fitting, as Ghost's neck manacle knocks on my shoulder as I shove him aside to get there first.

Our mouths attack her at the same time, taking a side of her jaw each as we push Mania back onto the blanket. Hands roam, occasionally bumping into each other. I slip my hand up her pink sweater, needing to feel her skin. A tearing sounds and I pause to watch Ghost go full hulk, ripping the offensive pink material in half, right through the heart detail. It drops aside, clinging to Mania's arms like a cardigan and the heat in her eyes flares brighter.

In my chest, the same fire surges. The throes of passion battling to be freed. Coaxing the eternal flame to the surface, my hand slides over her delicate shoulders and Mania moans. Energy dances between my touch and her skin, amplifying all of our pleasure. Peering up, I spot Hoax standing just inside the only doorway, his purple eyes glowing. I raise my head to call him over, when a Mute appears at his side. I vaguely recognize his pale pink hair, but I can't place from where. One spoken demand and Hoax retreats from view.

An impatient hand grabs my waistband and tugs, returning my attention to Mania. Ghost claims her mouth, driving his tongue inside. Chasing the fiery passion racing between us, my hands move of their own accord to her slender waist. I pin her to the blanket, shifting my thigh between her center for added pressure.

A moan fills the air. This time, it's not one I feel resonate in my chest. Cocking my head, I follow the noise. Across the yard, beyond the barred fence that no doubt is protected by Tate's force field again, movement draws me up onto my knees like a meerkat. The sister facility to Afterlife, the coveted rehab that has been dangled above the prisoner's heads as an end goal, has occupants.

"Hey, love birds. Check this out." When Ghost doesn't peel himself from Mania quick enough, I link my arm around her waist and hoist her to her feet with me. I know the guy's gorgeous and all, but even after taking on the entire asylum in her name, he doesn't need that many kisses plastered all over his face.

Me on the other hand, I'll take those kisses and put them in a little box inside my mind to take one out the next time I'm at Christopher's mercy. *No doubt it won't be long,* a small voice niggles in the back of my mind. The Afterlife owner is far from being done with me yet.

MANÍA

The boys take a side each, keeping pace until we stop about a foot from the fence. Yep, that bastard force field is practically humming, trying to lure our abilities to their deaths like an invisible siren.

On the other side, the rehab soaks in the sun's rays. Reflected in the shimmering water of the pool, it somehow seems brighter over there, despite only being a few feet away. Sun loungers frame the pool, each with a rolled towel at the ready. Cocktails with umbrellas sit on tiny, plastic tables and even a few pool floats are visible along the exterior of the whitewash building.

Way back once, I was prepared to do whatever it took to get into that facility. To live out my days in quiet peace, until death finally took a hold of whatever life I'd managed to procure. It's the opposite now, especially given the type of company the rehab seems to keep.

Olive green hair clenched in a tiny fist. A broad back, floral swim shorts. I don't know Camo well, but I can spot a snake in the grass, even when his face is currently buried in between Imp's thighs. Her neon pink eyes loll aside, the scrap of bikini fabric just about covering her nipples preparing to whip off from the heaving of her chest.

Looking around, I spy a hefty rock nestled in the ground. Not all of the labyrinth was fake, it would appear. Chucking it high over the fence, I hold back my choked laughter as the rock hits Camo directly on the back of the head in favor of smirking. Yeah, the cool kids smirk like whatever, I'm a sharpshooter, no big deal. Pyro ruins the facade though, raising his hand for a high-five and I can't leave him hanging.

"Hey!" Imp bitches, standing in an unnecessary pair of wedged heels to pull the bikini bottoms back up her stubby legs. "I was this close to finishing then." She holds up an index finger and thumb within a breadth of each other.

"You sure you weren't just measuring Camo's dick? I've seen it and I have to say, your fingers are at least two millimeters out." Ghost replies, wrapping an arm around my shoulders. I snort and lean into him.

Imp's eyes narrow on me as she stomps over, careful not to get too close to the fence. The forcefield on it would affect her ability too, but that's not what she should be worried about. I'd risk electrocution just to shoot my arm through and strangle the life out of her for betraying me. It'd seem none of my childhood friends were as genuine as they seemed. Camo joins her, wiping his mouth on the back of his hand and I shudder.

"So typical of you to be on that side of the fence, and still be making pathetic dick jokes," he directs at Ghost. The white-haired Mute merely shrugs, resting his cheek on my forehead.

"I've always thought my real ability was pissing people off." I beam at this, proud to be standing here with him clinging to me like a lifeline. No matter the situation, Ghost will find the opportunity to get beneath someone's skin and drag them back down from their pedestal. Even better than that, with Pyro back to take his natural role as leader, Ghost is free to be his usual, joke-cracking self. Linking my fingers in Pyro's, the three of us face our enemies with arrogant smiles, like we're the real winners here. Imp's anger bubbles beneath the surface of her pink face.

"Make all the jokes you want. You won't be around long enough to realize you're the punchline." Her nose scrunches up and she grips the back of Camo's waistband to tug him away.

"Pray tell," Ghost shouts, forcing them both to stop and hear what he wants to ask. "For old time's sake - what made you trade a life of freedom for a pool and pickpocket? You had your choice of female Mutes, not to mention your own club and more wealth than any other. If anyone's the punchline here, it's certainly you trading all of that for a thieving whore."

"How fucking dare you!" Imp turns back, only to be stopped with a wave of Camo's hand. His green eyes betray the relaxed pose he's trying to portray, brimming with irritation as he spears Ghost with a glare.

"It was going this way anyway. Pretending there would be a place for Mutes in this world is wishful thinking, but you always did live with your head in the clouds. Look where that got you," Camo tilts his head up with a condescending smile we all mimic straight back.

"With the love of my life, oh yeah you're right. Woe is me." Ghost drawls sarcastically. My brows rise and my head shoots up to grin at him. "Not to mention, Hoax is back from the dead and Mania's here too so I'd say I'm pretty set." Motherfucker. I slap him hard on the chest, ignoring his rumbling chuckle and how he reaches over me to high-five Pyro. Knowing what's best for him, Pyro doesn't reciprocate, turning with a roll of his red eyes and striding back to the picnic blanket with me in tow.

Remaining behind, I hear Ghost advising Camo to take notes of what a real orgasm sounds like, not whatever fake bullshit Imp was putting on while she robbed him blind. We make it to the blanket, where Pyro pulls me onto his lap, just in time to see Imp tuck the watch at her wrist behind her back.

"You know we're going to burn them all alive before we leave this asylum, right?" Pyro comments when Ghost returns to us. Stripping down to his Afterlife standard issue white tighty whities, Ghost drops down on his back at my side, hands behind his head.

"Mute fillet? Yum." I shake my head at him, placing a kiss on his lips just as the first snore leaves his mouth. It's been a long morning, bless him, and providing comedic relief in the worst of times is a feat in itself. Frankly, I don't know what we'd do without Ghost to liven the mood when it's needed at the most inappropriate moments.

Leaning back, I allow Pyro to envelope me in all that he is.

Comfort, belonging, hope. Throughout my entire stint in the dungeon, no matter what he was going through, Pyro never once left me to fan the fires without him. A love like ours doesn't need to be vocalized anymore. It's embedded into the very weaving of our connected souls. Knowing this, I relax against his body and briefly let all of my worries wash away.

The day filters by with us as bystanders, and I relish every second. The soft snores leaving Ghost show he feels safe. The gentle stroke of Pyro's fingers over my arms. And then there's Hoax.

"We seriously need to talk about him," Pyro whispers into my ear. He quickly kisses my cheekbone, as if that can soften the dread I feel emanating from his chest. It kills him to spoil our moment of peace, but conflict is never far away.

Standing beneath the canopy, watching intently from the shadows. Does he care to join, or is he following orders to observe and report back? Flicking my eyes north of his indigo hair, I note how every camera attached to its exterior is pointing directly at us. A growl lodges in Pyro's throat as our thoughts become shared.

We have have been allowed a day of peace, but conflict is brimming all around. This is all part of the game. Give us a meter and then tug us back a mile. Christopher seeks to catch us off guard, dangle the carrot long enough that we'll try to bite. But there's a longer game to be played here and in the end, it's not a prissy little fight Christopher will get. It's a full-blown war.

Pulling on the white tank and tucking it into an oversized pair of blue sweatpants riding my hips feels like a step backward in terms of fighting for freedom, but it could be worse. Squatting in derelict hotels, stealing hole-ridden tights for a start. Being without my men and slipping into a deathly coma follows closely behind.

Bouncing on my heels, I ready myself for a swarm of Mutes to attack me as soon as I leave my cell. I'm not naïve enough to this surrendering cooking duties to the newbies will be enough to hold them off for long. Nor am I foolish enough to think my men will always be there to fight my battles for me. It's me the new Mutes want. My blood in payback for those that they've lost. I understand their hatred; I just wish it was directed at the person who's actually responsible.

After we spent yesterday afternoon lazing in the sun while Mutes who were unhappy with the treaty loomed closer and closer, Christopher had called for an early lock-in. We must not be entertaining enough to waste his time watching us lie around in contented bliss. When no one, including us – especially us - bothered to comply, the cuffs at our wrists fried us all unconscious for the guards to drag us all to bed. Safe to say, I can already tell on this side of the door, tensions will be high.

Preparing my hand on the door handle, I send a wave of heat to my men, notifying them I'm ready to face our foes. My hand closes around the door handle and I yank it open, whilst holding one thought in the forefront of my mind. With my men, I'm stronger. Together, we'll be invincible.

Stepping out onto the metal platform with my head held high, the crowd gathered below for breakfast all halt their murmured conversations and look up. I brace myself on the railing, preparing to throw myself overboard and get a head start on the brawling until a familiar voice blurts out from their midst.

"Good morning beautiful, come on down!" Ghost's white hair pops up from the crowd, his beckoning hand poking out from the swarm around a cafeteria table. Pyro steps out of his own cell at the same time, adjusting his tank over the solid wall of abs flexing against his torso.

"You know he's talking to you right," I jest. The metal rungs of the staircase ripple through the platform beneath my canvas shoes and I watch Hoax descend into the chaos, parking himself on a bench nearby to watch with a vacant stare. My chest tugs at our bond, wondering if he can feel me or...anything, but there's no response.

Fingers link with mine, ones that were so recently caressing and claiming my body, drawing me to the floor below.

"The countdown began again, our hearts lodged in our throats as we decided which podium would seal or save our fate," Ghost's voice trickles through the crowd.

Spotting us, the Mutes part suspiciously, Pyro not releasing me once as we near the table to peer over Ghost's shoulder. Cracker podiums sit on cucumber stumps, a sea of lasagne sheets covering the table. Valleys of ketchup trail in and out of the podiums, with Ghost currently holding a chunky piece of red pepper with frayed hair and a dainty strawberry in his large hands.

"We knew we couldn't make it. There was no winning a game designed to kill us off. As the timer starts to run down, Py turns to me and says *'take her'.*" He deepens his voice before swapping out the pepper for an oversized mushroom.

"I didn't hesitate," Ghost adds, swooping in for his mushroom to hoist the strawberry over to the next podium whilst mimicking my scream. "But Mania wasn't having it. She's all *'you selfish motherfucker!'* and head butts me in the face." Cue strawberry and mushroom smash. "Next moment, she's slipped from my grip and thrown herself across the podiums just as the timer reaches two."

The whole crowd inhales sharply, entranced by Ghost's story and I risk a glance around. Suspense grips their expressions, a few brightly colored eyes drifting up to stare in awe at me. Ghost swipes his hand through a bunch of cucumber sticks, wiping out all of the cracker podiums except ours and the crowd gasps.

"Is it true?" a whisper sounds beside me and I flinch. The stroke of a rabbit's ear toys with my hair, a pair of chocolate eyes blinking at me through a watery glaze.

"Hare-iett?" I ask. A lone tear rolls down her cheek as she grips my wrist to pull me back from the crowd. I reassure Pyro I'm okay with a pull on our bond and he hangs back, but not without continuously checking where I am.

"Is it true Granite is here?" Desperation hitches her voice, and despite the clean tracksuit hanging from her frame, she looks scruffy. Her skin is ashy, as if she's tiptoeing the line of death with each shuddered breath that passes her lips. Her ear, the one that used to stand upright, is no more than a fluffy stump, charred along the ridge. I raise my hand to touch it and she flinches out of my reach, chewing on her bottom lip.

"Granite?" I echo and she nods.

"Stoney eyes, tattooed scalp. Creates buildings with his hands – I told you about him. But…well, I kinda left out the passionate affair we had. I thought I'd never see him again, but rumor has it – he's here?" A faint memory of the Mute retracting the very walls of the labyrinth comes to mind. There's so much hope in Hare-iett's gaze, I want to give her what she wants. But then there's the truth that her dream lover was integral in Christopher's plan to kill most of our species.

"Yeah he is, or was," I admit. "I'm not sure the male you once knew is still in the shell that's been left. Hare-iett, what the fuck happened to you?" I have to ask, hating that the perky dancer I met back at Camo's club is nowhere to be seen.

"The MRA raided the club, and they took everyone. Even the dormant Mutes who posed no threat. Whoever this Christopher Gordon is, apparently he's onto something big and needs as many Mutes as possible to pull it off. At least, that's what the agents in the front of our van were saying."

Now looking back, I realize I do know some of these Mutes and we're possibly not as alone as we thought. Or at least, with Ghost creating a marvelous distraction, they're not out for our heads just yet. Follicle gives me a nod from across the crowd, a shimmering Siren who's icy eyes still spear me with a glare at his side.

"I always wondered what happened to Granite," Hare-iett sighs and leans her head on my shoulder. "If a Mute like him can be turned, what hope do the rest of us have?" her voice hitches again and I wrap my arm around her.

"Everything is going to be okay," I lie. She's trembling like a leaf, a fearful bunny in a fox's trap. Refusing to let her leave until she's returned my encouraging smile, a nearby male who seems to know Hare-iett holds out his arm, beckoning her to slide underneath. She moves away, and I'm not surprised Hare-iett isn't at a loss for admirers. Rabbit ears or not, she's beautiful. I just hope the candle she's holding for Granite doesn't burn her in the end.

I resume Pyro's side. His heat eases from clawing at my chest, a soothing balm washing over the gaping hole that begins to erode at my soul whenever we're parted as his lips press a kiss to my forehead.

Ghost's tale has jumped, a wedge of watermelon creating a stage for a slip of red onion to stick into a pre-cut slot. Reaching beneath the table, he pulls out a half dome of fruit loops glued together with what looks like frosting and I can't contain a giggle. A Mute to my left glares my way and shh's me, leaning right over Ghost for the next installment of the story.

The fruit-loop cage is placed over Hoax's onion slice and so it continues. With graham cracker drones hovering overhead, the four of us in food form relive the worst days of my life between a cavern of thick bread slices. Up until the potato sculpture of a knobbly bull is produced from the box at Ghost's feet. Four stubby legs, a pair of crazed, tiny red onion eyes either side of a plastic fork with two prongs.

The mechanical bull clip-clops around the table making the strangest of gurgled roars as Ghost struggles to maneuver all of his characters at once. The strawberry is becoming smushed between his meaty fingers but no one else seems to notice. Too enthralled by the quickening of Ghost's tone, the exaggerated drama to his storytelling.

"Just then, the bull charged forward, spearing Mania in the gut," Ghost announces. This lumpy potato stomps over to my strawberry and I tap him on the shoulder.

"Yeah, I think I'll leave it here." The burst of panic that explodes in my chest almost floors me and it's only thanks to Pyro that I stay upright.

"You can't go!" Ghost spins on the bench and the crowd echoes his upset. "The best part is coming!"

"Where I die?" I twist my lips, unsure what to make of his pleading puppy dog face. We have different definitions of 'the best part'.

"No, the big finale, silly." He bops me on the nose and smirks. "I'll make this bit quick, I promise." Spinning back, Ghost instantly stabs the strawberry on the potato's pongs and spears me into the bread wall. "See, painless."

Pulling the bull back, the mushroom swoops in, becoming smeared with red juice leaking from my puncture wound. It's a stupid display that brings back too many painful memories and through the crowd, I catch Hoax's stoic purple eyes. All the while, Ghost's voice rings through the silence of a captivated audience.

"The light was dimming from her red eyes, her breath growing shallow as I scoop her into my arms. *Smile for me Ghost, let your smile be the last thing I ever see,*' she whimpers and naturally, I obey." Reaching into his pocket, Ghost pulls out a marker pen and draws a smile onto his faceless mushroom head.

"Then she fades away as I'm professing a love I never thought I could feel. Promising a life I can't provide, but in my heart the vow is already solidified. Grabbing the chain binding Hoax, I carry her limp body to Pyro, and he's all like *'this ends now.'*"

In the cage of his hands, Ghost shoves together the pepper, smushed strawberry, graffitied mushroom and slip of onion on a spaghetti leash. He shakes us all up like a cocktail, accompanied with the sound effect of a rocket preparing to explode.

Pyro's cheek leans down to rest on my head and as much as I want to question if we should be spilling our secrets to these strangers, the guys don't seem worried. It's nothing Christopher didn't watch in full HD anyway and these Mutes deserve to know why they are here.

Ghost's rocket erupts with the quick grab of rainbow sprinkles that he chucks everywhere, his beaming smile turning to capture me in his boyish charm. I shake my head slightly, smirking at the show only he could pull off.

Then, just like that, he slams his fists down on the bread walls, crumbling them to a mess that he brushes onto the floor. Between two of the slices which were leaning against each other, a trio of new characters are revealed between the crumbs. New to me at least, but everyone else shouts in shock. A brussell sprout, a pink marshmallow and a cracked pistachio with a single piece of sweetcorn wedged in the shell. Camo, Imp, the Blacksmith…and Serpentina.

"They took the child!"

"What the fuck!"

"Wait!" A male calls out from the back. "What happened to the labyrinth?" Ghost merely shimmers his fingers around and reaches beneath the table. He pulls up the box that contained all of his props, flips it over and slams down a cardboard version of the asylum over us all, artistically scribbled in marker pen.

"Holy shit, it was all fake," another Mute breathes and the crowd erupts in a mixture of excitement and dread. Many break off into their own conversations, finally giving me the reprieve to speak to Ghost.

"Um…good morning, first of all." I press a quick kiss to his lips. "What the hell is happening here?" His milky white eyes stare up at me, so filled with adoration while keeping a seemingly easy smile on his full lips.

"They restocked the kitchen," he shrugs and I punch him in the arm. Ghost winces, which is unusual because I'm weak as shit, so I grab the zipper of his hoodie and drag the jacket from him. Purple bruises simmer beneath the paleness of his skin, covering his biceps, bare chest and abdomen.

"Ghost, what the fuck?!" Pyro shouts, his hands flying to Ghost's torso to inspect him closer.

"Oh yes daddy, just like that," Ghost chuckles, gyrating into Pyro's touch until he straightens by my side, both of us with arms crossed and expressions glaring. "Fine. I slept too much yesterday afternoon, and got a touch of sunburn I might add, so I spent the night working on making posters and props instead." Following Ghost's eyeline, I only now notice the pieces of torn paper stuck on each plinth on the lower level.

For one morning only,
Witness a story of love and betrayal.
Discover who brought you here and why.
Cost of admission: One free punch to the host.

"You're such an asshole, you know that," I groan but can't deny the flutters claiming my heart. He did this, for me. Took on the entire wave of fresh Mutes ahead of them lynching us for their imprisonment. Put on a one-man show to convert everyone to our side. In terms of romance, I think this is Ghost's equivalent to a thousand bruised blue and purple roses.

Dropping into Ghost's lap, he nuzzles my neck and Pyro's hand strokes my hair as I risk a glance over to Hoax's bench. Only to find he's disappeared once again.

GHOST

Pyro's warm hands shift from my torso after healing all my afflictions, not that I was too bothered. Mania's kisses raining over each blemish was well worth the pain. The smile that has yet to slip her face is even better. If I can give her that glimpse of happiness in the dark, I'm doing exactly what I was put on this Earth to do. Entertain. Ease the suffering of those I love.

Our new fan base hovers close, soaking up our passion like leeches. A feeling bursts inside my chest and this time, it has nothing to do with the flames. It also has no right being there, but I let it expand and fill me up until I can't breathe without it leaking from my lungs. *Hope.*

I didn't know the eternal bond could feel like this. Now all of those years of mocking Pyro for his feelings have caught up to me, because I'm the sucker pining in the dark, yearning from a distance.

"Meet me in the bleachers in ten," Pyro mutters into my ear. Patting my shoulder, he gives Mania a nod and slips out into the crowd. I question her with my eyebrows and she shrugs. Fair enough, Pyro can click his fingers and I'll heel.

Rising from the bench seat, I leave Mania to speak with a female I noticed has clung to her side. Chocolate hair falls over one shoulder in bouncy curls which she uses to hide behind. One floppy rabbit's ear hangs limp beside the remaining stump of another. I recognize her and a few of the others from Camo's strip club and am fairly comfortable leaving Mania in their company. Just in case they get the wrong idea though, I lean into their bubble and spear Mania with my serious gaze.

"Any trouble, tug on my heartstrings Spitfire. I'll be back in an instant and heads will roll. No questions asked." The rabbit squeaks and I stride away, a smile cemented on my face all the way to the open hatch of the cafeteria. "Good morning, Sunshine. What's on the menu this morning?"

"For you," the female leans over the hot plates and bats her yellow eyelashes. "Spit soup or porridge puke." A tendril of her golden hair that has come loose of the hairnet blows in the steam from the pancakes and bacon laid out beneath, enough laid out to feed any army.

"Think I'll pass on the specials and help myself to some of this," I grab a plate and tongs. Three males step up behind her, their base instinct to protect their feisty female much like our own dynamic. But fuck me, if I was that hairy, I'd have booked into laser hair removal at puberty.

All three are similar enough in looks to be actual brothers; their hunched shoulders and matching snarls more animal than man. True, their shoulder-length hair looks rather smooth. One white, one brunette and one black, as if they co-ordinated it that way. But all three have purely black irises that stare me down.

"You'll have what you're given," the female growls, her hand flashing out to snatch my wrist. The rumbling sound is reverberated through the men at her back, daring me to challenge her. Well, if you insist.

"I think you'll find, I'll take whatever I want. I don't give a shit about any truce, we're not going hungry for the sake of a beating." Twisting my wrist out of her grip, I manage to get one fried egg on my plate before the males lunge forward. The white-haired one, I smash around the face with the plate. The brown-haired trips and lands on the hot plates, burning his front. And the last, I grab by his black hair and drag him over the counter. Really should have been wearing his hairnet too.

Wrapping my bicep around his neck, I hold the female's steady glare.

"Breakfast, Sunshine. Now." She smiles sweetly, reaching for a bowl. It's about time. Doesn't she know I'm an A-class entertainer? Holding the bowl beneath her chin she heaves straight into it. I let my arm slip, dropping the male in favor of holding my own stomach. Lumpy, beige liquid flows from her mouth, filling the bowl with each retch. Wiping her mouth on her arm, she places it on a tray and pushes towards me. Fuck, she really wasn't joking about the puke porridge.

"The name's Goldie. Happy eating." My nausea subsides and a laugh is torn from me.

"Oh, this is precious. Goldie, and her three bears? Someone really had fun with you, didn't they?" The male I dropped strides back to the kitchen door, obediently returning to her back with the others. *Riiiiiight.* "As for the porridge, how about we settle on you making me a coffee and I won't hand-shove this gloop back into your throat?"

A tense moment passes and finally Goldie sighs. Clicking her fingers, one of the bears pours my drink while the others add creamer and sugar. The sweeter the better. Weirdly, none of the trio take their eyes off me the entire time.

"Pleasure doing business with you," I grin when it's successfully passed over the hatch and Goldie mutters something about me being an annoying asshole. Guilty.

Victory coffee in hand, I send Mania a flare of fire through our bond. I'm really starting to get used to this shit. The curse of feeling every ounce of her misery locked in the cells is finally proving to be a blessing. Knowing she's close, feeling her contentment, discovering the depths of her love for us. That's all I need.

"You go ahead, I'll catch up!" she calls back and I smile. To be fair, I haven't stopped smiling since we were reunited with Py and at this rate, nothing will take it from me again. The tippy-toe of my canvas shoe touches the threshold to the outside when a screech from the overhead speakers makes everyone duck and wince. Smushing my ears between my shoulder and free hand, Christopher clears his throat and speaks.

"Requesting inmate Ghost to the elevator." A ding draws my attention to the door sliding open across the lower level, the opulent elevator empty and waiting. I scoff, finding the nearest camera to shove my middle finger at. Mania's scream pierces the air, her legs giving out as she writhes around. The cuffs at her wrists spark vigorously and before I can take a step in her direction, he speaks again.

"Last call for inmate Ghost to enter the elevator." I grit my teeth against the onslaught of agony I try to draw from Mania. Pyro skids into the room, like a bowling ball knocking all Mute pins out of his way to stop just in front of Mania's face. He draws her into his arms, red eyes seeking me out with a silent order blazing in their depths.

Go.

"Fuck's sake," I grumble to myself. There's a hindered drag to my feet as I take Mania's pain with me all the way towards the damn elevator. Goldie chuckles from the kitchen hatch, her chin balanced in the heels of her palms. Tossing the contents of my coffee cup in her direction, her squeal is music to my ears as the bears rush in behind to wipe the boiling liquid from her skin. Who's the asshole now? Oh right...it's still me.

The elevator ride is short, the doors reopening within a minute and I doubt I've actually left the asylum. Stepping out, I don't see much else than the chair bolted to the floor in the center of the room. Straight from a horror movie, leather shackles hang limp and protruding out of the back, a helmet awaits the unlucky bastard who's going to sit beneath it. Three guesses who that will be...

"Come on in Ghost, take a seat." Christopher takes a step forward, joined by four MRA agents that were lurking against each wall. Batons slap against their palms, mesh masks covering their faces.

"This BDSM setup is all for me?" I raise a hand to my chest. "My, my, fellas. You really shouldn't have. I'd only consider bending over for my brothers." An agent grips my shoulder, directing me to the rusty electrocution chair.

Christopher pays me no mind, lifting a remote control and

switching on the projector mounted to the ceiling. The wall in front of the chair lights and I figure, what the hell? Might as well get this over with so I can still keep my date at the bleachers with Py.

Dropping into the chair, the agents close in to strap my forearms and shins down. The helmet is placed over my temples and I giggle as an agent brushes my overgrown white hair behind my ear to secure a suction cup in place on my temple.

"Stop it," I wink at him. "I'm shy." His fist flies into my cheek before Christopher can bark at him to stand down and my laughter increases. "Okay, you got me. I prefer it rough." The agents shrink back into the shadows, leaving just me facing Christopher against the brightened wall. His face is plunged into shadow, those blue eyes peering out eerily. I'm pretty sure humans shouldn't be able to do that.

"I enjoyed your show this morning," he begins. I don't react, figuring nothing in the asylum would go unseen by the masses of cameras around. "So much so, I figured I'd ought to return the favor."

Stepping aside, the wall flashes forth an image from the maze. Boulders cascade, rubble rains down, the ground shakes and in the midst of it all, my hands are curled around Mania's ass. Our mouths are in sync, taking from each other the energy to carry on. To see out another day when there seems like nothing is worth fighting for. I remember it so keenly, my palms tingle. My lips warm. I could be reliving the moment if Christopher wasn't pacing back and forth, breaking the illusion.

"It occurred to me whilst you replayed the events of the Mute Games, how different the outcome would have been had I thrown Pyro in with Mania and withheld you instead. All those moments of passion in the throes of danger. All the times Mania was forced to rely on you to save her pathetic human life."

I buck against the restraints at that, fully intent on breaking free to kick Christopher in the balls for that comment. Dick move for a dick move. But then again, what's the use in feeding into his useless attempt to come between us? He must be desperate to be wasting his time watching home movies with me. I thought Christopher had an empire to build.

"This really is pitiful. Even for you," I roll my eyes. Undeterred and grinning widely, Christopher leans down with a hand on either side of the chair's arms.

"Do you really think she'd have fallen for you if Pyro had been there? She's moved on from Hoax quick enough. Pretends like he's not even there most of the time." I narrow my eyes at the bastard who could sell a television to a blind man. He has broken Hoax, yet is trying to make out we've made the decision to ditch him.

"I know what you're doing, trying to pit us against each other because even you're not stupid enough to see we're stronger together. Mania loves us all equally." My head jolts against the helmet, mere centimeters from headbutting the grin off his stupid face.

"Maybe, maybe not. But can the same be said for the rest of you? While you were fighting for your lives, Pyro was enjoying the pleasures of the human world." The screen behind his brown hair shifts to a setting I don't recognize and despite not wanting to seem interested, I look around Christopher to get a better look.

A ballroom splays out before the camera, littered with humans in masks. Pyro's red hair gives him away, but the sharp suit plastered to his body gives me pause. I've never seen him wear anything flashier than jeans, and that's only when I used to force him out into the human world. But there's no force being used here, especially when his arms banded around the slender waist of a lilac-haired woman. Tate.

"This is fake," I snort, shaking my head. Christopher moves aside to point at the time stamp in the top right corner. The date means nothing to me as I wouldn't know today from Halloween, but the year is correct. This was recent.

"You were fighting for your very lives. Fighting to save a man who took the pleasures I offered him without reservation," Christopher tilts his head, drinking in my every reaction.

Using the control in his hand, he fast forwards through Pyro and Tate laughing and dancing between the humans, before my brother exits to sit at the bar. Enzo joins him, the pair of them talking and drinking whiskey like old friends. Just like the way I always wanted to enjoy an evening out with him, but Pyro refused to leave the bunker. Something isn't right about this picture, I'm just not sure what it is.

Alarm bells ring between my ears, confusion settling in my chest. I try to send a questioning flare to Pyro, but the suction cups on my temple begin to glow and I'm shot with temporary darkness. As if I'd passed out, gone blind and lost all train of thought for five seconds. Blinking my vision clear, one MRA agent groans, passing a wad of cash to another while Christopher heads for a keypad on the wall and pushes a button.

"I wouldn't bother reaching out through your connection. The transmitter linked to your brain can pick up on the signals of the eternal flame being activated. While you've been crafting bulls from mushrooms and playing paper mâché, I've been studying the data *extremely carefully*. Turns out, you're much easier to predict than you think."

I don't have time to understand what he means by that as the screen behind him splits into four. Pyro at the bar top left. Next to that, him striding from a hotel room with a barely dressed human woman. Bottom corner, he's sitting on a plush mattress, flicking through Mute profiles on a huge flatscreen television. The expensive bedroom around him melts away as he bids on another Mute to win the Mute Games. I don't see who and I don't give a fuck in this moment. He could have aided Mania, or me if he was so pissed at her, but instead he chose a bloody stranger.

Finally, the last quadrant blinks onto a live feed from the asylum. The cafeteria area of Afterlife plays out in real time, Mania now sitting upright in Pyro's lap. A crowd has settled around them, cross-legged on the floor, finding comfort in numbers. In the background, Hoax sits stoic, staring at them.

"You've been so wrapped up in winning *her*, you weren't watching *him*." Christopher rounds the back of my chair. A hand cups my chin, jerking my gaze back to the cute couple cuddled up. Pyro draws Mania into a comforting kiss, completely unaware of the rising panic preparing to choke me out.

"You think your bond is split equally," Christopher chuckles, releasing my chin. "Pyro has been playing you for a fool. Using you to heal himself while he gets everything you've always wanted. A free life among the humans, string of ladies on his arm. He's been betting against you since the beginning. Resenting you, and the most poetic part is you've let him."

A phone rings from somewhere, only sheer willpower keeping me vaguely aware of my surroundings. The cups at my temple are doing more than blocking my connection to the others, they're marring it. Confusing my thoughts, muddling what my subconscious knows is true. A few grunts sound, but my attention is on the looped images on the screen.

I was risking everything in the maze: my chance with Mania, my own life, just to return her to him. All the while, he was sleeping around. Drinking in human bars, living his best life. Then why would he return to the maze – or did Christopher simply kick him out for enjoying himself too much? Did he see Mania was falling for me and decide to take her back?

And I permitted him. I welcomed him in. It was my job to protect her. To keep her alive. From the moment I gave into my passion, I was her loyal soldier. Put my life on the line multiple times, gave her everything she needed. And that service has not finished. My duty will never be complete. I'll continue protecting Mania against those who threaten her life and her heart. Pyro, Hoax or myself included.

"Sir, your visitor has arrived," a voice mutters through the darkness edging into my vision while Christopher moves to lean back over me. His icy eyes watch the light fade from mine as he pushes the remote control into my hand.

"Mania could have been all yours, Ghost. If only you'd be man enough to satisfy her on your own."

"Surely Ghost should be back by now," I frown at the elevator again. Drumming my fingers on the grass, I've positioned myself in direct line for when he returns. Not if, when.

I knew something was wrong the moment I couldn't feel his presence in my being anymore, but slamming myself against the internal brick wall wasn't helping.

"He'll be fine," Hare-iett smiles reassuringly. She shuffles over, handing me a daisy chain she'd been working on. "I mean, I only just met him properly this morning but it doesn't take a genius to see Ghost can hold his own." Sliding the chain over my wrist, her hand slinks into mine.

I lower my gaze, noting the bloodied scrapes across her knuckles. This Mute who's barely a size four fought like hell against the MRA agents. Not only that, the slight tremble through Hare-iett's hold stops me from pulling away. She needs reassurance as much as I do right now. Following my eyeline, Hare-iett tugs her long sleeve lower to cover her hand.

"Don't think you could spare me some of that healing juju I saw you guys do to Ghost?" she asks. I cover her hold with my other hand.

"I would, if it wasn't for these damn cuffs. We only seem to be able to heal away each other's afflictions from the inside but until I can test out Pyro's ability in me properly, I'm pretty useless." Dropping my hand away, the cuff knocks against the ground.

"Doesn't sound useless to me. I'm in awe honestly. You guys have been through so much, yet you've found one another. You've found love. That's something special in the best of situations." I nod, knowing she's right. It'd just be nice to go one day without having to worry one of us isn't going to return.

Pyro sits across the yard, hunched in the bleachers and talking to himself. He had kissed the crack on my forehead and said there was business he had to take care off. He hasn't moved since.

Hare-iett, Siren and Follicle are lazing nearby. Siren hums a tune to herself, her skin shimmering jade green to the deepest purple. Just like the first time I saw him in the strip club, Follicle's blonde hair flows to his shoulders, his face free of any stubble. He's one of many I've noticed without cuffs, apparently posing no threat to Christopher's plans.

All of the new Mutes seem to have quickly broken off into their own factions. A group of males who all meet the six-foot-plus mark have taken over the basketball court. More fitness junkies are owning the outdoor gym equipment or doing laps around the running track. I'm not surprised – many of these Mutes will have only dreamed about exercising outdoors. Many of those uncuffed lying around on the green, enjoying their mini pretense of freedom.

A buzzer blares through the main lobby, halting many of us. The guards slide open the gate, their batons charged and ready at their sides. Led by Christopher, a group of humans I've never seen before stride into the canteen under the careful watch of Goldie and her three bears.

At his side, a woman commands all the attention. Tall legs in tights and heels, a straightened posture in a blouse and pencil skirt. Blonde hair is pulled back into a flawless bun, not a wisp out of place. And on her face, an easy smile looks at home on her painted lips.

The Mutes around the yard abandon their chosen stations, nearing closer with hushed whispers.

"Who is that?" I lean into Hare-iett and she gasps.

"Don't you read the news?!"

"Been a little preoccupied recently," I give her a flat stare and she gives a small shake of her head.

"Oh, right - of course. Sorry. That's Octavia Horton. She's running for president in the upcoming elections." I bat her floppy ear out of my hair, peering around to see the Mutes are closing in step by step. There's static in the air, a low hum of curiosity and if I'm not mistaken, excitement.

"Since when have Mutes cared for human politics?" I ask, becoming whisked up as Siren and Follicle drag us up. I hunt around for Pyro but he's lost beyond the crowd. I do catch a pair of indigo eyes that spear me with their glow, Hoax always near but too far. Those behind sweep me up and soon enough, I'm being edged through the open double doors as Hare-iett rushes to fill me in.

"Octavia has spoken openly about Mute rights. She doesn't believe we should be condemned for our genes and has built her whole campaign around aiding us. At a summit a few weeks ago, she said it's the world that needs to change to accommodate us, not the other way around."

I don't have time to process all of the questions lacing my tongue as I come to a halt in the canteen and Octavia swings that relaxed smile on me. Christopher hovers over her shoulder, the lines on his face an obvious sign he isn't happy with her visit. Or that she seems to be taking a step towards me.

"Oh my," Octavia inhales. Sliding her hands out tentatively, Christopher growls a warning about catching a disease but she ignores him. Octavia gently lifts my cuffs and scoffs. "What are these for?" Her face crumples in disgust, easing my arms back down and twists to keep Christopher in her eyeline.

"Ability suppressants. They're necessary for those who can't control themselves." Icy blue daggers dare me to stay in line. Fuck. That.

"I can control myself just fine. It's my reactions to being-" a single shot from the cuffs zips up my arms, warning me not to say anymore. A warm, firm chest connects with my back. A reassuring comfort that

I have backup. But despite the confidence my man boosts in me, Christopher's expression has turned murderous.

This woman, whatever candidate she is and the principles she stands for, isn't going to help me. She's going to waltz out of here and not think twice about Afterlife.

"The cuffs need to go. You can't rehabilitate and aid these citizens if you simply cut them off from the source of their being. That's only teaching them and those living amongst them to fear the consequences of an outburst. Control doesn't come from suppression."

"With all due respect," Christopher grinds out. He hates this woman, and everything she just said. "You don't hold the power to make those decisions."

"Not yet, but the public are backing my Mute incentives. The days of treating mutants like immigrants are over. I have every faith my followers will come through and once I am president, restoring this facility to what it should have been will be my first order of business." Giving me one last kind smile, Octavia nods and shakes hands with the other Mutes like this is some sort of rally. It must have been one hell of a speech she gave to convince this many Mutes the world could change. I just can't bring myself to believe it.

Octavia's tour is continued through the asylum, or as she called it 'rehabilitation center'. Give me a break. She also referred to us as citizens. Call me cynical, but I believe she cares when I'm free of this prison. The Mutes follow her every move, just behind the hoard of MRA agents protecting her and Christopher from any of them getting too close. I'm not following her around, or hanging on her every word. I've heard too many false promises to last me a lifetime.

"What do you make of her?" I fold my arms and lean back on the chest bolstering me. Rolling my head across the firm chest, my cheek is met with warmth and my eyeline shifts to spot Pyro sitting on the bleachers outside. I freeze. Slowly turning, my head rises to find those indigo eyes blazing a trail into my skull.

"Hoax," I breathe. The wires in his torso spark, flowing freely between the circuits to his arms and back up again. A purple glow hovers beneath the fluttering pulse in his neck. I reach up to touch it, needing to feel the evidence of his life beneath my fingertips. He turns sharply, striding away but I refuse to let him go that easily. Tossing a look back to Pyro, I see he's risen from his perch and I hold up a hand.

I've got this, I tell him through our connection. Hoax reaches the wooden arched door at the back of the asylum, hidden in the shadows beneath the walkway above. He slips through the door and I race to catch it before it closes, silently ducking inside after him.

Nothing has changed except for the flood of memories that consume me whilst gazing upon the chapel. Hoax leads me down the central aisle, my fingers reaching out to trail the wooden pews. Light seeps through the three windows, the stained glass altering the colors around us like an ethereal rainbow. Turning away from the cross postered on a wooden podium, Hoax stops before a candle standing tall on a golden, floral stand. It's been burnt right down to the wick, smatterings of dried wax across the dusted, red carpet.

Inhibitions left at the door, I join his side.

"You won't remember this, but we've been here before," I mumble into the quiet. Raising my finger, I brush the tip of the wick, wishing I had the access to Pyro's flames to light it. "I'd come here to escape you all, but instead I met a flame-haired man who wished he could light this very candle for his dead brother." Hoax doesn't respond so I step closer into his side, linking my fingers with his.

"He was mourning you Hoax. He was so heartbroken, yet I knew you were here. You encouraged me to stay with him, to comfort him. And the whole time, I kept you my secret. I had some deep-rooted fear if I told anyone you existed, you might disappear. Or that somehow, you wouldn't be mine anymore." I huff out a breath. Rambling isn't going to help, but the silence feels even worse.

Closing my eyes, I call forth the memory. How Hoax overlooked mine and Pyro's first kiss. How he aided that first touch of the flame igniting my soul and setting me on this course. To an outsider, I may be trapped but in reality, I have everything I need. And if it wasn't for Hoax, I'd still be a lost girl stuck in Bellemare.

"Mania," he rasps, his voice raw and unused. My heart lifts at the sound. Turning my head, lips slam onto mine. My gasp quickly shifts into a groan. Burning need taints my bloodstream. Sparks crash through our eternal flame, causing my hair to shift with its strength. A desperate tongue seeks out mine, the rush of our flame intertwining just as easily.

I dare not open my eyes, frightened to break the illusion. Hoax's mouth skates across mine, his movements steady and curious. He makes no move to hold me, and that's fine. I throw myself at him. Fingers in his hair, nails along his nape. Fireworks burst through my soul, tearing down the last barriers that were barring me from Ghost as I drag mine and Pyro into this sensation. Connecting us all.

A rattle of the doorknob, aided by Christopher's voice announcing the chapel drives us apart. I cling onto Hoax's shoulders, dragging his stubborn ass behind a long, velvet curtain just as the door opens. Octavia's heels click inside, her voice relaying information back to her assistant. None of it matters though.

Indigo, glowing eyes have my full attention. I shift my hands over his bunched shoulders, along his neck to cup his cheeks. I need to feel him. Touch him. To commit him to memory. Groping Hoax when he's not responsive hasn't felt right, but he made the first move and I won't back down now. My thumb brushes his bottom lip, my fingers sweeping back his hair.

The others in the room retreat, closing the door behind them and I sigh. I need more time with Hoax, just the two of us. He watches me closely as I trail kisses along his jawline. Worshipping him for merely existing. The nights were twice as long when he was lost to me, not even his spirit appearing in my dreams. My heart squeezes at the thought, the rollercoaster of emotions not relenting. I grieve for him all over again, the ghost of the Mute that became my lifeline, all the way loving the shell of whatever is leftover. Raising a hand between us to rub at his chest, a frown pulls at Hoax's otherwise natural expression.

"I...feel you." His husky, unused voice stills the heart hammering in my chest. Tears well in my eyes. I try to beat down the sheer explosion of elation that's building within, the air leaving my body in short pants. Hoax winces, the sensation clearly uncomfortable. Being bonded to people you can't remember must be as confusing as it is terrifying. I peer up, laying bare the truth in my red eyes. As long as we're together, we'll be okay.

"I've felt you since the day I dragged you back from hell," I breathe. Those words are a relief to say. No more hiding my emotions, no more being coy. In the briefest moment of his clarity, Hoax will know exactly how I feel.

Our concealing curtain whips back and the bored stare of Christopher passes over us in one, lazy sweep. My hands on Hoax's face, my lips grazing his collar bone. I swallow thickly, feeling the tension line Hoax's body but he makes no move to protect me.

"Well, isn't this cozy." Christopher drawls. A tick beat in his jaw, the inhale and exhale of his chest too steady. No, he's not bored – he's pissed. "Hoax, report to Brainwave. Mania and I have some catching up to do." And with that, a simple command and no show of force, Hoax walks away to leave me in the hands of a monster.

My head rolls across the back of the plastic chair. The sun lowers just enough to grace the bleachers with a warm glow, heightening the tingling of my skin. So many emotions pass through me, I can't begin to pull them apart. All I do know is Mania has cracked him. Somehow, she's found a chip in Hoax's armor and pried it open to reveal what's underneath.

Until it suddenly changes. Fear claws from my lungs with the icy taint of frostbite. I gasp, my hand clenching the seat either side of me. Preparing to force myself upright, a voice calls out from behind the bleachers. The very one I've been calling for all day.

"Pyro? Are you there?"

"Shadow," I grasp out. "I-I've been waiting for you," I groan, doubling over. "But now's not a good time. Return tomorrow-"

"No! Pyro, listen to me. I'm risking everything by reaching out to you. This is the last time I can assist you. Suspicions are on the rise and the asylum is already erratic with Octavia taking a closer interest. Time's running out and it's starting to show."

The urgency in his voice gives me no reason not to believe him. But the warning flare in Mania's emotions are sending my base instincts into overdrive. The flame whips, lashing my insides with each moment I sit here while she's suffering.

"Pyro! I need you to focus. I've only got minutes until Mr. Gordon returns."

Mr. Gordon, huh? Faces begin flashing through my mind at who Shadow could be. I figured he was another Mute stashed away somewhere, but now I'm not so sure. To have access to the information he does, and to speak of Christopher with a sense of respect, could Shadow have been an employee this entire time? Does he help lock us up at night, shock us when we disobey a command?

"Speak," I rasp out, sealing my decision. My eyes lock on the chapel door whilst sending out a silent apology to Mania. I can feel her fear, and she doesn't scare easily. But this information could make all the difference to us surviving or dying in this place.

"This new campaign is bringing much unwanted attention. The experiments have been escalated with barely enough time to understand the resulting data before the next one begins. We're venturing into unknown territories and the fall-out will be catastrophic."

"And what is the end goal? Why is Christopher so hell-bent on pulling our DNA?" I query, trying to keep the frustration out of my voice.

"I don't know if he even remembers anymore. Our mission was to help, to cure. Along the way, the MRA became interested and the money started rolling in. Money changes everything."

"Sounds like you've been around for a while," I comment, listening carefully for clues. Shadow is a careful Mute, yet this may be the moment he slips up and reveals too much. "Where does that leave us – as lab rats?" I scoff. Even as the words leave my mouth, I know it's the truth. As if I expected to be anything else.

"Currently, you're his prize possession, Pyro. But even Mr. Gordon is beginning to realize your fires can't aid his mission. You need to guard those close to you, protect anyone you want to save for when he's finished with the child-"

The chapel door opens and Christopher walks out, closing it

slowly behind him. Straightening his suit, he heads directly for the elevator. Not a single Mute challenges him, cuffed or otherwise.

"Wait!" I shoot out of my seat, attracting the attention of the few littering the yard. "You mean Serpentina, right? She's still here? Tell me where," I spin around, hunting for a shift of movement in the darkened space behind the bleachers. "Shadow! Tell me where I can find the girl!" No reply; he's gone. For good this time.

My heart is pounding like the drums of war, my mind reeling with questions that won't be answered. Sprinting across the yard, I skid to a stop as the chapel door opens once more, revealing Mania. Blinking teary red eyes up at me, she falls into my arms. No physical marks are visible but the internal one splices through my soul. Ignoring the curious stares nearby, I walk Mania towards the staircase and help her up into her cell.

"Talk to me baby, what's happened?" I lower her onto the bed, where she instantly curls into my side.

"I had him Py. I was so close." Her voice cracks. A whisper so small, I can feel her spirit breaking. But that's fine, I will carry her until she's ready to walk on her own again.

"Did Christopher hurt you?" I ask again, softer this time while my hands check her over.

"No. Just the same threats as usual. It's Hoax I'm worried for. He was right there, just beneath the surface. Christopher won't permit such a slip up again."

"You underestimate our bond, beautiful. We'll get him back, don't you worry." Pulling her head back far enough for her to look me in the eye, my thumbs caress her cheekbones as I lean down to press a gentle kiss to her lips. A gentle connection filled with longing. A silent promise that we're going to survive this. All of us.

All it takes is a slight tilt of Mania's face to open her up to me. Her mouth opens, permitting me full access. My tongue sweeps over hers, my grip becoming tight. She presses into me, kindling our fire into something more potent. I feel the shift in desire the moment she does, gasping into my mouth.

Together, we shift. My hand moves to the back of her head, my body prowling forward to pin her down onto the mattress. Opening her thighs for me, I settle between them, my cock nestled against her warm center. I grind into her, drawing a frustrated groan from her lips. It's been too long. A single day is too long when all we want to do is explore our connection, discover every millimeter of each other's bodies.

Mania's nails claw at my back, ripping the t-shirt over my head. My hands grab at the waistband of her gray joggers in a rush to banish those too, and if it weren't for the cuffs, I'd have incinerated them straight from our bodies. But that would be too quick. I've made a mental promise to make this last, because fuck knows when I might get her all to myself again.

My cock is already hard, throbbing with an insistent need to slip inside her heat, thrusting as she clenches around me and drags me deeper. Mania swallows my groan at the thought. This won't be like the other times we've been together. No Ghost to speed things along, no doubts in the back of my mind. This one will be different. Slow and passionate. I'll take my time. Savor her sexual cues. Memorize her facial expressions.

I feel her fire flare to life inside of me, a burning desire that ignites our twin flame. She's a live entity within me. Her pleasure is my pleasure, and I can feel *everything. Everywhere.*

"Fuck, I love you, Mania," I whisper against her lips, the sweet taste of her teasing my tongue and blanketing my mind. My eyes fuse close as I fight to blink them open, to look at her as I lose myself in the wild crimson swirls of her enchanting gaze so like my own. Rocking my hips, I shudder. The raw, sensitive head of my cock grazes the inside of my boxers, while Mania's heat seeps through the thick material. She's more than ready for me.

I need to change that, fast.

Mania whimpers, begging me with her eyes. With deft fingers, I trail her sides, touching her everywhere I can reach and leaving no part of her unappreciated. Tenderly, my hands slip beneath the cotton of her t-shirt, over the warm expanse of her flesh and the higher up I explore, the more flesh that is exposed. Soon, I'm peeling off the layers of her clothing, one item at a time.

"Pyro," she sighs sensually, my name sounding like sin on her lips.

"Say it again," I rasp, dipping to place my heated mouth against her stomach, the tip of my tongue peeking out to leave a wet trail in its wake. I go back, blowing over the path I've just made, making her shiver from the coolness of my breath.

"Pyro, please! I need you. Your mouth, your tongue. Take me," She whispers in desperation, not wanting to be heard beyond these walls in fear we'll be torn from each other's arms. Not even Christopher can keep us apart. Nothing will ruin this.

Wriggling the sweatpants down her legs, I stop to stroke the black panties on her hips. I don't care that they're not classically sexy, or for Mania's flush of embarrassment. She could be wearing a garbage bag and I'd still think she's the sexiest damn creature on this earth. And she's mine.

Peeling off her underwear, she lies naked under me. Crawling from the bed, I fall to my knees and use her wrists to sit her up with my retreat. My hands firm on her ass, I move her to the edge of the bed, wrapping her legs around my head. Hands on her back, I devour her like a man feasting on his last meal. Savoring every bite, I spear her with my tongue. She gasps, arching her back, hands in my hair.

I know it's growing increasingly impossible to remain quiet. I pull her as close as I can, bury my face as deep as I can go. My thumb presses down on her clit and she denotes, gyrating against my face like a woman possessed until she comes into my mouth. Swallowing, I do it a few times until I've made sure I've well and truly licked away every part of her desire.

Only then do I stand, taking her with me. Legs around my waist, I press Mania's back against the door. Partly to act as a barricade, but mostly as a fuck you to this asylum and those who have trapped us in it. They can lock the doors, monitor us on their cameras, but they can't stop us from living. I'll never stop giving myself to the love of my life and proving to her why I'm worthy of her soul in return.

Impatience winning, I've barely shoved my sweatpants over my hips when my cock slides home inside her. Mania cries out, clamping a hand over her mouth. I pull it away, a dare in my gaze. Let them fucking hear. Pulling back to her entrance, I slam back inside. Once, twice. My fingers dig into her ass, the thread of my control preparing to snap.

"I want to be gentle," I grit out, more to myself. "I want to prove to you I'm enough for you on my own. That I don't need anyone else." I didn't realize I felt that way until the words fell out of my mouth, my head dipping in shame. Mania's thighs on my hips tighten, her fingers sliding into my hair to drag my head back up.

"You. Are. Enough," she growls. A burst of fire in my chest steals my breath, the ferocity of her glare dancing with the same flame. "You don't think I'd had the same doubts? That I'm not enough for three men? But then this happened, and I realized none of that trivial shit matters."

Her fires spark within me again, traveling down to my dick and forcing drops of precum out of me. I bite down on my lip to fight a groan, my hands slamming into the door either side of her. "We were meant to be together Py. Us, the others. I'm done questioning it and am ready to embrace it. Are you?"

Instead of answering her with words, I tilt my hips and spear her that little bit deeper. Without withdrawing, I rock my hips, stroking her g-spot with the head of my dick. I can't bear to pull away from her now, not even long enough to thrust back inside. Sweat prickles our skin. Our breathing turns into ragged pants.

Hooking my arm beneath Mania's knee, I hoist her thigh higher and bury myself in her. Our fires burn white behind my eyes just before Mania breaks for me. Like the bursting of a dam, she screams as her pussy convulses, squirming as I give her nowhere to go. I can't hold back.

Exploding, streams of my cum shoot inside of her with the force of a rocket. White coats my vision, the sounds coming from us too intangible to decipher. Our flames solidify into one, burning hotter and brighter than ever. I vow to touch her where the others never could. To leave my mark so deep, every time she's fucking them, she'll remember me.

Staggering away from the door, my legs cramp and give out just as we reach the bed. Twisting mid-air, I land heavily on my back, Mania straddling me. It's only when I peel my hands from her ass, I feel the scorching burn of my palms and spot marks seared into her skin.

"Shit, Mania. I'm so fucking sorry," I choke out, trying to shift her but she refuses. Not a trace of pain is evident on her face, her eye half-lidded and full of lust.

"Now we can take it slow," she smirks, rolling her hips. I'm still hard as steel inside of her, not nearly sated. But this time, I raise my still-tingling hands and place them either side of my head. Pretty sure my flames shouldn't be able to respond to my call through the cuffs, but I'm not surprised that Mania can draw such power from me either. If I'm the bomb, she's the fuse.

Time slows yet races by, Mania's body submitting to my dick over and over. She cries my name, scratches my chest raw. Her body runs so hot, I'm surprised she hasn't combusted entirely. Our kisses are lost to the daze of passion I never want to resurface from. Keeping my hands well away from her body, I order her beneath me. Our bodies slot together like the missing pieces of a jigsaw, the sweat slickening our movements. I fuck her until I know my dick will be tender for days, and I can't wait. I'll take any reminder of what happened here today, what I did to her body.

"You're my everything," Mania mewls just before she cums for me again. My lips trail her jaw, coating every inch of her salty, heated skin in my reach. I don't need to respond. The flames dancing between us reply for me. I'd burn the entire world down for my girl. My angel of darkness who's walked back from Hell hundreds of times to be with me.

"Get the fuck off of her," a growl penetrates the air. A hand snakes around my throat, ripping me away from Mania and tossing me into the opposite wall. Pain splinters across my back, ricocheting along my side as I drop heavily onto the floor. Naked and pissed, peering up at the furious male standing over me.

"Ghost?" I breathe, reaching out to smack his shin. "What the fuck, man?" Trying to pick myself up, Ghost kicks me in the gut. His boots stride away, and I watch through cracked eyelids as he scoops Mania into his arms. The lust-filled bliss flees her eyes, a look of panic sparking there. I raise my hand, sending a flare of reassurance through our bond.

Wherever Ghost has been and whatever he thinks he knows, it's best not to fight him like this. I'll give him his caveman moment, and make sure he regrets it later.

Sighing, I rest my back against the wall following the line of Ghost's bed. My legs are crossed, outstretched in front of me in the baggy gray sweatpants I quickly grabbed when Ghost carried me from my room. The Mute in question was decent enough to toss me a white tank of his before he started pacing, and that's where we are now.

The tension in his shoulders is geared to snap, the balls of his fists flexing in time with his ragged pants. Blowing out my own breath, I drum my fingers over my thighs.

"You don't really think Pyro, of all people, could fake his feelings? He's the most transparent person I've ever met, and it's hugely refreshing."

"I feel like that was a dig at me," Ghost grumbles, fisting a hand in his hair. "But you didn't see what I saw! I saw it Spitfire." Halting mid-stride, Ghost turns on me with so much sincerity in his white eyes, a boost of pity flares through our bond. I didn't mean to release it, but there must have been some insecurities already present in Ghost for him to be so easily persuaded that Pyro's love for all of us is anything but pure.

Sliding off the bed, I take Ghost's face in between my hands.

"I don't need to see anything. We've all done things that look shady, we've all been forced to play games to survive. If you'd just let him through the door, he could explain that for himself." Twisting Ghost's cheeks, his eyeline is forced to follow and gaze upon the door thumping behind the desk chair he's hooked beneath the handle.

"You can't waiver in what Christopher says or shows you. It's all about what we feel." To prove my point, I rest my head on Ghost's heaving chest and send a wave of love through all four of us. Hoax included. In my mind's eye, a rose of flame blazing into existence. Four petals peel back, unfurling into colored wisps that break away and re-join the base of the steam in a heart. Fuck, that was impressive, if I do say so myself.

Ghost sighs, his body relaxing and slumping onto me.

"Do you think…"

"That you allowed yourself to be convinced because with Pyro out of the way and Hoax AWOL, you'd have me all to yourself? Yeah, that's exactly what I think." I nod, bringing my eyes back to his narrowed ones.

"I was going to say, do you think I fucked up the chance at joining what I saw happening in your room?" Ghost draws his knuckles down my sides, not so accidentally catching my nipples with his fingertips. Smirking, I draw Ghost down to my mouth, speaking just before our lips touch.

"Oh Ghost, you've fucked up. Your balls are going to be blue for so long, you won't remember what them being empty feels like." Chuckling, I draw out of his arms and shift the chair barricading the door. Pyro whips in like a tornado, his eyes settling on Ghost on instinct where he instantly punches him in the face. Stepping aside to let the boys fight out their macho bullshit, the door slides closed just as the buzzer for tonight's lock-in rings through the asylum.

"Um, guys?" I say, trying the handle with no avail. They don't hear me, too focused on Ghost merely standing there looking miserable while Pyro goes to town on his face.

"That's for kicking me, you bastard. And that's for ruining my sexcapade with Mania. And that's for doubting me in the first place!" Pyro shouts out between punches until I decide enough is enough.

"Cool it, Py. He's doing that wounded puppy thing again and I can't handle it." Stepping between them, I place a hand on each of their exposed chests. Spearing both with a serious look, Ghost frowns and pitches forward. He grabs my forearm for stability, stumbling as his body flickers in and out of view. Almost as if his ability is fighting to be free. A violent shudder runs the length of Ghost's body as his cuffs drop to the floor. His, mine, and Pyro's.

Frozen in stunned silence, only the remaining echoes of Ghost's neck manacle spiraling around the floor can be heard until it finally settles. I don't move, expecting the alarm to ring out or agents to storm the room any moment, but nothing comes. Just the three of us standing there - my hand on Pyro's chest and forearm clutched in Ghost's tightened grip.

"Ghost..." I breathe. "What the fuck did they do y-" Ghost shudders again and the ground gives way. I somehow manage to swallow the scream that leaps into my throat as we pass through the floor, tumbling downwards. Pyro grabs for me when I almost lose touch of his skin, holding me close. Falling into the rec room below, we disappear straight through that floor too. Then another, until the wind rushing past and Pyro clinging to my back dislodges Ghost's grip and we slam onto concrete.

Ow.

"What the hell?" Ghost groans, rolling onto his back, clutching his arm. I dare not move, the threat of agony tethering on the edge. One wrong move and it'll explode. Pyro is the first to drag himself onto all fours, spitting a wad of blood onto the ground. The shadows of his face in the dim lighting deepen where blood coats his face, the crook of his nose glinting at a weird angle.

Raising my hand slowly, Pyro presses his cheek into my palm. Without the cuffs in place, flames answer my call instantly. My hand brightens, yet the tendrils leaking from my skin aren't hot. They wind into Pyro's pores, his skin glowing from the inside as I heal his ailments. His nose cracks back into place, as does another bone elsewhere on his body. Once finished, Pyro returns the flames through our connection and the healing balm washes through me instantly. Then, together, we deal with Ghost.

"Ahh, wait," Ghost hisses when we lay our hands on his chest. "Be gentle."

"For an asshole that's all talk, you're such a fucking baby," Pyro hides a smirk and presses down harder.

A bolted lock is tugged free from somewhere, the echo of the clang bouncing off the stone walls. We quickly half-heal, half-drag Ghost back behind a stack of boxes and in unison, clamp hands down over his mouth. His white eyes find me in the dark and I shake my head. *Don't glitch.*

A crack in the boxes provides a slither of a view, or as much as the faint lanterns on the wall will provide. Boots tap down stone steps, the male in question keeping his head down. A head of shortly cropped hair. Smoldering eyes swirling with liquid metal glow from beneath his furrowed brows. I suck in a breath, ducking lower. If the Blacksmith suspects our presence, he doesn't let on.

Crossing the length of the room, he stops before a tall, metal door. Placing his hands on the chain wrapped around the handles, he retracts them back into skin and heaves the door open, disappearing from view.

We wait a long moment, waiting for him to return. When he doesn't, Ghost shakes off our holds and sits upright so sharply, his shoulder knocks the stacks of boxes and sets them tumbling onto the ground. If looks could kill, Pyro and I would have disintegrated him right then and here. Yet no one comes so we take in our surroundings for the first time.

From the stone walls and floor, I would hazard a guess we're in a basement. A basement that's been kitted out like an old-style evidence locker. Metal shelving units stand in rows, each housing an uncountable number of white boxes. A long desk sits along the back wall, two chairs fitting comfortably underneath. A lamp on the surface hangs over scattered papers and a pair of the same cuffs we've just shedded.

Pyro helps me upright and guides me to the closest shelving unit to inspect the black marker pen on the side of the box. *Inmate #314.* We share a knowing look.

"Let's fan out. It won't be long before they realize we're not in our cells," Pyro instructs, taking the far side. Ghost dives for the middle and I start with the rear desk. Settling into one of the chairs, I put myself in the mindset of the previous occupant, scanning over whatever was too important to shove back into a box before they left.

Blueprints are concealed beneath the papers, a removable piece of acetate displaying how the maze was configured around and throughout the asylum. Jotted notes indicate the exterior stone walls were the responsibility of a Mute named Granite, whilst the interior was taken care of by the mirage twins.

On top, a mess of papers detail how Tate's ability has been infused with the MRA's electrical cuffs to short-circuit our abilities while delivering a minimum shock of twenty-five milliamps directly into our system. Enough to kill a regular human, it goes on to detail. How lovely. Turning my attention to the desk drawers, I pull out any that aren't locked, riffling through until my fingers land on a photograph.

"Hey guys, come look at this," I call out to the others. The withered edges match the sepia image of a man I vaguely recognize. Black hair is slicked back from his youthful face, a square jaw and straight nose jutting out. A relaxed smile has been captured upon his mouth, while a white lab coat frames his muscular frame. I wouldn't place him more than twenty years old, which begs the question why he's familiar.

"Here, there's something written on the back," Pyro eases the photograph out of my hand. Turning it over, we find 'Inmate #1' scrawled on the back.

"Oh hey, I found the box for that one." Ghost skips away like a kid in a candy store, trailing his fingers along the boxes either side of the aisle. "I worked out the system. The names that are crossed out didn't survive the experiments, the others were either converted into employees or transferred to another unit."

"Wow, Sherlock Holmes. You sure are a master at code breaking," Pyro drawls and I slap his bicep.

"What does that mean another unit? There's more converted asylums?" My question goes unanswered as Ghost reaches up and tugs the box off the top shelf. We huddle towards the closest lantern on the wall and drop down onto the floor beneath, emptying out the contents of the box. The papers are frail, discolored so much, the words on them have almost completely faded. Holding them up to the light, we try to make sense of the test results but it's the photos in the bottom of the box that are more telling.

A man. The same one from the desk, in this very asylum. The decor is different but I recognize the metal staircases leading up to the overhanging guard's quarters. What's strange is that, for an inmate, he seems to be the only one here. Posing for photos in and out of his lab coat, injecting and experimenting on himself. One faded image shows him peeling his skin off around the port wine birthmark on just over his shoulder, spanning the top right of his back. But that smile...I just can't place it.

"I've seen photos of that guy before. He's the original scientist, right?" Pyro asks, handing a photo to Ghost.

"Oh yeah, it was on the news for some anniversary tribute a few years ago. Dubbed 'The man who ruined the world'." Ghost nods, chucking the photo back in the box as if it means nothing. But it must mean something, right? To be hidden in a drawer in a creepy basement beneath the asylum. Closing the box, Ghost places it back on the shelf and I find myself pacing.

"Why would the scientist who detected blood markers for a mutant gene call himself inmate number one? We must be missing something." Ghost wraps his arms around me from behind, crushing me like a giant bear in an attempt of comfort. I wriggle against him, not wanting to waste time when an alarm pierces the air. We've been discovered missing.

Pyro tugs us to move, darting between the shelving units. There's nowhere to find within the four walls, just that one stack of boxes which will be too obvious. We run like wild, headless chickens until finding ourselves at the door the Blacksmith disappeared into.

Footfalls thunder overhead, a spear of light bursting from the top of the stone steps. My heart pounds in my chest and I reach out to take my men's hands. We might as well own being caught. Standing tall, the first glimpse of boots appear as Ghost jolts forward. I lose my grip on him, scrambling to help when he simultaneously burps, farts and blinks out of view.

Opening my mouth to call for him, a shoulder rugby tackles both me and Pyro through the door at our backs and we topple into the darkened room. Only, a giant goofy oaf doesn't fall on top of me as expected. Jumping to our feet, Pryo and I peer out of a tiny glass window, seeing Ghost stride forward with his hands held high.

"Alright, alright. You found me," he calls out and my gut drops. He's taking the rap. "You want to have a word with Tate. She messed with my ability and I fell straight through the damn floor. Been trying to find a way out this whole time." A guard removes the baton from his belt and slams it into Ghost's ribs. Pyro jerks and hisses as if that blow hit him too.

"Where are the others?" the guard bellows, using his boot this time to roundhouse Ghost in the stomach. But he doesn't fight back.

"What others? I left Pyro and Mania screwing in my bathroom, if that's who you're referring to. Going at it like monkeys. Sounded a bit like this," and Ghost proceeds to screech at the top of his lungs. A few hoo hoo ah ahh's and a bit of beating on his chest for dramatic effect before the manacle is clamped down on his neck.

I gasp at the sudden loss of heat in my chest, Ghost's presence now hindered from our flames. He's surprisingly cooperative, being dragged from the basement by his neck restraint but that's because he's covering for us. Fighting would only give the guards a reason to look behind this door. Speaking of which...

"Py, stop breathing down my neck," I whisper, shrugging off the heated puffs skating over my nape. When he clears his throat from a few feet to my left, I frown and click my fingers together to produce a single flame like I've seen him do. Except when I turn around, the pair of molten eyes glaring back at me are not Pyro's after all.

"Step away from her, Blacksmith, or I'll incinerate you where you stand." Calling for a fireball in the palm of my hand, the side of his hunched body comes fully into view. Chains snake around his arms, just deep enough to be considered as tattoos if I didn't know he could whip them into existence at any moment. His head shifts to me, but he doesn't move away from his spot towering over Mania.

"You can't be in here," he growls, his voice hoarse and unused. I'm fully aware we're trespassing, but when his clenched fists are so close to my soul mate, there's no backing down.

"I said, get the fuck away from her," I lift my hand. Just before the flames lash out of my control, a whimper sounds. The Blacksmith's shoulders stiffen just enough for me to notice in the glow, so at the last moment, I send my flames snaking around the room.

Swirling around the ceiling, glistening stone walls illuminate around huge bursts of foliage. Bark shifts beneath my feet as I step into Mania's side, now aware of the branches hanging low and vines threatening to trip us up. Humidity, which has nothing to do with my fires, seeps into my skin now the adrenaline is subsiding. And amongst it all on a small, single bed, is a girl peering up with worry held in her yellow-slitted eyes.

"Oh my god," Mania breathes. "Serpentina!" She goes to run forward but the Blacksmith is too fast, whipping out a chain to curl around Mania's waist and tug her back a step.

Snapping my hand closed into a fist, the fires from the ceiling shoot for the Blacksmith's neck. Spinning around his throat just close enough for the heat to pose a threat, he sighs and draws the chain back into his wrist. Mania shoots me a glare and I withdraw my flames too, leaving a single ball in the air to provide a light.

"What the hell is going on down here?" I bark when no one moves except the little girl sliding off the bed. Her white dress is filthy, her feet bare as she walks over the bark to hug the Blacksmith's leg. He lifts her against his chest, carrying her back over to the bed where he sits.

"You're protecting her?" Mania asks in a small voice. Similar to me, she must have made the quick judgment the Blacksmith meant this little girl harm. But as he strokes her yellow hair and rocks her gently back to sleep, it's clear his intent isn't to hurt her.

"I don't expect, nor do I care for you to understand. Just leave." He grumbles, pointing to the door.

"I'm not going anywhere until I know Serpentina is safe," Mania lifts her chin when the Blacksmith laughs bitterly and I step in behind her shoulder. That makes two of us. "Or why she's locked in the pitch black in some twisted vivarium bedroom."

"Firstly, Serpentina can see in the dark. And as for the bedroom… she was locked in the cells much like you were at first. Until I pleaded with Christopher to give her a room. After all, the experiments he's doing and still plans to do to her are extensive enough to warrant a decent place to recover. But this," the Blacksmith scowls at the walls and kicks his boot into the bark. "This is a fucking joke." The girl whimpers again and he's quick to soothe her.

Anger bleeds through our bond. Mania's chest heaves in short pants, her body beginning to shake. I feel every ounce of her frustration, and without words, we share the same thought. How the fuck can Christopher sleep at night after experimenting on an innocent child? But I can already hear the echo of his laughter and imagine his response. Mutes aren't innocent, we're abominations.

"We need to get her out of here," Mania takes a step forward and I stop her. Not because the Blacksmith tensed as if to mean her harm, because I'd take on him and anyone else who threatened my girl. But despite her sentiment, our hands are tied.

"Mania, where would we take her? It's no safer out there with all the cameras watching," I say into her ear. Pressing a kiss to her neck, I already know I'll be dragging her away from this room. Lack of uterus or not, Mania has a maternal streak she won't admit to. "We need to go before they realize Ghost was lying."

She doesn't move. The fires in my chest are battering around like a sledgehammer but on the outside, Mania is cool and collected as she raises her head higher.

"Why do you, of all Mutes, care about her? Why isn't Claire or Tate down here caring for her?"

"Have you seen Tate or Claire?" the Blacksmith scoffs, brushing Serpentina's hair back from her face. She looks even smaller in his large arms. "They're no good caring for anyone right now. While Christopher has been leaving you four alone for the most part, others are suffering." I don't like the edge to his tone that suggests we're somehow at fault. After all, he's the one working for enemy. The air taints with our resentment towards him, for the betrayal we never saw coming.

"We are going to find a way out of here," I announce confidently. "And when we do, we're taking the girl with us." Mania's head whips around, undying love gleaming in her gaze. I knew saving Serpentina was the right thing to do, but seeing Mania's reaction only confirms it. We'll give them both the family they need.

"You're all deluded and you'll get yourselves killed before you step foot out of this asylum." The Blacksmith lays Serpentina on the bed and tucks a tatty blanket around her curled up body. "Aside from the experiments, she doesn't leave my side, and I'm not running into the sunset with a bunch of convicts." Folding his arms, he steps between us and the bed as a clear warning. It's our time to go.

"I'd rather die trying then become a sell-out like you," Mania grits out. "Turning on your own kind and for what?! You're not exactly living the high life here." Her arms gesture at the tiny, dark room that makes him seem like a giant. In two steps, he's before us with the same menacing look directed at Mania that has my hackles rising.

"I was broken long before that maze. Playing my part ensures me a quiet life for the most part. You'd have done the same if you had nothing left to fight for. Besides, I don't owe any of you shit." Spinning on his heels in the dark, he moves to the back wall and drops down, forearms over elbows. I catch Mania's chin in my hand and shake my head. There's no point arguing anymore.

Peering out of the small window in the door, I find it clear and twist the clunky handle. My fires shoot back into me before I step outside, leaving the shadows to loom at our back. Turning to close the door, I catch the blink of those yellow, slitted eyes once more and my heart sinks. Leaving Serpentina down here goes against all of my morals, but we need to regroup. To plan and prep how the fuck we're going to get out of here. Pushing my weight against metal, a small, gruff voice seeps out just before the doors closes.

"I had a daughter once."

Arms wrapped around my neck, Mania burying her head into my neck as a sob escapes her. I hold her close, stroking her flame with reassurance I don't fully feel. Just when I thought I'd found a modicum of happiness, the reality of our situation comes crashing back down. How many have to suffer?

It's then I decide just escaping isn't enough. Not if this is what we're going to leave behind - history to repeat itself. To pass the torture over to a new, unsuspecting victim. No, we can't just leave. We need to tear this asylum down, brick by brick. Christopher's blood will rain upon the crumbled remains, his head clutched in my hand.

Ghost's faint flame stirs within, quietly asking if I'm okay. My thoughts went to a dark place he wouldn't expect from me. Hell, I wasn't sure I had it in myself. That's the thing about good guys. We love those we deem worthy ferociously; others perceive us as weak when it's quite the opposite. For the girl in my arms, I would go nuclear on the whole damn world, leaving only us and a select few others in the charred remains.

Pulling Mania away from the door and towards the small, stone staircase, I can't help the little voice in the back of my head that wonders if that's what the Blacksmith did? Or how much he had to lose to become the Mute he is today. Dammit, I don't want to sympathize with him.

Pushing the main door open a crack, I see we're on the ground level of Afterlife, between the chapel and other rec rooms lining the wall beneath the metal walkway where our rooms are. It's dark and quiet but there's no cameras in this corner. At least if we're caught elsewhere, we won't have to explain why we were snooping around the case files or that we found Serpentina's secret hidden room.

Keeping Mania close, I pull her behind me as I take the first step, keeping close to the wall.

"You sure took your time," Christopher's voice rings out and I know before the sea of stunt guns fire from above, we were kidding ourselves to think we'd make it out of this unscathed.

MANIA

Coming to, my neck rolls on a hard surface. A spike of pain shoots through the back of my head, and as I go to raise my arms, they splash through liquid to smash into a hard covering. *What the fuck?* Blinking my vision clear, a metal sheet stretches from my neck to my feet, fully encasing the tub I find myself in. Freezing cold water ripples across my body and I shudder.

"Mai," a whisper sounds and I twist my neck to see that's all Ghost could rasp out. Like me, he's trapped in a metal tank, much like a bathtub, with only his head visible. His white eyes roll back and in a panic, I look around to find Pyro in the same predicament on my left, his eyes cracked open but unresponsive, his lips blue. This is bad. Super fucking bad.

The open space resembles an old pool room, mold in the tiled walls. Mildew mixes with damp, making me want to sneeze if I weren't so distracted by the two metal cages either side of the frosted glass window. Shower heads hang over them, but the closed top and thick padlock give the impression not much choice is given in the temperature. Hell, it could spew out acid for all I know, my mind going a mile a minute.

"Seems the whole gang's awake," that voice comes and I want to shrink fully beneath the water, freezing or not. Christopher steps into view, the light behind him not masking the missing suit I'd expected. Standing tall in a white tee and blue jeans, he looks every inch the handsome man in his forties if I had to guess. Practically handsome, if I didn't know him better. His soul is black, his spirit doomed for Hell.

Walking around the front of the tubs, a line of MRA agents move into view to make a line before us. All for show, I'd imagine. Their hands are wrapped around the batons at their waists and it occurs to me the lack of guns I associate with the MRA. Can't have them killing Christopher's prized experiments though, can we?

"What do you even want with us?" I choke out, only realizing then how cold I truly am. Not just that, but the absence of our eternal flame in my hollow chest makes me shiver. It's too cold for Pyro, and if his flame goes out - all of ours do.

"Honestly?" Christopher's voice echoes around the room since I can't see him from this angle. "Nothing at all. I have all I need. But since the three of you decided to stick your noses where they didn't belong, I thought I'd have a little fun."

"Like you thought you'd have fun messing with Ghost's head?" I shout back, craning my neck to look at the Mute on my right. Ghost's eyelids have drawn closed and fear slices through me at how unresponsive he is. Even in the most dire situations, he can usually manage at least a tiny smile.

"Precisely," Christopher answers me at last. He reappears with a hand towel to dry off his forearms. "So, who's turn is it for some fun today?" Clearly Pyro and Ghost aren't in the frame of mind to reply and I bite down on my lower lip. It's a trap, I know that, yet knowing Christopher - he'll probably do the opposite I say. "No volunteers?"

Shrugging with a smirk, he whips the towel over his shoulder and clicks his fingers, pointing at Pyro. I shoot upright as far as the metal sheet at my collarbone will allow.

"Me. Obviously me, leave them alone," I beg. A faint voice in the back of my head screams to keep my mouth shut and my eyes slide to Pyro. He looks absent, but he's very much aware of what's happening. The agents circle around my tank, unclipping the top sheet to slide it off. And I'm completely naked. Fantastic.

The water is unusually blue, my limbs numb and unresponsive. Even if I wanted to fight the hands lifting me from the tub, I can barely manage to raise my hands for the heavy cuffs clamped back around my wrists.

Hauling me away, my head lolls to see there is in fact a swimming pool in here. Small, around the size of a Kingsize bed, and filled with the same tinted blue water. Black shapes shift within the liquid, although I can't get a proper look before I'm strapped to a metallic chair facing outwards on the pool's edge. Leather binds fix my forearms, shin and forehead in place.

Now facing the opposite side of the room, the doorway swings open and Hoax stands there. I flinch, for unknown reasons. My body's instant reaction to ask him for help while trying to cover my nakedness. Humiliation creeps up my neck and resonates in my cheeks, the warmest part of me currently.

Sparks dance beneath the wires inked on his skin, the purple glow disappearing beneath the short sleeves of his t-shirt and illuminating through the material. His indigo eyes capture mine, staring straight through my skull before he simply walks inside. Directly to Christopher.

Patting him on the back, the unhinged asshole passes Hoax an instrument that looks too much like a gun for my liking. No words are exchanged, making my hackles rise further when Hoax turns to me with deadened eyes and the strange-looking pistol in his hand. Finger already on the trigger, a curved needle points out of the end with some kind of capsule held in the transparent barrel.

"Hoax. Hoax, please. It's me. I know you know me," I try desperately to squirm aside when he approaches. There's no response, not that I expected one as I send out a flare of panic through my bond to the others. I can't help it, as much as I wanted to be the strong one here. Just a soothing balm of their comfort would have done wonders for my confidence to tackle this situation, but there's nothing. Hoax raises the gun, jabbing the needle into the skin of my neck where he halts, awaiting further instruction.

"Remember these Hoax?" Christopher muses and then laughs to himself. Of course he can't fucking remember; Christopher made sure of that. "These are the same capsules we test on the boys at the orphanage. Ironically, Pyro is the reason we know they actually work, since he's the only one who risked defying us enough to activate his."

A shudder rolls through my body. I hold Hoax's stoic stare, pleading with him not to do this. Pulling at my fire, I try to activate it enough to jolt some recognition into his soul, but it's pointless. I'm too cold, too stressed – and there's nothing to reach inside of Hoax anyway. My only saving grace is the gag resembling a small metal pipe he shoves into my mouth just before he pulls the trigger.

Sudden sharpness with the force of a bullet knocks into me, the click reverberating around my skull as a cold weight settles beneath my skin. I bite down on the pipe, tears streaming from my eyes that have nothing to do with the pain. Hoax shot me with whatever vial of poison I can imagine was in that gun. Or at least the version of Hoax that Christopher has manufactured did.

Then, he restocks it with a similar steel capsule and shoots it into his own neck, not even blinking against the pain I feel rush through him. Leaving me, Christopher directs him to take care of 'the other two' while I curse them both around my gag. A mechanical whirring sounds just before the chair flies backwards, dunking me into the water.

A thousand volts of electricity stutter through me, my screams lost beneath the surface. Convulsing like a woman possessed, a black shadow slithers across my face. My vision fades out as I submit to the excruciating pain. My ears pop and the whirring comes back to me, giving me an indication I'm being lifted from the water. I suck short breaths in through my nostrils as the machine powering the chair halts with me still horizontal above the pool.

Amongst the spectators who have come to witness the show, a dull memory from the back of my fried skull arises. The electrical eels from the maze were the only real aspects. Without recovering from the first drop, the chair gives out again and I'm plunged back under. Again, and again, until I lose count. Each time reality starts to ebb back, muttering filters in and Christopher's booming laughter slams another headache into me.

Finally being raised back to the platform, I slump in the chair. The slickness of my skin slides from the restraints, leaving me in an awkward heap. Performing a mental check on my body, nothing reacts as my limbs are rendered completely unresponsive.

"Take her away," I hear barked as a lilac-haired woman appears before me. I barely recognize Tate more than my instinctual decision not to fight her, even if I could. An agent swoops in to release me from the gag and binds, and lifts me into his arms. "Oh and Mania," Christopher calls out before I leave the vicinity. "Don't bother searching for Serpentina. She's already been moved."

Marching me out of the room, pinpricks spike across my skin and the odd leftover spark has me jolting. I don't care to pry my eyes open, focusing on the internal.

No flames respond to my call, and the sinking pit of Hoax's betrayal are becoming too much to ignore. I can't keep excusing him, regardless of my head telling me it's not his fault. My heart can't forgive his actions anymore. Being placed down on a mattress, I curl onto my side and sigh. The cover slides over me before a soft hand brushes the soaking wet hair from my face and neck. I lean into Tate's touch, just wanting to feel something. Someone.

"I'm so sorry," she soothes and I manage a twitch to my brow. "This is all my fault. I was ordered to put a block on Ghost's flame. An attempt to cut him off and make him more suspicious of you and Pyro not sharing your feelings with him. But I brought his other ability to the surface instead. I-I was trying to help, but I've made things so much worse. Again."

Tate's breath hitches and I manage to purse my lips enough to 'shh' her. It's the best I can do at reassurance at the moment. None of this is Tate's fault, and it warms me that fraction I needed because she tried. It makes the suffering worth it to know we have someone still fighting for us, even when all seems lost.

Still shivering, I slowly lift my arm beneath the cover and expose my body to her. It's nothing she, nor the entire asylum, hasn't seen by now. Taking my cue, Tate clambers into the bed with me and draws me into her arms. Her heat seeps into my cold skin, her breath fanning my face. I inhale deeply, drawing on her strength. How far we've come for me to not only consider Tate as an ally, but to trust her as a friend. To draw on her comfort in a time like this.

"H-how are you?" I breathe after we've remained silent long enough for me to gain some strength.

"I don't have an answer for that question," is the only reply I get. Closing my eyes, I take the last bit of heat Tate is offering and turn it inwards. The flame responds easier this time, although I'm the only one present.

Stoking it, I visualize a warm summer's day. A large apple tree with a blanket beneath, the sun kissing mine and Pyro's legs. Ghost runs across my fantasy butt naked, whooping as he disappears down the hillside. I leave Hoax out of the scene this time, knowing he'll only taint what I'm trying to achieve. Sure enough, the eternal flame brightens with orange and a dash of white, and at least in part - I know my men are okay.

"We're going to get out of here Tate. I promise."

"I've given up on these things. Hope, promises. Just today has proved there's always a way to trap us. Like overcoming the layer of resilience Pyro placed on you long enough to get the capsule into your neck."

"So that's what it was all about," I huff. With the possibility we could shake the cuffs at any time, the capsule is another way to control us. To scare us into behaving. Well, I'm done with that shit. If Christopher thinks this will stop me from rebelling, he's about to find out just how wrong he is about me.

Drawing myself upright, I hold the covers around my chest while Tate rises from the bed. Heading to my locker, she pulls out a towel and a fresh, folded tracksuit.

"Christopher is many things, but stupid isn't one of them. He knew you'd only let your guard down enough for Hoax to stick the needle in you. Pyro being slipped small doses of liquid nitrogen into his tank should have been enough, but he didn't want to risk it." I shudder at the thought of Py's flame being quelled like that, as well as Tate's notion I need to take a shower. Being under water again so soon doesn't sit right with me. She disappears into the bathroom and reappears with steam billowing at her back, one finger raised in a no-nonsense manner.

"Go warm up. You are no good to any of your boyfriends while shivering." Despite myself, I bite back a smile. My boyfriends. The title seems redundant at this point since we share an eternal bond, so why do I feel as giddy as a teenager hearing the label out loud for the first time?

Like a hero coming home from war, Follicle returns from the canteen with a tray piled high in each hand. His hair is thick and black, swishing to his waist while his beard is also dark and full. Behind him, Goldie is still panting, in a lustful daze as her bear-fetish-on-legs walks away with the entirety of her midday horde.

From around the table, Hare-iett, Siren, Pyro and I all cheer while helping him to unload. Steaks, burgers, chicken wings, fries, a pitcher of juice and enough crockery for all. A buffet for kings, or a worthy last meal if our sanity is the sacrifice we pay.

I don't know why Goldie and her three hairy minions bother cooking all of this food considering there aren't as many Mutes milling around as there have been. My guess is it has less to do with the possible alliances they could build and everything to do with the guards eying them from the entrance gate. If Goldie doesn't show that the kitchen staff are doing their duty, they will be replaced and her free rein on the food supply will swiftly end.

Dishing out our plates in a comfortable silence, we tuck into our meals while Follicle retracts his hair into a clean-cut army look, not a trace of stubble in sight and his blonde hair cropped short on top.

"If there's any porridge," Ghost calls out, hopping down from the bottom step of the metal staircase, "don't eat it." Pyro sighs, dropping his fork to temporarily step away from the table, punch Ghost in the face and return to my side. Ghost hiccups, mumbling that's what happens when he's caught off guard.

"Is this still happening? Dude apologized, let it go." I roll my eyes, bumping Pyro's shoulder. Ghost's arm slides around me as he takes my other side, pressing a hiccupped, blood-smeared kiss to my temple.

"No no, let him get it out of his system. I wavered in my commitment and then got us in a whole ton of extra shit, I'm always happy to pay for my mistakes." I shoot Ghost a look that says he's full of shit and he breaks into a grin. "And I've always got you to kiss my injuries better," he winks. There it is.

Playfully slapping him across the face, I press a heated kiss to his cheek and lips. Heated, a flare of the flame passes through my lips and seals the split in his lip.

It's been almost a week since that day in the old pool room. I've tried to block it out, despite the nightmares that arise each night where I think I'm drowning. Luckily, I've had the weight of two men pressing into my sides to ease my spluttering and comfort me back to sleep. We haven't spoken much about the capsules in our necks, preferring to live for each day and revel in what we have together until the next time. Hoax has yet to be seen.

"So," Hare-iett leans forward to whisper. "How's the escape plan coming on?" I still, fork in mid-air to flash a look at the camera pointed directly at us. Pushing a chunk of steak into my mouth, I take my time chewing and regulating my heartbeat.

"Don't know what you're talking about," I shrug after swallowing. Pyro's hand tightens on my thigh and I resist looking at either him or Ghost. Another blessing from the past few days, we've been giving the time to work on our mental connection.

Sure you do, Ghost communicates through our bond. *That vision of me streaking naked while you guys lie around being boring was pretty vivid.* I blush, concealing my smile behind another mouthful. His hand shifts to mirror Pyro's on my other thigh and apparently I was left out of the thought that has them both drifting their fingers up the inner seam of my sweatpants. Just before they reach the apex of my thighs, a Mute calls out for our attention.

"The election's taking place!" a Mute, they either call the Cheetah or Cheater, announces, popping his head back inside the rec room. Food forgotten, we rush over with most of the asylum's inmates at our back. They must have heard the announcement from the yard.

Piling inside the tiny room, the central table and chairs are shoved aside to make room. Ghost's hands wind around my waist before he plants me on top of said-table with Hare-iett and Siren scrambling up to join. A tiny, box television is mounted on the wall. Usually the source of arguments over the remote control, but not today as a young, female news reporter steps onto the small screen.

Good afternoon. I'm Rebecca Falls on behalf of Freedom News. I'm here live at the White House where Simon Beckett and Octavia Horton are awaiting the results of the recent election. Both candidates are in attendance with their families. The votes are in and I'm receiving word that they have been counted and verified. Your new president is..."

We all wait on tenterhooks. Not even a breath can be heard in the room of compacted bodies. I don't know what reason I have to be nervous, and I doubt a single Mute in this room has ever given a damn about the elections before. But our fate has never been in the balance before. For as long as I've been aware, we've been illegal. Hunted. Despised. And although I have my doubts Octavia would actually keep her hollow promises, there's a small chance. Right?

Octavia Horton! A flag unravels on the right side of the stage displaying a swirling OH on a personalized crest and the crowd watching burst into outrageous cheering. I'd imagine the scene akin to a rock concert, while the room around me echoes with a deafening silence. Side glances are shared, but no one is willing to admit the hope blossoming in all of us.

I spy Goldie and her bears by the doorway, her head dipping in a slow nod. For one moment, this moment, everyone in this room is equal. No enemies or alliances. Just beings searching for something to believe in. To live for.

"You've got to be fucking kidding me!" Ghost calls out, breaking the tranquility. I scowl at him before following his eyeline back to the television. Octavia has taken the center podium to deliver her speech, her arm outstretched for the camera to tilt to the stage's steps. A head of olive green hair leads the way. Right behind, a short woman in an outfit as pink as her hair bounces along, quickly followed by a bald male with head tattoos. Hare-iett gasps, her hand gripping onto my wrist.

"That's him!" she whisper-shouts in my ear even though I'm sure everyone heard it. "That's Granite!" I'm so focused on the male she told me about, I almost miss the pair of twins that are last to take their place on the stage. Mid-height with such pale hair and irises, they seem transparent. The Mirage Twins I'm supposing.

"Thank you!" Octavia calls out through her microphone. "Thank you all so much for your support. It is my privilege to stand before you today, not only with the tremendous backing of my deputy, treasurer and security general," she signals to the men and woman standing on one side of her. "But also with these fine citizens!"

Lifting her hand towards the five I recognize, the crowd goes wild again, applauding Imp and Camo like Gods. If I squint hard enough at the distorted screen, I can make out the bulging pockets of wallets and watches Imp has pickpocketed on her way through the crowd.

"Fine citizens, my puckered asshole!" Ghost shouts and receives a small applause of his own.

"Mutants have been exiled for far too long, and not because they pose a danger. But because we have been scared. We persecute what we don't understand, but I am here today to tell you - we are all residents of this wonderful country. We all deserve the right to live long and fulfilling lives, free from fear. The Mutants possess gifts that will enable us to create a better today, and a far greater tomorrow!"

The television goes black as the crowd erupts again, leaving us all looking around for the source. Mutes part to show a small man with saggy skin chewing on the cable plugged into the wall. His front teeth are overly large and stained yellow, his back hunched and legs bent.

"Fuck's sake," Ghost groans. "How long have we had a naked mole rat in our midst? Now I know where the droppings appearing in the yard came from." Groans filter through the room as people make their way outside. Sliding off the table, I move to follow when Hare-iett holds me back.

I'll be out in a minute, I tell the guys through our connection. Ignoring their worried looks, I drag two chairs into the center of the room and place them facing each other. Hare-iett sits, her eyes darting to Mole Rat and back as she chews on her nails.

"What's wrong? Surely the election is something to celebrate," I try to ease her mind. I don't believe the crock of shit Octavia said for one moment. Actions speak louder than words so the outcome of today will remain to be seen.

"It's not that. Did you see him?" Hare-iett shakes her head. Her floppy ear bounces against her brunette hair, the charred stump of the other now healed over with a thin layer of fur. "Granite. He looked completely lost, like a male who's been broken. He's literally made of stone, Mania. If he couldn't survive this place, what hope do we have?"

"What is it with you and him?" I ask the obvious. Hare-iett knows what's going on here. She's seen the aftermath of what Pyro, Ghost and I have been through. But suddenly she's worried about surviving Afterlife - or just that the male she pinned her hopes on might no longer exist?

"Maybe our 'thing' was more than I let on, or maybe it was all in my head. We had a passion filled week I've never been able to forget. It's stupid to think Mutes like us would find love in the basement of a strip club, but it was special. Or at least, I hope it was. He was dragged away before anything could come of it but...but I..."

"You never gave up on finding him?" I presume. Leaning forward, I take Hare-iett's hands in mine. "Having something to live for isn't anything to be ashamed of. Who's to say he's lost to you forever? If I can find my men in the pits of hell, you can reach him. Don't give up." Sharing a smile I'm not sure either of us feel, a glimpse of indigo beyond the doorway catches my eye. Speaking of males being lost to us...

Leading Hare-iett out and telling her to go finish her lunch, I spy Ghost and Pyro leaning against the staircase. They jolt upright but I raise a hand to halt them, my feet moving as my eyes remain trained on the canvas shoes disappearing up the steps.

Give me one last chance, I tell them mentally, already walking past. *One more attempt to reach him. If there's nothing left to save, I'll walk away for good.*

We all will, Pyro replies, nodding to me. Inhaling deeply, I jog up the stairs and brace my hand on the cell door, finding some inner strength before pushing my way inside to find Hoax.

HOAX

Thu-thump.

Christopher stands from behind his desk, fully invested on the phone pressed to his ear.

"And how long can we expect to see results? If his bloodwork isn't showing signs of accepting the gene, scrap him and start on the next one." The frustration tainting his tone, a hand being scrubbed over his face.

Thu-thump.

Rounding the desk, he wears the rug thin with the circle he prefers to pace in, almost tripping over my outstretched legs.

"Fuck's sake," Christopher grumbles and snaps his fingers in front of my unblinking eyes. "Move your damn feet Host."

Thu-thump.

He took to calling me Host a while ago, an insult on the mind he continues to rob from me. Pulling my feet back as he says, my eye line remains on the heart pulsating in a jar on his desk.

Thu-thump.

I could stare at the colors for hours. Gold gleams through the crevices, catching the light of the fireplace. It always glows brighter when close to the flames. As if it knows. Cracks snake around the blackened organ, the outer level seeming to be hardening inside the jar of yellow-tinted fluid.

Ending his phone call with a barked order, he heads over to the drink's cabinet. The clink of the whiskey bottle on the rim of the glass rings through my ears. Soon enough, a measure of strongly scented amber liquid in placed beneath my nose. An offering. A trap.

I don't take it. I know what's coming.

"As if I'd waste good whiskey on you," he snarls, tossing the contents of the glass in my face. My threaded fingers twitch, hidden by the slow rise of my abdomen. "You're lucky I have use for you."

Returning to his leather chair behind the desk, Christopher sips his drink, watching me closely. I'm his favorite object. An ornament to add to his collection of stuffed heads mounted on the wall behind me. After all, that's why he put me here. In this chair, where I await further instruction.

Bored of our staring contest, Christopher opens his laptop and gets back to work. His phone vibrates across the desk with a string of calls and messages, all of which he ignores. Sighing, his fingers go to his temples where he rubs small circles to relieve stress. One black strand of his hair drops forward and he's quick to push it back into place.

"I never intended for this to take so long," he mutters to himself. His hand curls into a fist. Slamming it onto his jittering cell phone, he lifts the empty glass and throws it into the fireplace. "It never should have taken this long!"

A tentative knock sounds at the door. Righting his shirt and smoothing down his hair, he stands, telling the intruder to enter. Feet softly scuffle inside. Not impressed with who he sees, Christopher strides forward and snatches the files from her trembling hands.

"T-there's been a development you should know of, Sir." Lilac eyes trace my features, concern pitched in her brows.

"Speak freely. We've run extensive tests. There's no brain activity going on in here," Christopher grabs a handful of my hair, dragging my head around in wide circles. Tossing me back into the seat, he lays the files onto his desk and flicks through them, his back to me.

"The election results," she hesitates when Christopher whips around. The female flinches, her voice almost too small to be heard. "President Horton has given her acceptance speech. She's entering the White House as we speak." Icy blue eyes flitter with panic. Reaching for his phone, Christopher frantically scrolls through the missed calls and messages he should have responded to.

"Sir, we should reach out first. Congratulate her and build up a healthy

relationship that will benefit us," the female tries but her words are lost to Christopher's bitter laughter.

"No one permitted you to talk," he chuckles as if finding the glimpse of her backbone humorous. "We continue as normal. Backup every file on hard drive and wipe the servers. We're too close to be hindered by some hippy liberal now. If it comes to it, we move all of the important test subjects to a secure facility and leave the rest to starve."

"You can't just leave all of these beings to rot. It's not humane. Especially with a new President taking such a close interest," she continues to argue. There's no use trying to change the opinion of a bitter old man.

"Fine. We'll shoot them where they stand. Is that humane enough for you?" Dismissing her, Christopher returns to the files. A photograph of a small girl with yellow-slitted eyes flutters to the ground, her skin red and scratched. She was in here briefly yesterday, picking off the scales growing along her arms.

I draw my attention back to the thumping heart, unaware the female in the room has stepped closer until her hand brushes my arm. I remain still. Trailing her cold fingers down to mine, she pries my hands free of one another to give me a squeeze. In reassurance maybe, but the notion is lost by the tremble in her limbs.

Catching onto the lack of a closing door, Christopher looks over his shoulder. She gasps, dropping my hand and returning to her previous space.

"Why are you still here? I've given my orders."

"Sir," she swallows loudly enough for me to hear it. "You promised you'd release Claire to me after the child was finished on dialysis." The tension in the room thickens, ridding the air of oxygen. Even the fire flickers, struggling to stay a light as Christopher wipes an arm across the desk. The files scatter across the ground, the heart jar wobbles before righting itself.

"That little serpent has rejected every other animal mutagen we've thrown her way! Until her antibodies are stable, you will continue with your work."

"But that's not-"

"Fair? Is that what you were going to say, Tate?" Christopher spins now, puffing his chest out. His dress shoes eat the distance between the two, bringing him within breathing space of her paled face. "I don't think you *rendering an entire society of Mutes defenseless against the MRA was very fair either, but you still did it."*

"I was only following orders," Tate whimpers, shrinking away from him. Grabbing the lapels of her lab coat, Christopher holds her in place.

"And you will continue to do so, unless you need a reminder of all the ways I own you?" His arm raises, his hand flat in preparation for a slap that doesn't land.

On my feet before he can blink, I catch his wrist and throw it backwards. Pushing my shoulder between the two, my forehead slams down on Christopher's nose. Small hands press aside my shoulder blades, a brief 'thank you' on Tate's lips before she flees the room.

Blue eyes filled with venom return to mine, before a sadistic smile spreads across his face.

"Base instinct is still present," Christopher mutters to himself. Evaluating every move I make, as per usual. Reaching for the cell phone that also dropped to the floor, he doesn't take his gaze off me for one second. I stand there. Arms relaxed by my side, legs open in a solid stance. No trace of emotion on my face. Calling for his guards, the door bursts open and hands seize me. I don't fight.

"Get him out of my sight," Christopher growls, pulling an embossed handkerchief from his pocket to dab at the blood spilling from his nose. "And for fuck's sake, someone find Brainwave. I swear that bastard is taking avoiding his duties to a whole other level."

team slips out of the crack in the bathroom door as I enter Hoax's room. I pause by the bed, wondering if I should sit and wait when his low murmuring catches my attention. Hoax speaking at all is a miracle, but it's the female tone replying that has my heart hammering in my chest. No one else entered with him. Yet I hear her speaking just below the spray of the shower. Has he been playing us for fools this whole time?

The door to the bathroom wavers and I panic, deciding in a split second to dive into the locker-style wardrobe instead of leaving altogether. Pulling the door closed on myself, I shimmy back, thankful for once I'm practically skeletal. Spears or light through the slits in front of my face give me a hindered view of the room as Hoax steps out of the bathroom.

Topless, his circuit tattoos are pulsing with purple light. It's been a while since I've seen so much of him so up close but damn. Hoax has been working out. His shoulder blades shift as he reaches for a wooden pole of some sort, tucked beneath his bed. Thick biceps match the traps at his collarbone, and when he turns, all of the saliva in my mouth runs dry. Abs stretch over his torso, the overhead light dipping into each crevice between his tattoos.

"I told you not to bring them here anymore. It's too dangerous," he grumbles. At first I thought he was talking to me, or himself, until the replied hiss comes from out of sight.

"Just hurry up! I've got my own workload to manage without having to cover yours too." I frown, vaguely familiar with the tone but when the shower is beating down into an empty tub, it's hard to tell. At least I hope it's empty, my teeth grit together and jealousy spills into my bloodstream. Hoax's head whips up and looks around, his palm rubbing his own chest. Shit, I forget he's still bound to me when my feelings are rarely reciprocated. I have to control myself.

Returning to the bathroom, the door remains ajar just enough for me to watch his hazy reflection in the steamy mirror. Another figure joins him as he taps the wooden pole on the floor and something shifts. I can't make it out at first, the silhouette of his reflection growing in height. Dark shapes grow from his head and before I can stop myself, I've left the safety of the locker.

Stepping up to the bathroom door, I peer around at the ruggedly beautiful male that steals my breath. Thick horns protrude from Hoax's indigo hair, his eyes filtering into all black while his tattoos shift and refigure into skulls trapped in silent screams. On his neck, the image of an eye becomes visible, all-seeing and ever binding. The pole in his hand is transformed into a staff, wooden claws clutching the large onyx jewel trapped at the top.

If I didn't think my heart was about to give out, I'd have shrieked at the sight of Azella moving in by his side. She's dragging a body with her, shoving the handful of hair into Hoax's grip to take. He raises the staff once more and knowing what's about to happen, I burst into the room and grab onto Hoax's bicep.

"Wait!"

Skin tears. Limbs stretch. My organs spill out and then shoot back inside, my body reconfiguring itself in my new surroundings. Charred grass crunches beneath my canvas shoes, the scent of burnt flesh clogging my nostrils. A smell I was once so accustomed to, but now it's no more than a distant memory.

"Mania?!" a chest rumbles beneath my cheek, the voice so raw and annoyed that I flinch. Peering up, Hoax's irises glow purple while the rest of his eyes remain black. I shudder, and not in fear. "What the fuck are you doing?! You can't...I- you can't see me like this!" Shoving me away, Hoax drags the body clutched in one hand across the grass. Dumping it, he places his hand on the dead guard's chest and draws the soul out of him. Wait, what the-

"That's a fucking guard, Hoax?! What's going on here? And why do you look like that, and since when have you had horns and..." the breath saws out of me. My fluttering heart subsides, turning into a cannonball in my rib cage as my thoughts come tumbling in. Azella appears a moment later, two more guards are heaped at her feet. Tears prick in my eyes at the sight of my formidable adoptive mom, but I push them back and fold my arms.

"You need to go," Hoax grunts without looking my way. Not fucking good enough. Launching myself at him, I manage to build up just enough momentum to flip him over the dead body and slam his back into the ground. Scrambling up to straddle him, Hoax's reactions are too slow to catch the fist I deliver into his face.

"Answer me!" I scream, throwing another punch. He catches this one, twisting my wrist sharply. The jolt of pain gives him the edge he needs to buck his hips and throw me aside like yesterday's trash. Standing and brushing himself down, he moves over to talk to Azella in a low voice, neither of the two beings I love paying me any attention.

"Wow. And to think I liked you better as a fucking zombified slave." Dragging myself to my feet, I start striding towards the iron gates. I know enough demons here for any of them to give me a ride home before Pyro's bond kicks into gear. Unless it works differently this time because I didn't arrive by death, I hitch-hiked.

I make it within an arm's-length of Asher, who's manning the stone pillar holding up the iron gates, before Hoax's hand slips beneath my arm and he nearly drags me off my feet. Clawing and digging my heels in, I'm no match for the amount of muscle he's gained.

Raising my arm, I'm about to sink my teeth into his knuckles when he whips us into a small, stone structure. One that used to be for caging souls that weren't ready for their reaping. Long before everyone stops caring if sinners were ready or not and threw them into the fires to meet their fate.

"Get the fuck off me you-" Hoax's mouth crashes onto my mine, silencing me. I punch against his chest, refusing to be subdued so quickly. It's useless, a battle I could never win but I put up a good front. Grabbing my wrists, Hoax throws them over his neck and grabs my ass. Hoisting me up, he rams my back into the stone, gripping me tight enough to bruise.

Prying my eyes open, I watch the purple glow shimmering beneath the skeletal tattoos of reaped souls pulsate, and surrender. This is Hoax. My Hoax. The one I've been hunting for in the blankness of his stare. The male I'd convinced myself wasn't coming back. He may appear different, but I'll take him any way I can.

Pushing my tongue into his mouth, the last thread of resistance between us snaps. Leaning into me, chest to chest, crotch to crotch, there isn't a breadth of space between us. The waistband of his cargos rides against my pussy, softened by the thick material of my sweatpants, yet the barrier has me growling in frustration. Reaching for his zipper, my fingers grace the steel-like erection inside and Hoax nudges my hand away to do it himself.

Bracing myself on his neck, his dick thuds against my ass and I realize I don't have any cuffs on down here. A smile graces my lips between his heated kisses. When his tongue next takes me hostage, I tug on the heat welling up inside and direct it to my legs, burning all clothes south of my waist into nothing but ash. Hoax groans at the gentle kiss of my flames, breaking apart long enough to watch the speckles of ash drift around us.

"So beautiful," he breathes, nudging my chin aside with his nose to access my neck. The glint of his horns catches my eye and I stroke the curve, holding back my questions for later. Now isn't the time.

Hoax's hand shifts from my ass, using the pressure of his body to hold mine against the rough wall and dip his fingers between my thighs. Finding my clit instantly, he circles it three times before dipping to my pussy. I'm surprised at how wet I am, but his satisfied chuckle is all masculine ego.

For too long he teases me, spreading my wetness around my clit and back down again, never once entering me. I'm thankful for that, because the frenzy building in my core will denote as soon as he does, and it'd better be for his cock.

"Fuck me Hoax," I groan, writhing in his hold. Raising his head, the smile that stretches across his face makes my heart skip a beat. Hoax is beautiful regardless, but the two lengthy fangs spearing his gums is my undoing. "Actually, *fuck*. Bite me, fill me, do *something*."

A simple jerk of his hips and the large head of his cock is pushing into me, stretching me. Guttural sounds leave my throat as I clamber for air, being sucked into the void that is Hoax in his true form. Oh my demon.

Pulling back and easing back in, I spread my legs wider to accommodate him. I don't know why I didn't think this far ahead, but I'm pleasantly surprised to find *everything* has grown. He fills me without any room to spare, my body wriggling to adjust while he patiently waits. Or watches me whimper, the fucker.

Then, he moves.

Thrusting me into the wall without restraint. Dragging his fangs across my jaw. His dick slams into my g-spot over and over, yet every time my pussy begins to flutter, he's gone and I'm left reeling. My nails are embedded in his back, the flames inside me reaching fever pitch. Sweat breaks out across my skin and when I close my eyes, his purple strand is all I can see. Dancing just out of reach, taunting me. The tremors of my orgasm sets in again and his flame fades out of view.

"You're hindering me!" I gasp, realizing Hoax is not only playing with my body, but my climax too. He chuckles against my neck and I fight a swoon. I don't know who this Hoax is, but I love it. I want it. Every hour on the hour for the rest of my life.

Not now Mania, not when it's your pleasure we're discussing.

"Do you have any idea what it's been like watching you from afar?" Hoax asks, ramming into me harder to punctuate his sentences. "To see you kissing Ghost. To hear you fucking Pyro. While I'm stuck in the background, yearning for you." My heart breaks between the screams being pulled from my throat.

"You could have had it all too," I cry, tears prickles at my eyes from the intensity of it all. His words, his cock driving me into oblivion. His glowing purple and black eyes lift to seek out mine, his body stilling and I whimper at the friction halted inside of me.

"I almost broke once, in the chapel. It would have been so easy to take you then, and ruin everything I've been preparing in the process." His grip on my ass turns punishing as Hoax sinks a hand into my hair and yanks my head aside, exposing my neck to him. Picking up the pace of his thrusting again, his head dips and those razor-sharp fangs sink into my neck. My toes curl as everything clenches, my orgasm ripping through me.

Wave after wave is torn from my core, my vision blacking out. I squeeze Hoax's shaft so hard, he has to force himself to keep moving inside me until he's roaring his own release into my neck. Ripples roll through his shaft, drawing out my pleasure until I'm sure my voice box has dislodged and my heart won't ever beat again.

"I love you so fucking much," I mutter softly, a tear finally falling from my eye. Hoax slumps against me, his body heaving heavily as I feel this moment quickly coming to its end. Despair claws at our bond, trying to hold on when I know it's useless. I can already see his flame dimming, feel his soul withdrawing. Shoving my hands into his indigo hair, I clutch him to me for as long as he'll permit it.

"You can't tell anyone Mania, especially not *them*." His voice cracks through us like a physical divider. Releasing him, Hoax lowers my feet to the ground. Pulling the t-shirt over my head, he uses it to clean me up and then steps out of his boxers to gently ease them up my own legs. Standing before him in merely underwear, I fold my arms, watching him tug up his cargos and tuck his still-hard dick inside. I was right, he's huge with a thick vein curling around his shaft, but that moment has passed.

"I can't keep secrets from Pyro and Ghost. It'll be our downfall," I tell him when I'm sure he's about to leave.

"And if you alert Christopher to what I've been doing, it's all for nothing. I've been suffering so you won't always have to. Don't undo it all now," he bites back, a crease in his eyebrows.

Is he angry at me? I haven't been the one lying and sneaking around. My subconscious bats around, trying to make sense of how he's acting and although deep down, I know my best interest is his goal, I can't get over how he's treating me now.

"As you wish. After all, it's you who shot a poison capsule into my neck. So much for not having to suffer anymore." My head raises defiantly, even when Hoax spins to slam me back against the wall, his hand on my neck.

"You really think I'd put you in danger?" he growls up close. The streams of blood from my neck trickle down his chin in two straight lines and it takes everything in me not to do something stupid. Like lick them clean or offer myself up as his breakfast, lunch and dinner.

"Your words don't match your actions," I breathe, a shiver running through me. There's a tug on our eternal bond, a visceral yank in my chest that tells me Pyro is looking for me. The way Hoax's eyes glow that little bit brighter shows he felt it too. We're running out of time.

"Christopher's plans are bigger than all of us. It's not good enough to kill the bastard and be done with it. There's a fail-safe on his life, meaning so many more would die. So. Fucking. Many, Mania. Don't make me choose between my head and my heart."

"Seems like you've already made your decision," I mutter when he hangs his head. A stab of pain resonates through us. As good as Hoax is at hiding his emotions from me, evidently he's not good enough.

Throwing his fists into the wall either side of my head, Hoax roars to the ceiling at the same time a sinner screams from the fires. I remain there, not backing down when his eyes return to mine, full of frustration. This time when he speaks, it's through our mental connection.

If Pyro and Ghost know I have my spirit back, they will treat me differently. Look at me differently. I need you all to hate me to pull off what I've been trying to do. Christopher has eyes everywhere Mania, even among the Mutes. You can't trust anyone.

Stepping away, Hoax calls for his staff. It appears in his hand and I drink in one last look at my bonded mate. My darkest desire. My demon.

GHOST

"She's in here!" Pyro shouts from the doorway of Hoax's cell. Racing up the hallway from hers, I skid inside to see Py lifting Mania's body from the floor. Steam billows from beneath the closed bathroom door, the sound of the shower hammering down making my fingers curl into fists.

"What the fuck did he do to you?" I shout, unable to control my voice. "I'll fucking kill him where he stands."

"No," Mania rasps. Black boxers hug her ass, her legs and torso bare aside from a crop top bra. Blood is smeared over her collarbone, although I can't see the source. Mania only ascended the stairs to follow Hoax up here a few minutes ago, but Pyro knew something was wrong. He felt it before I did. "S-someone else attacked me and pushed me in here. I didn't see who," Mania breathes and curls into Pyro's chest. We share a look that screams bullshit.

Stomping to the bathroom door, I use my foot to open it. Slamming against the tiles, I approach the shower cubicle and rip the glass divider open. Hoax faces away from me. Scratches disappear into the circuit tattoos spanning his back. Merely standing there beneath the spray, I grab a fistful of his wet hair and shove my foot into his lower back.

"What happened to her?" I growl, yanking his head back as far as it will go. He doesn't react, refusing to even look at me so I drag him out and slam his head onto the floor. "If you put one hand on her, I swear," I cut myself off, seeing red. Never have I wanted to hurt someone so bad and if it weren't for the gentle pull of Mania on our bond trying to hold me back, he'd already be dead.

"Who...are you?" Hoax says in the blandest, most hollow tone I've ever heard. Closing a hand around his throat, I tremble against the desire to squeeze until his light fades out of our bond completely. He's a goner anyway, this would merely be a service to the Mute we once knew.

"Come on Ghost, let's go. You're not going to get any answers from him," Pyro says from the doorway. Mania weakly pushes against his chest to be put down on wobbly legs.

"Leave him," she agrees. "He's not our Hoax anymore." Sorrow glints in her red eyes and I clench my jaw. Something happened, I know it, and I don't like being kept in the dark. The pair shuffle away, leaving me to make the decision for myself. I growl, tearing my hand away but getting all up in his face regardless.

"Braindead or not, touch Mania again and I'll snap your fingers off one by one and stuff them into your ass." Shoving myself upright via Hoax's chest, I walk away from him lying too still on the floor. I don't give a fuck about loyalty anymore, my love for that male has gone.

Finding Pyro on the walkway outside Mania's room, I join his side with a loud huff through my nostrils.

"You should have let me kick his ass. I don't like this guilt-trip shit."

"Save it, you've got better fish to prey on." Following Py's eyeline over the railing, I watch Camo, Imp and a bunch of other misfits step out of the elevator. Oh fuck yes, I needed this today. Cracking my knuckles, I barely manage to hold on long enough for Mania to reappear. In a tank top, sweatpants and bomber jacket I haven't been gifted with in my locker, there's a twinge of color to her cheeks and she won't meet our gaze. Weird.

Leading the way down the metal stairs, my canvas shoes ring out through the asylum like the countdown of a timer. The timer on

Camo's existence. Not listening to a word he's babbling to the crowd of Mutes that's circled around him, I stride through the center and throw my fist into his gut. Nails scratch at my shoulder until I shove Imp aside to deliver Camo with another blow, this one to the ribs.

"Woah, woah, hold up!" Camo cowers like the little bitch I know him as. A male steps in behind, circling my waist with a meaty arm and tosses me aside like I'm nothing. Landing on my ass, I jump up as a wedge of stone forms around my feet, anchoring me in place. Gripping the stone and trying to break it free, more grows around my hands and I'm stuck to the ground with my ass in the air. Perfect.

"Granite," a small voice gasps as the bunny girl pushes her way to the front of those watching. She slides in by Mania's side, staring up at the huge Mute that pays her no mind. His stone-cold eyes are narrowed on me, a tightness to his jaw that accentuates the tattoos on his bald head. Dusting himself off with the help of Imp, Camo pulls his suit jacket straight and clears his throat.

"As I was saying, before we were so rudely interrupted, we're coming to you directly from the White House. President Horton is eager to put her plans into action, briefing us to start work right away." No one answers, and Camo sighs, hanging his head.

"Look, I know I've made mistakes but I'm a reformed Mute. Octavia has shown me a way forward, and I'm here to help rehabilitate you all in a similar manner. Can't have crazed mutants with childhood trauma roaming the streets now, can we?"

"We're never getting out of here," Mania replies, popping her hip out and crossing her arms. Her words are a lash to my chest but on the exterior, I boost her confidence with a wink. That's my girl.

"So much negativity. Let's start with you." Imp taps a pen on the clipboard now in her hands. She's been playing costume shop alongside Camo, wearing a short skirt and white blouse. Trotting past in heels, she bops her pen on my head, guiding Mania and a few others Camo selects into one of the side rec rooms.

Granite approaches, slamming his hand down hard on my back. The air rushes out of my lungs and the stone crumbles, being retracted into his suit trouser legs as he walks. Where does he store it all? I swallow thickly at the thought of being imprisoned in his shaft stone before jogging to catch up with Pyro just before Imp can shut the door on me.

The room has been pre-set. A large circle of twelve chairs facing inwards. Nudging Follicle out of the way, I sit down and find my eyes level height with Goldie. Her three bears take up the opposite side of the circle, with Follicle now sitting between Siren and Hare-iett. With Mania and Pyro on my right and Granite deciding to stand in front of the door, that leaves a spare chair for Camo and Imp to settle into.

"Welcome everyone to your first group therapy session. The feedback Imp and I provide to Octavia will be critical in choosing who will be first to enter her Emergence program." I snort at the name, bringing everyone's attention to me. Give me a break.

"Who says we want to be a part of her bullshit program in the first place?" Imp places a hand to her chest, gasping in fake shock. Give me a break.

"For your information, the program not only includes rehabilitation, but an integration back into society. It'll be an uphill battle, but we truly believe this is the first step in changing the human's perception about us."

Camo leans over to place a hand on Imp's thigh, the fakest smile I've ever seen upon his face. This asshole couldn't sell Viagra to a retirement home, and now he's sitting here trying to convince me he's been brainwashed into selling his soul to the humans? I'm not buying it.

"What's the catch?" Goldie asks, her chin held high. I've never heard any of her bears speak but they sure are giving me evils from their narrowed eyes. If it's a harem-off they want, I'd be more than happy to oblige.

"As part of gaining the human's trust, we'll need to work for them. Show them we're valuable assets to their world," Camo places his forearms on his knees and I snort.

"And if this experiment should fail, the program is pulled and we're all stuck here anyway," Imp adds. Good to know she feels as trapped as the rest of us, even from her blissful oasis across the fence. Slapping my hands on my thighs, I push to stand.

"Well, I don't know about you guys, but I've had quite enough of experiments to last a lifetime." Going to walk away, Granite grinds his teeth and spits out chalk-like dust, challenging me to try and get through that door.

Challenge accepted.

"Yeah, probably for the best. Leave the hard work to those who can handle it. My men and I will happily take the credit," Goldie mutters. *On second thought...*

"Credit?" I muse, spinning back around and lowering into my seat. There's not a lot in this world that powers my motor, but global credit for being the first integrated Mute sure could be one of them. Bracing my chin on my fist, I gesture for Camo to continue with my free hand. He rolls his olive-green eyes.

"Anyways, as I was saying. You lot have been selected as the first ten to undergo therapy and depending on our report, may be invited to partake in the program. So Mania, we were going to start with you." All eyes swing to my Spitfire, who looks like a deer in headlights. Still slightly flushed and tugging on the sleeve of her jacket.

"There's really nothing to talk about," she looks around and settles on me to help her out. Dropping my head on her knee, I give her a light squeeze.

"It's okay to speak your truth Spitfire. I know it was traumatizing to wake up with my dick in your-"

"Okay fine," she huffs and shoves my hand aside. "You want to analyse me? I was born human, murdered at eight after my birth parents used me as a drug mule, brought back to life by a soul mate I didn't know I had, grew up alone in Bellemare with two friends that both turned into backstabbing bitches. I went from being stalked by a spirit to being trapped in an asylum, my emotions torn to shreds by three assholes that just wouldn't leave me alone. Turned back to human, tortured in a maze, now I'm trapped as a Mute again, sitting before the male who sold us out and telling him why I deserve to be *rehabilitated.*"

Mania slumps back in her chair after straightening her spine with each sentence, her chest heaving as the room falls silent.

"Damn. That's a lot," Goldie raises her brows, staring at a spot on the floor. Imp scribbles away on her clipboard before looking up to Mania.

"How are you spelling factitious?" she asks, tilting her head and Mania shoots out of her seat. Mine skids back too as I lunge to catch her, dragging her backwards to sit in my lap. Pinning her arms by her side, I press kisses along her neck.

Later, my love, I say through our mental connection. *If we truly have a shot at some time in the real world, we need to take it. One sneeze and I could slip us into the sewers.*

Solid escape plan, Pyro pitches into our connection. I give him some serious side-eye. It's not lost on me how quiet he's been this entire time. Whether he's trying to avoid talking about his turbulent emotions or he's been trying to prod around in our bond to see what's up with Mania, I'm not sure. Yeah, I feel you in there, Captain Sneaky.

"Goldie, we can come to you next. Get the females out of the way. We all know how much you ladies love talking about your emotions," Camo smirks behind his hand, covering his mouth in a I'm-pretending-to-be-interested-but-really-I-just-want-to-be-unalived kind of way. However, I'm also particularly interested in what Goldie has to say.

"No backstory here. I was born in Underlife, was there my whole life until the transfer. Everything in my life has been carefully designed and orchestrated. Now I get to listen to a Mutant who'd had the chance to live freely complain and whine." Her yellow eyes slide to Mania and me.

"Wait, rewind," I say, pushing Mania to the floor. Sorry babe, I need to make sure I hear this correctly. "What's Underlife?" Goldie looks at me as if I'm fucking stupid.

"Another facility," she shakes her head, mocking me. "Pretty much the same as this one, except there isn't fancy bathrooms in each room. There's a communal shower block that we ran." The bears beside her grunt - the first sound I've heard any of them make. Pyro has perked up too, his back ramrod straight.

"Who ran the facility?" he asks in a calm and collected tone that contradicts his alarm bells going off in my head. Mania retrieves her chair to join us.

"The same person that runs all of them - Christopher Gordon," Goldie rolls her eyes. Camo and Imp bristle at his name, looking back to check Granite is still blocking the doorway. Interesting. The trio wouldn't have made it in here without Christopher's knowledge, but if Camo's cagey behavior is anything to go by, I'd say Christopher isn't on board with our new President's program. Which only makes me more interested.

All of them, Pyro echoes through the bond. I nod absent-mindedly, letting him know I caught that too. I caught it all.

"So, in your carefully orchestrated life," I tilt my head to the ceiling, "who got carried away with the nursery rhymes and gave you these three goons? Is one too big, one too small and the last just right?" I fight my own smirk, not surprised when an animalistic growl rips through the room. The male on the far right stands up, slamming his fist into his palm.

"Ahh, there's the little dude. Always the one to overcompensate first," I chuckle, standing to accept his challenge. I've been waiting for a decent fight all day. Goldie snaps her fingers and he swiftly sits back in his seat, more like a hairy lapdog than a bear.

"We've heard all about you from your friend. We're not here to play your mind games. Surviving one day at a time is the only way forward."

"My friend?" I frown when Imp shoots up.

"Well, that's enough for today. I've got all the notes I need and these findings will be extremely helpful when it comes to the selection process."

Skipping between Goldie's stare on mine, the neon-haired sprite mutters to Granite something about putting and misery, before slipping out of the room. Camo does the same, straightening his ridiculously cheap suit and thanking us for our time as Granite steps up to me. Stone trickles from the cuff of his sleeve, forming around his fist just before he smashes said rock fist into my temple.

I feel myself falling weightlessly, my consciousness slipping away before I hit the ground with one last thought. About fucking time.

MANIA

I t's raining. Absolutely pouring as water openly falls from the heavens to drench the yard beyond the open rear doors. Despite our numbers dwindling with each passing day, it's not enough to know this amount of Mutes have to huddle inside. They need to taunt us with it too.

Tensions are already running high since Goldie has closed the kitchen shutter early and her largest bear is barricading the door. The moans coming from inside and thoughts of contamination would usually put us all off our food, if it weren't for the fact we were forced to skip dinner last night too. She hasn't been the same since the group therapy session, or perhaps this is her way of asserting her dominance after Ghost challenged the masculinity of her men.

"Come on Babygirl," Pyro kisses my forehead, wrapping his arm around me. Tugging me away from the open doors, we head for the rec rooms in search of something to do. Hare-iett is leading a yoga session in the largest, with Granite not too far away hovering by the door. Whatever happens between the two of them is none of my business, as long as he doesn't toy with her. Then I'll be the one hurting him, stone balls that would break my knee or not.

Heading into the library, a tiny woman with no neck jostles past.

Layers of clothes cover her body, a page of literature hanging from her mouth.

"Bookworm?! You're still here?" I stare after her until she disappears between the bookshelves. Pyro shares a look of what the fuck with me before I link our fingers and lead him into the aisles. Turning towards non-fiction, I follow the alphabetic genres down to D. Demonology.

"Something you want to tell me?" Pyro quirks a brow. I shrug.

"Just interested in what the humans have to say is all." Turning to bury my face in the books, I run my finger over the spines. The Dark Scarcement, The Day the Devil Called, The Exorcism of Anneliese Michel. Nothing that'll help me understand the demon ritual, but then again, what was I expecting? No demons have sat between reaping souls to write down their experience. I'm just that desperate to understand what I saw.

"Look, I know what this is about," Pyro mumbles, brushing my hair from my neck where the healed fang marks are hidden beneath my sweater. I freeze, wondering when I gave it away. I've been so careful to avoid Hoax completely, in topic and person. "You miss Azella."

"Oh," the air whooshes through my parted lips. Pyro places a kiss to my neck.

"It must be hard not seeing her anymore. She was the closest thing you had to a mom." Reaching out to gently take the hand clutching the shelf, Pyro turns me with the grace of a ballroom dancer. His red eyes are hooded, his lips seeking mine.

Concealing the wobble that threatens to draw me to tears, I push up the last inch. His mouth skates across mine, loving me so tenderly - the damn tears fall anyway. Easing one hand into my hair, the other still holding mine between us, Pyro pours his love into our bond. His lips warm but he doesn't rush his exploration.

Tipping my head back, I open my mouth and coax his tongue inside. He's everything the others aren't. Transparent being one of them. An open book, a hopeless romantic. My Pyro, who never wavers in his commitment. Guilt laces through my chest at the thought of lying to him, and if he feels it, he doesn't let on. His long fingers massage my hair until his heated mouth pulls back, leaving me yearning and breathless.

"I know it isn't the same, but until we meet our fate, I promise to be all the family you need."

"Yeah, and I'll be that pervy uncle that gets too handsy on holidays," Ghost cuts in, thoroughly ruining the moment but I laugh anyway. Postured further down the aisle, he leans on the bookcase with his ankles crossed and an apple in his hand. Taking a large bite, the red, smooth surface beckons me.

"Where did you get that?!" I gasp, rushing over. Saliva pools in my mouth. Ghost holds out the apple for me to take a bite, only to whip it away at the last moment.

"Sorry Spitfire, I had to risk my eyesight to steal this when bear number three couldn't watch any longer. A trio of hairy dicks coated in porridge isn't something I'm going to forget anytime soon." Shoving at Ghost's chest, I jump to reach the apple but he's too quick. The grin on his face shows he's thoroughly enjoying my efforts and I groan, not having the energy for this anyway.

"Selfish asshole," I roll my eyes. Turning my back on him, his arm bands around my chest to stop me from walking away. The apple catches the corner of my eye and I smile, opening my mouth. Rolling the sphere across my cheek towards my lips, Ghost pulls it back at the last moment and sinks his teeth into the side, right beside my ear.

I buck and groan to be free from his grip. Taking his time to finish crunching and smacking his lips together, Ghost tosses the apple core to Pyro and proceeds to tickle me. I try to hold back the laughter, wanting to stay angry because fuck him. But then again, I knew exactly what I was signing up for with Ghost. Hell, those days in the maze where his goofiness was a distant memory were some of the worst.

Pyro leaves us to sort it out, hunting through the shelves for whatever book he thinks I was looking for. I wriggle downwards, trying to twist out of Ghost's hold. When that doesn't work, I take to stomping on his feet and throwing my head around in hopes of connecting with something. Still, his fingers are relentless and I'm not responsible for the hyena cackles that are ripped from my throat.

Finally releasing me, I shove him back with my shoulder and put on my best scowl for show. He won't get the better of me.

"All of this because I forced myself to eat that apple so I could save this for you," he pulls a packet out of his pocket. It's smushed and crumbling, but the double chocolate muffin still has my heart skipping a beat. Snatching it from his offering hand, I maintain my scowl.

"Fuck you."

"Yes please," he winks and I link my arm with Pyro's, tugging him backwards. Once at the small table in the center, I push Py into a seat and carefully pry open the packet. Taking a clump of chocolate fluffiness in my fingers, I throw my leg over Pyro and feed him the muffin piece by piece. Ghost tries to steal a chocolate chunk and I slap his hand away. Two can play this own game. Once it's finished, I stand, only to wipe my hands down the first of Ghost's white t-shirt.

"Now go get me another one," I order. Ghost raises his brow, refusing to indulge me. I know I won't win this battle of wills, but it sure feels good to try. He could at least pretend I have a slither of power over him, for one millisecond. Just as I'm about to waiver, he sighs.

"Fine," he pulls a second muffin from his other pocket. "But this one, I'm feeding to you, washed down with some double cream from my dick." A flash of purple halts any response I may have had. Hoax rounds the corner, hammering a piece of paper onto the wooden shelving with his fist and a metal pin. My heart seizes at the sight of him, then sinks at how he doesn't pay any of us the slightest bit of attention.

I understand, sort of, but it doesn't help. If anything, it makes it worse. Hoax isn't vacant or being controlled. He's very much aware, yet unable to give into his feelings like the rest of us. Prevented from taking part in the love we share. Disappearing from sight, the three of us move towards the hanging sheet of paper.

Delegated Jobs, the title reads. Apparently they've finished the fake counseling sessions with the Mutes that are left. I recognize the writing as Imp's because she always puts a stupid heart on her i's. Always has.

Graffiti removal – Polar, Grizzly, Yogi.
Litter picking – Misfortune, Telecom, Simplify.
Road maintenance – Pyro, Ghost.
Woodworkers – Strimmer, Tremor, Decay.
Metal fabrication – Alchemy, Follicle, Ash.
Entertainment sector – Hare-iett, Goldie, Mania, Desire.

"Typical," I roll my eyes and Ghost grunts in agreement.

"Right?! Couldn't they think of a more original bear name than Yogi?" Ghost lowers his chin onto my shoulder and I shrug him off. Idiot.

"It's no coincidence they are separating us," Pyro growls. His shoulders hunch and through our bond, a thick cloud of smoke becomes clogged in my throat. Twisting into his side, I press a hand over his heart.

We've survived worse than this, I tell him and Ghost through our connection. I've been even more careful after Hoax's warning - Christopher has eyes and ears everywhere. But still, I don't like any of it. The fake therapy, the selection process. As if we didn't have enough to contend with, now we need to play nice and work just for the same rights as humans who don't deserve them? But for my men, I need to remain strong.

Road maintenance sounds promising. There will be shovels and machinery. Possibly other objects you could stash as weapons, I try to sound hopeful through our connection.

We don't have to go. Trapped or not, at least here we are together, Pyro does his best to be rational. He should know by now this isn't a game we can win playing by the rules. Only by cheating.

No one is going to give us a future. We need to take it. Sliding my eyes back to Ghost, he nods. All trace of humor and playfulness gone. I hate that this place does that to him, but it only serves as another motive on the list to escape. Somehow, someway.

Taking both Ghost and Pyro by the hand, I lead us away from the library and into the central lobby. Mutes have gathered outside the elevator, being called forward by MRA agents a group at a time to have their cuffs checked. The 'entertainers' are called amongst the bodies and my chest clenches. Kissing each hand in turn, I step forward before turning back.

"Everything's going to be okay. I've got this," I force a smile. Don't ask who I'm trying to reassure. In response, a barrel of mixed messages seep through our connection.

Be safe Babygirl. Keep your head down and come back in one piece.

Give them hell, Spitfire. Fuck 'em with their own dicks and return our queen of dismembered cum.

My eyes widen, a hand tugging my arm to pull me away. Hare-iett leans into my side, holding both of us upright as we step into the elevator and the doors close behind us.

Boxed in by the MRA agents, I peer around the elevator. Aside from Hare-iett and I, there's Siren, Goldie and a Mute I'm vaguely familiar with crammed together in the shaft. Desire, I'm presuming. The doors open again and if I wasn't nervous already, my gut just dropped.

"Welcome ladies," Camo beams the biggest, shit-eating grin. Hair slicked back, a suit on his lean frame and a glass of wine in hand. Strobe lights flash behind him in an otherwise dark and empty club. Hare-iett sucks in a breath, her grip on my arm becoming tighter.

"What the hell?" I scowl as the agents push us from the elevator and ensure we follow Camo towards the stage. I refuse to look at the metal poles and extravagant backdrops, still haunted by the last time I was in Camo's club. If it wasn't for finding Ghost so easily, I'd have been up on that stage. Something I also refuse to do now.

"As part of the Emergence program, you fine specimens will be working for me. Hot meals and uniform included," he sniggers to himself, knowing full well there's no real 'clothes' in the dressing rooms beneath our feet. "Six hours a day, five days a week, per your rehabilitation. You'll return to the asylum after your shifts to rest."

Pyro chooses that moment to tug on our bond, asking if

everything is okay. I swallow hard, shutting down the line of communication rather than lie to him.

"Just to be clear," I hold up a hand when Camo tries to walk away. Hare-iett is still clinging to me like a lifeline. "We've gone from prisoners to slaves." Camo flashes me a smile and I grit my teeth. No need to guess whose bright idea it was to start up the Emergence program, considering we're putting money straight back in Camo's pocket. He's living his best life while we work for free. This can't be happening.

Prods of electric batons at our backs make sure we follow the slime bag's trail to the back of the stage and down the hidden staircase. If I didn't have men waiting for my safe return, I'd have taken death by electric shock over this. But knowing they'll all feel my pain as freshly as if it were they're own, it's not fair to put them through that. Who knows what they've ended up walking into.

Standing before the dressing room door, Camo's eyes glint a brighter shade of green as he pushed it open. *Holy fuck, what is that smell?!* The room is a mess of broken dressing tables and costumes strewn everywhere. Feathers from the boas have been ripped free of their strings, fluttered over the carnage like sprinkles on a shit-pie.

Hare-iett clasps a hand over her mouth, suppressing a sob. Following her eyeline, I see what has her dropping to her knees and clutching her gut. Amongst the mess, one lone rabbit's ear lies beneath a coating of maggots and flies. This is where she was taken from. Where the MRA agents stormed to see through Christopher's demand for more Mutes. Giving Siren a stern look to get rid of it, I crouch to block Hare-iett's view.

"Hey. It's okay to cry. Let these fuckers see what they're putting us through." Camo and the agents can hear me, and that's the point. We're real people, not numbers on a piece of paper. Not objects to be used and disposed of. Anger brims inside of me and this time when Ghost reaches out, I respond.

This is the last day we abide by the rules. When we return to Afterlife tonight, it'll be for the last time.

I get a solid *fuck yes* in response and close off my emotions. Being erratic won't serve anyone. Easing Hare-iett up on shaky legs, I hold her against my side. If only we had a telepathic thread to communicate on, I'd promise her of all the ways I'll make this right. As it stands, I have to comfort her with pathetic words like 'let's just take it ten minutes at a time' and 'we can get through this'.

Moving into the dressing room, Siren's aquamarine eyes flicker to a watch box where she must have hidden the ear. I push it aside with my canvas shoe, stashing it beside the wall for later.

"You've got an hour before the club opens to clean yourselves up. There's plenty of eager humans already queueing to see our new star attractions," Camo grins, almost giddy. Righting a stool and propping Hare-iett on it, I spin my hardest glare on him.

"I'm not dancing."

Allowing the agents to step inside the room, Camo steps into the center. An intimidation tactic I refuse to acknowledge. Keeping my chin tilted high and eyes fixed on his for a full minute, he finally groans and rubs the back of his neck.

"Disappointing. I was looking forward to gloating in Ghost's face about watching you strip." I smirk. The guys are going to flip either way and I can't wait to see what's left of Camo when they do. "But we happen to need someone to bust tables. Considering you have the least experience, I guess you pulled the lucky straw."

Striding from the room and leaving the agents behind, my eyes slide to Goldie. She hasn't spoken. Helping Siren to lift the dressing tables and prop them against the walls, a mask of indifference is fixed upon her face. How much experience could she have with stripping from being raised in a facility? Then again, Christopher owns it, so I really don't want to know. Giving her a sympathetic look, she purses her lips and flips me off. Okay then.

The room falls into silence, apart from Hare-iett's small sobs, and with every passing minute, the air thickens. It's hard to breathe. Picking up costumes from the floor, I hang them onto the railing Desire puts back together. The ones splattered with blood I toss into a pile for burning. Siren's mermaid tail included. The MRA really didn't hold back when kidnapping them.

Guilt claws at me for being so stubborn about dancing on stage, when the other women in this room simply hung their heads and accepted their fates. Lifting Hare-iett's bowler hat, I place it upon her head with a small smile.

"This is temporary," I whisper. Wiping away her tears with my thumbs, I cup her reddened face. "Put on a smile, fake it for today and tomorrow will be different. I promise." Hare-iett gives me a small nod but I don't think she understands the message I'm trying to convey. Siren drops down beside me, a make-up palette and rider's crop in her hand, and together, we get Hare-iett ready.

By the time Camo returns, we're all dressed and visibly seething. Obviously, the agents didn't give us any privacy to change, and the paper divider we could have used looks like it had a body thrown through it. Camo whistles low, rubbing his hands together.

Somehow, I managed to find one outfit that wasn't torn or spoiled, and actually covers most of my body. A leather catsuit with a teardrop cut-out on my cleavage. Studded heels on my feet make me unsteady but I'll manage. Siren did my make-up, covering the crack in my forehead and black circles around my eyes. A pop of red lipstick and an inch-thick layer of concealer and I practically look human.

"Glad to see everyone is excited as I am," Camo grins sarcastically. Hare-iett has her old English hunter's routine ready. Siren went for a glitter bikini and heels that highlight her shimmering scaley skin. Desire has chosen an outfit consisting of leather straps, and Goldie found a tiny yellow dress with a pot of honey on the chest. Even I had to snigger at that one, presuming it must have been selected for her. The malicious glare on her face is a far cry from the fairy-tale though, despite the pigtails hanging either side of her head.

Clicking his fingers for us to follow, Camo leads us to the staircase where another male awaits. Bland on the surface. Brown curly hair on top of his head, a relaxed tracksuit on his body and hands in pockets. Music plays from the stage area and once in a while, a strobe light catches his sharp face, highlighting his bored expression.

"One more thing. This is Mute," Camo points to the male blocking our ascent.

"Yeah, we're all Mutes," Goldie speaks for the first time. Crossing her arms, the cuffs we all wear clunk together awkwardly until she drops them back down by his sides.

"No, it *is* Mute." The male moves swiftly, whipping his hand out of his pocket to press it over Goldie's mouth. Her yellow eyes widen but her struggles are fruitless with the agents that step into her back. Removing his hand, Mute steps back to slide it back in his pocket, as bored as ever.

Goldie opens her mouth, but no sound comes out.

"A fail-safe to make sure you don't ruin the humans experience with too much chit-chat," Camo explains and I roll my eyes. Don't spill Christopher's secrets more like. "You'll get your voices back at the end of your shift, if you behave. I have no problem sending you back the way women should be - silent."

Oh, I'm going to kill him.

Camo takes in my expression and bursts out laughing. "Don't bother getting all murderous on me. Without my permission, Mute won't return that smart mouth of yours." Grabbing my chin, Camo smushes my lips up and I jerk out of his grip. He's loving this - being in control. Power-hungry because he sold out all of his employees to Christopher and wormed his way in with the new President.

Glaring, I step up to Mute and stand still while he takes my voice. Just when I thought I had nothing else to lose. Voices filter in from the club and Camo checks his ridiculous diamond-studded watch.

"It's showtime. Oh, and ladies? Welcome home." I give Camo a middle finger before managing to climb the stairs with more grace than these heels should allow. Behind me, I hear him direct the others to either backstage or the private rooms.

Heading directly for the bar, I round it and take a black, circular tray. A few human bartenders eye me suspiciously but I'm not dragging this day out any longer than it needs to be. Filling the tray with tiny shot glasses, I pour a measure of vodka in each and stride into the club.

Men are just sitting down, filling every seat while more stream in from the doorway. I spot a poster on the bulletin board, announcing 'Mutes, Music and Mischief' as a new regular act. Maintaining a level head, I make my way around the tables, handing out shots to the men who don't smack my ass or order me to sit in their lap. Then it's back to the bar for refills.

"We're not supposed to give out drinks for free," a young female leans in to tell me. She can't be more than twenty. Extremely pretty and if she had any hint of mutant genetics, I'm sure Camo would have her on that stage too.

I shrug and smirk. The slimeball reckons he's got a nifty little business agreement with the President going on. Watch me drain his profits. It's petty, I know. But while I'm working on hatching up a plan, it's the best I've got. The music quietens long enough for a welcome speech to ring through the speakers and announce the first act for the night - Hare-iett.

Here we go.

Maneuvering towards a darkened booth at the back, I lean against it. Males whistle, trying to get my attention for a drink but I ignore them. Hare-iett steps on stage, accompanied with Pony by Ginuwine and strolls up to the pole, dragging her feet. Her eyes flutter closed, her hand raising to grasp the metal.

Then, as if the beat dropping awakened a kindred spirit in her, her eyes snap open and she dances. Throwing herself around as if she weighs nothing, spinning with full splits in the air. The crowd goes wild and if I could speak, I would too. The confident creature on the stage may be a front, but it eases my worries Hare-iett is able to compartmentalize. Watching her roll her body and play up to the audience, I smile. That bitch is the strongest of us all.

Catching Camo glaring at me from the shadows across the room, I wander between the tables. Serving free shots, taking orders I don't intend to charge for on a notepad the bartender hands me. The males don't pay me much attention now they're fascinated by the stage's display. Siren is introduced to join Hare-iett and together, they put on one hell of a show.

Siren's body glimmers under the lighting, her lips curved upwards. Strolling around Hare-iett, she lifts the hare's body onto her shoulder and flips her up onto the pole. Remaining up high, Hare-iett hangs upside down while Siren uses the space underneath. Rolling her hips, appearing to have the time of her life in a well-choreographed routine the pair must have done many times before.

Song after song, my worries ebb and I find the smile on my face isn't as forced. If those on stage can fake this so well, so can I. Each step of the heels becomes easier and soon enough, there's a saunter to the way my hips move. The cat calls don't seem as degrading as they do powerful.

"Hey skinny thang," a bloated man in a too tight suit calls out. I raise a brow. "You look like you could use a bit of meat in you." His friends all laugh and I smile along. Sleazy and cheesy, but I appreciate the sentiment. Maybe being a Mute in the real world isn't going to be so bad. I'm a committed woman, but appreciation from humans isn't something I've ever experienced. There's power to be found in confidence, and all of the eyes currently on my ass is boosting mine.

So that's how Hare-iett and Siren do it.

Returning to the bar for the hundredth time, the next tray of drinks is slid my way. "For the private group in room 4a," the bartender shouts over the music. "Through that curtain, second door on the right." I switch the tray with the empty one in my hand and follow her directions. Rasped laughter leaks from beneath the door of 4a and I stutter, wondering if I should knock. But then again, they ordered the drinks.

Pushing down the handle, I enter a dimly lit room. Desire doesn't pause her lap dance, bending in half with her ass in a tattooed bikers face. She doesn't need access to her ability to have the room full of muscley men drooling. Edging around the side, I place the drinks one by one onto the table in front of the others watching on. None but one pay me any attention. Stark blue eyes beneath an eyebrow piercing have teardrops inked on both cheeks.

"You're way too good for a place like this," he breathes. *Tell me about it.* Frowning, his finger slips beneath my cuffs and nearly makes me drop a glass. "I was locked up once. Drains your soul, makes you feel worthless, alone. Forgotten about." My breath hitches, my head lowering to hear his barely whispered words closer. "I can show you how to slip these cuffs, if you like. Just let me know."

Opening my mouth, I remember I can't speak. And more than that, with the hammering of my heart, I wouldn't know what to say. Withdrawing his hand from me, I finish placing down the drinks and slip out of the room. There's no one else in the hallway so I pause to rest my back against the wall. I can't escape now. Not when my men are still trapped. But what if I took him up on his offer? Let him show me how for when the time is right.

The door beside me opens and I nearly drop my tray. The man who was receiving the lap dance steps out, asking me where the bathroom is. I point down to the clearly labeled doorway and watch him walk away, struggling to walk around adjusting his erection.

Pulling myself together, I walk back into the club on numb feet. This is what I need, a possible way out. It was my whole reasoning behind taking the stupid job. Lifting the pen out of my cleavage, I head to the bar for a napkin and write down two words. *Show me.*

Wrapping the napkin around a whiskey that was left on the side, I head back to the private rooms. A tremor of excitement thrums through me. This is the first step. The first time we will have an advantage. And what's better, I won't be that damsel in distress waiting to be saved. I'll be the one leading my men to freedom.

Gripping the door handle, movement shifts by the wall and Camo materializes just before his hand wraps around my neck. Slamming me into the wall, his camouflaging ability washes over me. Pressing a finger to his lips in mockery, the tattooed biker returns from the bathroom and walks straight past us, entering the room of laughter and lust.

I struggle against Camo's hold, clawing at his arm when he delivers a sharp hit to my abdomen. I scream silently, doubling over. Rounding me, his arms band around my chest, pinning my arms down as he drags me backwards and tuts in my ear.

"Failed at the first hurdle, I see. Appears I get to gloat in Ghost's face after all."

"Ironic, don't ya think?" Ghost muses to himself. "Making us fix the road you destroyed. Like we've gone full circle." I tune him out, digging out the rest of the rubble with a shovel. He hasn't done much more than watch the cement churn in the mixer, but with Imp as our warden, there's not much motivation.

Like he said, the crater in the road is all that remains of our old bunker before I blew it to shit. While Ghost finds humor in irony, I can't help to let old thoughts sink in. This is where I hid myself from the world. Where I mourned a love I didn't get to know. How can I have come so far, yet not be any closer to having the life I want? The one I damn well deserve.

A fist connecting with my gut cripples me, yet there's no one close by. An alarm rings in my head, the flames of our bond blazing in my ears. *Something's wrong.*

"Ghost," I rasp out and he's by my side in a second.

"I felt it." Helping me to straighten, I look at the sea of MRA agent's eyes on us. We're the only two Mutes here, aside from Imp. She's busy robbing them all blind while they pay her no attention. Whistling, I beckon her over and turn my back so the agents can't pry on our hushed conversation.

"Imp, you're in charge here," I whisper, eyeing the key card to the elevator attached to her hip. I have no idea why anyone thought she was a good choice to watch over us, but I'm not complaining. Ghost and I are the smallest of groups that were taken away from Afterlife, but in my opinion, the most problematic. "We need to get to where Mania is. It's important."

Imp rolls her pink eyes and tries to walk away. I stop her with a hand on her arm and the agents growl. Raising my hands, showing I mean no harm, I try again.

"She was your friend once. Surely you'd want to help her if she's in danger?" This time, it's Ghost that groans and shoves me out of the way.

"Take us to Mania so we can make sure she's safe. When we get back, I'll help you rob….that bank," he points to a tall building at the end of the street. Imp's head perks up.

"There's money in the bank," she mutters to herself, licking her lips.

"And gold," Ghost adds. Imp rubs her hands together.

"Ooooh, I like gold," she nods. Biting down on her lip, I can see the cogs turning in her brain. "How do I know I can trust you? Camo told me not to listen to a word you say," she tilts her head. Instead of answering, Ghost slowly raises his hand and produces his pinkie. Imp gasps. "Pinkie swears are unbreakable," she agrees and accepts it with hers. I twitch at the display, eager to get going. Turning to face the guards, Imp clears her throat for a big announcement.

"We're going for a threesome. We will be back when I'm sated." And then she turns and leads us back to the train station we came from. Shuddering at the thought of people thinking I'd ever hook up with Imp, I send a reassuring flare through the eternal bone to let Mania know we're on our way.

Entering the elevator shaft that appears innocent enough, Imp pushes the key card into a slot and types in a code on the displayed buttons. The doors close and Ghost shoves a hand into Imp's hair. Shoving her shoulders one-way and twisting her head the other, she drops to the floor in a heap of tangled limbs and a snapped neck.

"Cameras?!" I shove Ghost in the chest, ignoring the red flashing light in the corner. Snatching the key card out of the slot, I pocket it and hope to all hell we haven't just been redirected. The doors slide open, revealing a strip club in full swing and I frown.

Deciding Imp was serious about the threesome and has sent us to the wrong place, I reach for the card when Ghost grips the back of my neck and directs my head to the stage. Hare-iett and Siren are gyrating on each other, a sheen of sweat slickening their skin. My gut drops.

"I swear to fuck," Ghost grumbles and strolls out of the elevator. Staying on his heels, he navigates the room as if he's familiar with the layout. A young bartender smiles at the sight of him, before she realizes the bunch of his shoulders and her expression drops.

"Five eight, black and red hair, blood red eyes," Ghost reels off, his fist on the countertop.

"I-I last saw her taking a drink to 4a. Camo followed her out," the human girl blinks a few times and Ghost curses. He's moving again, down to the other end of the bar. Reaching over the slick surface, he produces a pot of pepper. I open my mouth to ask what the fuck he's doing, but don't get the chance. Fisting my t-shirt, he tugs me towards the nearest wall and throws me against it. Raising the pepper, Ghost dips and shakes the contents into his nose, showering me in the process.

"Ghost, you fucking nut-job. Get off of me!" I struggle against his stone-like grip. The manacle on his neck wobbles as he sucks in deep breathes, drops his head and proceeds to squeeze on my face. Taking a step towards me, I vaguely realize we've passed through the wall. My own fist snaps shut, preparing to knock him the fuck out when his white eyes widen and I look behind me.

A collar holds Mania's neck in place. Her hands bound above her head. In a black catsuit that's zipped down the front, exposing her breasts and the length of her tattooed abdomen, to the top of her panties. Those same panties that currently have Camo's hand pushed down the front, tears streaming from Mania's eyes while she bucks and screams. But no sound comes out.

His green eyes flick to us and with the hint of a smirk, he fades into the background and disappears from view.

"Get her down," I barely manage to grit out to Ghost. The reddened hand print across her breast is my final straw. Roaring at the sky, fire scores a network of lines from my chest to my shoulders and down my arms. Crusting over the cuffs, they melt away and drip onto the floor like molten lava.

Ghost grabs a letter opener from the desk and quickly cuts Mania free, her body flopping over his shoulder and they're gone. Out of the room with the door slammed closed behind them. My nostrils flare, my eyes scanning the room. Camo may be able to blend into his surroundings, but he can't pass through walls like Ghost. He's still in here, evident by the heavy breathing I hear to my left.

Lashing out with a fiery whip, it slams into the wall, missing my target. It doesn't matter. Nothing will survive this room except me. Christopher's previous cuffs may have done a good job while I subconsciously allowed them to cage me, but nothing can contain the rage coursing through my bloodstream. Strolling to the door, I hear a soft, surprised chuckle.

"Always knew you were weak," Camo whispers, quiet enough that I can't pinpoint his position. Eyes on the wood of the door, I raise my hand just south of the handle and twist the lock. Then I call for my fire.

I don't need petty words of vengeance. I don't need the flames Christopher thinks he stole from me. Mania and my brothers re-stoked my fire, brought me back from the ashes. With their strength boosting my own, I'm rejuvenated, and with that thought, I unleash the true extent of my ability on this room only.

A tornado of fire spirals around the walls, careful not to touch the edges. Turning, the silhouette of Camo being closed inside presents itself to me. His shouts are lost to the roaring passing through our ears, inaudible to anyone passing by outside.

Using my whip again, I catch my prey this time. Tugging him closer, I add a second. Not hot enough to burn yet, only to hold him in place. That's what he likes right? A bit of bondage and a lack of consent. Pulling Camo to me until we're nose to nose, I feel the eyes in my skull ignite into burning coals. I'm going to enjoy this.

Applying heat, oh so slowly, I watch Camo struggle. I relish in his suffering. The first scream is a balm to my fiery soul, giving me the validation I needed. The whips sink into his skin, disintegrating all they touch. Skin, flesh, bone. A rancid smell coats the back of my throat, giving me a sick sense of satisfaction. Camo's green hair bleeds orange, coated in the glow of the tornado.

Beyond his screams, there's no sound of bones splintering or any evidence of his impending death. Simply the slice of my whips like a knife cutting through butter. One minute he's here, the next he's not, with my contorted and flame-lit face being the last thing he ever saw.

No one, outside of her harem, touches my girl.

Stretching my neck, I walk through the pile of ash on the floor, setting a light to his desk. Whatever personal belongings he stashed inside will not be kept for sentimental value by whoever cared for him enough. Camo is no more, and it's my mission to see that he never existed in the first place.

Once satisfied, I retract the fires. They seep into me, righting my soul and reuniting me with the male I once was. The one I should always have been. Straightening my tracksuit, I go in hunt of Ghost and Mania. The door across the hall is ajar, Ghost's white hair visible in a slip of lamp light.

"It's okay, she's okay," Ghost breathes. I don't know who he's trying to reassure, but it's definitely not working for anyone. Easing him away from where she's perched on another desk, I take Mania's face in my warm hands.

"He won't be a problem to anyone anymore," I tell her softly. Ghost has zipped her back into the catsuit, but the red mark is still visible in the teardrop cut-out. Spreading my fires through her, I heal her of any physical injuries, but it's the internal ones I'm worried about.

"We will replace every scar with a memory of pleasure. Tonight won't even be a memory you have to think of once we've finished proving to you how incredibly special, beautiful and loved you are. I will fix this," I vow, holding Mania's eyeline.

The tears have stained her make-up, but underneath, she's still my girl. The feisty woman that walked back from the pits of hell to find me, the one my soul deemed worthy of reviving again and again just so I could love her. Worship her.

Ghost nudges my shoulder, producing a wipe which I gladfully accept. Cleaning her up, I smile at the gorgeous face lying underneath and pour the extent of my love through our bond. Ghost feels it too, his hands eager to be a part of mine and Mania's moment so he takes to massaging my shoulders.

"Let's get out of here," I tell them both. Removing Mania's heels, I ease her off the desk and into my arms. Nothing will stop me from holding my girl as close as possible until I know she's okay. Ghost marches ahead, calling for the elevator while Mania's head nestles deeply into my shoulder.

"Let's get out of here," I tell them both. Removing Mania's heels, I ease her off the desk and into my arms. Nothing will stop me from holding my girl as close as possible until I know she's okay. Ghost marches ahead, dodging some MRA agents lurking around the club. Calling for the elevator, Mania's head nestles deeply into my shoulder and I fight the urge to drum my fingers impatiently on her thigh. We need to get out of here, now.

The doors slide open. Before Ghost can enter, I stick out my leg to stop him and send a flame slithering up to the camera. Once the glass lens cracks from my heat, I permit us to enter and tell Ghost to use the card from my pocket. He pushes it in the slot and freezes.

"Um…" he says, and then starts pressing all the buttons in random order.

"Ghost! Stop that, you have no idea where you're sending us!" I kick him and Mania twists to see what's going on. The doors begin to close as an agent passing catches sight of us and a very dead Imp on the floor. Reaching for his stunt gun, he doesn't make it in time, but it's safe to say our cover is blown.

Pushing away from me, I place Mania down, trying to stand in her way of seeing Imp but she's too fast for me. I wait for something to pass over her face, either shock or glee or…*anything,* but she doesn't react. Instead, Mania bends to tug the biker boots off Imp's feet and pushes her own inside.

Next, she strips off the jacket, unfazed by the blood lining the collar. I help her into it, taking her cues by zipping the front up to the neck and tug the back down to cover her leather-clad ass. She wants to be covered, protected. I want to say something to reassure her we'll get past this, that a little time and love will heal all, but Ghost speaks first.

"So, cat's got your tongue huh? You can always borrow mine," he smirks and I clench my fist. If it wasn't for Mania's hint of a smile, I'd knock him on his ass. Pointing to her throat, Mania uses our mental connection to speak instead.

There was a Mute called Mute. He won't return our voices without Camo's approval. So that's the end of that.

"It's fine, you can scream my name on the inside," Ghost shrugs. I groan, pinching the bridge of my nose. Do the issues ever stop coming? I don't feel guilty about Camo's death, but fuck that fucker. We'll find a way to get Mania's and the others their voices back. A ping at the top of the elevator announces we've arrived and as a trio, we step out of the opening doors.

A corridor stretches as far as the eye can see, not an exit visible in the darkness that closes over it. The bite of a bitter chill tries to penetrate the heat coating my skin and I make sure to send a blast Mania and Ghost's way too. Either side, old-style cell doors line the stone walls, their metal bars mirrored another two floors up. Ghost whistles, the sound echoing through the dungeon-inspired space.

"Shhh!" I nudge him and we start walking. To where, who knows, but hanging around doesn't seem like the best idea. Each cell is as dark as the next, no sign of life inside other than the hairs standing on the back of my neck that scream of being watched. Our footsteps ring out as we walk for longer than I care to count, until finally a red light can be seen up ahead. Fuzzy at first, until Ghost jumps with joy and skips the rest of the way to flash his jazz hands at the sign that displays 'EXIT' in bold lettering.

"This is it! We're finally getting out of this hellhole!" Ghost cheers, fist pumping the way. Mania stops in her tracks. I quirk my brow, holding out my hand for her to take.

"Mania? Everything okay?" Small shake of her head.

We have to go back.

"What?!" Ghost shouts. Something shifts within one of the cells nearby. "Are you insane? After the ridiculousness we just dragged you out of. We have a chance to leave and you want to run back?" Mania bites her bottom lip and when Ghost steps towards her, she shrinks away.

"Give us a minute," I tell Ghost, patting his shoulder. Keeping my hands raised in submission, I slowly creep closer to Mania and keep our mental conversation private from whatever is stirring in the cell.

Talk to us, we just want to understand. That's all. Ghost scoffs through the bond and I ignore him.

We can't turn our backs on those we care about and run. This is...bigger than all of us. Mania frowns at her own thoughts and nods, as if she's only just come to that conclusion. Easing her hand into mine, I hold it between us when Ghost pipes up again.

"Fuck everyone else!" he kicks the cell bars. A growl comes from inside, followed by the opening of hazel eyes glowing through the dark. Now he's done it. Trying to tug Mania away, she tears herself out of my grip and starts moving backwards the way we came.

I can't leave him behind. A tear falls from her eyes, a pulsation of grief bleeding through our connection. She's hurting and I have no idea how to fix it. Making a last-ditch attempt to comfort her, my arms have almost closed around Mania's shoulders when she lifts the key card from my pocket and runs. I stand frozen to the spot when Ghost barrels through me, a curse on his lips.

She ran away from me. Stole our way out, and ran. Shock roots me to the spot, as well as a slice of betrayal. Many emotions batter around me, not all my own but all I know is, something isn't right.

"Py....Pyro?" A cracked sound comes from the cell. I'm too wrapped up, too confused by Mania's actions that when I glance over the metal bars, I don't fully compute at first. But then I double take. Matted dreadlocks hang loose, a pair of slender ebony hands gripping onto the bars with what little strength they have left. Those hazel eyes blink open again and this time, recognition settles within.

"Enzo?" I peer closer. On my next heartbeat, I'm rushing to the bars and pushing my palms against the metal. Melting them away, the male falls into me, his body skinnier and breathing raspy.

What the hell is happening here? I call to Ghost through the connection, asking for a little help back here but he shuts me down.

Fuck it. Scooping Enzo up in my arms, much like I had been carrying Mania not long ago, I run as fast as I'm able.

Enzo's dreads slap me in the face and he groans in pain but I don't slow. Not until I'm catching up to a terrified looking Mania, pressing the elevator button. Ghost closes his arms around her, hoisting her away and the card drops to the floor. His white eyes connect with my red ones and I shake my head. *Don't ask.* Putting Enzo down with his back leaning against the wall, I retrieve the key card and exhale harshly.

Okay, enough, I tell Mania. *Whatever it is, we don't run from each other. There's nothing you think or feel that we won't understand, so tell us. What's really going on?* Her head drops and she stops struggling in Ghost's hold.

I've been keeping something from you both. Please, don't be angry. I hate how small her voice is, even in my own head. Ghost releases her and folds his arms.

Tell us what it is first and then I'll decide how angry I get to be, he clenches his jaw. The elevator doors chose that moment to open and Mania heads for them, holding her finger up to signal we should wait. Grabbing Imp's ankle, she drags her former best friend across the ground to re-join us. Ghost and I share a look. Sighing, Mania closes her eyes.

A blast of yearning slams through our bond, knocking the air out of me. Mania pours her misery and grief into the notion. Coating her flame in enough desperation, I can see it darken and wither in my mind's eye. Pushing a foot forward, intended to shake her into stopping this, a word is leaked through the flames. Not just any word, but a name.

Hoax.

HOAX

The staff appears in my hand on instinct, hitting the floor before I have time to consider those around me. I've made a habit at sitting out of sight of the cameras, and hopefully the Mutes returning from their hard day of labor didn't pay me any attention in the corner of the canteen.

The next time I blink, darkness envelopes me. Only a dead body could have pulled me through space, but it was Mania's call that alerted me to its presence. Wherever there's death and Mania, I'll never hesitate to respond to her call. Sighing in relief that the pink-haired Mute on the floor isn't someone I care about, I turn my attention to the trembling female before me.

"What's wrong? Are you hurt? What happened?" The questions rush from my lips and I drop the staff aside in favor of cupping her face. Tilting her head up to face mine, my nostrils flare at the slight of her tear-streaked face. My lips kiss away their existence, my eyes fluttering closed. I can feel her pain through the bond and I'm used to dealing with it better than this. But when she's so close and leaning into me for comfort, she's impossible to deny.

"Give me a name and consider them dead," I rest my forehead on hers. A throat is cleared behind me.

"You're a little too late on that front," Pyro strolls into my eyeline to join Ghost. The fucker is casually leaning against a wall with his ankles crossed, but the bond says otherwise. He's currently pissed, confused and particularly impatient.

Releasing Mania, I can't help the way my lips purse. I knew she wouldn't be able to keep my secret to herself. Maybe it was selfish to ask, but when it comes to her protection, there's nothing I wouldn't do.

"Someone had better start talking," Ghost runs a thumb over his nails, faking his cool exterior. "And since Mania's had her vocal chords hindered, that person will be you, *brother*." He sneers at me but I turn my glare back to Mania. She quickly relays what happened to her voice through our connection and I lash out my hand. The staff answers my call and within a split second, I've appeared at the strip club, grabbed Mute, the mutant and returned to Mania.

"Give her voice back," I demand. The male doesn't appear intimidated by my all black eyes and horns hovering over him, nor the growl at watching him press a hand to her neck. No one outside the three of us should ever touch Mania, and the second she sighs at having her voice back, I tug the soul from his body. Flesh and limbs hit the floor while my hand is wrapped around his nape in spirit form.

"I'll deal with this. You deal with them," I jerk my chin to the males glaring at me, "and go back to the asylum," Mania, sensing I'm about to leave, grips onto my arm. "Mania," I growl. She knows I can't take her with me. Between calling me here to be exposed and an emancipated Enzo on the floor, this is all her mess to deal with. Shaking her off, I drag Imp's soul free of her body in the same hand as Mute and slam the staff on the floor.

"Back so soon? I've only just processed your last kill," Asher inquires the moment I appear in Hell. Lava pulses through the open crevices on his face from scars that refuse to heal. Or he won't allow them to. A clear and painful reminder of his own sins and the love he lost. A strike of lightning flashes in the distance, breaking free of the thick cover of black cloud. Spying that the prisoner line is particularly lengthy today, I shove the souls into his hands.

"Take these. I need to get back and handle some shit." I huff.

There's not a shred of doubt in my mind Mania will stay exactly where she was, hoping I'll return. I just needed a little space, a moment to think before I fucked everything I've been working so hard to achieve.

"Trouble in paradise?" Asher chuckles, handing off Imp's soul to HogFace. She's just revived and realized where she is. Beyond screaming, her arms and legs kick out wildly, cursing Ghost's name on repeat.

"Go fuck yourself," I grunt. Asher knows I don't fully mean it. We've spent enough time together now for me to consider him almost a friend. An ally, at least. Peering over his black, circular specs, his golden eyes watch me too closely.

"I may understand your motives, but you haven't given Mania the same opportunity. Don't ruin the love she has for you whilst trying to preserve it." He taps me on the shoulder and strolls back to his post outside of the gates. Azella hovers just inside, nodding her head to me. She knows better than anyone the turmoil I'm experiencing. Will my conscience allow me to save the love of my life, over the rest of the world as we know it? That's a question I struggle to answer every damn day.

Using the staff, I return to the dank corridor I recognize from some of the bodycam surveillance footage on Christopher's laptop. He became convinced I was so lost, he didn't even bother to hide his plans from me. It's how I knew Enzo was alive, as are most of the Mutes that supposedly died in the maze games. They've merely been moved to facilities around the world, awaiting a full gene reconfiguration or death. Whichever comes first.

Keeping my face placid, I don't reveal how unsurprising it is that no one has moved since I was last here. Except Enzo, who's curled up and fallen asleep. He's definitely not dead, or I'd feel it. But he's close.

"We will discuss how cool that was later," Ghost points a stern finger at me. Walking over, I knock his hand aside and pull him in for a quick hug. It's been too long since I've felt the comfort of my brothers. The men I thought I'd survived hell with in the orphanage basement, until I found out how cruel hell really could be if you're on the wrong side of it.

"No, we won't," I shake my head. Pyro stares at me and I don't bother trying to reconcile with him. He's far more stubborn and the crease between his eyebrows won't be easily assuaged. "Upon returning to Afterlife, none of you can talk to me. Don't look at me, don't even think about me. Forget I fucking exist until it's safe not to do so."

"What's that supposed to mean?" Pyro asks, only to be groaned over by Ghost.

"Not you too. There's an exit at the other side of this hallway, and we're all together now," he pleads to Mania. "We can just disappear." Putting his hands together, Ghost spreads his fingers apart and makes a sound very similar to a 'poof'.

"We have to return to Afterlife," Mania nods, looking to me for backup. I can see she's trying to do right by me and Asher's words echo in my head. She can't possibly understand my struggles if I don't voice them, but neither will I put her at risk. "But it'll be better this time. You don't have to do this alone anymore. We can help you."

"No, you can't! You'll just make it worse!" I explode, throwing my hand out and she flinches. Shame washes over me instantly and I take a step back from all three of them, careful to keep my voice low.

"Don't turn me into the villain here. Just go back to the asylum, have your fill of threesomes. Keep your heads down and do the job assignments you were given. It will all be over soon."

"You hear that, Ghost? We have to wave Mania goodbye as she heads back to the strip club. Maybe next time she'll get raped for real." My head whips from Pyro to Mania and the truth of his words are plastered all over her face. Fuck. Mania looks about thirty minutes from having an emotional breakdown and I have to clutch the staff to my chest to resist pulling her into me.

It wasn't supposed to take this long. I knew Mania would suffer from the experiments, but I also knew it wasn't anything she couldn't handle. But this. My confidence in mine and Azella's plan falters. The urge to take Mania to another astral plane and live with her in peace filling my mind. But the demons would find me. They'd torture us both for eternity if I break my vow. Pyro turns his back on me, muttering low but I hear it just fine.

"And here I was, thinking we all loved her the same."

Dropping the staff, I lunge at his back. Tossing Pyro into the wall, I'm right behind him, twisting his arm high behind his back.

"Don't test me," I growl. Ghost grabs me by the horns, throwing me aside with all his might. I skid to a stop, remaining upright. Mania steps between the three of us before I can attack again, but my focus is held on Pyro.

"I love Mania more than you can contemplate. I literally sold my soul to the devil to bring her back from the dead. It was my demon ability that triggered your eternal bond back into existence and I've had to watch her praise you every day for giving her a love I can't participate in."

"Hoax…" she gasps, reaching for me. I twist out of reach and kick up the staff with the toe of my boot.

"Leave it alone. Once my job is done screwing with Christopher's plans and I've seen you to a safer life, I have to take my rightful place in Hell. That was the deal I signed. There's no future for us Mania, so the least I can do is ensure there's one for you."

With that, I stamp down the staff and return to my cell in Afterlife. Stripping myself of my demonic appearance and sliding the bland-looking stick beneath the bed, I throw my fist into the locker. Then the wall, then my own face. Anger and frustration burns me from inside, flaying the underlayers of my skin. Biting down on my fist, I stifle a scream and quickly flick on the shower in the bathroom.

My chest heaves erratically. Come on Hoax, get a hold of yourself. Gripping the edge of the bathroom counter, a figure with two full horns appears in the mirror's reflection.

"I can't do this anymore," I tell Azella, hanging my head. I refuse to let her see me cry. I'm a demon for fuck's sake. Petty emotion should have been burnt out of me long ago.

"Breathe," she tells me, rubbing a circle on my back. I've come to understand how Mania grew fond of Azella so easily. I've never had a mother myself, but sometimes it's easy to pretend there's one with me now. "You're far from alone, Hoax. You can love her from a distance," she says softly.

Sucking in air, I level my breathing. Slow my heart rate. Unclench my fists and allow the swirling sensations of all four of us battering around our bond fade away. I've had enough practice closing off my link to the others. So much in fact, I manage it with barely any thought. Raising my purple eyes to Azella, I straighten and nod.

"Loving Mania from a distance is all I know how to do."

Tightening my arms around myself, I gently rock back and forth. Ghost shifts, snoring as he rolls over on the adjoining mattresses. If Christopher is watching, he didn't let us know of any objection to Pyro and Ghost dragging their beds into my room. And trust me, they made enough noise about it. The door doesn't open fully and we have to crawl over the bedding to get to the bathroom, but I hoped it'd help.

It hasn't.

Pyro stirs, reaching out for me but I don't want to lie back down. The images that dance across the ceiling refuse to let me sleep. What Camo did…what Hoax said. My heart is torn to shreds and my body – there's not enough shower gel in the world to wash off the dirt crawling beneath my skin.

A ping sounds from the floor below, seeping through the crack left in between our door and the shoe I used to jam it open. Nothing and no one will allow me to feel caged in right now. Crawling across the mattress, I peer around the door and spot the open elevator doors through the metal platform outside my room. A bald headed male exits, a sleeping or unconscious Hare-iett in his arms. Fuck, I can't believe I forgot about her. Even if I'd wanted to, we wouldn't have been able to find our way back to the strip club.

Somehow, Ghost guessed the right code for the keypad on his first try. Or there was some intervention on Hoax's part. He doesn't wear cuffs like us, so there's no telling what he gets up to whilst being ignored. I suppose that's the point. A row of guards were waiting to tear Enzo from us the moment we returned, clamping cuffs back on Pyro and forcing the key card from Ghost's grip. *Back to square one.*

Siren hobbles out of the elevator afterwards, the limp in her stride more from the pinch of her high heels than an injury. Goldie by her side appears unaffected, and Desire is nowhere to be seen. Grabbing Ghost's discarded sweater, I pull it over my tank and slip out of the room. Pausing briefly outside Hoax's room, I force myself to move onwards to the staircase. Granite pays me no attention, disappearing into Hare-iett's room and the door locks into place after closing. A part of me worries for her, but even if I could have followed, it wasn't them I was waiting for.

Goldie's yellow head pops up from beyond the railing and when she makes it onto the platform, I force my arm into hers.

"We need to talk," I tell her, no questions asked. Pyro will kill me when he finds I've disappeared, but I can't keep letting myself be controlled by others. When there's so much at work I don't understand, I need to start carving a path for myself. Starting with an alliance that will serve us all.

Entering Goldie's room, I leave the door wide open. Still in her tiny, yellow dress, I perch on the bed and wait for her to wash up. Time clicks by slowly. My cuticles barely exist by the time she saunters back inside in an oversized shirt that's clearly from one of her bears.

"State your business fast. I'm tired as fuck and need to be back at the club by tomorrow lunchtime."

"Good to see you've got your voice back," I sag my shoulders. This conversation would have been so much harder if only one of us could speak. Perhaps Mute's death absorbed all of his abilities back from his victims. Nothing surprises me anymore. "And for the record, you're not going back to the club. None of us are."

"Oh yeah? Finally found a backbone?" she chuckles and gets beneath her covers. Nudging me out of the way in the process, I opt to drag her desk chair across the room and sit backwards on that. Seems more intimidating that way.

Opening my mouth to argue, no words come out. She's completely right. This almost stranger that barely knows me has been able to see how fragile I've become as of late. Another aspect of my life Christopher has taken.

"I haven't always been this way," I sigh. "I used to stab myself in the neck just for a vacation in Hell. I stole for fun and screwed with people for kicks. Mainly MRA agents."

"What do you want – a medal?" Goldie pulls the length of her yellow hair over her shoulder and snuggles down further onto her pillow. Her eyes are heavy so I need to get to the point.

"No. I'm just saying, I've been through a lot of shit. But you're right, I've lost track of who I once was. Become too content hiding behind the three men that have sworn to protect me. Something I thought you'd be able to relate to – but I've seen how you are with your bears." Goldie peeks a yellow eye at me, her attention returning. "You haven't let yourself become lost in their masculine egos. I commend you for that. It's not easy to do."

"Yeah well," she shrugs. "When I publish my autobiography, I'll be sure to reserve you a copy. Now if that's everything?" Running a hand over the back of my neck, I stand and make my way over to the door. Using one finger, I slowly push it closed until the lock clicks into place. Goldie groans, realizing I'm not going anywhere. Nudging her over on the bed until she's in line with the wall, I snatch the pillow from beneath her head and use it to prop myself up.

"It makes no sense for us to be enemies when we can aid each other. Our men provide the muscle, but we have the cunning. The finesse to carry out what I have in mind."

"And that is?" Goldie drags herself upright beside me, crossing her arms.

"A full-blown riot. I'm beyond caring if we survive this place or not. You were raised in captivity - you know better than anyone there's no escape for us. But that doesn't mean we need to roll over and obey." Silence follows. Goldie's head is turned up to the ceiling, deep in thought so I continue.

"You said it yourself. I have lost my backbone. But with you at my side, I know I can stand up and fight. Not watching from the sidelines, but leading the parade with our men trailing behind."

"So, this is your little plan?" she clucks her tongue. "To become allies and ruin what little freedoms we have? For the first time in my life, I have a job. I get to leave the asylum and see the outside world. Not only that, I have total control of the kitchen and incoming food supply. Why would I give all of that up? They're only going to throw us back in the dungeons for acting out."

"You're not thinking big enough. I'm not suggesting we 'act out'," I finger quote, "and bend over to receive a spanking. By the time we're done, there won't be an asylum left standing. We'll burn this place to the ground, along with any bodies that didn't care to join us. I'm ready to cause havoc. The only question is; are you content receiving Christopher's handouts, or do you want to take control of your own life for once?"

Silence follows again, but this time, I don't need Goldie to speak to know what she's thinking. The answer is all over her face. Uncrossing her arms, she holds out a hand that's covered in waterproof, speckled glitter from the club.

"You'd better not go soft on me. I don't make deals lightly," Goldie warns, holding her hand just out of reach. I set my jaw, an expression of seriousness taking over my features.

"I'm doing this, with or without you. But you'd better make sure when the time comes, you don't stand in my way." Thrusting my hand forward, I take hers and give it a firm squeeze. A tingling stirs in my chest as Pyro wakes and asks what the fuck I'm up to, but I don't respond. Right now, I need to keep my nerve because I have a whole night of scheming ahead.

"That's more like it," Goldie smirks. Settling back, she tugs a packet of chocolate chip cookies out from the secret stash at the side of her bed. I know Hoax told me to lay low, but he also dented my pride in shouting at me. I may have lost his trust, but I refuse to let my own self-respect fall any further. With Goldie and our men backing us, we can make enough noise to distract Christopher from whatever Hoax is up to.

Accepting a cookie from Goldie, we knock them together with one thought uniting us. Let's stir some shit up.

Sitting across the canteen with a coffee in my hands, I watch Goldie raise the kitchen shutter. The bears spot me instantly, giving me a nod in unison. They're ready for a busy morning, with aprons strapped around their chunky bodies and hair nets over their bushy manes. Not many are awake yet, leaving me in the company of the MRA agents. A pair pass through to open the back doors and allow a brief chill to sweep inside.

"Morning boys," I smirk, lifting my coffee to them as they pass. They ignore me, disappearing behind the safety of the entrance gate. Sighing contentedly into my coffee, I can't help but smile. Today is the first day I woke up feeling like the old me again. Never mind that the small amount of sleep I did have was on Goldie's floor and my back is paying the price for it now. Speaking of which…

I hear Pyro stomp up behind me and place my cup down before he yanks me up by my ribs. Dragging me from the bench seat, I'm spun into his chest while Ghost steps into my back.

"Do you know what I woke up to this morning?" Pyro growls and I raise my brows. "Ghost giving me a fucking hand job." I cover my mouth, unable to stifle my laughter. Ghost chuckles too, his arms banding around my middle.

"I put on a high-pitched voice and everything. Think I would have gotten away with it if he hadn't put his hand in my hair. Are you proud of me, Spitfire?" I'm too busy laughing, pushing Pyro's chest away for the space to double over. Ghost comes with me, his erection lining the center of my ass cheeks in Goldie's sweatpants.

"So fucking proud," I spin in his arms and put my arms around the back of his neck. "Always looking out for me, even when I've snuck out."

"Yes, where did you go exactly?" Pyro grunts, folding his arms but Ghost clicks his tongue.

"It's rude to ask a lady where she's been. But it's obvious, she went to Hoax. How is he doing? Did you manage to screw some of that bad temper from him?" My laughter dies out and I give Ghost a serious glare. We're not allowed to discuss Hoax for fear someone might find out his secret. I push back, returning to my coffee on the bench.

"For a matter of fact, I was with Goldie."

"Goldie?! Why?" Ghost whines, sounding disappointed. I dread to think what he's imagining I did with her. As if summoned by her name, she appears with two more mugs in her hands and places them down for my men. They eye her suspiciously, making no move to take the coffees until I order them to do so. Goldie gives me an appreciative look and I practically glow with confidence. To think, yesterday I was merely some dead guy's victim.

"Mania, what's going on?" Pyro asks, sitting down on the bench with his legs spread either side of me in the center. I give him a bob of my eyebrows and gesture to the kitchen hatch, almost giddy that it's me doing the spontaneous shit. Talk about pride – Ghost will be beaming with it later on today.

Mutes stream from their rooms, drawn down the stairs by the smell Goldie's bears are cooking up. Goldie returns to her spot, standing tall inside the serving hatch with a grin plastered on her face. If anything, I reckon she just likes the mischief of it all.

Pre-wrapping bacon rolls in the stack of napkins on the countertop, she hands them out to those passing with a mug of coffee. Follicle appears with Siren and I point, directing them to go get theirs. Hare-iett surfaces next, Granite striding out of her room and heading for the guard's headquarters without looking back. Once she's received her breakfast, she sits opposite us, a blush on her cheeks and eyes remaining downcast.

"Don't ask," she mutters.

"Wasn't going to. Eat up, we've got a big day ahead of us." Follicle and Siren share a quizzical look, until they unpeel the napkin around their food and discover their job for today. Roles in rolls. I can't take credit for that genius idea. Catching Goldie's eye to share a cunning smirk and push myself up from the table.

"Mutes, listen up!" I announce. Pyro's hand wraps around my ankle, half in support and half in a *what the fuck are you doing?!* I'll take the former.

"Today, everything changes. Today, we take back the control that's been stolen from us. Whether you've been personally targeted by Christopher Gordon or not, I know you've noticed we're disappearing. Soon, there will be no one left to rebel. No one left to stop this malicious asshole from taking more of our kind. Silencing us, destroying our species. We didn't ask to be born this way, but it's time we stopped living in shame for it. If you're with us, you'll find your job in your napkin. If you're against us…"

I glance over to Goldie and she nods.

"Then get the fuck out of the way." I hop onto the bench, then the floor and sit, my chin held high.

Okay, seriously, Pyro dips into our connection. *I will back you in whatever you want to do, but you have to tell me what it is.* Wrapping his arms around me, he pulls me into his warm comfort and I drop my head into his neck.

We're causing some trouble. Whether to give Hoax the distraction he needs or just to get some revenge for the bullshit we've been dealt, it doesn't matter. I'm done with sitting around and waiting for whatever comes next.

Okay, is all Pyro replies while Ghost goes for a more enthusiastic response.

Fuck yes!

Mutes settle down with their food, many pausing to read what job they've been given. Follicle nods, scrunching up his napkin and stands. With his jaw set, he walks to the back door with the others that received the same instruction. Another handful of Mutes head to the security gate where a lone guard can be seen, reading his newspaper just beyond. Moving out of Pyro's embrace, I look up into his red eyes.

I need you at the bleachers. Oversee the crew there, tear off whatever materials you can and get them to the basement door within the hour.

Pyro presses a kiss to my forehead and leaves, no questions asked. That's why I love the shit out of that Mute.

Ghost, you're the most important part of my plan, I turn to him. His doggish smile makes me melt inside but I force on a stern expression and push a finger into his chest. *You need to stand beneath the platform and stay there. Don't move from that spot.*

With my eyes, I look across to direct him the right way. He doesn't move, however. Instead, he pouts.

I want a cool job. With a weapon. And a costume.

I'm all out of resources, but trust me. Your task is the coolest of all, and it ends with you emerging as a badass warrior, covered in blood.

Sold! Ghost jumps up and stops himself from running off for just long enough to lay a heated kiss on my lips. Then he skips into position and gives me a double thumbs up. Taking the three cups, I leave Hare-iett to share steamy details of last night with Siren and walk up to the kitchen hatch. The three bears are just leaving through the side door, and ascend the staircase, headed for the top.

"You ready for this?" I ask Goldie. She takes the cups from me and tosses them over her shoulder to smash on the floor. I'll take that as a yes. Peering around the asylum, I see a Mute beneath each of the ever-watching cameras, except for one. That one is for Christopher's benefit, to watch us ruin everything he's created. Including ourselves.

"It's been long overdue," Goldie agrees. There's a hint of emotion in her voice but I can't place what it is. She moves to stand at my side, the two queens who orchestrated the fall of their kingdom, ready to sit back and enjoy the carnage. Once the bears reach the headquarters entrance, all three braces themselves on the railing and roar to the sky. A frighteningly realistic sound that acts as the claxon for our riot to begin.

In unison, Mutes rip the cameras from the walls or smash them by any means necessary. Sitting on each other's shoulders, swinging around chairs. A buzzer sounds as the security gate slides open and close to seven guards steamroll into the asylum. Those waiting in the wings pounce, overpowering the guards by sheer strength in numbers. Batons are grabbed, coffee mugs are smashed into temples and in a short space of time, the guards are rendered unconscious.

I'm not surprised when a few make a run for it, the first one with any sense slamming his fist on the control panel to send the asylum into lock down. A grate criss-crosses over the elevator door and his neon orange eyes light with freedom just before a metal shutter slams down over the only other entrance, just before the spray of bullets can be heard on the other side. Poor fucker should have heeded my advice. Work with us or die.

Unfortunately, his sacrifice was exactly what we were counting on. Now the lockdown procedure has been initiated, we have four hours until the highest security detail of the MRA arrive and try to bargain with us for the safe return of their men.

"How do you know so much about asylum protocol?" I ask Goldie as we stride across the canteen together. She keeps her lips pushed shut, refusing to answer while we shove a table closer to the last of the cameras. Standing on the table together, she slips an arm around my shoulder just in time for the lens to focus on our grinning faces. Giving Christopher our middle fingers, Goldie slams her fist into the camera and the red flashing light stutters out. Damn, the girl is hardcore.

"Time for phase two," I jump down from the table. Ghost hasn't moved and I reach up to stroke his hair like the good boy he is. Those waiting nearby toss their captive guards into a heap at Ghost's feet. Taking his cuffed wrists, I lower him down to press his hands onto the back of the guard dumped on top. "Have all the fun you like, but you can't kill them. Yet." I wink. Ghost follows me with his eyes as I step back, his head tilted upwards.

Grabbing the hem of my sweatshirt, I whip up my top to give him a full-frontal view of my lacking underwear. Jiggling my breasts about, Ghost's eyes widen in surprise and he hiccups, falling straight through the floor into the basement with his soon-to-be victims. Worked like a charm. A throat is cleared behind me and I drop the hem, turning to find Pyro's quirked brow.

"Where do you want this lot?" he sticks a thumb towards the group of Mutes approaching. Each one is carrying their bodyweight in metal and broken plastic that used to be the bleacher seats.

"Barricade the basement door. If Ghost leaves any of the guards with the ability to walk, we have to make sure they can't get out."

"And how is Ghost getting out?" Pyro tilts his head. He has yet to show any emotion on how he feels about all of this; pity, pride or otherwise.

"He'll find a way. If there's anyone I don't have to worry about, it's Ghost." I shrug, preparing to walk away when Pyro's hand catches my bicep.

"Do you ever worry about me?" Pyro asks, pulling me into his chest. His hands rest on the small of my back, his red eyes searching mine. I smile sadly.

"Every minute of every day. I worry that you won't have the life you've been waiting for. That I'm not always going to be enough for you." I turn my head but Pyro grabs my chin and tilts me back up to his lips. Hovering just above my mouth, his whispered words seep into me as if Goldie hasn't begun smashing the furniture to shit with a tenderizer in the background.

"There isn't a second of the day you are not all I need, want and desire. Having you, holding you, that's my future. The place and predicament doesn't matter." Lowering his head, he kisses me slow. An unhurried connection that blossoms in our chest and I openly groan against his mouth. His lips warm, his jaw tight beneath my palms. We both want more, but now's not the time.

"Come on lovebirds, we need to stoke those fires of yours," Goldie shoves her shoulder between us. She shakes a pair of gas lighters in her hand. Her yellow eyes are alight with mischief and I chuckle, pulling Pyro after me towards the stairs. Hare-iett and Siren are already on the second floor, throwing mattresses over the railings to form the burn pile below.

"Go help out," I tell him, smacking his ass on the way up the steps. Who knows where we're going to sleep, but that's what the demands are for. If we're lucky, Octavia will respond to our SOS. In aiding our cause, she's also shown her weak side. One I intend to take full advantage of. But…If I'm being truthful with myself, the entirety of my plan counts on her seeing our desperation for change. Surely she won't leave us all to rot if we make a big enough noise.

Heading beneath the platform to listen through the basement door, intending to check on Ghost, a hand wraps around my mouth and I'm jerked backwards into the cleaning cupboard next door.

"What the hell are you doing?" I grit out, holding back the full force of my anger. If I hadn't been hiding in here, forcing a wedge between my emotions and the bond that linked her, Mania would have collapsed under the weight of my rage. As if I wasn't clear enough she is to do as she's told, her rash actions today could have set me back weeks.

Mania rubs her ass against my crotch and pries my hand from her mouth. "Sorry – am I taking all the fun from you and your sneaky plans?" I growl low, wondering where I went so wrong. How I messed everything up this bad whilst trying to keep it ever so simple. Be the brainwashed robot everyone expected, bring down Christopher's empire. But the deeper I looked, the larger it grew and now everything is out of hand.

"If this is about getting my attention," I start but Mania's harsh laugh cuts me off.

"Oh please. You can't control me, Hoax. And you can't expect me to sit around, twiddling my thumbs just because you say so." Breaking away, I feel the cold of the distance between us. Even cramped in this tiny cleaning cupboard, she feels like a million miles away and I know I'm losing her for good. Hanging my head, I sigh.

"Don't blame me when you don't like the outcome." Reaching out for the door handle, Mania shoves me in the chest.

"Oh I will, because if you'd have just told me what you were up to – I wouldn't have to guess!" She shoves me again. This time, my back hits a shelving unit. Pots and cans rain down around me. When she tries to put her hands on me again, I grab her forearms and twist her around.

"Is this what you want?" I bite down on her ear lobe, until she doesn't resist anymore. Watching her from a distance is one thing, but having her here, so close and so disobedient, the last shred of my control snaps. "You want me to tell you what I'm feeling. Give you everything I've been holding back?"

This time, my fangs extend and I sink them into her neck. Her hiss quickly turns into a moan and I shove them in harder. The taste of blood does nothing for me, but the lust leaking through the dam I'd cemented between us is my undoing.

Removing my teeth from her punctured skin and wrapping a hand around her neck, I use the other to shove down the back of her sweatpants. No underwear greets me from her creamy skin.

"You want me to bare my secrets?" I spank her ass hard. There will be a handprint mark left for Pyro and Ghost to see. Just to make sure, I do it again. Mania arches her back, pushing into me. I reach for my button and rip the zip for my erection to thud against her.

The desire is too much, just like when she followed me to Hell. I know I should pull back, leave before I ruin the last of my hard work, but I can't. I must have her. Without the practice they have had, my passion flows through the bond, reaching everyone who is connected by it. Ghost cheers me on in my head, but Pyro isn't so understanding.

Hoax, stop. She went through a traumatic event just yesterday.

Stop and I'll burn your fucking dick off if it's the last thing I do, Mania growls through the mental connection and cuts the others off for me. I grin a full-fanged smile, pushing my dick between her thighs. She's soaking wet and with a simple jerk of her ass, permits me access. There's no holding back.

Using my grip on her throat, I keep Mania in place while I fuck her tight pussy relentlessly. Her strangled cries are drowned out by the clap of her ass on my groin, my balls swinging to slap her clit on each rough thrust.

Pyro seems to think our girl isn't strong enough to overcome everything life throws at her. He forgets she's a survivor, but he didn't see her the way I did. He wasn't present every step of the way, watching over her from beyond the veil. I've lost count of the amount of times I've watched Mania pick up the pieces of her soul and slot them back together. She's walked back from the fires of Hell too many times for a piece of scum like Camo to affect her. But just in case, I focus on erasing every trace of trauma that may still linger.

Removing my hand from her throat, I slide my arms beneath hers, creating a cross over her chest. My dick slams home inside her, my groin pressed flush to her ass. Instead of thrusting, I use my grip on her shoulders to rock her on me. Impaled, so impossibly filled and unable to escape the pressure the head of my cock is applying to her g-spot.

Mania's screams fill the small closet, her hands gripping the wooden shelf for stability. It isn't fastened into the wall, so if anything - it just makes our fucking more obvious to those lingering outside.

Lifting her thigh, I wrap Mania's leg around my hip, opening her to me. With my dick buried to the hilt, Mania whines and drops a hand between her legs. I snatch her wrist, pinning her hand behind her back. I won't let her rush this. And I won't let her finish until I've imprinted in her so deeply, she won't be able to forget me when I'm gone.

"Hoax, *please*," she begs and a smile graces my lips.

"Yes, my love?" I answer, not waiting for a reply. Using my grip on her leg and wrist, I hold her still, stretched across the room as I quickly pull out and slam back in. Again and again.

Harder.

Faster.

Deeper.

More ruthless than I ever planned on being with her. But I'm not the man I once was. Not the Mute she fell in love with. That person died when I took the demon oath and all that remains is someone calculated and cut off from reality. Except when she entices me with her body and look where that's got us.

Thrusting like a mad man, I feel her pussy closing in and clamp a hand over her mouth just before she screams into it. Shattering beneath me. Crumbling for me. Mania falls to pieces while waves of her cum slicken my movements. Biting down on my cheek, I draw the blood rushing through my cock back, focusing on the blood seeping into my mouth instead. My vision starts to dance, but I manage to see her orgasm to its end before withdrawing completely.

Mania stumbles forward, turning back to grab my dick but I step out of her reach. Her cheeks are flushed, her eyes swirling with fire that quickly dim as I tuck myself back into my cargo pants. The zipper is bust so I tuck my erection into my waistband and cover it with my t-shirt.

"I don't understand, let me…" Mania steps forward and I hold her back by the shoulders.

"We're done here," I grit out. My dick is pulsating to be back inside of her tight cunt, my balls so taut, they're giving me a stomach ache. But I refuse to obey either.

The desire to empty myself into Mania will be my painful reminder as to why I need to keep her at a distance. I can't make her happy. I can't stick around once my demon vow is complete. Popping back to Earth once in a while is the best I can offer, and when it comes to my soul mate, she deserves better. It'll be easier for her not to see me, while I relish the anguish of an unsated cock and curse fates for the rest of eternity.

A tear trickles down Mania's cheek, highlighted in the dim, overhanging bulb. The hurt in her expression is echoed through our bond, carving a hole through my being. A hollow cavity that will never be filled. I will my feet to move, for me to walk out of that door. It'll be easier that way. To leave her with a reason to hate me. But my hand raises instead, my thumb wiping away the tear and those that continue to fall. Cupping her cheek, I tug her to my chest.

"You've picked a battle you can't possibly win," I sigh. Mania jerks her head out of my hold but doesn't step away.

"Don't," she spits angrily. She doesn't look at me but I can see the crease in her eyebrows, the hard set to her jaw. "Can we just leave this as it is? I don't want to fight every time we are together." Her heavy exhale rushes over my chest. "Hold me Hoax, before something else happens like Brainwave takes your memories or some shit."

"That'd be impressive," I grunt, "considering I killed him weeks ago." Mania stiffens for a moment, as if she's holding a stranger. A male she doesn't recognize anymore. But I'm still the Mute who fell in love with her, risked his life to protect her. So, as if I had any other choice, I give her exactly what she wants.

Straightening her clothes and brushing the hair back from her damp face, I lower myself onto the floor, pulling Mania into my lap. My lips rest against her forehead, her even breathes fanning my collar bone. Beyond this room, a war rages. The crackle of fire glimmers around the doorframe. Mutes shout for direction, Goldie shouting orders and the rise of a rebellion thrums through the asylum.

A naive and pointless attempt to anger Christopher, but Mania's right – I can't control her. Especially when I won't include her in my thoughts. Wrapping my arms around her, I steal a few more precious moments. If it wasn't for Pyro and Ghost knowing Mania was with me, I'm sure they'd have stormed inside by now.

The ticking of my mental timer is growing louder and before long, I feel the tug of a nearby soul in need of reaping. The first of many, if the stench of thickening smoke is anything to go by. Riots cause deaths, and I'm a demon with a commitment to fulfill.

Tipping Mania's head up one last time, I press a kiss to her lips and gently set her aside onto the floor. She tracks my movements as I stand and call for my staff. My appearance changes the instant it responds, solidifying in my hand. Raising it just above the floor, I hang my horned head.

"Keep yourself safe, my love."

T he last of the mattress' is tossed over the railing and I grip it tightly. My knuckles turn white, and for the thousandth time, I try to reach out through the eternal bond. Mania has snubbed me out. It's not just the emptiness in my chest that pisses me off; it's that anything could have happened and I'd have no idea. Hoax could be tricking us and have marched Mania straight into Christopher's clutches for all I know.

"Just go find her already. Your moping isn't helping morale," Goldie barks at me when I descend the stairs. She's got the fire going strong, a thick plume of smoke spiraling to the glass roof. Multiple guards and agents have attempted to leave their headquarters, but the bears have a system going. Two attack and the third dips low to chuck their attackers over the railing to their death.

"Fine," I grunt, realizing Goldie is still standing in front of me. I had been worried about what I'd walk in on, as well as wanting to give the pair their privacy, but enough is enough. Grabbing the door handle to the room beside the basement, it twists under my grip and Mania steps into my body.

"Oh hey. How are we getting on?" she smiles, sliding past me. I don't miss the droplets of blood at the neckline of her sweater, but when I look inside the cupboard, there's no one else present.

"Everything okay?" I ask, frowning hard. Mania throws me a cheeky wink and smirk over her shoulder.

"Of course." She accepts a firelighter from Goldie's pocket and heads outside. Thick lines of blood trail the floor where the dead guards have been dragged out to the yard, exactly in the same direction Mania is headed. I stride after her, joining her side before she can breach the sunlight.

"I'm not buying it," I grunt, winding my arm around her middle so she can't get away this time.

"Well that's good, because I'm not selling you anything," she giggles. Peering up at me, her forced smile doesn't reach her red eyes and in the brightened light, I can see she's been crying.

"Oh yeah? Release your emotions to me then," I dare her. A flicker of uncertainty flashes in her expression before she twists out of my hold. Goldie joins Mania as the pair share a nod and spark their lighters. Mutes run around the heap of bodies, throwing anything minutely flammable onto it. Flour, sugar, cooking oils, creamer.

I'd be worried about the mess we're sending to Hell if Hoax didn't appear across the yard in his full demon attire. Thick horns protrude from his head, black like the leather tunic on his muscled frame. His eyes have bled black with purple irises, matching the onyx stone held in his staff. This time, he has friends.

Azella takes the lead, hauling the souls out of the nearest bodies before Mania barbeques them. Asher is at her side, joined by Hoax and a demon I'm unfamiliar with. His face resembles a hog with a gold ring joining the nostrils of his snout. It hadn't occurred to me until now how a demon's features could change and that Hoax might not look anything like his old self one day. He's a far cry from it now.

Mania makes a point of ignoring him, lowering her gas lighter to the first body. Clicking the trigger back, a meager flame melts into the dead guard's flesh, but nothing beyond that. She tries another part of him, scorching mini holes all over his torso and chest. Goldie does the same, their plan only going up in flame figuratively.

A band of Mutes, who have decided not to take part in today's riot, snigger in the background. I shoot them a glare and they shrink back from the metal fencing of the basketball court they've locked themselves into. So much for taking a stance. When Christopher takes back control, I'm certain they'll be the first he kills.

"Need a hand?" a familiar voice says from behind. Ghost steps into view with a female under each arm. I'd scold him, if it wasn't for the flash of lilac hair that catches my attention. Tate smiles, tossing the heavy manacle in her hands onto the body heap. Claire holds Ghost's wrist ones and does the same, and suddenly those trapped in the basketball court want out. Too late fuckers, you made your choice.

Tate makes quick work of disabling my cuffs and with the full force of my fires, I crack them open. Next, she does Mania's, then Goldie's and all the other Mutes rushing forward with their hands held out. Forming a production line, Tate works on deactivating the cuffs while Ghost, Mania and I crack them open. Our body pile becomes littered with mechanical cuffs that probably won't burn but it'll be fun to watch.

Together, with Hoax watching on with a frown, the three of us place a hand on Mania's test dummy and call forth our fires. Warmth spreads through my veins until an explosion of color bursts from my palm. Orange, blue, purple and a hint of white, all swirling into the inferno we're finally able to release. I sigh at the feel of it, like an animal of flame unfurling in my chest. The pile is instantly engulfed and Mutes all around cheer.

A smile graces my lips. Mania has given us all a new lease of life. If only for morale's sakes, I already know this rebellion was worth it. To see our kind beaming from ear to ear, hugging strangers and whooping to the sky, the scene plays out before me like a movie. A fantasy I didn't know I had. For us all to be united as a species. Tate draws Claire into her arms, pressing a kiss into her hair. To them, I'm sure the moment is reflected tenfold. Their escape from Christopher's rule to be together. Do they even know Enzo is alive yet?

"Come on then, tell us," I pat Ghost roughly on the back with a blast of heat. "How did you get out of the basement in the end?"

"You don't want to know," he grunts, running a hand through his white hair.

"Well now I really do," Mania smirks, wrapping her arms around his middle. She stares up at him with such admiration, my brow twitches. Why do I suddenly feel like I'm on the shit list?

"Later," he pats her on the head like a dog. *A dog.* Her tongue rolls out and she nuzzles further into his chest. Fuck it, I don't understand what is happening here.

"All you need to know is after I figured out a way to trigger my ability, it was easy to stride into the guard's headquarters and find Tate. On my way out, I shoved the bears inside and they legit shifted right before my eyes. Well, through the glass. One polar, one grizzly and the other an American black bear. You've never seen anything like it," Ghost whistles low and his eyes glaze over as if he's remembering the best moment of his life.

"They fully shifted?" Goldie steps closer to listen in. Ghost nods, still day dreaming and Goldie sighs. "Ah fuck, I better go sort them out. They can't shift back without my command." She strides away and a moment of calm settles as she stands to watch the fire. I'm distracted by the demons that keep popping up, strolling into the inferno as easily as air. Above, a thick of smoke trails into the clouds, signaling to anyone in a three mile radius that those at Afterlife mean business.

"So...what do we do now?" Ghost asks, drumming his fingers on Mania's shoulders like the impatient fucker he is.

"Now we just have to wait for the MRA mediators to turn up. Could think about what our demands are. We should get everyone's input," Mania raises a hand and Ghost quickly pushes it down.

"Orrrrrrrr, we have the opportune moment for a threesome in the chapel. You know you've always wanted to do something unholy with a cross," Ghost bobs his brows. "Soak the alter in your baptism batter, take a shower in my satanic semen?" Mania bursts out laughing while I look to the ceiling for my fleeting patience. I push the heel of my palm into my chest, still very much aware that she's hiding the true nature of her feelings from us.

"I think Mania's had her fill for now," I say in a much gruffer tone than intended. I'd meant to be protective but now I just sound like a jealous prick.

"Perhaps Mania should decide for herself when she's had enough," Ghost growls. His arm tightens around her and I know I'm fighting a losing battle. My brother draws her inside and I'm left to follow, keeping my tight fists by my sides. When Ghost's hand travels down Mania's back to graze her ass, I send a blast of fire into his being, resonating in his palm. Ghost yelps, jerking away as his skin audibly sizzles and the smell of burning flesh isn't just outside anymore.

"What's your problem?" he shouts, swinging around to face me. "Bitter asshole or not, I was going to let you watch?!" I inhale sharply and rear my fist back.

"I'm really sorry about this," I manage to grit out before my fire-engulfed knuckles crack into Ghost's temple. His body flies into the air with the added force of the flames, landing hard and skidding across the lino on his back. When he doesn't immediately rise, I figure I have at least a few minutes and grip Mania's forearms.

Tugging her with me, I spin her back into the wall and crowd her with my body.

"I don't understand why you're fighting so hard to pretend everything is okay. If this is a retaliation to what happened with Camo-" Mania sucks in a breath at the name and throws her fists into my chest. I don't move.

"Oh my god Pyro, just leave it alone! Everything is fine and I'm happy."

"No, you're not," I state roughly, lowering my head. "You're hurting. Let me in so I can help." Shuffling my thighs in between each of hers, I pin Mania to the wall without an inch of space for her to move. My chest is solid against hers, my jaw brushing across her cheek. She tries to struggle, muttering that others are watching but I don't budge. Fuck who sees, this needs to be settled now.

"You know better than anyone, ignoring your pain doesn't make it go away. It'll resurface at the worst possible moment, and I need to know you're okay before we go any further with this riot. I'll have your back beyond death do us part, and I'll always be here to call you out on your bullshit. Now let. Me. In."

Mania's head tilts ever so slightly to close the distance between our mouths to mutter softly, "fuck you." But regardless, the dam blocking our bond disintegrates. Emotions, so raw and gut-wrenching, flood my system. Hatred, anger. Loathing, both for our predicament and herself. A hint of vulnerability and shame taints the love we share and in turn, I hit her back with my own feelings.

The adoration that radiates from me is stronger than I've ever felt. Encased in pride, layered with passion, I pour it all into Mania's heaving chest. A golden glow emanates between our heaving chests, widening and wrapping the two of us into a cocoon no one can penetrate.

"Don't you know by now," I whisper for her ears only, "your strength to overcome such travesties only makes me love you more. We will never have an easy life, but I don't need you to fake your happiness." Pressing my forehead onto hers, I fill her. From toes to temple and everywhere in between, there's not a hidden crevice of darkness I don't fill with my light, erasing the suffering she refuses to deal with. But that's okay, I'll deal with it for her.

"Let me carry you until you're strong enough to stand again. If there's something you can't handle, I'll do it for you. There's no concealing what's in here," I tap her heart with a finger before trailing it up to catch the tear about to drip from her jaw. "I want it all. And when you refuse, I will take it from you."

I could have easily opened her bond to me by force, but I needed it to be her choice to trust me enough. Mania's had enough ripped away without her consent. I'm in no hurry to join that list until she gives me a reason to.

Her tears flow freely. I hold her up physically when she curls into my body, giving her as much time as she needs. Slipping past her defenses, images flutter behind my eyelids. One's I wouldn't have wished to see, but relieving her of them is what this is all about. I witness how Camo dragged her away, using a marble paperweight to beat and subdue her, before taking full advantage of her lack of voice. He openly mocked her for continuing to scream when no sound could be heard.

I grit my teeth, wishing I could pull him back from Hell to kill him again. Maybe that's something I could speak to Hoax about.

Backtracking, scenes play out from the maze, and even before that.

During the month Mania was purely human and struggled to survive in the harsh world that wouldn't accept her. My chest squeezes, my lungs constricting. Every ounce of her pain is drowned in misery, a weight I only now realize she's been holding back. But with a flare of my fire, I burn it all to ash. Scrub it from existence so when Mania next exhales and peers up at me, I see the real her. Weightless, reassured and peaceful.

"I'm sorry, for pushing you away," she mutters and I silence her words with my mouth. There's no apologizing between us. Shit isn't always going to go our way, but it's how we face it that will define us. Her lips part for me, eager for more but I refuse to give it to her. This isn't about passion. This kiss is a promise to love her forever and protect her always.

On the edge of my subconscious, a faint buzzing sounds and I withdraw the glow surrounding us. Mania refuses to let me pull away, her hands fisted in my t-shirt so I take her with me. Wrapped in the safety of my arms, Ghost is just rousing to see the drone hovering a meter from my face. Much like those in the maze, the outline of a parrot twists sideways to present a camera lens as the robotic creature's eye.

"As touching as that was," Christopher's voice crackles through the speaker in the animals mouth, "it seems your precious soulmate has become complacent." I crush Mania to me, even though there's nowhere else for her to go, and twist her away from the parrot's view. It flutters around my side and Mania stands tall, pulling on my strength to boost her own defiance.

"I'm sorry my facility proved too boring for you, my dear. Allow me to spice things up." A sound echoes from the top of the asylum, the door to the headquarters bursting from its hinges. Goldie, who was standing outside in a bid to get in, flies over the railing, gripping onto the bar just before she falls to her death like many before her.

Squeezing into the open doorway, a huge creature of black fur and patchy pink skin peeking through holds an actual polar bear in his large jaws. Red taints the white around its teeth as the creature jerks and tosses the bear down the staircase. Throwing his head back, it roars at the glass ceiling tainted by the billowing smoke trying to escape.

Christopher's laughter leaves the speaker just as the drone turns to fly away, sending a message out to all of the Mutes standing and staring up in horror.

"Enjoy this moment with your loved ones. It will be your last."

"What the fuck is that?" Ghost hops to his feet and runs over to touch shoulders with Pyro, creating a barricade between me and the asylum. Tate and Claire bolt towards us from their place hovering in the open doorway, both clinging to Ghost's arms and hiding behind him.

"Experiment 23," Tate replies, a tremble in her hushed tone. My red eyes scrunch closed, shielding me from the look of horror I briefly caught. "They must have transferred him over from another facility using the internal elevator."

"Him?! That thing is a Mute?" I ask, another roar reverberating through the asylum.

"It was," Claire whimpers, ducking her face into Ghost's back. Risking another peek, I hold Pyro's hips for stability and push up onto my tiptoes. A creature, the size of a house, snarls over the railing, swiping a gnarled claw at Goldie. My heart is in my throat, watching her cling on for her life.

A brown bear leaps out of the headquarters, slamming into the creature's back and as a pair, they tumble over the edge, just missing Goldie. She screams a word I can't decipher but the brown bear instantly shifts back into a man. A hairy, naked man that lands on the creature's back and rolls off groaning. I take a step to the side but Pyro holds me back. The creature pushes up on all fours, shakes out his fur and licks the blood from its lips.

"Chapel, now," Ghost orders and starts moving. I link my fingers into Pyro's as we run around the mattress burn pile, using the smoke to cover our movements.

"There's no time for your religious threesome! We need to work out how the fuck we're going to escape that thing," I hiss, bumping into Ghost's arm. He draws me underneath it, pushing the chapel door open with his free hand. Somehow, amongst the sheer panic radiating through our bond, Ghost manages to find a second to wink at me.

"I like your thinking, Spitfire, but that's exactly what I was doing." Ushering us inside, Ghost pulls the old-style, wooden doors closed and pushes the handle of a nearby mop through the handles.

"Game plan," he barks and snaps his fingers at Tate and Claire. "Go."

"Um…well, I suppose," Claire strokes the length of her side braid for comfort. Ghost growls and she flinches, so Tate steps in between them.

"Our best bet would be in the headquarters themselves. There are bunkers in case of a containment issue. That could be where the rest of the guards are hiding out if they haven't left the building altogether via the elevator. Failing that, the operating theaters have heavy-duty locks." Pyro nods, pulling me back into his side. Since I unleashed the full extent of my emotions onto him, he's being extra clingy. And I love it.

"And Christopher?" Pyro asks, rubbing his jawline.

"He'd have been the first one to jump ship. He could be anywhere in the world at one of his other facilities," Tate sighs and the rest of us visibility deflate. All of this was to get his attention, to piss him off, and he's not even here.

"Shit," Pyro finally curses and I brush a hand over his chest. His annoyance is seeping through me now that our connection is so fresh and I need him to keep his nerve. A rumble precedes a line of stone crumbling from the ceiling as the creature runs the length of the metal platform on the level above.

Pyro drags me against the wall while Ghost uses his size and ability to cover Tate and Claire's crouching frames. I give him a quick smile and nod when he catches my eye. It wasn't so long ago Ghost would have thrown Tate into a wood clipper just for fun.

But to survive this place, we all need to work together. Our forced proximity and unconventional relationships are churning into something deeper. Something I've never considered to have before. A family.

I decide in that moment the three of us, hopefully four including Hoax, can quit and run the first chance we get and never look back. I won't be able to leave without Tate, Claire and Enzo. Then there's Serpentina, who seems to be a package deal with the Blacksmith, Hare-iett and whatever is happening with Granite, Goldie and her bears…

I swallow. The list is getting longer and longer and the sense of dread in the pit of my stomach tells me I won't be able to save everyone. Now, the idea of a riot, when I have so much to lose seems like the worst idea. *Fuck!*

"It's too late for regrets," Pyro mutters. His hands brush away the goosebumps prickling on my forearms, but I'm not cold. I'm fucking terrified.

"Okay so it's simple," Ghost states when the creature has moved on. "I keep us transparent, we skip up to one of those bunkers. Kill everyone inside. Maybe play with a few control buttons on the way past and hide out until the negotiators turn up or we starve to death. Whatever comes first," Ghost shrugs with a smile that's far too easy for our predicament. Tate makes a sound in the back of her throat and we all turn to face her.

"Experiment 23 had my blood markers installed into his thyroid glands, along with the capability to generate my mutant into a gas."

"In Englishhhh," Ghost groans, holding his hands up to the ceiling as if he's praying. Pyro slaps a hand on Ghost's nape and yanks him away from Tate before he gets too ragey.

"Meaning?" Pyro tries a softer approach.

"His breath can debilitate our abilities," Claire answers on a quickened exhale. A moment passes where Tate refuses to meet our stunned stares before Ghost has an outburst.

"Oh for fuck's sake Tate!" He kicks a pew, knocking over a candlestick in the process. The creature roars on the other side of the door and my eyes widen.

"Quickly, there's a backdoor. This way!" Tate whisper-shouts, darting down the aisle, her hand linked with Claire's. My heart jolts in my chest, and I dart for the main door – despite Pyro's protests. Removing the mop and wrenching it open, I grab the back of Ghost's t-shirt and shove him outside.

"New plan. Ghost distracts it while we get to the bunker!" I shout, already slamming the door closed as a pair of giant, orange eyes swivel through the plume of smoke. Shit. I vaguely hear Ghost yelling 'come get me muff-nut' as I run, a thud slamming against the door a moment later. All that spurs me to keep moving is that the weight behind it, joined by the further crumbling of stone, was too heavy to be Ghost.

"And how do we plan on getting Ghost out of there alive?" Pyro asks, crowding me into the secret exit behind a curtain I saw Tate disappear through. I half shrug, starting up the spiral staircase.

"He's like a cockroach. There's nothing Ghost can't survive!" I shout back, finding Tate and Claire waiting at the top. Pyro closes the gap between us, just in time for Tate to dislodge the wall panel and permit us entry into a supply closet. We pass straight through, nothing aside from paint thinner catching my eye. Unlocking it from the inside, we peer out tentatively.

The monster batters around the level below, slamming from wall to wall. Black fur in matted patches expose the raw, pink skin underneath. Its teeth stick out at various angles, dripping with drool. A faint, green gas passes along the line of the tongue hanging out of its mouth, swinging wildly as he runs after Ghost. Using his ability, Ghost dives through the mattress fire before the debilitating gas can touch him. Spotting us edging out onto the platform, Ghost bows to me like a matador, putting a random fork from the floor into his mouth like a rose.

"For you my love, I shall slay the beast!" Experiment 23 leaps through the fire and snaps it's teeth around Ghost's legs, tossing him aside like a ragdoll. My heart judders and I grab Pyro's hand, sending a blast of flames through our bond to heal Ghost's injuries before the monster can pounce again. Rolling aside, Ghost just misses the stomp of a giant, gangly foot. A roar penetrates the air and a ripple rolls through the monster's back.

"We have to go!" Tate shouts, giving a vague warning as the monster body shifts and contorts. A tail bursts from the base of its spine, its arms lengthening and cracking until it's hunched onto all fours. Bucking, it grows in size, slamming its back into the platform beneath our feet. We're thrown to the edge of the railing and stumble back to the wall. The metal groans and crunches, and with another buck, gives way completely.

My stomach lurches and I'm freefalling until the clinch of metal at my wrist yanks me to a swift stop. Pyro is caught too, left hanging as we peer up at the molten eyes of the Blacksmith. Serpentina is wrapped around his body, her face buried in his neck. Retracting the metal into his hand, he pulls us to safety, with Tate and Claire at his side.

"Where," I breathe, barely able to rub two braincells together. "Thank you," I mutter instead, happy my feet are back on solid ground but as the monster roars, I feel like we won't be for long. Leaving the gaping hole in the platform behind, we run for the final staircase separating us from the guard's headquarters.

At the foot of the stairs, Goldie is bent over the male who must be her polar bear. His white hair, the same shade as Ghost's but much longer, spills over the metal platform. His chest is riddled with holes, only visible through the sheen of blood by the gaping, darkened holes dotted throughout. Goldie uselessly tries to cover all of the punctures at once with her hands and forearms.

"Goldie," I sink down, placing a hand on her back. Her sobs rock beneath my palm and I look to Pyro with desperation in my gaze. Nodding, he tries to scoop up the male but he proves too heavy. A chain wraps around my waist, hoisting me up and a small sound of shock is torn from my lips. The beast below doesn't like that, mimicking the sound throughout the asylum tenfold. The Blacksmith glares at me, tearing the child from his front and easing her into my arms.

"Try to take her from me and I won't be responsible for my actions." His chain remains tightened at my waist, anchoring me to him as he helps Pyro lift the bear. Tate bravely takes the lead, running up the stairs while Claire hangs to the back, her hands briefly touching me every now and again to remind me she's there.

I hug Serpentina to my body, a hand sinking into her yellow hair. I can't describe the attachment I feel to the small child, considering I haven't spent much time with her, but knowing she came from Bellemare like me, that she has no one left and the Mutes who adopted her in the maze are gone, the level of protection that rises in me is fierce.

Breaching the headquarters, we tentatively look around, but there's no one here. Whoever was deemed invaluable enough to remain have been ripped to shreds by the monster that passed through. A clear line of blood shows his journey, from elevator to the main door. The stench of copper in the air assaults my nose, the limbs and heaps of flesh strewn across the room making me push Serpentina's curious gaze back into my shoulder.

A strangled cry and blast of actual fear through our bond has me turning and making Claire get out of the way. I rush back to the railing, scared to look. The Mute I've given a third of my heart to is clutched in the monster's jaws, its teeth snapping closed. One last thought pierces my mind as the white thread of our bond is completely shut off.

I love you Spitfire.

"No!" I scream, pushing Serpentina into Claire's arms when she hovers nearby. I grip the railing, fighting against the Blacksmith's chain to throw myself over the edge. With the creature directly below, I could drop down and hit him with a blast of my fire before it even noticed I was there. Tears pour from my eyes, my frozen heart refusing to beat as Ghost's body falls from its jaw in two halves. An image I can never unsee, imprinted inside my mind. This is all my fault. My idea, my riot. My loss to bear for eternity.

I grip the metal as my legs give out, huge sobs and an impending panic attack making it hard to breathe. To think. To live without my comical asshole to boost me when there seems to be no hope left. And there isn't. It's over. There's no point surviving with a third of my soul withered. A hand touches my shoulder and I try to shrug it off, but it holds on tight.

"Wow, Spitfire. I didn't realize you cared so much." Blinking up, Ghost's white eyes have me blubbering something inaudible. Hoax, in full demon form, stands off to the side.

"Keep a leash on your mutt," he drawls, smacking his staff down and disappearing from view. Ghost smirks, brushing the ash from his shoulders. Back to his full cocky self. I just sit there, consumed with elation and the reprise of his being merging with mine.

"This eternal flame shit is incredible. I'm fucking invincible baby!" Ghost shouts, running to throw himself over the railing just for fun. The chain at my waist flicks into action, wrapping around Ghost's ankle just in time to yank him back onto the platform. The Blacksmith stares at the pair of us with daggers and my attention is brought back to Pyro hovering over a still body.

"Next time, I won't pull you back," he grunts. Holding his hands mere centimeters from the naked man/bear's chest, I feel the tug inside our bond that Pyro is using to heal a male he doesn't even know. I aid him, filling myself with the warmth that allows me to raise back to my feet. Where Hoax makes my heart race for all the wrong reasons and Ghost provides me with the humor that allows me to see this bleak life through with a smile, Pyro is our strength. The solidity we rely on, and his kind-hearted nature gives me so much pride to be his. The generous, selfless male I rejected so many times, but wouldn't exist without. I feel so much love in this moment, only the snarl of the creature brings me back to reality.

It's close. A shudder rolls through me and Ghost yanks me back into the doorway, his eyes wide. Hovering into view, a pair of withering and broken wings flap, barely allowing the creature to rise high enough. But one glimpse of his huge orange eyes is all I need. The Blacksmith helps Ghost grab the metal door that's been cast aside, slamming it over the open archway before a flare of green gas can reach us.

"A fucking dragon, Tate?" Ghost shouts. "Are you shitting me right now?!" The female shrinks back, a flush of shame gracing her cheeks. It's not her fault, but I understand Ghost's need to blame someone since Christopher isn't here. I retreat further into the headquarters, my eyes snapping to the wall of surveillance screens.

Many Mutes have taking to hiding outside, relying on Ghost's distraction technique. Those in the basketball court are huddled together, others have ducked behind what remains of the bleachers. From the broken equipment to the fire of bodies still raging, the riot is taking place exactly how I envisioned it when cooking up a scheme with Goldie last night. So why don't I feel good about it? Where's the fun in being a rebel when the man we're trying to fight is nowhere to be seen?

I spot Granite before I notice Hare-iett huddled in his arms, crouched behind the rack of yoga mats in the largest rec room. Siren and Follicle are in there, beneath the table with a few others I can't make out through the grainy screen. The creature's wings give out and he crashes into the ground, his tail slamming against the rec room door. Granite's hand clamps over Hare-iett's mouth and luckily, the creature doesn't find them in his search. It pulls itself outside with one leg dragging behind and screams to the smoke-filled sky. Actually, not so lucky for those who have chosen to stay out there.

"Come on, while it's distracted," Tate says, ushering us further into the headquarters. The Blacksmith and Ghost drop the door, giving each other evils as they follow. The bear on the ground groans, being pulled up by Pyro and Goldie to stand. Claire keeps Serpentina, those yellow slitted eyes spearing me when she braves a look up. I close the gap to run my hand over her hair and smile as best I can.

Winding through the lounge area, Tate storms ahead as if the furniture isn't thrown aside and broken all over the floor. I tiptoe around the limbs lying amongst the mess, only stopping when Ghost makes an 'ooh' from behind. He's spied the vending machine that's been knocked over, quickly emptying out a sofa cushion of wadding to fill it with cans of soda and snacks. The Blacksmith uses the chain on Ghost's ankle to tug him along, leading to a full on man-fight.

"We don't know how long we're going to be in the bunker!" Ghost shouts, throwing a punch in the Blacksmith's face. "You'll thank me when I have a can to piss in and you're not starving!" The Blacksmith doesn't hold back his own fists and a part of me thinks he's just enjoying the physicality. It mustn't have been easy sitting around a little girl's bedroom for who knows how long. Whistling for Ghost to heel, he instantly obeys with a smile, tossing the makeshift bag over his shoulder.

Beyond the lounge area and away from the kitchen I spot, Tate leads us to a few steps just around a sharp corner. Out of sight from the main headquarters, a large metal door conceals what's below. No handle, no peephole. Just a chrome slate with a keypad on the side wall. Blood is smeared across the buttons. Pyro eases the bear against the wall and moves to stand beside Tate when she punches in the key code. We don't know if anyone has decided to hide out here, so I aid Pyro's fires as he raises his fists and coats them in flame.

The door releases and Pyro punches out, sending a flash out light through the darkened room beyond. A figure is sitting hunched at the far end of a bench, unreactive to Pyro's invasion. Matted dreadlocks fall over his face, his body barely able to move as he forces a pair of dazzling hazel eyes to peer up.

"Oh my god," Claire gasps, handing Serpentina to the Blacksmith and rushing through Goldie and her bear. Tate joins in her surprise and the pair tackle Enzo on the bench, causing him to groan loudly. They don't seem to care. I almost turn away, not wanting to invade their reunion, but the roar rocking the asylum on its very foundation doesn't give me much choice.

Ghost starts to shove from the back, pushing everyone inside and twists to close the door when another sound pierces the air. One that both excites and terrifies me. The shrill ring of a landline telephone. Turning his white eyes on me, Ghost winces and I shoot a burst of fire into his chest as a warning.

"Ghost…" I say, feeling Pyro's firm chest come up behind me with the same threat radiating through our bond. "Don't you dare." Ghost bites down on his lip, the ringing beginning to echo through my mind as the moment stretches on. Crowding the doorway with his frame, Ghost's head tilts slightly before his foot raises.

"Sorry babe." He kicks my stomach with such a force, I fly into Pyro, losing track of all the air that's supposed to be in my lungs. The blast of Ghost's healing flame doesn't help soften the blow that this fucker just booted me backwards without a shred of remorse. In fact, I see his faint smirk amongst the shadows. "Snooze you lose," he shrugs and makes a run for it.

GHOST

"Hello?"

"Who am I speaking with?" a female asks and I watch her step into view on the surveillance screen. Only a handful of feeds are left and all are on the exterior of the asylum, but luckily so is she. Confident in her stance, an upturn in her straight nose. A pinstripe skirt, pressed white blouse. Her light-colored hair is flawlessly swept into a high ponytail, blowing slightly in the breeze as she stands tall in a pair of flats. Ooh, she means business.

"This is your friendly mutant resident, Ghost. Called Ghost, not an actual ghost. That's my brother, or it was, until he had a make-over. But you can just call me Ghost, or your highness. I'll respond to both." Mania walks up to slap my arm and I cover the receiver to bat her away. "Babe, I'm on the phone," I tsk, turning my back on her.

"Ghost, this is the president, Octavia Horton."

"Yeah, I know. I'm looking at you." Her head turns this way and that, before glancing up to the camera I'm watching through. I wave, even though she can't see me.

"Excellent. Then you can see I'm unarmed and ready to listen. I've currently got the MRA standing down, but if you don't show some form of compromise, I can't argue with their riot protocols."

"Threatening already? At least take me to dinner first," I smirk. Pyro tries to wrangle the phone from me this time so I stick my ass out to hold him back. He scoffs and backs off, as I knew he would. Dude is so scared of coming off as gay, he'll avoid my ass at all costs. Even when the cost is me being lead negotiator in a hostage situation.

"No, no. Not threatening. I'm purely explaining the procedure to you. Now why don't you come down. I'm told there is a holding room off the central lobby that we can speak in privately."

"Sure, sounds swell. If you can just shoot down the wild monstrous experiment that's eating the inmates, I'll be with you in a jiffy." There's a pause on the other end of the phone. On the screen, Octavia presses the cell into her chest and shouts at someone out of view, pointing her index finger and everything. Muffled shouting reverberates through the receiver, demanding to know who and what is going on inside the asylum.

Agents raise their guns and stalk around the building, showing up around the back fence. They open fire on the poor bastard and within seconds, it stumbles and collapses, right on the fiery heap of disintegrated bodies. I kinda feel bad. If I'd been deemed expendable by Christopher for such a fate, I'd have been pretty bloodthirsty too. Its name, Experiment 23, makes me shudder. What happened to the other twenty-two?

Returning her attention to the phone in her hand, Octavia rights her skirt and lifts it back to her ear.

"You have my attention for thirty minutes. Send whoever is leading this rebellion to meet me in the holding room. After that, I'll be forced to make decisions based on my gut instinct." The call ends, but not before I hear her loaded sigh.

"So, what did she say?"

"I'm sorry babe," I sigh, "she wants my cock so I'm going to need a hall pass." Mania rolls her eyes and this time, it's Tate that walks up to give me a healthy dose of attitude.

"What. Did. She. Say?!"

"Okay, okay," I lift my hands. I don't know how these females can get the Afterlife standard issue granny-panties in such a twist, but they've managed it. "The President wants to talk negotiations with one of us, and clearly that Mute will be me."

"Have you lost your damn mind?!" Enzo croaks from the bunker. His silhouette peeks through the shadows, lying on his back across the bench. Claire is tending to him, and not in the good way.

"I should go," Pyro states, trying to pat my shoulder. I shrug him off with a frown.

"Why? I'm just as capable as the next handsome devil." Stepping forward, Mania's hand gently rests on my chest and my eyes fall to hers.

"I think what we're concerned about," Mania pitches in and I don't like this general use of 'we', "is that you won't have everyone's best interest at heart. This fight was about *all* of the prisoners here, not just those you deem worthy." Mmmhmm, I think, still watching the rise and fall of her tits. I can't see them through the sweatshirt, but I know they're there. Round and perky in all their tattooed glory. Wait…

All the prisoners? Mania's hand travels to stroke my stubbled cheek. I do not reciprocate the intended comforting gesture. I'm pretty sure she just called me selfish, but whatever. I won't apologize for only caring about the two and a half fuckers that ever gave a fucking fuck about me. Hoax is the half measure, just to clarify.

When my posture doesn't shift, Mania dives into our connection. Pushing her love into me, filling my head with silly notions like doing as she says. Luckily, I'm too pig-headed to listen to that little voice.

Taking her hand in mine, I pull Mania across the headquarters to talk in private and end up at the wall opposite the bunker. It's not as private as I would have liked but it'll do to convey the message I need Mania to hear. After all, she's the one who started this fight – so I suppose she has the final say.

"Can you just trust me this once? Please? I've got this. I want to be the one that comes through for a change." Searching my eyes, her red ones soften and she nods.

"Okay, Ghost. I trust you."

"You'll all lost your damn minds." Enzo grumbles from inside the bunker. Tate returns to him, pulling the door mostly closed to block out the light spilling in. Kinky.

"It's fine. I have a plan." The grumble doubles as if that somehow made Enzo feel worse but I'm already leaving too fast to give a shit. Mania keeps pace, rubbing my back the entire way and slamming into me when I abruptly stop.

"Sheriff, there's a snake in my route," I frown at the creature slithering into my path and hissing at me. Lowering slowly, I tilt my head. Green scales with a yellow twinge coat its lengthy body, all the way down to the rattle shaking at the end of its tail.

Hissing again, a spray of venom lands on the floor beside my feet. As quickly as it appeared, the snake returns to the small, yellow-haired girl who is standing not too far away, her eyes closed and brows pinched in concentration. Slinking up her leg and body, it coils around her shoulder and seemingly sinks into her skin, vanishing from existence. The Blacksmith lingers nearby, watching her with curiosity. Her slitted eyes snap open, staring at me with an open stance but clear hatred in her gaze. Whether she doesn't like me or the idea of our futures being in my hands, I'm not sure. Nor do I give a shit.

Mania ducks past, with Claire right behind. They soothe the girl and I stand, taking my exit before Pyro can stop me. He's too interested in helping the other of Goldie's bears anyway, checking over his wounds as he hobbles across the main room and drops down on some sofa cushions.

I didn't see the point in healing the first shifter Mute or whatever they are, but Pyro can make his own mistakes. Heal the rest of them for all I care. The bears have no *bear*ing on my plans. I laugh inside my own head, drowning out the memory of Mania saying something about including everyone. I don't really remember; my eyes were too focused on her tits at the time.

Descending the stairs, the smoke has dwindled to a thin pipeline of wisps. With nothing left to burn on the base level, all that's left is the gulpy mess and putrid smell. Not a castle fit for my Queen in the slightest. Dropping down from the third step, the platform wobbles. Oopsie daisy. I tiptoe from then on, using the railing that's bent beneath the hole missing in the metal to the fireman's pole down to the bottom level.

Ash coats the floor, dirtying my canvas shoes. A puddle of blood creates the silhouette of where my two halves lay because Hoax did a fixer-upper on me. I shudder, rubbing my abdomen where there should be a vicious scar. Shards of wood and cracked plastic are still shoved up against the basement door, barricading the guards I hear shuffling around inside.

Eyes peers around the door of the rec room and I give Follicle a solid thumbs up. It's all going to be okay. Approaching the entrance gate, the shutter lifts and reveals the entire MRA army standing behind it. Octavia barks at them to stand down, considering all of their guns are pointed at my face. On the outside, I grin and wave, although on the inside – there's a hint of poop poking out of my butt. I'll never get used to the threat of gunfire riddling my body, immortal or not. I need to protect my beauty.

Forcing the men to step back, even though their guns remain in place, Octavia calls for the dividing gate to be opened and leads me to a closed door left of the lobby. I look around as much as the mass of bodies allow, spotting a receptionist's desk and waiting area. I didn't realize we attracted many visitors. Opening the door, Octavia turns to make sure I'm following whilst dragging her eyes over my uncuffed wrists without subtlety.

"Ghost, I presume?"

"The one and only," I nod, gesturing for her to enter the room first. Swiftly shutting the door behind us, the MRA agents are forced to wait outside. A red light flashes in the corner, letting me know I have an audience from the headquarters. I hope Mania figures out how to switch the audio on. I want her to hear what a negotiation boss her boo is.

Pulling out a chair for Octavia like the gentleman I am, I walk to the other side of the large table dividing us. Taking the chair waiting there, I drag it across the floor with an ear-piercing screech and swivel it to sit backwards. Leaning over the backrest, I raise a brow and wait for her to begin.

"So I understand-"

"Here's my demands," I cut her off. "I want every Mute that's still alive escorted into the sister facility next door before we leave this room. As a safety measure." Aka, proof that those I care about and those I don't give a shit about are tucked away in case these discussions go south.

Octavia nods, pulling out her phone. A reasonable demand, if I do say so myself. They were never going to let us walk out of here, but a more luxurious facility with a pool? Count me in. Finishing the tippity tapping of her manicured nails on the screen, Octavia lifts her head to face me expectantly. Shit...erm, I hadn't thought that far beyond this. "And snacks. So many snacks. Only decent ones though. And real clothes, like jeans. I look good in a fitted pair a jeans."

Octavia raises one eyebrow so I lean across to tap her screen, encouraging her to write it down.

"Anything else?" she asks, starting to look pissed off. Anyone would think I was wasting her time or something. Sitting back in her seat, my eyes catch the hem of her skirt riding up and the frill of a garter concealed underneath. Aha! I snap my fingers in her face.

"We get to choose our own jobs. I'm all for rehabilitation, but only in industries that are badass. Like rock and roll bands, or modeling," I flex my biceps, practically auditioning for either role. Hell, I'd do both and be hailed as the first Mute billionaire. On that note – "I suppose there isn't any point in asking to be paid and recognized as regular citizens for when I'm ready to buy a mansion?" I get a 'dick please' look through her lashes and Octavia places her phone on the table.

"The remaining Mutes are being transferred as we speak. I've given orders to the public relations director to investigate the food and clothing companies that provide your necessities. As for the employment," Octavia leans forward to link her fingers on the desk. "I understand there was a disagreement with your partner and Camo." I growl, low in my chest and her back straightens further.

"Certain industries are lacking and if we appease the humans, more money will be put into the economy. Hence, more opportunities for your kind. I know you're frustrated, but this is how we get the ball rolling."

"All I'm hearing is you tried to hand my girlfriend over to a gold-digging backstabber with the intent of stripping for rich humans and she was nearly raped instead. We might not be upstanding citizens, but we're not slaves." Octavia bristles, leading me to think she didn't know that tidbit just as there's a knock at the door. I scowl at the MRA agent who nudges it open.

"These two refused to be escorted out," he grits through a clenched jaw and I already know who'll they'll be before the agent steps aside. Mania and Pyro. Arms folding, faces set in hard lines that dare me to tell them to fuck off. Pushing up from my seat, I walk around the room and tug the pair of them inside.

"I told you, I've got this," I hiss low. Pyro surprises me by being the one who answers.

"We know, but we wouldn't let us be separated. We're a team, remember?" I roll my eyes, hating his logic and the fact something in my gut flutters around like a little boy on a sherbet high. Or maybe I just really need to pee...

"Fine, sit in the corner and stay shtum," I use my fingers to squish Pyro's lips together. A glare from both sets of red eyes says I'll pay for that later, but for now, they do as they're told. The door is closed and I pass around the back of Octavia's chair, shifting it at an angle so she'll have to focus on me. Retaking my seat, I realize too late the agent that brought Mania and Pyro here has stayed, his hands on the gun strapped to his front. Eavesdropping fucker.

"As I was just saying," Octavia tries to turn to talk to Mania but I grip her chin and twist her back to me. The agent's gun is in the air, the safety knocked off as my final warning. But I don't let go. Octavia raises a hand and the gun is slightly lowered, but not enough.

"My turn to talk," I tell her, at the same time I send Pyro a mental instruction to cover me. He frowns in my peripheral but sidesteps towards the guard anyway. "Octavia. You seem super lovely and all, but you're too late. This country is too broken to heed your carefully written speeches. A quiet cover-up would only serve to damage our message. To prove we're easily ignored and bought with simple amenities humans take for granted. Pretty words don't change worlds; rebellions do."

"Ghost, no!" Mania screams but it's too late. Twisting with the speed of a whippet and force of a...gorilla? I whip Octavia's head aside. The crack of her neck is masked by Pyro diving on the agent, the ring of gunfire zipping around the room. Wrapping an arm around the agent's neck, Pyro squeezes so hard, the veins in his forearm pop out and soon, the agent has joined Octavia in a heap on the floor. Messy business.

Mania's has her arms spread and mouth hanging open. This really isn't the time for a blowjob, but I'm nothing if not an opportunist. Standing, I reach for my waistband and her eyes widen. Okay I'm getting really mixed messages here.

"What the fuck, Ghost?!" she whisper shouts. I shrug at her. I was merely keeping the president in here as a stalling tactic whilst the rest were ushered to safety, but my mates sure are stubborn asses. If anything, it's their fault for accelerating my timeline. Not to mention – it was Mania's idea in the first place. *No one is going to give us a future. We need to take it.* That's what she said. I know, because I was actually listening that time.

"Well I hope you're proud of yourself," Pyro grunts, stepping over the guard and folding his arms. I don't know what he looks so pissed about, half of the casualties in this room were caused by him. As for pride, yes indeed I am. "You've just killed our only real defense against Christopher." Oh yeah, right… I forgot about that asshole. Oh well, no going back now.

"Not to mention, what could have been the best shot at a semi-normal life for the entire Mute species," Mania says, dropping her hip against the table. I narrow my eyes. I thought she wanted to stir shit up. I make a point to remind her not to issue me a challenge in future.

"Oh yeah? If Madame President was so goody goody," I pause to search Octavia's pantsuit and find concealed pockets in her tight skirt. How suspicious. I drag out the first item my hand wraps around. "Then why did she have this in her pocket?!"

"That's a lipstick," Pyro points out.

"Or this?!"

"A tampon…" Mania rolls her eyes. Dammit. Third time lucky, I rummage into Octavia's cleavage.

"Or how about this!!" I hold up the small, black cylinder. Ugh, how many tampons does one woman need?

"Wait, what is that?" Mania pushes off the table. I hold it out of her reach as she approaches but in the end, hand it over. Pyro is over her shoulder in a millisecond like the protective prick he is. Rolling the object in her hand, Mania spots two tiny buttons on the end and presses one.

"**A**nd *where is the girl now?*" Octavia's voice rings out of the tiny device. My eyes flick up to Ghost. There's a pause on the recording and for a moment, I didn't think there'd be an answer.

"She's secure," the grunted reply comes. I know that voice. Christopher shuffles, clearing his throat. *"Forgive me, Ms. Horton, but I'm a busy man. The object you'd requested is not for sale."*

"I wouldn't refer to a young child as an object, and I wasn't offering to buy her. I have a court order for Serpentina to be released to me. I will be relieving her of you. Today."

A bitter, manly laugh sounds.

"How about this? If you can find her, she's yours. But as it stands, that mutant is the key to unlocking a huge advancement in my research."

"Because she can Astro-project, or because her body is equally merged with reptilian DNA as it is human?"

"You have a lot of information I'd only trusted to my closest employees. Seems like a purge may be in order." Amongst the soft crackle of fire, a cupboard is closed and a cork squeezed free of a bottle. I close my eyes, envisioning Christopher's office. The glug of liquid being poured

is followed by a long sigh and squeak as I imagine him dropping back into his desk chair.

"Serpentina's blood work is the most intricate I've come across. She could provide the answer to armies the world has never seen. Soldiers mixed with animals that can project across the battlefield. We could win wars without ever leaving the training camp."

"My concern, Dr. Gordon, is with the wars you're planning to produce. A power-hungry man is never satisfied. What lengths will you go to in order to prove your elite soldiers were worth the billions of dollars this country has invested in you?"

"Previous presidents have always understood what I'm trying to create here."

"As do I. It doesn't mean I condone it. You're to hand over the child or I will seize every asset you deem of value." Octavia's voice is drowned out by a throaty chuckle.

"We're not so different, you and I. You interrupted a critical surgery to request one Mute child, and have yet to mention obtaining any of the others. You'd sooner see them rot then I would."

"I've read the case files and you've been humored for long enough. You wanted to create a mutagen, then you sought to control it. Then came the shifters and again, you wanted more. We're not going to discuss your fruitless attempts at immortality," Octavia scoffs. Christopher growls and the squeak sounds.

"We're done here. I have a surgery of my own to prepare for. You want the girl, you'll have to find her yourself." Shuffles leading to the hard slam of a door closing and I exhale.

"Holy shit Ghost, you were right," I breathe.

"Holy shit Spitfire, I was right," he agrees. Pyro is tense behind me, our jumbled thoughts battering around the bond. I lower my hand, my thumb hovering over the button when another voice sounds from the device. One that spills dread into my system and makes my stomach flip.

"Her location hasn't been shared, nor recorded. Trust me, I've searched." My eyes fly back to Ghost's white, widened ones. The air around us goes cold, a tremor rolling through the room. Hoax.

"One of us needs to find her before it's too late," Octavia sighs. *"If*

Christopher gets what he wants from her blood work, the world as we know it will be over."

"I will find her, but I might need leniency for some...creative license." Hoax's voice is stoic, devoid of all emotion.

"What do you have in mind?"

"I can coax my mates into being reckless. They get under Christopher's skin, make him act on impulse. He'll lash out and reveal the girl's location without realizing."

"I'm trusting you, Hoax. Leaking those files to me was a smart move, but I need you to be even more cunning. Once Serpentina has been revealed, you know what must be done."

"I'll ensure she has a swift and painless death, and that she's taken care of after the fact. You have my word."

My heart squeezes. My limbs go numb and the recorder smashes to the floor. It was all a lie. A trick. Hoax pushed me into rebelling, playing my heartstrings like an instrument for his enjoyment. Snapping at me to lay low, he knew I'd do the opposite. He orchestrated this whole thing and we've played straight into his hand.

"Where is Serpentina?" I spin on Pyro, unable to remember where I last saw her.

"She should have been transferred into the facility next door with the others," Pyro replies, his eyes moving back and forth in thought. "But I didn't see her or the Blacksmith when the agents came for us. I can't...I don't," he stammers and twists, slamming his fist into the table. Frustration ripples beneath his skin in lines of flame just beneath the surface. I soothe him while Ghost takes the other side, stroking the veins popping out of Pyro's arm.

"It's going to be okay buddy," Ghost says just as a knock sounds at the door. We all freeze.

"Madame President? The thirty minutes is up. Is everything okay in there?"

"Yes!" Ghost fakes a high-pitched voice and I pinch the bridge of my nose. Pyro's arm twists beneath my hold, gripping me as he slams Ghost's wrist into the table. The jolt causes Ghost's ability to wash over all three of us and Pyro storms through the table and wall behind it with us in tow, just as the door to the holding room opens.

"Secure the facility! President down!" the agent shouts, kicking his colleague aside. The wall solidifies behind us. An alarm breaches the air but Pyro doesn't slow. His grip is punishing and I hold back my whimper, understanding his anger. The main facility comes into view, flashing red while the alarm is pitched high enough to render us into submission. With the broken staircase mocking us, Pyro twists and shoves our joint hands against the elevator button. Orders are barked over the noise to get the entrance gate open, but we have our own problem. Entering the elevator, all three of us stare at the empty key card slot.

"Well, it's up or down," Ghost announces. The doors begin to slide closed, giving us a moment's reprieve to consider the repercussions of both scenarios. Climb the chords supporting the chamber we're standing in, or drop through the floor and pray there's more to this elevator shaft then an abrupt end.

The door nears the jam as a bloodied hand cuts into the small margin of space remaining. I jump back, while Pyro and Ghost prepare themselves for a fight when the door slides back and the Blacksmith topples inside. He crashes to our feet, his eyes too swollen to open and a key card in his hand.

"Eight-four-two..." he croaks out, coughing up blood in between. "S...s."

"Ahh fuck it," Ghost snatches the card, pushing it in the slot and punches in the code with a six at the end. The doors slide closed fully this time, punctuated by gun fire as the agents manage to breach the lobby.

I force my fingers free of Pyro's grip, bending down to look for any wounds on the Blacksmith that may prove fatal. His skin shimmers with the metal flowing just beneath, his narrowed molten eyes dimmed. Checking behind his t-shirt, a rounded bruise that's already blue sits central on his sternum. Much like the one Hoax's staff would cause.

Sharing a look with Pyro, I hold my hands out over the Blacksmith's broken and bruised body. Heat answers my call instantly, brightening my palms with a golden glow. Until Ghost snatches my hands and tosses me aside.

"Don't you dare. This is the least he deserves," Ghost grunts, and kicks the Blacksmith in the ribs for good measure. Glaring at him from the floor, I generate a shard of my eternal flame into a sharp knife point and deliver it into Ghost's gut. He pitches forward on a strangled shout, eyeing me with shock. I merely shrug, allowing Pyro to help me up for the elevator door opening again.

Yes, the Blacksmith may have appeared to be picking sides with Christopher, but we've proven time and again nothing is as it seems. We don't know what lengths Christopher went to in blackmailing or torturing the Blacksmith.

A darkened room is revealed and I find us right back in the guard's headquarters. Gunfire can still be heard on the lower floor, the agents emptying their magazines into the closed elevator door. The lights are off, only the glow of the surveillance screens reflecting across the space. I thought it looked like a wreckage before, but Hoax has taken it upon himself to redecorate. What isn't burnt is torn to pieces, the furniture unrecognizable amongst the shadows. The vending machine is a heap of shredded metal amongst the ruined packets splayed around it.

"No! Not the snacks!" Ghost tries to run forward but Pyro stops him. A fire whip extends from his hand, snapping across Ghost's front. When he turns his steady gaze on me, all I find are flames in his eyes. Movement shifts from the kitchen area, beyond the wall that no longer exists. I make out Enzo's outline, his dreads hanging over the other two bodies he's protecting. Deciding if they're moving, they're alive and that has to be enough for now, I turn my attention to the bunker.

With Pyro in tow, we creep around the tiny wall that hides the silver door from view. It's ajar. A soft cry leaks out from inside. I storm ahead, not needing any more evidence to know Serpentina is in there. Whipping the door open, I gasp to not only see Hoax, but Azella holding the little girl's arm. Her eyes widen, but Hoax doesn't react. No doubt he could sense me coming.

"Let her go," I demand of both of them. Serpentina's head whips around, her yellow-slitted eyes begging me for help.

"I'm needed elsewhere. Clean up your mess," Azella barks, not bothering to acknowledge me. For now, I push the hurt of that aside, but it'll resurface later. The woman I considered a mother, the one I relied on to always be there for me…taps her staff and disappears. A fresh crack splits down the center of my heart.

"Just leave Mania," Hoax sighs as if I'm the problem, one hand rubbing his chest and the other wrapped around Serpentina's tiny wrist. My jaw clenches and nostrils flare.

Shifting to grab his own staff, which is propped against the bench, I rush forward. Kicking it out of his reach, I skid out, grabbing the wooden stick and toss it to Pyro in the doorway. Metal clinks as a pair of chains race passed, circling Serpentina's body and ripping her from the bunker on a tiny scream. I catch Pyro's blazing eyes, sending him a mental instruction and he immediately obeys. Pyro slams the bunker door closed, with myself and Hoax locked inside.

"There's no time for this," Hoax groans, his body shuffling to find the light. Long fluorescent tubes blink to life on the ceiling, temporarily blinding me. Pushing to my feet, I dust myself off and fold my arms.

"Make time. You have so much to explain to me." Ignoring me, Hoax's appearance shifts back to normal. The horns retract, his skeletal tattoos bleed back into the wires and circuits I used to dream about tracing with my fingers. In the days when he was always available to me, yet untouchable. Now he's the exact opposite. Too focused on the internal keypad, Hoax searches for the correct combination to let himself out. Seems like without his staff, he's just the same as the rest of us.

"It's best you don't know," Hoax finally replies. I storm across the bunker, yanking his shoulder back so he's forced to look at me. Look at the one he claims to love, yet is hell-bent on excluding, deceiving and betraying. Hoax must feel me through our bond because in the next second, he's growling and tossing me against the door by my throat.

"Everything I've done and sacrificed has been for you."

"How can you say that?" I spit back, not phased by his close proximity. "I'm done being your scape-goat." His lips inches from mine, his eyes dropping to where he holds me in place. Shoving himself away, Hoax runs a hand through his purple hair.

"You'll realize one day all of this has been about ensuring there's a world for you to live out your eternity in. Securing your safety after I'm gone is paramount. Don't test me when I say, I will do whatever it takes to make that happen."

"Like killing a child, Hoax? Is my life really worth more than hers?" A tense silence follows. His jaw ticks. His breathing is hindered. He doesn't have an answer. Fisting his hands, I stand tall, fully prepared for him to hit me. I don't know the Mute before me and I can't foresee his actions.

"You have no idea how selfish you're being right now," Hoax huffs, flexing out his fingers. Me, however, I see fucking red.

"How dare you call *me* selfish?!" I stride forward and slam my hands into his chest. He doesn't budge. "How can I be selfish when you've been making all the decisions for me? I never stood a chance to be anything else. Had you simply asked me, or involved me in the slightest, I'd have told you we'll find another way. We always do." My hands slam again and curl into his t-shirt, desperately trying to find the Mute I knew. Amongst the blank expression staring down at me, it cuts deep to realize he isn't here. Not really.

"You decided to be the hero," I accuse. "You decided we were no longer a team. We never stood a chance." I shove at him and stride away.

"I have one single purpose," Hoax reiterates from behind me. So deluded by his so-called mission, he's blind to what really counts. "Nothing else matters," he growls, reading my mind through our connection again.

But when I turn on a bitter laugh, I can see in his eyes that even he is doubting his words. He's lost sight of what he's doing, yet I don't try to reach him. If this is love, sacrificing others, lying to those closest to you, sneaking around and backstabbing…well then I don't want it. Pushing away from the door, I raise my chin.

"You're relieved of your duty," I state, devoid of all emotion. Before anything can slip through, I slam down the barrier between mine and

Hoax's bond. His eyes travel up my body, landing on mine with a spark of purple in his irises.

"Think about what you're saying," he warns and I continue.

"I'm safe in Pyro and Ghost's arms. Your deal has been fulfilled." My eyes prick but I refuse to let him waiver. Inhale, exhale, don't think about the way my heart's breaking. Just see it through. "You're the only one causing me harm, Hoax."

"Mania," he steps forward and I move back. "You...you won't be able to take this back." I see it then. The fleeting worry cross his face. For me? Or for the mission he's set himself on? I vowed to love this Mute, to be everything he needs. But he's lost his way. He's hurting, even killing people, in my name and that's something I can't allow. What Hoax needs is to be removed from the destructive path he's following.

Ironically, I'm pushing away the one I wanted so bad, the one who was always just out of reach. I've loved this Mute since the instant he appeared in my hospital room. And now, for the good of everyone, I have to let him go.

"Then so be it," I declare, somehow devoid of all emotion. Azella reappears in an instant, her grave expression angled at me. Like the day she also found me, scared and alone, she's been my rock. My constant who guided me from afar. Yet the demon staring at me now is a stranger.

Her fangs hang over her bottom lip, a taloned hand curling around Hoax's bicep. I can't make out her expression amongst the shadows and the tribal tattoos on her face. Her chocolate brown hair spills over her shoulders, blending into her leather jumpsuit and boots.

"You heard her," Azella mutters to Hoax, not taking her eyes off me. "We're done here." There's a sigh of disappointment huffed from her pierced nose. For me? At me? I can't tell, but her hand wraps around Hoax's wrist slowly, as if waiting for me to take back my words. If this was a normal break-up, I'd say my adoptive mother has taken Hoax's side – but it's so much more than that. This is a goodbye to them both, to that part of my life, for good.

In two steps, Hoax has closed the distance between us, Azella walking along beside him. His free hand reaches up the cup my jaw and my lip threatens to wobble.

"It was all for you," he breathes, placing the tenderest of kisses on my cheek. His purple eyes drink me in one last time.

"I know," I nod slightly. "But you chose the wrong soul to sacrifice." The faint click of wood on the concrete floor sounds like the slice of a guillotine to my ears, and right before my eyes, he vanishes. They both do. I stumble forward, the warmth at my cheek the only lingering evidence Hoax was even here. My eyes close. Internally, the purple strand of our bond fizzles out, taking a portion of our heat with it.

I crash to my knees. The walls I'd built around my heart crumble. I vaguely realize arms are closing around me as I scream to the sky. A roaring, uncontrollable sound filled with the extent of my anguish. With the tragic despair I'm drowning in for a Mute I could never truly have. My cries are echoed by the two huddled on the floor either side of me, feeling the cut of loss just as deeply.

This was my choice. A conscious decision I made on all of our behalf. Maybe Hoax was right – maybe I am selfish. But I couldn't watch him destroy his morals and obliterate what was left of his soul in the name of saving me. I couldn't let him kill a child who hasn't had the chance to live. I've made plenty of mistakes, ones I'll pay for as long as I'll live. But at least I've been able to make them. Serpentina deserves the same fortune.

I hold Mania until she doesn't have any more tears left to cry. At some point, Ghost weaseled himself into her lap, curled up like a Great Dane trying to be a lapdog while Mania absentmindedly strokes her fingers through his hair.

"We have to move," I say when we've been here too long. Last I saw, the Blacksmith had created a metal barricade to block the elevator doors from closing and hence, prevent the guards from arriving. But it won't be long until they find another way.

I repeat myself, not sure if either of them heard. Mania's head slowly turns and for the first time since meeting her, I see a truly broken woman. The fire in her has dimmed, her eyes barely crimson as they stare through me.

"After all this time," she mutters and Ghost sits upright. "We fought to bring back Hoax, yet when I truly had him, I let him go."

"The decision you made was a selfless one," I tell her, cupping her face. It took Ghost a whole five seconds to locate the speaker button on the outer keypad so we could listen in to Hoax and Mania's conversation. I could feel her emotions at war with her words, battling her conscience to do what was needed. The truth Hoax is gone hasn't hit me yet like it has the others, but I won't blame Mania when it does.

She made the choice I wouldn't have been man enough to. I'd have kept fighting, kept struggling against the secrets Hoax kept. All in my selfishness to have him nearby, but it wasn't right. Not when so many others would have suffered at his hands.

Pressing a kiss to the crack in Mania's forehead, I ease my hands onto her ribs. Ghost winds an arm around her waist, aiding me to lift her with the delicateness of a China teapot. Drawing Mania from the bunker on numb feet, I hear the muttering of those crowded in the elevator before I see them.

Enzo slumped on the floor, cradling Tate and Claire. Goldie surrounded by all three of her three bears, looking much more alive than I last saw them. Blood covers their t-shirts and matts their hair, but none of that stops them from fawning over Goldie more like primates as she bats them away. The Blacksmith stands in the threshold, his chains preventing the doors from meeting in the middle. Serpentina clings to his back, her sharp, slitted eyes watching us approach.

"Get us out of here," I grumble, sliding past. Obeying, the Blacksmith retracts his chains, allowing the doors to shut and punches a code into the keypad. There's a limp in his step and his hand carefully holds his side, but he's upright and breathing. That's more than Hoax intended when beating the shit out of him.

I don't bother asking where we're going. Just like everyone in this elevator, I have someone to take care of. Mania shivers in my hold, a strand of our bond now missing. Ghost strokes her hair and I nuzzle her, but there's no response. No solace within the icy crack I can sense in Mania's heart. The elevator jolts to a stop and I sigh, standing tall to push Mania behind me. As exhausted and disheartened as we all are, the fight isn't over just yet.

The doors slide open and my stance widens, braced for an attack that never comes. Frowning, I hold up a hand to keep everyone back and peer out at our surroundings. A path of bark crunches beneath my shoes, a soft breeze of fresh air prickling at my skin. Jasmine and lavender surrounds me, as do trees that touch the sky. Spears of sunlight penetrate the canopy, creating a lazer field of light. A rogue butterfly flutters past and a small hand slips into my slackened one.

"Where are we?" Mania breathes, her eyes re-focused on the world around us. I break my trance on the forest to briefly glance at her.

"I'm not sure, but don't let go of my hand."

"Okay," Ghost says, interlinking our fingers on the other side. I roll my eyes but don't let go. Let's face it, he's probably safest holding onto me. Twice my size in muscle, yet always that young boy looking for his next compliment. The fact I don't shrug him off should be telling enough. I've always got his back.

Gingerly creeping forward as a trio, movement crunches behind us. We whip around in time to see the trees themselves moving, cutting us off from the elevator and those still sitting within. Roots slither into place, linking the trunks together in an impenetrable wall. Both sets of hands in mine tighten and I exhale deeply, soothing their erratic flames.

Setting my jaw, I draw us further into the woodland. Anxiety batters around at the corners of my mind but I push it away for now. I can't let my emotions overrule basic instinct. A squirrel runs the length of a branch overhead, birds tweet from the glimpse of a blue sky. I inhale the fresh smells, catch off guard by the serenity seeping through me. Everything around us is green, full of life and perfect. Too perfect.

Breaching the treeline, I stop first and yank the others back. Sand spans a private beach, framing the gentle lap of water beckoning us closer. The lake shimmers crystal blue and reflects the mountain range beyond. And the sun. The sun bathes our skin with a stroke of warmth and I can't fight the close of my eyelids to drink it in for one, single moment. My biggest mistake.

Ghost's hand is whipped from mine before he releases a whoop and is gone. Running. Stripping. Cheering. His clothes float onto the sand before he hears me yelling for him to come back. Struggling with his socks, Ghost leaves them in place and rips his sweatpants from his waist, diving butt naked into the water.

"Asshole," Mania and I say in unison. A thread of jealousy wriggles through me. I can only imagine how incredible the water feels, gliding over his skin. Cooling the flames we've been forced to rely on for too long. For the few minutes I'm prepared to give him, Ghost's slice of freedom is more than I'll ever feel. There won't be a time I'm not looking over my shoulder, protecting the harem my mate has created. Or I suppose, we're more of a menage now.

Mania sighs, trying to walk forward but I hold her back. I don't trust anything my eyes are showing me. As if a jigsaw piece falling into piece, I pinch the bridge of my nose and curse. That's it. The fucking Mirage Twins. It's too easy to pretend the Blacksmith knew the keypad code for a forest - and it's naive to think we've left Christopher's clutches.

"We should go get him," Mania urges me. Bubbles rise to the surface, popping and fizzling out into the gentle flow of water.

"He'll be fine," I nod, ignoring the twinge of panic at my chest. I rub it with the palm of my hand and Mania gives me an expectant look. "Ghost is the strongest of us all. Both physically and mentally. He'll be fine," I repeat.

"You really think that?" Mania asks, genuinely curious. Multiple expressions I can't read filter behind her red eyes before she ducks her gaze from me. "We can't rely on Hoax to bring him back this time." A pinch of guilt mars her beautiful face and I tug her into my hold.

"Ghost hides behind acting childish, but yeah. I truly believe there's nothing that Mute can't handle. His coping mechanism protects his heart, and let's face it. There's been times the rest of us have faltered in our bond, but from the instant he allowed himself to love you, he hasn't. Let me say what Ghost probably can't understand enough to vocalize - you're everything to him, Mania. The mother he never had, the love he's been yearning for. You've given him back the life he lost. I don't know how you managed to crack him, but I'm so glad you did."

"Pyro," Mania mutters into chest. A damp patch seeps through my t-shirt, her watery red eyes peering up at me. "Shouldn't we maybe go get him then?" I peer back at the water, groaning that he still hasn't resurfaced. Knowing Ghost, he'll have found a pod of dolphins and have piggy backed a ride of a sight. But I guess I'd better at least look for him if I want to stay in Mania's good books.

Repositioning her to remain by a tree, I take a step onto the sand as it shifts beneath my feet. Slipping into a spiraling valley, taking me down with it. I flail for something to grab onto, my hands sliding through the particles. Mania's scream cuts through the rushing around my ears, my limbs unable to resist the coiling cyclone. Plummeting downwards, darkness falls over me like a cape before I'm spat back down, deposited onto the forest floor.

My back protests as I roll onto my side, a groan of pain slipping from my lips. Coughing, I splutter up sand and scrape the sand from my tongue. Dragging myself up onto all fours, I shake the rest out of my hair and struggle to catch my breath. Bark cuts into my palms and through the sweatpants at my knees. This time, the spears of sunlight seem to be mocking me. Caging me in. A muffled cry sounds from above and I jerk myself up as quick as my legs will allow, hunting for Mania. But it's not her I find.

"Serpentina," I gasp. Hanging suspended amongst the branches, a spill of yellow hair hangs from an otherwise concealed, tiny body. Wrapped from toes to shoulders, the sheen of spider's silk glints in the light. Twisting her head, her yellow-slitted eyes spot me and another scream reverberates from her mouth, through the patch of webbing there too.

Pain forgotten, I scramble to the nearest trunk. My arms are slow to respond to the urgency carving through my chest. Each branch I try, cracks off in the palm of my hand. Remaining close to the trunk, I shimmy upwards, finding the one thick branch that doesn't seem to be hell-bent on killing me. Allowing my legs to dangle, I swing myself along the length, one hand in front of the other until Serpentina is within reach. Just beyond a three-foot gap I can't cross.

A tear falls from her eye and I bite down on my tongue. Staying subjective would allow me to think logically, but it's impossible not to let my emotions take control.

Stretching as far as I can, my fingertips graze the webbing around her body. She's trembling, causing the branch she's precariously attached to, to wobble. A sharp sting punctures my side where my t-shirt is riding up but I pay it no mind. I must reach her. Placing my hand back on the branch, I opt for a more dangerous strategy, but it seems like something Ghost would do. That fucker always seems to win somehow.

Swinging my legs, I opt for clamping them around Serpentina's body and ripping her free of the thread holding her, hopefully not dropping her to her death in the process. But I don't make it that far. Another sting comes, this one on my nape. Then another, and I realize the buzzing too late. The flash of black and yellow in the corner of my eye is joined by more, until I'm forced to take stock of my own predicament.

Wasps. Everywhere. Spearing any patch of skin they can find. My arms are surrounded, thousands of sharp pricks piercing me. I hold on for as long as I can, my eyes locked with the slitted ones begging me to save her. The small jabs of pain combine into one, overriding agony and before I know it, my fingers have slipped. The wasps circling my body hang back, watching me fall. I don't bother fighting this time, sending a blaze of love directly to Mania wherever she is. I came into this forest adamant she wouldn't lose another mate, and she's possibly just lost all three.

Large arms band around me, breaking my fall. I fear opening my eyes, not wanting to know who caught me as easily as a ragdoll and when I do, I wish I never did. Stone gray eyes stare down at me, a jaw cut from rock. Ugh, Granite. Shrugging out of his hold, I mutter a thanks and brush myself off. Then, my eyes snap straight back to Serpentina. I still need to get up here.

"It's hard to watch, but he won't hurt her. He needs her," the male to my right states coldly. No need to ask who 'he' is, when it's blaringly obvious. Christopher. Still, I start looking for sticks on the forest floor with some absurd plan to build a ladder. Hopefully by the time I get to that point, I'll have come up with a better idea.

"There's no use fighting it. We just have to ride out the illusion," Granite grinds out. His jaw is clamped tight, his teeth crunching like tiny bricks shifting against one another. At least he's confirmed what I suspected about the Mirage Twins being involved.

"If it's all the same, I'm not going to sit around and wait. Neither am I going to trust you," I point a stick in his direction. The very Mute who created the maze that trapped and killed so many of us. Granite holds his hands up and mutters something about looking for someone anyway. He strides into the forest, leaving me with a small pile of sticks I've collected and I sigh. Turning my hand over, I call forth a flame. Maybe if I burn the trees down and sever her connection, Serpentina will drop into arms as easily as I did in Granite's.

Huff.

Air blasts against the side of my head. A glint of metal catches my eye. I don't look, taking a moment to close my eyes and steel myself.

Huff.

Cracking one eye, I peer at the mechanical bull inches from my face. His eyes glow, his body squeaking as he takes a step back and prepares to charge. It's all an illusion, I tell myself. Standing to face him, or it, I fold my arms. I won't be intimidated by Christopher's attempts. A billow of steam leaves the bull's large nostrils, a guttural sound twinged by the crackle of a speaker splitting through the air as he rams forward.

Wielding his chrome tusks, the machine sweeps me up and tosses me over his giant body. I fly for the second time in ten minutes, no one there to soften my fall this time. Landing on my shoulder, I scream in a blinding agony. White covers my vision, which I blink clear just in time to see a pair of round, metal hooves about to trample on me. Rolling aside, the bull misses me by inches and I scramble to my feet.

Running for the nearest clearing, I don't look where I'm going. The bull takes chase, crashing through fallen logs and trampling over white and purple flowers. Holding my shoulder, I turn my head in time to see a wall of vines directly ahead without time to stop myself from skidding into it. The impact of my fall causes the vines to bounce and jerk into action. Closing around me, a cage is created before my eyes. Before I can escape. A vine bolt is slammed into place, the echo of it breaking the illusion. A lab spans around the very real and metallic cage I'm trapped in.

"Oh hey Py," Ghost calls from the cage next door. His hair is wet and there's a puddle beneath his hands hanging through the bars. "You took your time."

The rumble of the boulder hell-bent on chasing me remains just a few feet behind. No time to think, no time to judge my footing. Just as it has since I watched the sand swallow Pyro whole and fled, the gigantic rock doesn't give me a second of reprieve. It veers in whichever direction I turn, unstoppable and relentless.

Crashing through the trees, huge chunks of wood hurtle overhead. My arms cover my hair, the stitch in my side becoming increasingly crippling. Rolling my ankle on a jagged root, I whimper but keep moving. Hindered and hobbling. Cries of pain and frustration flee my open mouth. When I'm sure the boulder is about to crush me, I brave a look back. It is there, but…still around a foot behind me.

My eyebrows pinch as a crazy thought comes to mind. I slow. The boulder slows. I come to a stop, and it copies. Taking one hobbled step forward, it rolls just enough to remain close.

"You've got to be fucking kidding me," I pant, bashing the side of my fist against the stone. *Ow.* It hasn't been chasing me; it's magnetized to me. Leaning my weight on the boulder, I sigh. Removing the canvas shoe, I rub my tender ankle and wonder what I'm supposed to do now. Especially with this giant crater refusing to leave me alone. How did it all come to this?

At dawn, I was back to my old self. By morning, the entirety of the asylum was behind me in taking back control. Before lunchtime, I was in Hoax's arms with the bond to my others solid and raging. And now the afternoon rolls into evening…and I've lost it all.

Stars begin to twinkle through the blanket closing over the sky, pre-empting a blissful night. In the universe, maybe, but my world remains to be the exact opposite. The scamper of tiny feet quietens, the changeover for nocturnal life happening all around the dense woodland. Squeaks turn into hoots, the scratch of claws in soil become powerful flaps of wings. Moments fizzle by, the churning of my stomach increases. Regardless of where I've been dumped and what dangers may or may not await, I need to move.

Watching the pale blue overhead shift into navy, I thrum my fingers on the stone, waiting for the pulsating pain to ebb from my ankle. It's not going to heal fully, not when I can't pull on my connection to Pyro or Ghost. A fact I've been trying to ignore up to now. They're big boys, they can handle their shit. Me, however…

Huffing, I start limping onwards. Carving a path through the dark, keeping to the pathway and figuring it must lead somewhere. A long stick presents itself in the light of a moon I didn't see rise, beaming down like an omen. With the aid of the stick, I take the weight off my ankle and keep going. On and on for what feels like an eternity until I breach the tree line once more. A beach doesn't await this side of the forest, but a field filled with white peace lilies.

"This isn't going to be good," I sigh. No idea who I'm talking to, the boulder I suppose. Yet, faced with the options to either retrace my dragged footsteps or cross it, I know which I'd prefer. I've never been one for backtracking. I already know what's behind me.

Braving the first step onto the field, the yellow stems within the nearest lilies brighten and begin to glow. Puffs of golden dust burst from each flower, wafting into the air around me. *Oh here we go.* There's no point trying to fight a death trap that's clearly designed for me, so I continue onwards. Fireflies drift in on a breeze, dancing through the flowers like teeny, tiny wings beating against my coffin. Luminescent dust glows against the night, sparkling like diamonds.

Razor-sharp diamonds that seep into my nose and slice the inside of my throat and fill my lungs.

I splutter, jerking forward and the boulder nudges my back. I topple, landing hard amongst the flowers. My organs seize, cramping in my torso. I grip my sides, wishing the pain away or for my lungs to burst and get it over with. Yet I know in the back of my mind, Christopher isn't done with me yet.

The lights around me brighten, blinding me with a flash of white light that disappears on my next blink. That's when the darkness seeps in. Muffled cries ring through my ears, the smell of chemicals drawing me back to life. The pain within has gone, despite the lasting glitter of golden dust on my arms as I drag myself up and brush myself off. Thick, damp bars close me in, beside the Mutes I'd been searching for.

"Mania," Pyro breathes in a 'thank fuck' kind of way, but our predicament is anything but a reason to rejoice. The whole gang is here, from Follicle, Siren and Hare-iett also trapped in upright, cylinder cages. Goldie and her bears have been granted the luxury of a seemingly glass cube. Slumped together in a huddle of comfort, but confined nonetheless.

Tate, Enzo and Claire are in electrocution chairs, their heads and limbs strapped down with rags knotted tightly across their mouths. To the left, either side of a double fire exit, a row of Mutes sit patiently. Granite, the Blacksmith, a pair of conjoined twins with wired helmets on their heads.

The lab is larger than any other I've seen. Shiny white floors, pristine workstations in neat rows, each with an assistant at the ready. Lab coats hang from their frames, gloves upon their hands and a look of complete indifference in their eyes. Equipment lines the desktops, between vial and test tube holders. Large machinery has been pushed against the back wall opposite the row of cages that are out of place amongst the cleanliness within.

But it's the huge screen Christopher is staring at that attracts my attention. Data flashes around maps of countries I can't pinpoint, an expanse of military grade equipment spread across a desk that takes four agents to man. I shrink back in my cage, only reminded I'm not alone by the flare of heat that surrounds my ankle and Pyro's partly reassuring smile as he heals me. An agent whispers to Christopher, who turns and smirks at me.

"Ahh, all here at last." Clicking his fingers, the agent shifts enough for me to see the wheelchair Christopher is sitting in. Gripping the handles, the agent then wheels him over to us in expensive, dark jeans and crisp white sneakers, a fraction of the man I first met. Slick, black hair is smoothed back on his head, his skin blemish-free. His profile holds resemblance, the hint of a port wine birthmark lingering at the edge of his fitted t-shirt. Icy blue eyes match the mirth of his easy smirk, his body muscled and as lean as a college athletic – aside from the wheelchair aiding him.

"Where's Serpentina?" I half-shout, looking around for her with a wash of panic claiming me. After everything we've been through, after she was so recently in my arms, my heart hammers from her lacking presence. Christopher merely chuckles, his youthful face stretched wide. I'd place him at no more than twenty, if I had to guess. But his voice, as melodic as it is, still holds the ring of an older man with too much knowledge and even more confidence.

"Lorraine has seen to hiding the girl, even from me. She's the future. She must be protected. Whether I'm leading the parade or not, this world will turn to ruin without those prepared to fight. To invade, destroy and start over. The world is going to change, one way or another."

"I don't care for your riddles," I growl, shaking the bars of the cage. The spark of Tate's ability bites at my palms, trickling down my arms. Another reason for Christopher to laugh mechanically.

"You've been quite the pain, my dear. Annoying, yes, but it sure has been an entertaining watch. The most amusing in all my years, in fact," he chuckles to himself, rubbing his stubbled jaw. I straighten and grip the bars in front of me.

"And how long has that been exactly, inmate number one?" The glint in his eye increases. His index finger points my way.

"Clever girl. I wondered how long it would take for you to figure out what you saw in the basement. Those case files should have been burnt long ago, but I've always been one for nostalgia." Taking the wheels of the chair in his own hands, Christopher nods to dismiss the agent and proceeds to rock himself back and forth.

"People are fickle. They believe any story they're told. I was on my third run of life when I was finally ready to announce my Mutant program to the world. Advancements in technology, you see. My greatest achievement and biggest downfall. I could no longer rely on taking people from the streets, not when too many disappearances were being traced back to me via DNA tracking. But why do I need to kidnap when there are those who so willingly volunteered? Suddenly, the rise in mutants across the country became expected and no one tried to trace just how far back the genes ran in their family trees."

"So what exactly is your ability, since you're awfully chatty today?" Ghost asks, his hair crinkled and damp. I spare him a look, realizing too late he's utterly naked and doesn't care to hide it. Christopher nods but continues to direct his answer at me.

"I like to call myself BounceBack. Living between eighteen and eighty on repeat. It's only natural the first successful Mute of the program should be the very scientist who discovered it." His smile is all slick and no charm.

"So what changed? You practically have immortality – why go after Pyro's eternal flame with such desperation?" I ask through gritted teeth.

"You should know the answer to that one. Love," he raises a brow and all three of us burst out laughter. Give me a break. Not amused by our eruption, Christopher clears his throat to silence us. "My wife's dementia took hold before I realized she had it. Working long hours, you see. I can spot faults in blood matter within an instant, yet I failed to recognize the disease tearing my wife's consciousness from me. No matter what I tried to fix it, she only seemed to get worse."

"Boo hoo," Ghost drawls. "Grab me a fucking tissue. The evil bastard who tortures and abuses mutants actually has a heart." Christopher smiles again, his own humor peaked by something Ghost said.

"On that note," he clicks his fingers. All four agents from the far desk respond, striding over to shove electric batons into Ghost's cage. A vision flashes before my eyes as Ghost recalls a group of electric eels stinging him and dragging him further into the lake, their bodies writhing with the debilitating spark of Tate's ability. The same spark that is still flooding his body and preventing him from slipping through their hold.

Ripping the cage open, Ghost is dragged out by his hair and neck, multiple hands and guns shoving him to stand beside Christopher. All the while, the asshole in the wheelchair has been slowly tugging off his shirt with obvious anguish. A puckered, red scar lines the center of his chest, the skin around it bruised.

"Heal me," Christopher announces, holding his arms out wide. Every eye in the lab, Mute or not, raise to watch the interaction. Ghost barks a laugh and tells Christopher to go fuck himself. The butt of a gun cracks across his mouth and Ghost spits out a wad of blood onto the floor.

"Heal me," Christopher repeats. Breath tickles the back of my neck. I spin around, finding no one there, but when I return to eye ghost, the breath comes again.

Tell him to do it, a voice echoes in my head. I know that voice. I banished that voice to Hell without hopes of ever hearing it again. Snorting, I shake my head and Pyro gives me a quizzical look from the cage next door. *Tell Ghost to heal Christopher, or you all die.*

I huff, withdrawing my hands to knot them together. Hoax isn't a fool, he knows more than I do. But am I willing to let myself trust a man who only has my best interests at heart? Saving me despite everyone else isn't the way I want to live my life. I have friends now, a family, and those I hold even closer. But he was also in the latter category. He still is. I gave my heart and soul to Hoax once, I have to trust in myself to do it again.

"Heal him Ghost," I announce, my gut twisting. Ducking my head away from Ghost's open-mouthed gape, I send a message back to Hoax while the connection is still open.

Now will you tell me why? Please? Desperation leaks from my tone, even in my own head.

Pyro's heart beats in Christopher's chest. He holds the core of your eternal bond. If anything happens, you all suffer the consequences alongside him, on earth or in hell.

The breath leaks from my lungs. My eyes slowly travel to the scar on Christopher's chest, unable to comprehend just how...and why... and what that means.

You had no right to keep this from us, I growl in the space between my ears.

I know, Hoax's response comes. And then he's gone. Disappeared again, and fuck does it hurt just as much as the first time. Will it always be like this? Hoax popping into my head to drop a bombshell and abandon me again, or will he be gone for good this time? Will he allow me to mourn the loss of him like a loved one should?

Christopher's smile makes my skin crawl as Ghost obeys, taking great pleasure in slapping a hand heavily on Christopher's chest. I feel the tug at our bond, Ghost using us to aid him in healing the scar. Deceit curdles in my chest, both pairs of eyes from my men glaring at me in confusion. I can't bring myself to tell them the truth, and instantly feel that sour regret of being a hypocrite. I don't want to worry my men with information I know will crush them, yet condemn Hoax for doing the same.

"What's the phrase - if you can't beat them, join them?" Christopher laughs, fully healed and jumping to his feet. Kicking the wheelchair away, it slams into the nearest counter. The lab assistant quickly rights the test tubes that threaten to topple over and returns to her microscope.

"You were always one of us," Pyro grits out, speaking for the first time. I brave a look at my mate, noting the tight clench to his jaw and the way he's pointedly ignoring me. I can't blame him, I wouldn't look at me either. There's a wash of shame across my face and still, I can't bring myself to tell him his heart is currently beating in Christopher's chest. I don't even understand it myself, my eyes dropping to the even fall of his chest.

"On paper maybe, but I've proven time and again I am far more superior. Look what I've been able to achieve," Christopher holds his arms out wide.

"All I see is a man who has locked himself in the last laboratory he still has possession over," a voice pipes up from the glass cube. Goldie has risen to stand, her arms folded and yellow hair spilling over her shoulder. Her chin nods to the door, which I look at more intently now. Thick, metal chains have been threaded through the handles, a bulky lock keeping them in place. Not to keep us out, but to keep others out. Christopher regards Goldie with a warmer smile than I'm used to.

"Observant as always, my dear." The tension in his shoulders eases as he looks at her, wagging his finger like a father reprimanding a child.

"Thanks to your little outburst, the public relations director has seized all of my other facilities. The rehabilitation center is heavily guarded, the Mutes inside now withdrawn from my possession. The Afterlife project as we know it is over. However," Christopher hums to himself, returning to our cages with a skip in his step as Ghost's is slammed closed again. "I was able to strike one last deal for the ownership of Octavia Horton's killer, and as far as I'm concerned - that's all of you. You all had a part to play. You're all I have left to prove the solider program can succeed."

The agents surrounding Ghost's cage stomp towards Follicle's, tearing him free of his confines. Hare-iett cries out, much to Granite's displeasure as he sits straighter in his seat. He doesn't get out of it though, which makes him a whipped assmunch in my books. Follicle resists the tug of the agents, but as muscled as he is – it's all for show. The fine physique flexing beneath his t-shirt has been carefully sculpted for performing on stage and making humans drool, but not combat.

Crouching, Christopher opens a small panel in the floor and reveals a metal hoop imbedded into the concrete beneath the lino. A chain is wrapped around Follicle's neck and attached to the loop, pinning him down on all fours. The lab assistants take their cue, banding together in the center of the lab. Whatever they've been working on, the result of each sits in a syringe in each hand.

A choreographed routine takes places before us, unspoken commands being given as Christopher calls out numbers one through eleven and there's nothing we or Hare-iett's screaming can do to stop it. Even Siren tries to sing a tune and deafen everyone but it just adds insult to injury.

Follicle jerks against each stab of the syringe, his hands quickly bolted to the same loop when he tries to punch through one of the assistants over his shoulder. The MRA agents linger close, pointing their guns at his face. They won't shoot, not until Christopher sees his experiment through, but they're threatening enough to subdue Follicle's attempts at struggling.

As the last syringe is pushed into his neck, a beat of silence follows where we all still to watch. That beat stretches into ten seconds, then thirty and I allow myself to believe it hasn't worked. Until Follicle's shoulder blade cracks out of place. The other side mirrors it, his arms contort at unnatural angles.

Screaming to the ceiling, his mouth stretches, his teeth lengthening. His eyes scrunch closed and yellow ones snap back open. Follicle's hair ripples across his entire body, breaking free of his clothes as his back hunches and tears his t-shirt. The hair sprouts in bursts of color, unable to decide which shade to be, giving him a patchy Dalmatian look. The chain at his neck hinders his movements, but there's no doubt Follicle has gone.

A grotesque version of a lycan is sprawled before us, its hollow howl splitting through the room. Hare-iett drops to her knees, reaching out for him just as the creature snaps his jaws towards her fingers. Granite shoots out of his seat, much to Christopher's amusement.

'Settle down everyone, the true test is about to begin.' I dare myself to look away, not to give Christopher the audience he wants, but I'm too fascinated. Follicle's altered body judders, as if another mirror image of himself is trying to break free, but not quite. It snaps back into himself, drawing a pained groan from the creature's mouth. Or should I call him experiment twenty four now?

"Jess," Christopher snaps, calling for a brunette in a lab coat hanging back. She gloves up, puts on a pair of protective glasses and reaches for an object beneath her work station that resembles a whip. Letting the end unfurl, a spark of electricity ripples along the length just before she strikes. Lashing the creature's back, he screams, his arms doubling with another set. Translucent, but each time I blink, I can't convince myself they're not real.

Again, she strikes. A duplicate lycan jolts out of the first, spitting and growling. Iridescent, mostly see-through, but there's no denying the glint of those sharp teeth. Freed of his restraints, the second version leaps over the first and clamps his jaws around Jess. She barely has time to scream, her blood splattering over the white lab coats lingering nearby.

"Oops," Ghost's brow raises and he flutters his fingers through the cage's bars. "Bye Jess." The shimmering beast turns his head, a crimson snout twitching in the air. He stalks towards Ghost, smelling his extended hands with interest. Ghost doesn't withdraw them, in fact he slowly tries to stroke it but the creature twists his head and settles a pair of bloodthirsty eyes on me.

Ahh, fuck. I don't have a good feeling about this.

HOAX

Leaving the isolated chamber on the outer wall of Hell's gates, I exhale harshly through my nose. This is the only place I can find enough solace to check in with Mania, but my disappearances are becoming apparent. The distraction from my duties, the intrusion in my vow. I promised once she no longer needed me, to let her go. But I can't. Not when my heart is filled with turmoil, and despite the break in our bond, my senses are erratic. Mania is still in trouble, and that wasn't the deal I made.

A lengthy line of prisoners, waiting for their turn to enter the fires, eye me, having the good sense to no longer beg me for freedom. As if my appearance isn't formidable enough, the last human that clung from my staff in desperation found himself impaled by it. Tensions are high and no amount of reaping worthless souls will fill the void inside.

I have considered the possibility of reaping Mania's soul, wondering if that would mean we could finally carve a place in this world to be together. But while Pyro's heart still beats, that's not an option I can consider. My new purpose from afar is to ensure that heart keeps beating, regardless of who's chest it currently resides in.

"Hoax," Asher calls from the gates. Still on guard duty, still being punished for a crime I'm yet to uncover. Not even his agreement to bring me in has managed to save him from an eternity of boredom. But somehow, amongst the shit hands we've been dealt, a friendship has begun to form. Not much of a consolation prize, but currently – that's all I have to cling onto. Approaching Asher, fires radiate from beneath the scarring on his cheek, his jaw set in a hard line. "You've been summoned."

I frown, looking to the staff in my hand. It thrums with energy, seeming to understand the instruction whereas I do not.

"Summoned for what?" Instead of answering me, Asher plants a heavy hand on my shoulder, resignation obvious in his golden gaze.

"Good luck," he nods, lowering his hand onto the onyx stone at the top of my staff. Tapping it on the ground for me, the scene contorts, reforming around me to reveal a cave. Standing at the mouth of it, a warm glow emanates from inside. At the back of my heels, a sheer drop into a valley of bubbling lava gives me no choice but to walk forward.

The cave curves into the center of a mountain, the damp coating the walls beaten away by warmth pulsing from my destination. With every step, the glow brightens until I turn another corner and stumble upon a fireplace. A fur rug is stretched before it, two tall armchairs either side. A walnut coffee table awaits, ready with a glass of whiskey, a pair of ice cubes floating inside.

Sit, a voice booms. I hunt for the owner whilst pushing myself into complying. I became too complacent taking orders from Christopher in my rouse, allowing him to believe I was braindead, that doing so now goes against my instincts. To be controlled and ordered around, its not a feeling I am quick to submit to again. Yet when faced with a pop-up lounge in the middle of Hell, I'd do well to leave that stubbornness at the entrance.

Lowering myself into the high-backed armchair, I smooth my hands over the black leather. The chair opposite remains empty, my company preferring to remain faceless.

I've been watching you, Hoax. Sitting forward, I brace my elbows on my knees and take that whiskey intended for me. Sipping the amber liquid, I wait to see where this one-way conversation is going before deciding which answer to give.

You've been forced to sacrifice where others have asserted a right they don't deserve. You were delivered here before your time. The decision for you to become a demon was orchestrated on false pretenses. You took an oath you didn't understand, and whilst I am unable to restore life, it is increasingly clear to me – you don't belong here.

Finishing the whiskey, I carefully place the glass back on the table. My eyes remain on the leather armchair opposite.

So what do you propose I do with you?

"Do I have a choice?" I reply, sitting back and threading my fingers over my stomach. To hope is a dangerous thing, and to voice my wishes would only prove the desperation in my non-existent soul. The anguish of rejection I felt through our eternal bond before I severed it. The weakness in me that couldn't hold out Mania's request to leave. It may have only been a day up there, but down here it's been far longer.

Seems you've caught yourself in quite the predicament, but it so happens – so have I. One of the astral planes is out of balance, a revolt that ended in the death of a prisoner before his time.

"What do you mean – a prisoner?"

For some, facing the consequences of their sins are not enough. I have a host of astral planes which are reserved for the hunting and torturing of such souls. I believe, we can help each other counter the balance, whilst giving you back what you've lost.

A tremor rolls through my back. My claws extend, pushing into the leather while my teeth cut into my lower lip through my soft heaving. Am I foolish to believe trading favors with the devil won't have repercussions, or am I too blinded with need to care? I fucked up saving Mania once, I broke her trust and threatened the love we share. A mistake I will never repeat, if lucky enough to be given the chance.

"Tell me what you need me to do."

T he creature bashes against Mania's cage again, hellbent on crushing the bars inwards. To her credit, she hasn't screamed, but I see the terror in her gaze. It cuts through me with the sharpness of a blade and my efforts to reassure her I'll break out of here and come to her rescue are no use.

Throwing my hands against the locked door yet again, my palms flare with fire but make no difference. Whatever has been welded to contain me isn't standard metal. My eyes slide to the Blacksmith sitting on a chair beside the fire exit, his impassive expression watching the scene unfold. No mention to Serpentina's whereabouts has been mentioned, and for a male that claims to care for her safety, he doesn't seem too worried.

The creature bucks, slashing giant claws against the bars. In his crazed haste to get closer to her, the hairy beast wrestles his way between our cages, nudging mine to the right. A little bit more and I'm knocked into Ghost's, his arms wrapping around me from behind.

"Brother!" he cries out, banding me into a tight man-hug. I grit my teeth, wrestling to get free when I still. Of course. Grabbing Ghost's arms, I stop the war battling in my mind and clear it, freeing myself of the turmoil Mania is stirring up. The beast's grunts fade away as I struggle to focus, slipping into our connection. Ghost is there, his strand of the flame burning white amongst the purple sparks flaring around it. The lasting effects of the electric eels from the lake supressing his power.

Tightening my brows, I let my own flame blaze. Spiralling, expanding. I engulf his, drawing out the last of Tate's ability. Then, I do the exact opposite of my base instinct, and give Ghost full reign. Boosted by my fires, he slips through the bars and into mine, a triumphant cry escaping his lips. Without pause, I rush forward, still holding his arms in an awkward piggyback. Launching myself through the cages, we knock Mania through the bars of hers and land heavily on the floor just as a crippling jolt of pain seizes my chest.

"Na ah," Christopher singsongs. Stepping closer, I manage to see his sneakers through the haze of my narrowed lids, the agony within making me twist and writhe. Mania's hands are on me, her healing flame warming up as the creature tackles her aside.

"Save. Her," I gasp out to Ghost. He scrambles off me, narrowly grabbing the jaws of the monster before it gnashes at Mania's face. This time, she does scream. I hear it in the pits of my soul, echoing around my ears and seeping into my mind. But I can't respond. Christopher crouches down, grabbing a handful of my hair in his hand and waves a small device in his other. A control of some sort.

"Don't get any ideas of chivalry. I need you one last time before the three of you become expendable to me. Then, I'll relish in killing you all." Dragging me along the floor, the lab assistant partner and MRA agent follow. I try to look back at the screams and gaggled grunts behind but Christopher's hold doesn't let up for a second. Not until I'm planted in the wheelchair and strapped down in front of the giant screen. Red pinpricks blink across the countries, surrounded by coding I don't understand. *If only Hoax was here.*

"I have nothing left to give you," I grit out, my head being strapped back and secured in place. The only ones in my peripheral are Tate, Claire and Enzo, and they're not fighting. Not struggling, or screaming. They've accepted their fate and their sagged postured suggests I should do the same. Not likely.

"Luckily, it's not you I need," Christopher says, placing my hands over the keyboard. An agent steps in from each side to pin down my wrists so Christopher is free to lean over my shoulder. "I know you're still linked to Hoax, and as you've just proved, you can access the abilities of your bonded ones. Why else would I inject Follicle with just enough of Mania's DNA to make him crazed with hunger for her?"

I jerk, trying to headbutt him and Christopher chuckles.

"Here's the deal. Access Hoax's ability, undo whatever he's implemented into my files, and I might call off Follicle before your mate is almost raped. Again." This time, I reserve my energy to send an internal alarm to Ghost. *Get Mania the fuck out of here, leave everyone else.* Selfish, yes, and I'll accept my punishment later. For now, Mania is the only one in immediate danger and beyond all others, the only one I'd care to protect. Damn, now I sound just like Hoax too.

"If not," Christopher continues, patting my shoulder, "then I suppose I'll have another creature/mutant offspring to add to my roster. Not a total loss, but you should know," he leans in to whisper, the curve of his smile lifting against my ear, "none of the surrogate mothers have survived the delivery as yet."

I've never been one to give up hope. Even when my heart is shredded. Even when I was orphaned, left to rot in a home for abused mutant boys. But in this instant, as my eyes drift shut and I search my soul for the ability of my dead brother, the notion takes me. The urge to fight, which I rely on to pull me through each day, weans and a small voice in my head says, there has to be more than this. Even in hell, there has to be a place where the suffering pauses long enough to enjoy the rewards.

Our flame responds to my call, but I've never seen it so weak. Faint in color, fragile in strength. The three strands we cling onto so tightly struggle and flutter like weeds in the wind, unable to wrap into the one, unified strand we depend on. Ghost bellows from behind me, a burst of pain drawing me away from my aim. To find a remaining fragment of Hoax within.

Here, brother. Allow me. A gravelled voice replies inside my head. I frown at the rush of power flooding my veins, the purple flame behind my eyes sparking to life. His presence leans into me, flowing from my chest to shoulder, down my arm and seeping from my fingers. My consciousness is pushed, once, twice, and suddenly, I'm falling. Only held in place by the straps on my head and torso, and the hands pinning me to the keyboard, a rush of circuits and wires race behind my eyes. My stomach rolls, the notion of claustrophobia seizing me before the wires open up, and a world I never knew existed is displayed before me.

Networks of flashing lights, a universe of colour beyond the unknown. I'm urged through before my mind can grasp what I'm seeing. Diverting through balls of light akin to stars, with Hoax as my guide, we hurtle forwards. My stomach dips as we do, the motion of a rollercoaster rushing through me. On the edge of my awareness, Christopher's voice sounds as he barks at me for an update, but I don't respond.

Before I know it, files appear behind my eyelids. Yellow, like those of a desktop, but with a nudge forward, we enter inside. Lines of text filter into view, documents flashing, blueprints shifting aside for more information to be drawn to the forefront. Plans become apparent and I suck in a sharp breath.

A base profile, accompanied with test results, statistics and observations. An image of a small girl with yellow hair and slitted eyes. And lastly, a surveillance live feed. Serpentina is curled into a tiny ball, hugging herself amongst the straw bed she's been given. The room is stark white. Too harsh for her eyes by the way she cowers her head and amongst the straw, small slithering snakes peek in and out. Their scales not quite green with an iridescent shine.

What's happening to her? I ask Hoax, still sensing his presence in my head. The file of statistics is brought back to the forefront, a bunch of numbers and lines I can't make sense of.

Serpentina's blood markers present a new strand of metamorphosis. Whereas our abilities work alongside our genetics, hers are embedded within it. Her projected snakes display a psychic connection, while her appearance is down to her mutation. I groan inside my head, trying to make sense of it all. The comfort of Hoax's hand touches my shoulder.

She has dual abilities that Christopher has already utilized into a gas form. Predictions have shown with age, she'll only grow stronger and become more of an asset. The plans are extensive, and they have been passed onto military generals around the world. Whether Christopher is alive or not, her DNA samples are already being sold to the highest bidder to create Mute weapons. The longer she's alive, the more of a risk she presents. We have to end her now, Pyro, before she single-handedly destroys the human race.

I snort to myself. Since when have we given a shit about the humans? They've done nothing but isolate us. Hunt us. We're the vermin they'd sooner see exterminated than to even give us a chance. How the Mutes could have thrived with the same rights. I know in that instant, Serpentina must live. We have to look out for our own kind when no one else will.

As much as I enjoy the sentiment, Hoax interrupts my thoughts, *you always were driven by passion. I rely on logic. Humans are greedy and with power, they will be their own downfall. Countries destroyed, a world on fire. Animals, plants, all gone. The advancements in electricity will halt, causing masses of floods and gas emissions.*

A sigh sounds between my ears and I feel it then. The ache Hoax has been carrying alone. The turmoil that he's burdened himself with. Seeing a world through the eyes of technology leaves nothing to the imagination, and I can only guess at what point the male I knew broke off into a bitter version of himself that alienated those who love him.

Serpentina's location isn't trackable, but I can submit an order right now for her to be determined. Mania's made it clear how she feels about my decisions, so It's your choice Pyro. Mania thinks she wants the weight of this decision, but I assure you, she does not.

Internally, I shake my head. No, I'm not being pressured into risking the bond Mania and I have by presuming she's not strong enough to handle this decision. There has to be another way. Hoax hears my every thought, commenting back.

That's not what I was doing. I'm not the villain here. You want the death of a child on her conscience or just the undoing of the entire world? If we return to the lab without submitting the order, it'll be too late. There's no other way.

But still, I pause. I can't make such an enormous decision without Mania and Ghost's input, yet there's no time. Can I have either scenario on my conscience? Then again, why would it be? Nothing up to this point has been down to me; I'm merely a pawn. Let the world reap the undoings of their own kind. I feel Hoax's presence hanging his head in defeat.

Good luck with your happily ever after when there's no world left to live it out in. With that, Hoax abandons me and I'm drawn out of the hardware. Thrust back into the wheelchair, my wrists still pinned by agents who eye me suspiciously.

"Well?" Christopher stomps into view. "Did you find the bug your poor excuse for a brother embedded in my life's work? He thought he was real clever leaking my files to the presidential candidates, but Hoax should know by now. I always win."

GHOST

A satisfying crack reverberates throughout the room, silencing the snapping beast once and for all. Hare-iett sobs, resting her head against the bars of her cage, but what else had she expected me to do? Let that version of a male that no longer existed rape my mate? No thanks, I'm pretty sure Mania's going to cost me an arm and a leg in therapy once we get out of here as it is. Speaking of which…

Looking down at my blood-soaked arm, I yank out the lengthy tooth embedded in my skin. Mania jerks upright, shoving the dead carcass of the beast off her to shout at me.

"Never take out the object stemming your blood flow, idiot!" Scrambling to yank her t-shirt over her head, I raise one brow at the sight of Mania's perky, small boobs in a crop top and wish I'd pulled out the tooth earlier. The perfect handful. I reach out with my good arm to give her left tit a squeeze and she blocks me, delivering a sharp slap to my face. Feisty. I love it.

Twisting her t-shirt around my arm and tying it extra tight, Mania's attention is drawn to Christopher as his voice travels from across the room.

"...He thought he was real clever leaking my files to the presidential candidates, but Hoax should know by now. I always win."

"Sure about that?" the answer comes, just before a figure appears at Christopher's back. Thick, black horns break through his disheveled indigo hair. Leather hugs his tattooed body in the form of a tunic vest and tight slacks, disappearing into a heavy set pair of boots. The staff in his hand contorts into a claw, holding a large onyx stone that gleams in the lab's lighting.

Hoax! My heart flutters and a stupid smile tugs at my face. I knew he'd be back. Mania, on the other hand, despite the same elation spiking within her, jerks on the knot at my arm, causing me to hiss. Hoax grabs the back of Christopher's t-shirt in one hand and throws him across the room with little to no effort. I clap wildly, ignoring the blood splatter dripping from the t-shirt bandage onto the floor. I really should sort that out.

Winding a hand into Mania's hair, I twist her around and plant my lips on hers. She tries to struggle, but there's no resisting my charm. Or the fingers gripping her scalp. Gliding my mouth over her cracked lips, I draw out that hint of warmth I need. Those ability-debilitating eels really did a number on me. After Mania surrenders, aiding me with her fire and my arm has healed, I still hold her there. This time, it's because I just want to solidify our connection for a little longer.

Tipping her head back, her lips part and I slide my tongue inside. Mania bites down, causing me to yelp and pushes away at my chest. Touché. Time and place might be less than desirable. Christopher pulls himself up on a workstation, keeping it between him and Hoax as my brother stalks closer. Damn, where's the popcorn.

"You can't kill me. Pyro's heart beats in my chest. My death will seal the same fate for the rest of them," Christopher waves a hand in mine and Mania's direction. Wait, what? I drag Mania into my lap, using the dead carcass of Follicle's beast as a prop-up cushion. The scar on Christopher's chest, the same one Mania told me to heal…

"We're going to have a chat about open communication," I grumble in Mania's ear and proceed to stroke her hair. At times, I want to be mad at her in the ways I used to find so natural, but I can't. Not when I do stupid shit on an hourly basis. I have no right to tell anyone else what to do, but knowledge such as Hoax regaining his memories or Pyro not having a heart might have been useful information to know.

Hoax grins, twirling his staff in his hand like a cheerleader's baton. "Good thing I've made pen pals with the Devil," he says, low and spooky-like. Goosebumps prickle my skin and I swear my own dick just jolted. Yes please, demon daddy. Mania eyes me suspiciously, feeling the evidence of my thought train beneath her ass.

"Even better that I don't *have* to kill you." Hoax swirls his staff, the onyx stone glowing a midnight shade of purple. The same color streams behind, creating a circle in the air. Expanding to ten-feet wide each way, a misty grey void hangs inside, vacuuming anything nearby towards it. Chairs skid, equipment wobbles. Machinery tugs closer and paperwork flies from the work surfaces. I grip Mania's middle, dragging her back towards the cage she so desperately tried to escape and shove her inside.

"Shhh Spitfire," I place a finger on her lips when she protests. "I have a plan." Mania rolls her red eyes but it's too late. The plan has taken root in my head and now I have to see it through.

"At least put some pants on," she mutters around my finger. I look down at my own nakedness, offended she'd ask such a thing. But as my now-dry clothes skid past, on their way to Hoax's portal, I grab them.

"Fine," I huff, dragging the pants up my legs whilst holding onto the bar of the cage. The strength of the gateway grows stronger. Christopher ducks behind the workstation like the pussy I always knew him to be, but Hoax is having his own problems. Machinery on the opposite wall flies free of the screws holding them down, snapping at the sockets. Wires whip and snap, sparking at the end, threatening to squash him if he doesn't dive out of the way. Army crawling across the floor, I head in the other direction.

A row of Mutes eye me, their fingers white from gripping onto the seats they've yet to vacate. Never mind the fact these traitors are happy to sit and watch the rest of us struggle, not one reaches out to help me. So instead, I clamp a hand around the Blacksmith's ankle and pull myself up his body like a sexy sloth climbing a tanned tree. His molten eyes are wide, his inked skin cold to the touch. Actually, as I pull myself into the Blacksmith's lap, I would go as far to say he's frozen solid. And not in a good way.

"Wakey wakey," I click my fingers in his face. Those same molten eyes shift aside and I follow his eyeline. Readjusting myself to straddle him, wishing I was still naked so I could tease him about this for years to come, I peer over the Blacksmith's back. A tube attached to the wall and beyond has been inserted to his nape. Clear in color, pale smoke akin to liquid nitrogen is pumped through. The others have the same, although Granite is doing his best to fight the effects of the gas. His fingers slowly curl into a fist, his hard stare not leaving Hare-iett for one second.

Tilting my head, I frown at the Blacksmith and his scowl that is frozen in place. Okay, well, maybe I can forgive the lack of hard-on he has for me being draped all over him. I'm a fine catch on the worst of days. The word Adonis rolls around my mind, before a sharp slap of heat lashes at the inside of my cheek. Rubbing my face, I peer back at Mania. She's glaring at me, her eyes and hands on fire. Better get on with it.

"Tether me, big boy!" I grab the Blacksmith's wrist, pinching the chain tattooed around his forearm. Nothing happens and I end up digging my nails in until he bleeds. On a strangled, inward moan, a glint of metal is forced through his skin and I snatch it. Aha! Dragging the length of chain out, I wind it around my waist, up my arm and wrap around my hand a few times. That's as good as it's going to get. Standing with my bare feet on the Blacksmith's solid thighs, I dive into the wind tunnel the open gateway has created. This is as close to skydiving as I'll ever get.

With the agility of a bulky flying squirrel, I swoop across the lab, narrowly avoiding the microscope that flies by. Ducking my head, I slip beneath the overhanging lip of the counter's surface and barrel into Christopher.

"Hello old friend," I grin my slimiest grin, propelling him out from behind the workstation. The wind grips us immediately and I snake an arm around Christopher's waist. We're in this together, you old/young evil bastard. I won't be satisfied until I've seen his banishment to the end, if that's actually what's going on here. Might be a bit presumptuous on my part, but my harem prefers to keep me in the dark when it comes to plans, so here we are.

With Pyro's and Hoax's protests being lost to the whirring I'm hearing, I fly through the gateway. My brain scrambles, my eyes unable to track the worlds churning and changing around me. Instead of trying to, I focus on Christopher, slamming my forehead down on his when he insists on struggling against me the entire time. Buildings appear through a layer of smoke, righting themselves and I slam onto a hard, concrete road.

An empty town. A thick layer of cloud preventing the sun from shining. Withered flowers decorate the sidewalks like botanical graveyards, trees with no leaves left to shed casting spindly shadows. Christopher doesn't waste time looking at his surroundings, scrambling for the portal that zooms closed behind us. The only evidence it existed at all, aside from us, is the metal chain hanging from my waist that seems to be cut short. Yet when I double tug on my end, there's a response on the other side.

A round of gunfire cracks on the road beside my feet. The person responsible remains hidden from sight so I wrap the length of chain in my hand around Christopher's wrist and tug him along.

"No need to be shy!" I call out, sincerely hoping Hoax knew where he was sending us. Figures shift out from the shadows, every single one holding a machine gun in my direction. I wave, putting on my most cheery smile. "Good news! I have some firing practice for us!" I point to Christopher's paled face and then frown myself. "Actually, scratch that. You can't kill him, but feel free to wire him up to a ventilator before draining him like a human colander."

Apparently, I said something right. Excited chatter picks up, following the crowd that rush forward. I take a step back myself, needing a double take at the familiar faces sizing up Christopher like their next meal. Heavy dreads shake around a skinny version of Enzo, dressed in fatigues with bullets dripping from his waist. Camo, dressed in full camouflage appears amongst the crowd and I point a finger at his face.

"You," I growl. "I'm going to fuck you up."

"On what grounds?" a female responds, walking through the

centre of the crowd as they part for her. At her back, three males remain close, the one on the right piquing my interest the most. White eyes stare into mine, large muscles shift beneath a white t-shirt with an LMG strapped to the front. When he tilts his head towards the female in the center, a scar becomes visible at the back of his head, cutting through his white hair.

"Wait," I gasp, suddenly feeling my own. My hands brush a slit in my silky, cropped locks and I see my life flash before my eyes. Motherfucker! How long has that been there?! The female stops before me, sighing at me wasting her time. Brown eyes follow the chain at my waist, linking me to Christopher. She pulls her chocolate hair over one shoulder, revealing a trio of skulls inked onto her neck.

"Mania?" I raise a brow. It's her, but she's not my Mania.

"Mia. You must be Hoax's friend," she nods in understanding and I get the impression she doesn't mean the male on her left side. An easy smirk lives upon his lips, his indigo hair left to grow out in a shaggy, too-cool-to-brush kind of way. Definitely not my Hoax, but damn. Do you think anyone would notice if I swapped them out? Most likely.

"Yeah, I am," I agree, realising too late she's still waiting for a response. "Hoax has sent me to hand-deliver you a present." Tugging Christopher forward, the Mutes around him close in with cruel smiles. Mia pushes the gun strapped to her front around to the back. Her full curves draw my eye and an arm quickly bands around her from Pyro. Or a copy of Pyro that looks like he doesn't cry when he jerks off.

"Hmmm, the bastard that tortures and kills Mutes for sport I'm guessing?" Mia purses her lips, ignoring the testosterone around her. "Hoax spoke of him. Alas, he appears like a human, but these would suggest otherwise." Grabbing the chain I'm holding, Mia inspects the hundreds of pinpricks covering Christopher's forearm. He growls at her, then immediately regrets it when every Mute close enough throw the butts of their guns into his face and body. Camo's at the forefront, stepping between Mia and Christopher in a protective manner. I narrow my eyes at him, and Mia narrows hers at me.

"Was there anything else?" she asks, tearing my attention away from Camo. I can't resist giving him a little shove back, needing him out of my space before I separate his head from his shoulders. My version of Camo or not, I didn't get to take out the revenge burning in me on the last one.

"Yeah, a condition. As much as it pains me to say it, you can't kill him. Our Pyro's heart resides in his chest. If he dies, we all do," I grit out, remembering I've yet to give my own payback for that sneaky trick. A grave look passes not only Mia's and her harem's faces, but everyone's. It doesn't take a genius to figure out she is their leader.

"Understood." Cracking her neck side to side, the crowd takes their cue and begins to disperse. Retreating into the shadows they came from. I catch a glimpse of a golden-haired female and her three bears. A pink-haired Imp holding hands with a little girl who looks back to stick out her fork-shaped tongue at me.

Seems the whole gang is here, but soon it's just me, a struggling Christopher and Mia remaining. I say struggling, the weak tugs on my waist only go to prove without all the gadgets and minions, Christopher is just a weak prick with some serious little-dick-syndrome going on.

"Well," Mia raises a brow. "What are you waiting for? Release him." Her tone drips with authority and I can't fight a smirk.

"You sure you don't want me to tie him to that fountain or something?" I spot the cement structure that's run dry of water in front of an abandoned church. Just beyond, a pile of bones stretches high with a single, cawing crow sitting on top. Mia pops her hip, an equally bored yet amused expression upon her milky face.

"That would defeat the point of hunting him, don't you think?" she smirks. "We like to play with our food before we eat it." A small sound escapes Christopher and I take great pride in knowing I've never seen him look so small. I bet he's seconds from pissing himself, but the tug of the chain on my waist starts to pull me back. Shit timing Hoax! I want to stay! I want to play hunt the human and flay his skin off inch by satisfying inch. Another tug yanks me a few steps back so I sigh and drop the section wrapped around Christopher's wrist.

He runs and my heart sinks. Rolling my head back to Mia, she's already checking over her machine gun.

"Remember, whatever happens – that heart has to keep beating.

The rest of it is fair game. And Mia," I manage to tilt her head up with my index finger before I'm jerked further back. "Give that bastard hell."

"I intend to," she nods. Allowing myself to be pulled away without resistance now, the whirring of the portal opens behind me. Just large enough to fit my body as I'm whipped through, waving goodbye to Christopher as he tries to make a run for the portal. The echo of his 'nooooo!' will be forever embedded in my mind, and I'll use it each night to lull myself to sleep.

The lab comes back into focus as I'm spat out onto the floor. The lino slaps against the skin of my torso and by the time I've rolled onto my back, a sexy minx dives onto me. I wrap my arms around her slender body, nuzzling my face into her hair. This is *my* Mania. The female who owns my soul. Who loves me without reservation. Not despite of my quirks, but because of them, and I'll travel to any astral plane to ensure she knows I feel exactly the same.

G host squeezes me until no more air can access my lungs, and I let him. Everything happened so quickly, and despite feeling like it's not over yet, all three of the men I gave my heart to are currently alive and in the same room. An experience I've yet to fully appreciate. Shifting to sit upright, Ghost takes me with him and huddles me in his lap. Wherever he's been and whatever he saw, he's not ready to let me go yet.

"That's what you meant by not killing him, right?" Ghost looks up to Hoax with such raw emotion in his white eyes. He knows it's too late either way, but he not-so-secretively wants the recognition for a job well done. I raise a brow to Hoax, mentally telling him what to do. After a beat, he rolls his black and purple eyes and pats a clawed hand on Ghost's head.

"Good boy," he grits out. Both Ghost and I beam up at him with smiles that break through his irritated façade. The corners of Hoax's lips lift and his eyes drift closed. The staff gripped in his hand shrinks to a simple stick which he drops onto the ground, the tiny pebble of onyx stone rolling beneath one of the workstations. His horns retract, his tattoos turn back into the circuits that thrum with purple light.

Leather attire becomes a comfortable tracksuit, talons pull back into lean fingers.

Opening his eyes, Hoax's indigo irises hold mine and in a rush of emotion, his eternal bond snaps back into place in my chest. My gasp is echoed by Ghost, and Pyro from across the room as he releases the Mutes still trapped. My Hoax is back, and something tells me it's for good this time.

But there's no time to celebrate. An alarm blares to life, the screen on the back wall flashing with a large X. Hoax rushes forward, his fingers connecting with the mouse and his expression drops. Everyone else jumps over sporadic piles of charred ash and littered broken glass to rush to his side, including Granite and Hare-iett, the Mirage Twins, Goldie and her bears.

I share a worried look with Tate as she re-enters the room with Enzo and Claire at her back, their search for Serpentina proving useless. It was decided the Blacksmith would work on barricading the elevator to prevent agents from intruding, while Pyro unleashed his flames on any that were stupid enough to remain after Christopher was gone.

After what feels like too long to remain still, the alarm is shut off and Hoax returns to us with his eyebrows pinched.

"What's wrong?" I place a hand on his bicep. The first time I've touched him since telling him to leave, but now's not the time to appreciate the zap of desire that floods me from the contact.

"I thought," Hoax curses under his breath and stalks away, leaving my hand to drop. Pyro catches it in his, pressing a kiss to my forehead. "I mean, I'd hoped," Hoax pushes a hand through his indigo hair. Everyone waits for his next words, growing impatient when they don't come. Releasing Pyro's hand, I stomp through the remains of dead scientists this time and push my hand into the center of Hoax's chest.

"Spit it out. No more secrets," I demand. My glare gives him no room to argue, not if he wants to start repairing the damage that has been done. I want Hoax with us, in our unit, not always on the outside looking in. Without looking at me, Hoax tugs me beneath his arm, drawing on my presence for comfort.

"There's a failsafe on Christopher's life. I'd hoped instead of killing him, simply banishing him wouldn't have triggered it. But, I was wrong." Retracing his steps to the crowd by the computer, he speaks to us all.

"Serpentina's DNA holds the power to Astro-project. She shows this via her snakes, but Christopher understood what it really meant. Her blood markers hold more mutations than any of us. All of us combined, in fact. There's also evidence to prove she could fully shift in and out of snake form too, making her the first with dual abilities. She's beyond the most powerful Mute to have lived, and not even nine-years-old. So he took his samples and used machines to duplicate it, transferring it into a gas form. Those mutagen gases were in facilities all over the world, ready to be released."

"*Were?*" Goldie folds her arms. "As in, they're not there now?" Hoax rest his cheek on my head.

"They were released around five minutes ago. Anyone who doesn't have the blood markers to survive the mutations will die."

"That's...almost the entire world's population," Tate shudders, her voice barely audible. Hoax tries to step away, but I won't let him by holding onto his waist. Ghost and Pyro step in also, boxing Hoax in.

"I tried to hinder his experiments, but my focus was...distracted." He peers at me. "I think Christopher knew I was onto him, because he kept throwing me curveballs to keep me distracted. Disabling the capsules before they were injected into all of your necks, keeping up the ruse while communicating with Octavia."

For some unknown reason, a wave of jealousy flutters through me at the mention of her name. It's uncalled for and out of place, but nothing about our journey has been 'normal'. Thinking about Hoax having secret meetings with the ex-president while I didn't even know he could form a sentence doesn't sit right with me, and he knows it. Pulling me in front of him, Hoax's arms wind around me, the weight of his body leaning on me a little too heavily.

"None of this is any of our fault," Pyro comes to Hoax's defense, pulling Hoax's shoulders upright to lean on him instead. There's no end to what Pyro can sense through our connection. "We didn't start this. All repercussions are because of Christopher's decisions and actions. He was a bitter, power-hungry man. If he even cared where the moral line was, I doubt he could see it."

A moment passes where we all stare at the floor whilst the Blacksmith grunts. Chains fly from his wrists, shooting through the base and roof of the elevator shaft and severs it from the cords holding it in place. Whipping them back just in time, the elevator shaft shoots south and crashes at the base. Who knows if that will be enough to keep the agents away, but a short window to escape is all we need.

"What – what about Serpentina?" Claire asks tentatively through the bleak moment. Hoax lowers his chin onto my head and sighs again.

"I couldn't find her. The surveillance feed has been disconnected, and all traces erased. If I had to guess, I'd doubt she's even in the country. There's been a bidding war for her for a long time now. It would have been too easy for Christopher to lose her anywhere in the world at a moment's notice."

Surprisingly, it's Ghost who stalks away to kick one of the lonely cages and screams in frustration. I didn't think he cared much for children, but I believe his anger lies elsewhere. With a man that, even though will be punished for eternity, in Ghost's eyes – got away. He seeks to feel revenge at his own hands, and not having the closure is gnawing at our connection.

"Come on," I announce, pushing Hoax a step back. "We have to move. This isn't helping anyone." My feet are twitching with the need to get going, all of this standing around is making me anxious. Banding together, we stride for the main exit. Regardless of whatever is about to hit the world, I'll be glad to never see the inside of an asylum or scientific lab again.

Leading the parade, my hand outstretches for the door a light flashes above and the audible click of the lock sliding into place resonates through us all. What the-

"No." Hoax's voice can be heard, and it's only then I realize he isn't behind me. Those at my back separate, allowing me a clear sight of Hoax's hand on the master computer.

"No?" I ask, trying to keep the attitude from my tone and posture. I failed on both fronts.

"We can't leave. I've already locked the outer gates and rigged the fences with the electrocution switch Christopher designed with Tate's ability. We have to stay here, for good."

"Hoax, I'm only going to say this politely once," Ghost manages to grind out. His fists are curled to the point of whitening. "Release the fucking door, or I'll dismember you limb from limb and fuck your ass with each one in turn." The bears all take a cautious step to the side, the message clear to not get on Ghost's bad side. Hoax doesn't stand down though, his hand still attached to the mouse.

The screen behind him fills the entire wall with an image. A village encased in yellow gas, humans running for their lives to avoid it. Clutching their child and the belongings they deem valuable enough to risk their lives for. Most collapse, coughing, holding their throats. The live feed shrinks into the corner, accompanied by others until the whole screen is filled with different corners of the earth. All being swarmed with gas. All thrust into a war they didn't have any chance at understanding.

I take a step forward, my stomach plummeting. Hoax enlarges one particular surveillance feed in the center and I freeze in place. The release of a missile from a facility that looks too much like Afterlife for my liking. It soars into the sky, no doubt about what it's carrying. Trailing my gaze to Hoax's hard expression, my heart breaks.

He knew. He's been carrying this burden. Protecting me from it. Trying to prevent it all by himself. But even with his ability, he wouldn't have been able to unweave the web Christopher has been creating for decades.

The dam between our eternal bond crumbles and I fight a sob. Love fills every corner of my being. Not the soft and fluffy kind – but rather a raw ache. Twinged with desperation, doused in longing. Hoax is my backbone when I'm weak, my defense against the decisions that will haunt me. I pushed him away, yet here he is, just as steady as ever. Regardless of my stubbornness to be free of anywhere Christopher has been, there has to come a time I hang up my reservations and have to trust Hoax completely. And I do. I trust him.

"Okay Hoax. We'll stay," I nod. Joining his side, his arm welcomes me and together, we give the others the same choice. Ghost will be able to tap into his ability soon enough. He can deposit those who want to leave in the outside world.

"So that's it?" Pyro asks, remaining across the room, his expression unreadable. "You want to stay here, after everything we've been through?" I close my eyes, not able to comprehend the words that are about to come out of my mouth.

"The place we found each other, yeah. There's nowhere else I'd rather be," I nod, gripping onto Hoax tighter. A beat pauses before Ghost throws his hands into the air, slaps them down on his thighs. Striding over, huffing the entire way, he drops into a desk chair on wheels. Pyro shrugs, leaving those gaping at his back. His steps are unhurried and when he does reach us, his hands slide into my hair, drawing me out of Hoax's hold.

"My home is wherever you are baby." His red eyes are alight with a flame I feel burning deep inside. His mouth presses against mine, savoring the small glimpse of freedom we've finally found. It may not have looked the way we'd envisioned, but what's a building compared to our safety? Having my men all together at the same time is a feat in itself. The rest is secondary.

"Oh great," Ghost groans, scrubbing his hands over his face. "Look at the smooth talker. I should have said something like that." I break apart from Pyro on a laugh, dragging his wheeled chair over by his wrist and perching myself on his leg to face the others.

"Well? What do you say?" I ask, more worried than I thought I would be they might all leave. I came into Afterlife the way I'd lived up to that point, solitary and alone. I'd isolated myself from the world, unaware of the reason I couldn't join Azella in Hell permanently. Yet now I'm surrounded by those very reasons, their hands all finding a way to touch me as we stare at the others.

Tate breaks first, linking her hands with Claire's and Enzo's. Joining our newfound pack, I share a nod of understanding with the Mute I once resented for trapping us here. Her lilac eyes gleam back, with Claire popping her head forward to smile at me too. Granite moves next, drawing Hare-iett into his side to cross the expanse of the room. Siren shifts her blue gaze to the Blacksmith, looking at him with such longing and desperation to be held.

"Don't even think about it," the Blacksmith growls. Siren shrieks and rushes over to join us, while he remains behind and seething. "Sit around and pretend in your happily ever after. I'm going to find Serpentina." Coating his fists in a metallic sheen, he beats a hole into the wall big enough for him to leave through. Granite stomps his foot, sending a ripple of rock to cover the gap after he's gone.

That leaves the Mirage Twins, who slink our way and remain distanced by a few feet, and Goldie with her bears. Her golden eyes are narrowed, her arms folded. Her three bears stand tall, awaiting instruction. Their black eyes stare forwards, their chests rising and falling evenly in black t-shirt. All that separates them are the different shades of their shoulder-length hair.

"We're safer here, and we're together," Hoax reaffirms. Goldie has much the same reaction as Ghost, huffing and rolling her eyes.

"Fine. We stay. But we're not coming all the way over there to hug it out. Release the doors and let's find out what shithole we've resigned ourselves to."

"If we're lucky, not everyone has evacuated," Granite speaks and I flinch at the deep rumble. He cracks his knuckles, his harsh jaw set. Hare-iett smiles, stroking his hard chest and he visibly melts for her. Not that I have time to watch as Ghost tosses me on the ground and shouts that he gets shotgun on the best room. I can't even complain as Pyro pats me down when I stand, falling into his hold.

Watching Ghost and Goldie fight to be the first one out when Hoax releases the door brings a smile to my face. This place won't be perfect. It'll hold all of the memories that became my hell on earth. The shithole we spent all of our time and energy to escape. But with a little love and a whole load of optimism, we'll make a home. I have my men and an irregular family that tagged along on the way. What more could a mutant ask for?

EPILOGUE

"Seriously, it's perfect. Stop messing about and get over here," I groan from the bed. Pyro lifts his hands away from the bouquet he's been arranging for far too long. First supply run out of the exterior face, with Hoax disabling the forcefield just long enough for Ghost to drag Pyro through, and this is what they prioritized on bringing back. A flourish of beautiful red roses, and possibly the last of its kind. Not to mention, the first bunch of flowers I've ever been given.

However, Goldie hadn't been too happy her list of requests was ignored, and vows to go with Ghost next time. That's a duo I would not like to cross paths with.

This facility isn't dissimilar to Afterlife, minus the burn pile of mattress' and bodies we left behind. Multiple levels of padded cells, a few extra games rooms in the base around the abandoned canteen. None of the facilities appear to be used, and the yard is a work in progress, to put it politely.

None of us venture down there too much, not when the staff quarters here are bordering luxurious. To me, at least. At the top of the building, floor-to-ceiling windows provide a 360 view of the mountain ranges surrounding us. The sun shines more than it rains, filling our oasis with more light than I'm used to. The kitchen and lounge areas are communal, fitted with all the latest gadgets and comforts. Solar panels cover the roof so we don't run out of electricity or hot water.

Although, a favorite spot for us all is the rooftop terrace. A sanctuary of AstroTurf, potted plants, a canopy overhanging wooden furniture for us all to lounge in and best of all, a hot tub. It didn't work at first, until Hoax had his way with the mechanics. Better yet, each bedroom is fitted with a balcony for easy access.

With more than enough bedrooms for us all individually, there's plenty to spare. Especially as my harem, Goldie's and Tate's have all bundled into our own. Hare-iett has roomed with Granite and I've seen Siren disappearing with the Mirage Twins more often than not. Speaking of which...

"Pyro! Leave the roses alone and come to bed!" I call out, disappearing beneath the covers. A hand grips my ankle, dragging me further downwards. The baggy man's t-shirt I'm wearing rides up, revealing just a lacy thong underneath. The other essential from their supply run, apparently. A giggle escapes my mouth as that hand finger walks up my inner thigh, a flash of white hair appearing between my legs.

"I didn't hear you shouting for me to come to bed, so I invited myself," Ghost bobs his brow. Burying his face into the lace covering my pussy, he inhales deeply. "Fuck yes. So damn sweet." Another body joins us, Pyro finally obeying my request. Sliding beneath the cover, his mouth is straight on mine. A hand skates across my stomach, holding me flat as Ghost's tongue drags up the outside of the lace. Heat pools at my center, the material growing wet instantly.

Using the bond to stay in tune with each other, Pyro's teeth nibbles at my lip as Ghost's drag the lace aside. Their tongues enter me at the same time, causing me to gasp into Pyro's mouth. My back arches as Pyro swallows my soft moans. The hand travels up my stomach to my breasts. Teasing my nipple between deft fingers, I recognize them as

Pyro. Ghost is a rough grope kind of guy, always in a rush to bring me to climax. Pyro is the opposite.

Like hot and cold, the two of them play my body like an instrument. Calm and sensual up top, hurried and carnal down below. Two fingers spear me, Ghost's wicked tongue lapping at my clit. I moan, fisting my hand into his hair. I could easily break apart for him in an instant, but there's something missing. I call for Hoax through our connection.

Be up in a minute, his reply answers instantly inside my mind. Not good enough.

Now, Hoax! Ghost shouts through the bond on my behalf, sensing the yearning in my being for all of my men together. Having been separated for so long, I refuse to have it any other way. Pyro kisses a trail across my jaw, down my neck and tugs the t-shirt over my head. Back arched, chest flushed, he lowers to take my nipple in his mouth. Swirling ever so slowly, I fight against the need rising within.

My thighs squeeze Ghost's head as he curls his fingers within me, drawing on the climax I'm holding back. Retracting his fingers, Ghost replaces them with his tongue, spreading my wetness around to my back passage. Applying pressure there, I bite down on my lip to prevent myself from crying out.

The cover is whipped off us, an utterly naked Hoax ready and waiting. I drink in the muscles he's retained from his demon days, the shadows of his abs appearing through the circuit tattoos covering his torso. His dick stands tall in his fist as he strokes his hand up and down his shaft.

"Lie down, right now," I tell him, trying to shift. Ghost's hands clamp on my thighs, his tongue spearing me.

Not this time, Spitfire. It's all about you, he communicates to me without pausing his assault. White dots appear behind my eyes but I fist his hair harder, tearing him from me.

"Yeah no, I don't think so," I groan. Pyro shifts aside, giving me the space to shift out of Hoax's spot. A hidden smile lifts Hoax's mouth as he complies, laying on his back with his hand still caressing himself. It's not like there's an official roster or anything, but we seem to have a rotation going on that suits us just fine. Pyro and

Ghost stand, removing their clothes while I have a moment alone with Hoax.

"How's he doing?" I lean down to whisper in his ear, pressing a kiss to Hoax's cheek. There's no need to mention who, as we both know I'm referring to the Blacksmith. The Mute that Hoax has been sitting in the lab tracking day and night. It's surprisingly easy to track a man of metal; he shows up on all thermal cams still active.

"Still searching. I'll keep an eye on him and continue to hunt for word on Serpentina. If anyone is still active on the dark web, I'll find them." Hoax's purple eyes shine with sincerity.

"I know you will," I smile, brushing a hand over his chest. Hoax has been working overtime to prove his loyalty, to the point where the exhaustion is evident beneath his purple eyes. There's no use telling him he's doing enough, when ultimately it's Hoax who needs to forgive himself. Lifting my leg, I straddle his hips and lower myself directly onto his erection. Stretching me, I shift to accommodate his thick shift. Another demon trait I'm thankful for. It seems like Hoax was left with all the best attributes.

Hoax's hands lay on my hips, helping me to roll and pull him that bit deeper inside. I lean onto his chest, slowly lifting to put on a show for Ghost. The resulting groan makes me grin so I speed up, Hoax's traps creating the perfect handlebars. The mattress dips as Ghost shuffles in behind, his lube-coated fingers finding my ass again. You guessed it – another necessity.

Pyro appears at my side, standing for his dick to jut out at the right level. A bud of precum waits there, beckoning me to sit upright on Hoax and take him into my mouth. The smoothness of his shaft slides into my throat, coating my tongue with saltiness. I accept him greedily, licking everything Pyro has to offer and sucking out what he didn't think he was ready to give.

With Pyro's hand curling into my hair, Ghost's fingers inside my ass and Hoax rocking my hips back in forth, I come apart instantly. My vision blacks out, only the sensations racking through my body remain. Tremors squeeze Hoax's cock, pulsating and forcing his fingers to dig into my flesh. Ghost pumps his more vigorously, riding out my climax as my skin grows tight.

Releasing my suction on Pyro, I come back to the present as the dull thud of Ghost thumps at my back passage. He does it on purpose, tapping his plump head on my opening before pushing forward. My nails dig into Hoax's abs, scoring lines into his skin. Taking my hands in his, he sits up. Burying my face into Hoax's shoulder, he holds me, rocking his hips to give that small amount of relief needed while I adjust to Ghost's size.

Pyro sits on the edge of the bed, sending a flare of our fire to make me more comfortable. Just like the first time we ventured into anal alley, the three of them concentrate on my comfort above all else. A tear escapes my eye as Ghost seats himself fully and I release the breath I'd been holding. Then, they start to move. Hoax reclines, watching me with the hunger of a predator, his arms behind his head to allow Pyro some room.

Scooting closer, Py slides my hair out of the way to bite down on my neck. I sigh on a smile. I've developed quite the thing for biting since Hoax's fangs showed me pleasure to be found in pain. Taking on a life of my own, I ride Hoax, keeping in time with Ghost. My pussy throbs, Pyro spreading my legs wider to gain access to my clit. Rubbing in small circles, I whimper, ready to give them the satisfaction of making me come again so soon. But this time, I'm taking at least someone down with me.

One hand between my legs, Pyro's other rubs over each of my nipples on its way to my neck. He holds me in place with the effectiveness of a collar, only my lower body able to move. Bucking, jerking. Two dicks stretch and pull inside me with each thrust, Ghost taking over our movements. Gripping my waist, he lifts and slams me onto them both, a trio of groans penetrating the air. Sweat prickles at my chest, aided by my fire which Pyro is working into a frenzy.

The flame trickles lower, spiking in my core with the intensity of a fever. Each time the dicks within hit home, Pyro zaps me with a jolt of fire that seems to connect them. Like dripping wax directly onto my g-spot, I hold onto Pyro's arm for stability and break for him. For them all. Screaming, I clench down hard. Hoax's cock swells, his groans stifled by the fist he pushes between his teeth.

Riding out both of our endless orgasms, Ghost slows and Pyro remains close for me to slump onto him. Heavy breaths are all that sound within the room, my heart rate erratic. Scratching his neck and chest, Hoax pulls himself upright, the jolt of his dick making me gasp. My eyes pop open, Hoax's satisfied smirk waiting for me there. Wrapping his arms around me, Hoax gives Ghost long enough to pull out of me before moving to stand. I moan at each movement, wrapping my legs around Hoax as he carries me to the shower.

"I have to get back to work," he mutters, placing a kiss on my temple as my feet re-join the floor. The faucet is turned on and Hoax pulls himself free of me, washing up with lightning speed. Pyro's chest is at my back in an instant, reminding me this isn't over. Jabbing a finger in Hoax's chest, I give him my sternest, after-sex glare.

"One more hour, then you're coming to bed to sleep with the rest of us." Kissing me hard and fast on the lips, Hoax wraps a towel around his waist and exits, only to be replaced by Ghost holding a pair of nipple clamps.

"They'd look good on you," I snigger. Ghost's resulting smile is all mischief, yet the look in Ghost's white eyes makes my heart melt. Like I'm his entire world, his perfect girl and the missing piece of his soul, all wrapped into one.

"You owe me an explanation, by the way," I push a finger into his chest when he is close enough. Ghost quirks his brow, snipping the clamps in preparation to attack me with them. "You never did tell us how you escaped the basement with your manacle on." Pyro steps in behind, wrapping his arms around my breasts to both protect me and listen in.

"It's not my proudest moment," Ghost *blushes* and that's when I buckle in for the next words that spill from his lips. "You know when you sit on your legs long enough to get pins and needles, but then you really need to pee," he huffs and I twist away, clamping my hands over my ears. Nope, I'm good. Ghost dives into our mental connection instead, forcing me to listen to the rest of his story.

Imagine your lower half racked with tingles and then having the best pee-gasm of your life. Apparently that's my sweet trigger spot.

Pushing my forehead into Pyro's chest, I shout at Ghost to stop before he utterly ruins the moment. Pyro manages to save it though, working up a lather of shower gel in his hands, spreading it across my back and I melt against him.

Love blossoms in my heart, mirrored by all of those around me. Even Hoax as he makes his way back to the lab to witness more horrors. Turns out he was right in the end, I don't want to know what's happening outside of our bubble. In here, it's just the four of us, and dare I say I've earnt the right to be selfish. To be worshipped and adored. To give my men that and more in return. The world's not perfect but we've got each other and that's all we need.

Fingers shift into my hair, massaging my scalp. Stream envelopes us, the walk-in shower removing our need for sight. In here, all we rely on is touch and taste. Lips skate over my wet neck, those skillful hands teasing me into a frenzy. My body turns, enjoying the scolding spike of water cascading over my front. A sharp tug pinches at my nipples, causing me to gasp and jolt upright. Ghost's inked chest is just visible a few inches from my face, one hand lifting my thigh and the other shoving me back into Pyro's chest.

"There'll be time for sensuality later, Spitfire. We're not nearly done with you yet."

EPILOGUE

I used to be able to disappear into the wide web for hours. Days, even. But since…well, everything, I'm becoming a victim to the headaches. They're increasing each time, crippling my ability.

I must find Serpentina. I owe her that much, after I was prepared to kill her for merely existing. Christopher had been doing the same to all Mutes, yet I was blinded. By love, by some sense of loyalty to a world that never wanted us. Yet here we are, in the face of an apocalypse and the last wrong I can right has been lost without a trace.

So instead, I'm tracking the Blacksmith via his molten heat signature. Maybe he knows the best places to look. Maybe he's wandering around without a clue. Currently in the remains of a once-thriving city, the Blacksmith is navigating the empty streets. There's no life nearby, or the heat signatures would be pulsating red and orange. I've been tracking him for almost forty minutes this time, and with the pounding in my head, I won't be able to last much longer.

He stops to rest beside a building and internally, I groan. Withdrawing my consciousness from the heat camera, I do one last sweep of the city using a satellite image. The only fault in this plan would be that Serpentina is cold-blooded and wouldn't be easy to spot on the heat cams. Her body would reflect in blues and greens, much like the maps I've been staring at.

Sighing, I pull further back when something catches my eye. A ball of red light. I push my focus towards it, narrowing in on the ball that seems to be pulsating beneath the concrete surface. The closer I zoom in, the more I'm able to see it's not a ball, but a device. Wires surround it, and with a quick calculation I can see it's hidden beneath a post office. A bomb someone had planted before the interruption of mass genocide, only one street over from where the Blacksmith is currently resting.

Throwing myself back into the system, despite the paralyzing headache that's about to throw me out, I find the nearest electronic billboard. It's at the far end of the street from the Blacksmith so I flash a few times to capture his attention. Then, I use the last of my willpower to display one word. RUN. His heat signature straightens, a pause in his movements before he obeys.

Rushing down the street towards the billboard, I manage to display an arrow to the left, leading him away from the bomb. Within a minute, it's detonated. Colors burst to life, blinding me from the map's view. My head spins, a kaleidoscope twisting before me. My stomach rolls, my grip on the computer loosening. It's only when I see the signature of a man successfully running away from the blast that I allow myself to retract, and slump in my chair.

"Everything okay?" a soft voice asks. I can't manage the flinch that judders in my chest, peeking an eye at Tate in the seat beside me. She smiles weakly, offering me a steaming coffee I'm not able to take yet. Placing it on the desk, she pulls a thick cardigan around her, tugging at the ponytail of lilac hair that was caught in the collar.

Settling her eyes on the screen, she watches the live feed I'd left on. Hermitage home for boys. Being Mutes, none of the boys playing in the backyard were affected by the gas leaks. Watching them play eases me, but who knows how long they'll be safe behind their fence for. The humans that successfully turn into Mutes will want answers. Their abilities may be erratic, but that's a fight for another day.

"They seem happier than I remember ever being," I comment when I've recovered enough to lift my coffee. Tate's smile is still in place.

"Lorraine will have gone into hiding with the rest of the Gordon family after Christopher's disappearance. There are protocols for all eventualities. It appears Shadow has taken over the boy's care." Tate points and I narrow my eyes at the porch. The outline of a figure can just about be seen against the darkness.

"Shadow?" I ask. I've heard Pyro speak of him. He slinks back from view, disappearing into the house where no lights are on. Tate makes a noise in the back of her throat.

"He was a guard at Afterlife. A kid that didn't know what he was getting into really, but he soon found out. He was exposed to a premature leak of the mutant gas. Christopher thought he died, and Enzo worked hard to keep it that way. Instead, he slunk around in the Shadows, helping those where he could. Those boys are in good hands," Tate assures me.

I return her small smile and sip my coffee, allowing that weight to be lifted from my shoulders. One less worry I have to contend with. That just leaves a sea of others rising up, and the headache returns with a vengeance. People are depending on me. My harem is depending on me. Rubbing my temple, I try to breathe deeply until the tightening in my chest subsides. Mania's flame within me flares, soothing me for a while longer.

"I can't do this much longer," I admit into the silence, hanging my head. "But the thought of not being there if something should happen doesn't sit well with me." Tate's hand lowers onto my own, her body twisting in her seat.

"You can't save everyone, Hoax. The Blacksmith made his choice to leave without help. He didn't even give us the chance to join him."

"Would you have gone?" I raise my eyebrows. Tate's lilac eyes drift back to the screen, a small shrug at her shoulders.

"Maybe. I've been inside these facilities for far too long. Whether I'd have given up the peace we've found for the chance at a real adventure...it's difficult to say. But not all hope is lost. We will find her." Tate's gaze returns, filled with determination. I place down my cup and shift my hand out from under hers to run it through my hair.

"We?" I question, an unknown emotion constricting my throat.

"Yeah, we. You might be the one with access to the entire world, but we're not completely useless, you know." Tate reaches into her cardigan and withdraws a piece of folded paper. Unraveling it, she gives it to me to read through. Front and back, lists of words have been scrawled, separated by associated names, places, companies and suppliers. "It's all Claire, Enzo and I could remember, but we hoped it would help."

Nodding a thanks, my eyebrows pinch in concentration as I read through. Many of the names I'm aware of. All cooperations associated with Christopher ceased to exist prior to the release of the mutant gas, almost as if they didn't want to be tracked. I've mentally tracked all of the facilities, noting which ones still house Mutes and which have been abandoned. Many of the names come from sponsors of the Mute games and all of which are no longer alive. Except for one.

"Who's Victor Peroni?" I ask. Tate peers over at the name my finger is pointing to and shrugs.

"No idea, Claire had overhead his name once. Sounds like a gangster from the early nineties."

"Sounds like a lead to me," Mania responds from the doorway. Her brow is quirked over blood-red eyes, her hair wavy and damp from a recent shower. Wrapped in a bathrobe, she pads her way over to me on bare feet. "But not for tonight. You need to rest," she strokes a hand through my hair.

"I should investigate this quickly, just in case," I plead to her, scrunching the paper in my hand. Tate slips out of her chair and leaves us to it. Wrapping her arms around me from behind, Mania's cheek presses against mine.

"I can feel your pain and stress through our bond. If you overdo it and find yourself unable to use your ability for long stints, possibly forever, you'll only hate yourself more than you already do." I sigh, resting my head back on her shoulder.

"I fucked up, Angel. In so many ways."

"And once you take my hand and leave this lab, you're going to forgive yourself for all of it. I can't sleep sensing you down here, knowing you're struggling. We've fought our fight Hoax, it's time to start living."

Tipping my head further back, Mania kisses me. A soft promise from her lips that she'll always be here for me. A vow to love me while I'm unable to even tolerate myself.

Perhaps it is time I let go of the resentment I'm holding onto. At Christopher, and myself. I've been to hell and back, fought endlessly to be right here. In Mania's arms and her heart. Her love flows through my veins. Twisting the chair around, I pull Mania into my lap and deepen our kiss. With a sigh of contentment into her mouth, I release the piece of paper in my hand and slide it into her hair instead. My battle is over, and my prize is right here.

BONUS CHAPTER ONE

WHEN HARE-IETT MET GRANITE

Music sinks into my soul. The roll of my hips, the coolness of the pole against my overheated back. The Hare-iett who was struggling to cope has been left downstairs. Her inhibitions are hanging back at the asylum where she's imprisoned. The one out here, dancing on this stage for the audience watching on in awe, is thriving on the minimal escape she's been provided. This is where I'm comfortable. This is where I'm safe. Hidden in plain sight.

Siren's hand winds around my waist, spinning me slowly. She lowers, my hip rolling seamlessly onto her shoulder in a routine we're practiced for years. Settling myself into the spot between her shoulder blade and neck, my head hangs as Siren's hands splay across my upper back and I flip my legs upward, clamping my ankles on the pole. The tails of my waistcoat flip forwards, revealing the thong beneath that perfectly fits around my bunny tail. My bowler's hat slips and Siren catches it, popping it on her head.

We make it look easy. We've learnt to mask the pain.

The music smooths into the lead-up to the chorus, my hands smoothing down Siren's arms. Taking hold of her slender biceps, she times the drop of the beat perfectly. Kicking off the floor, her legs curl beneath her and I use the momentum to spin us both, upside down via my ankles. The crowd goes wild. Roaring over the beat of the music and reminding me they're still there. I become so involved in my movements, in forgetting there's a world beyond the stage, it's easy to forget.

The sound grows, drowning out the beat and I momentarily falter. Siren plants her feet down, returning the grip on my arms to lower me onto her. Our bodies roll together, still putting on a show for the strobe lights flashing over our sweat-slickened skin. A body vaults onto the stage, more muscle than man, a hand gripping my wrist with bone-crushing strength. I yelp, pulling back until a bald head covered in tattoos blocks out the spotlight, a pair of stone-gray eyes consuming me.

Holy wow.

My heart squeezes, making it hard to breathe, move or think. Not when he's looking at me with such interest, touching me with his calloused hand. I manage a heavy swallow, wondering if he's planning on joining the show. Instead, I'm whipped over a shoulder again, except this time I wasn't expecting it. My mouth opens on a rasped scream, my voice raw. I tend not to use it after leaving the dressing rooms, preferring my solace when performing.

The male jumps from the stage, my ass up in the air and hair swishing down past his ass. A rock-hard buttocks in black cargos that struggle to hold him. In fact, every part of him is in proportion, just larger. Harder. Girthier. My mind wanders to a dark and deprived place as a scream penetrates the air. Jerking upright, I use my hold on the male's waist to prop myself up.

The music cuts out, the lights brighten. The sound I'd mistook for cheering is revealed to be screaming. Humans flee in all directions, scrambling for the exits. A SWAT team storms the building, aiming their guns at every passerby in search for someone in particular. Their attention is caught by a couple at the bar, clinking champagne glasses together. Neither seems affected by the chaos taking place all around, too enthralled by their mini-celebration. Orders are barked from behind SWAT helmets for the pair to get on the ground. They don't respond, aside from the male with slickened-back hair who raises a tattooed middle finger in their direction. Apparently, that gives the SWAT team a reason to open fire.

I scream at the sound, dropping heavily over the male's back to cover my rabbit ears. A hand grips the back of my waistcoat, dragging me around until I'm being cradled in a pair of thick arms. Not once does he falter in his long strides. I don't look at where we're going, preferring to take comfort in the solid chest cushioning my cheek. Raising his foot, a door is booted inwards, then slammed closed behind his back. I'm finally set back on my feet, whether I was ready for the loss of his heat or not.

"W-who are you?" I breathe, holding onto a rounded booth for support. We're in one of the exclusive private rooms. Red drips from the wall, contrasting with the all-black furniture. The leather, circular booth is pushed against one side, facing the singular chair opposite that is reserved for lap dances. A black pole stands in between the two and in the glass case across the room, an array of sex toys is on full display. My stomach drops.

I've been in here before on the odd occasion a human with a rabbit fetish and thick-lined pockets has requested it, but I've never once gone beyond dancing. Is that what this male wants? For me to dance for him, or more than that? I stare at him with widened eyes, taking another step back to come flush with the booth.

"What do you want from me?" I ask, both nervous and partially excited for the answer. Losing myself into my performance is one thing, but dancing for a male that actually peeks my interest...that's a whole new game I'd like the chance to play.

"I'm not...sure," he admits. Confusion tenses his brows, the harsh cut of his jaw twitching. Pushing his hands back against the door that wobbles on its hinges, a wall of rock begins to appear. It seeps from his very skin. Rippling from his shoulders, through his muscles and along his forearms. The wall is cemented in place, preventing anyone from entering, or me from escaping. I should probably be worried about that aspect, but my pussy is already fluttering with possibilities.

"I saw you," he grunts out, stepping forward and then halting. His hand extends, then retracts and I leave the safety of the booth. He truly doesn't know what he's doing here. Closing the distance between us, I reach out and take the same hand that's now by his side.

"You saw me, and what?" I ask through my lashes. His stoney eyes grace my old English hunter's attire. A diamante waistcoat that only has one button beneath my bust, exposing the lacy bra and thong underneath. A bow tie sits at the base of my throat. On my legs, stockings stretch from cute ankle boots to the top of my thighs. It's not complete without the hat and crop, but still hot as hell if I do say so myself. The male releases my hand to take one of my loose chocolate curls in between his fingers.

"That's it. I just…saw you." His gray eyes hold my brown ones, a moment of lust and new territory being shared between two Mutes who haven't been properly introduced.

"I'm Hare-iett," I tell him, laying my palms flat on his chest.

"Granite," he responds, still seeming confused by his being here. His name, his own presence in general. His chest shifts beneath the cotton t-shirt, his heart thumping against my hand like a hammer.

"Well, Granite. Seems you've brought me here, locked me in. I don't get much time for recreational activity. So if you don't mind me being forward," I drift my hands lower and push the t-shirt up. His abs flex, tattooed with similar tribal designs to the ones on his scalp. He remains still, until I tug at his arms and force him to remove it. In all honesty, it doesn't take that much force.

Granite tosses his t-shirt, standing before me like a sculptured statue. I'm a great appreciator of art, but I'm also the kind of girl that seizes an opportunity when it arises. Popping the button of his cargos with clear intent, I slowly walk backward, undoing my own waist jacket. It slides down my shoulders, pooling at the floor. Next, I unhook my bra. Then goes my thong, until I'm naked and hanging from the central pole for support.

Circling it slowly, I give Granite a show of his own. After all, that's what enticed him to go all caveman on me in the first place. His instincts told him to take me, to barricade me in a room created for pleasure, so here I am. Rolling my hips in an invisible rhythm, my bunny tail bounces. My nipples are tight, my pussy becoming wet under the scrutiny of his hard gaze. On the surface, one would presume he doesn't care. But there's an underlying hunger, an unquenchable thirst I'm ready to fulfill.

When he doesn't move, I lean my back against the pole. Taking my nipples between my fingers, I twist them and moan. My head falls back, my eyes fluttering closed. This male can watch me bring myself to a climax if he wants, but I'll be damned if he sees me chasing him. Hot as sin, or not, if he wants me, he has to be willing to come the rest of the way.

My hair tickles my lower back, one of the hands puckering at my nipples traveling down south. Grazing my hip, my wrist is suddenly caught and wrenched back to be held at the pole with a large hand. I blink my eyes open, spotting Granite on his knees before me.

Oh my.

He captures my other hand to pin that one behind me too and throws my thigh over his shoulder. Without warning, Granite *feasts* on me like a man starved. My back arches off the pole, a guttural groan being pulled from my lips. His tongue is everywhere, lapping at my pussy. The rough pad scrapes over my clit before he begins to suck hard. Keeping me pinned in place with one hand, his other grips my ass until I'm sure the bruises will be permanent. All I can do is pray to the ceiling this never ends and rock my hips in encouragement.

Shifting his hand, two lengthy digits enter my slick channel. I shatter instantly, coming over Granite's fingers. He curls them and remains fixed in place, applying pressure to my G-spot. I cry out, my body no longer my own. In this moment, it's his to do with as he pleases. His assault on my clit continues, alternating between licking and sucking. I can't wait to be sore for him tomorrow.

Once my screams and the stars behind my lids have subsided, Granite removes his fingers and lifts me in one, smooth movement. My legs wrapped around his waist, and it's only then I realize, he's completely naked. His cargos are discarded on the floor behind him, the thud of his blunt head bopping against my ass.

Standing tall and without unwavering, Granite holds my stare and lowers me onto his cock. I gasp at the sheer size stretching me. Squeezing my eyes closed, he lifts me up again and waits. I wait too, for my impending impairment, but it doesn't come. Cracking an eyelid, his gray eyes ask for my entire focus, before lowering me down again. This time, I don't shy away. His hands hold my ass mid-air as if I'm weightless, his dick sliding into me deeper and deeper. I whimper, biting down on my bottom lip until finally, with a little wriggling, he's fully seated.

"Fuck me Granite," I beg, unable to hold off any longer. The fullness of him nestled inside me and the painstaking slowness of his stoic actions are driving me insane.

He bucks. I scream. The hint of a smirk lifts the corner of his mouth, then it's game on. Granite's hips move with a ferocious speed, his cock slamming into me with equal force. The room is filled by the sound of his balls smacking against my ass, while all I can do is hold on to his thickly-corded neck. And even still, those eyes pierce me, drinking in my soft sobs without a hint of regret. In fact, I'd say he's fascinated.

My core tightens, my nails piercing his skin. I'm bordering another climax, preparing to tear myself apart and let this stranger piece me back together. He can use me as his puppet, pull my strings. All ideas of being a strong, independent woman vanished the moment he entered me. I'm ready to throw my inhibitions away and let this man ruin me. Dropping my head onto his shoulder, I pant his name. On a grunt, Granite whips out of me and I honest-to-fuck cry out in desperation.

Walking me to the booth, I'm tossed around and planted on my feet. My boots dig into the leather, my chest pushed against the backrest. Granite spreads my legs, the seat providing me with enough raised height for him to stand behind and re-enter me in one slick thrust.

"Holy shit!" I cry out, gripping the back of the booth. Granite's hand wraps around my throat, holding me in position and seemingly punishing me for something. Fuck knows what, and I'm not that mad about it.

Pounding into me, over and over, his grunts are drowned out by my own hindered screams. The grip on my neck is too tight, my breathing coming in short pants. As a wave of dizziness washes through me, my head lolls. All that anchors me is the male battering my g-spot and stretching me beyond repair. His free hand dips between my legs, and if I'd thought he was going to show any relief from his harsh movements, I'm sorely mistaken.

Granite doesn't seem to do soft.

Gripping my pussy around his shaft, the heel of his palm pushes against my clit. He holds me tight around him, leaving no room for my cum to escape from as I detonate for him again. Blinded by the sensation, dizzy from the lack of oxygen, I'm unaware of the guttural sounds leaving my restricted throat. My core twists tighter than ever before, a rush of waves fluttering through my inner channel.

My head drops onto the coolness of the leather and my legs give out. Slumping into a mess of limbs over the back of the booth, Granite pounds every last drop of cum I'm able to give him and then some. With nowhere for it to go, I feel the slickness of his hand sliding against me. His hand at my throat suddenly withdraws at the same time as his dick, and his fingers are straight in me. No warning, no reprieve. He draws the cum from my body and moves his fingers to my back passage, just beneath my bunny's tail.

No one has ever gone there before.

I slide further down the backrest, until I've pooled myself onto the seat with my ass high in the air. There's no fighting it. My desire for this man has surpassed my self-control. I want it all, everything he's willing to do to me. Give him everything he's willing to take. His fingers pressed against my anus, causing a hitch in my breathing. But instead, my hair is grabbed and I'm dragged up into a seated position. Those cum-covered fingers are shoved into my mouth.

"Clean them," Granite rasps. His tone is no different from when he announced his name, but the tension in his jaw is more pronounced. Good to know I'm having some sort of effect on him. Sucking his fingers clean, as instructed, his teeth sink into his bottom lip.

Still holding me up by my hair, because I'd collapse otherwise, the fingers are quickly replaced by his cock. For a brief second, I saw the thickness of it and my eyes widen. Granite pushes himself all the way to the back of my throat and holds himself there. My air supply is cut off, tears streaming from my eyes before he finally releases me. Only to do it again.

His own saltiness mixed with the evidence of my climax coats his smooth shaft. I grip his balls, twisting them in my hand whilst clawing at the inside of his rock-hard thigh. Two can play this game. The harder I squeeze his balls and scratch angry red lines into his legs and abdomen, the harder Granite thrusts into my mouth. My throat burns, and I scrunch my eyes shut.

"Look. At. Me." Granite grinds out, tugging my hair back further to open me up to him. My eyes settle upon his face just as he explodes down the back of my throat, holding my eye contact the entire time. Stone gray irises, dilated pupils. An intense stare that solidifies this moment in time. A cry is held back behind his closed, full lips, but the grumble resounds from his chest away. Muscles ripple and I consider too late if this Mute could accidentally pump me full of concrete.

Withdrawing from me, Granite stands there another moment before turning in search of his pants. His plump, purple head glistens as he tugs up his cargos, the tip of his dick poking out from his waistband. Retrieving my clothes, he returns and with surprising gentleness, cleans me with his t-shirt. The thong is pulled up my long legs, the bra reclasped at my back. Granite dresses me slowly, reluctantly. Up until he lifts the waistcoat back onto my shoulder and pauses to run a hand over my floppy rabbit's ear.

"Kiss me," I breathe softly. His eyes shift to mine, a trace of panic in their stoney depths. When he doesn't move, I shuffle to the edge of the seat and lay my arms over his shoulders. "You don't get to do me like that, and not even kiss me."

Without giving him a choice, I plant my lips on his. He doesn't react, but I don't give in either. Moving my mouth over his, I lick his full bottom lip from corner to corner, and then repeat the process on the top. Pushing my mouth against his again, I get a twitch of response. Then a jerk. My hands scrape over his bald scalp, drawing a groan from him. Planting one last peck on his mouth, I pull back with a smile.

"We'll work on it," I promise him. It doesn't take a genius to figure out Granite is well versed in fucking, but the sensual, softer touches – not so much.

Buttoning my waistcoat, I use his shoulders to push myself up onto shaky legs. My boots are still in place, the bottoms of my feet aching for a soak. Sauntering my hips, I make my way to the wall blocking the door and lightly knock my knuckles against it. Granite stands, tugging his t-shirt into his waistband to cover his dick, and recalls the rocks into his body. I swear his muscles grow before my eyes, rippling as the rock settles beneath his inked skin.

As if someone has been listening or trying to get in for a while, the doors bursts open. Camo stands there, a strand of his green hair falling out of place. The fury on his face subsides as he glances over my disheveled hair, and towards Granite.

"Ahh, Hare-iett, I've been looking for you," Camo rightens his posture and smooths his hair back. "You weren't on the register for our lockdown procedure and I'd started to fear the worst. I should have known my best girl was showing our newest employee the ropes."

"Employee?" I frown, looking over my shoulder to Granite. It never occurred to me to ask why a Mute I wasn't familiar with was at Camo's club, but to be fair, I haven't done much thinking since I entered this room. Base instinct took over instead.

"That's right," Camo nods. "Meet Granite, he's going to be our newest main attraction." Camo's hand extends to me and I take it, being pulled into the hallway and towards the dressing rooms.

I hear the buzz of whispers from the females we pass on the way, and note the lack of SWAT team in the main area of the club. None of that really holds my attention though. Not as much as the male keeping close to my back, and the sting of jealousy at the thought he'll be on stage for human women to gawk at. I'm not naïve or desperate enough to think one fuck entitles me to a claim over Granite, but this feels like more than that.

Instinctual, primal. The connection I feel to Granite is a living entity I plan on investigating. One way or another, I'm going to make that man mine.

BONUS CHAPTER TWO

WHEN GOLDIE MET HER BEARS

I despise porridge.

The bland taste. The lumpy texture. The way it sticks to the back of my throat, followed by the burnt aftertaste that accompanies it every time I'm forced to vomit.

Yet without it, I'd be dead by now. Left to rot in my own feces with only the regurgitation to keep me going. I don't know why I bother. Bringing myself back, only to continue suffering. Hell would be a better alternative to this.

The sound of keys jingling echoes through the hallways beyond my cell. It won't be for me. It never is. I haven't spoken to another person in so long, I'm not sure I still can. But I won't be caught screaming and pounding on the doors like others in the facility. They can keep me contained, tear out my humanity, but they won't have my soul. They won't hear me beg or cry.

Creaking pierces the air, the unused hinges of my door protesting as a beam of light spears my cell. I squint, turning away from the light and the shadows that hinder it. Hands grab me, dragging me off the floor when my legs won't respond. The tops of my feet drag through the mess I've made, scraping over the rough stone of the hallway. I manage to pry my eyes open as we turn the corner, leading into the shower block. Tossing me onto the floor, a spray of freezing cold water beats down on my back.

I grit my teeth. Clench my jaw and take the icy burn hammering down onto my frail limbs. The yellow hair around my face becomes heavy, obscuring the view of bare feet padding towards me.

Stopping just before my face, the owner bends to sweep back my hair and I'm presented with a gigantic cock inches from my face. Jerking back, the harsh movement draws a groan from my lips. Fingers curl around my cheek, lifting my gaze to a pair of endless, black eyes. A waterfall of inky black hair tumbles forward and I resist the urge to test if it feels as silky as it appears.

Arms ease beneath my body, lifting me slowly as the water bleeds warm. Twisting my head, I see two more of them. One holding me, the other just out of view while he tampers with the showerhead to ease the harshness of the spray. Like the first, both are completely naked.

I may not have surfaced from my room in…fuck knows how long, but the last time I was permitted to shower, the one-gender rule applied. Out of fear we might jump each other's bones and breed before the guards could tear us apart. Nothing happens in Underlife without Dr. Gordon's permission, and unplanned pregnancies are his biggest pet peeve. If we're not carefully engineered by him, we're abominations.

Refusing to be held like a meek submissive, I shove away from the male's hairy chest. His eyes are the same, swirling pits of dark beneath furrowed brows at my action. Setting me down, the three of them close in around me. My heart picks up a beat. Is this a test? Or have the guards been paid off to look the other way while I become a victim of gang rape?

Large hands press against my back and I suck in a breath. My eyes close. No screaming, no begging. Biting down on my lower lip, I prepare myself for when the hands begin to move. Except they don't drift down to my ass, or force me to bend over. They maneuver my muscles, massaging the kinks from my shoulders through a layer of suds. Blinking upwards, the male in front of me accepts the bar of beeswax and works it over my skin. Across my collar, down the valley between my breast to my stomach. I suck in a breath, watching him watch me.

Brown hair trickles from his scalp to his shoulders. Dark, due to the water's spray, but hints of honey amongst the dry strands hint to its natural color. Muscles ripple across the expanse of his body, solid pecks into washboard abs, the defined V of his groin leading to...

My head snaps back up as his dick jolts. A blush flares at my cheeks. Not that I'm shy in any way, but going from solitary confinement to a steamy shower, in many senses, has me feeling weak in the knees. Maybe that's the point. To catch me off guard, but at this point, I really don't care. Handing the bar to the next, the male works the soap into my body. Deft fingers smoothing over my torso with just enough pressure. Gently gripping my hips, he turns me to face the last of them and I gasp.

His eyes and height match the others, but I can't stop staring at his stark white hair. Giving into my urge this time, I reach up to test it between my wet fingers. His jaw, cut from stone, twitches and I quickly retreat. Working up the bubbles in his huge hands, he tosses the bar aside and plants his palms on my breasts. Rubbing, kneading. He works me into a frenzy without paying my nipples any special attention, but the contact is all I need.

Ripping the shower head from the wall and shielding me from the concrete that rains down, the male with black hair at my back washes off all evidence of soap. Then passes it to the one with white hair to do my front while Honey Locks focuses on my hair. I smell the shampoo before I feel it, seeping into my scalp with the accompaniment of skilled fingers. Another groan escapes me. If this is a test, then sign me up.

Keeping my lip beneath my teeth, I let go of my inhibitions. If Dr Gordon hadn't wanted these men here, they wouldn't be. Maybe it's my time to reproduce the next mutant spawn, and the way these hands are smoothing over my skin, I couldn't resist whether I wanted to or not.

After spending an age on my hair, the shower is switched off and I sigh. Back to reality, and my cell, I suppose. A fluffy towel is produced and wrapped around my middle. I stand awkwardly, but the males take my hands and tug me along. Out of the shower block via the exit at the far end where there aren't any guards. The end that takes us back to the main facility. Tensing, I refuse to believe I'm being returned until the metal gate is opened for us and as a four, we enter the lobby.

Cheers erupt from those who spot me first and I quickly whip my hands out of the male's boxing me in. Greeting my fellow Mutes with a wide grin, I'm enveloped in a mass of group hugs. Damn, it must have been really long this time. I wouldn't consider myself a very personable Mute. Alright – I'm a bitch on the best of days. But a large group of us here grew up together. Reared from the test tubes we were created in.

"Good to have you back, Goldie!" a female my height with a shiny, hairless head slaps me on the back. One of the male's I entered with growls audibly. "Things were really starting to crumble around here without you," Alo winks. Having alopecia is only part of her ability. With one touch, Alo can cause the hair to fall off anyone's body. I should know, she's given me the full works from neck down on a weekly basis since I hit puberty. As long as I don't piss her off, I don't need to worry about waking up one day with my luscious locks decorating my pillow.

"Yeah, right," I scoff. "You just miss the entertainment when I'm dragged away by the guards." We share a snigger, bumping shoulders and ignoring the males hovering over me like a shadow. Adjusting my towel, I sit on a canteen table and pick at some cheesy fries that have been wasted. Oh good god, *real food*.

"I don't think we need to worry about lacking entertainment anymore," she chuckles, eyeing the males with glorious hair. When I ask further, Alo merely points to my room on the seventh floor. All the way up the top and great for the calves. Peering up, I spot Dr. Gordon leaning on the railing outside my room.

"Better see what he wants," I quirk a brow. Leaving my fan base behind, I ascend the stairs, surprised when the three males automatically follow. Every time I stop, they stop. By the time I've reached the fourth floor, I lean on the railing for a break. I'd forgotten how much of a ball ache trekking these stairs could be after my calves have lost their muscle memory.

Honey Locks scoops me up, carrying me the rest of the way and I can't find it in me to protest. Not until I see Dr. Gordon looking at me with the smuggest smile and I force him to put me down for the last three steps.

"I've never known anyone to go into confinement and put *on* weight," the Dr. chuckles and I cross my arms over the towel at my breasts. I mean, Porridge isn't the best diet and it's not like I'm one of those steroid freaks that spends all their time working out. Popping my hip, I give the Doc a flat glare.

"And I've never known an old man who refuses to opt for a skincare routine, even when he knows his acne stage will be back soon enough." A moment of tense silence is broken by the Dr's gavelled laughter. He taps me on the shoulder and guides me into my room.

Call it Stockholm Syndrome or whatever those books in the library say, I can't help the relationship that's formed between the doc and I.

Aside from the string of nurses and scientists that pop in to take my blood or counsel me after I've lashed out, he's the only consistent adult I've ever known. A father figure, if I'm being honest with myself. We can't pick our parents and sure, I've heard rumors about what he does in his other facilities, yet he's never needed to force me into anything. I talk a big game but resisting the experiments when my name is called suicide. Even I'm not that stupid.

Opening my door, I stop short. The single room I left behind has been tripled in size, the walls knocked through to the rooms either side. A kingsize bed is propped against the back wall, beside a double wood wardrobe. The door is open, revealing a range of men's clothing between mine on the hangers. Canvas shoes from tiny to giant sit in the base. Stepping inside, I spy the extended bathroom with a giant tub, walk-in shower and four toothbrushes on the counter.

"What's...all this in aid of?" I spin to ask the Doc. The males hang back on the platform, standing side by side with the exact same placid expression.

"Your honeymoon suite," Doc announces and my stomach drops. My...what?! Ten minutes ago, I was all for these males taking what they wanted from my body, but honeymoon implies...I'm stuck with them for good.

Sucking in a hitched breath, I focus on exhaling deeply. Calming the erratic voice in my head that wants to send me directly into a panic attack. My rules are all that's kept me sane. I won't lose them now, no matter how much the doc tries to bate me. I'm sure he prefers when I'm misbehaving. It provides him with more entertainment, I suppose.

"What happened to the wedding?" I ask, trying to cover the pounding of my heart. I swallow thickly, avoiding the three black stares peering through my doorway.

"I didn't think you were the flamboyant type," the Doc shrugs. "We can always throw a ceremony, if you'd like. I do enjoy a good party and it'd be an Underlife first." I laugh bitterly, presuming he's joking.

"So...you've given me not one, but three males, to what? Co-habit with?" I drop down onto the edge of the bed before my legs give out. My breathing is short, my head beginning to spin.

"Do whatever you like with them, my dear. My Goldilocks needs her bears." I bristle at the nickname. The fairy-tale that's haunted my life and defined me since I was a baby. While others struggled with croup and jaundice, I was throwing up porridge non-stop until an extra valve was inserted in my throat to cover my larynx. Now I can vomit on demand, not that I take much pride in doing so.

Dr. Gordon begins to leave when I push to my feet and grip the towel when it almost falls free.

"Why?" I ask and he pauses in the doorway.

"Trial run," he shrugs.

"I'm gonna need more than that," I purse my lips.

"You'll get whatever I give you." Dr. Gordon snaps, quickly

reminding me who's in charge here. His face softens in a second and he reaches out a hand that I accept. "But to ease your curiosity. There's a harem forming in one of my other facilities. A dynamic I'm unfamiliar with, so consider yourself lucky. You've been presented with three males, manufactured to adore you. There's worse fates to suffer here than the gift of love."

Leading me into the bears, they each wrap one arm around me as the doc takes his leave. I stand still, my flesh coming alive beneath their touch but my thoughts are racing. As a result of being punished, I've now been given three men. Will they fall at my feet, do as I say and abide by whatever rules I set in place. Or maybe I'm still being punished, and the challenge itself is keeping them all happy. After all they're been made for me. Hang on, wait just one minute...

"What do you mean manufactured?!" I jump forward and shout over the railing. Dr. Gordon smiles up and me and gives one of his signature winks. The one that says 'good luck'.

AUTHOR NOTE

Well, that's it folks – the end of the crazy ride that was Mania's turbulent time at Afterlife Asylum! Thank you for reading the All My Pretty Psychos Series. This series took me on a journey of its own and it nothing like the plot I originally planned. The characters took on a life of their own!

I hope you've enjoyed discovering the cruel world of Mutants and found solace in the glimpse of happiness Mania managed to carve out for herself.

ACKNOWLEDGEMENTS

There are so many people who boost me on a daily basis, picking me up and giving me strength to continue when the words seem to evade me.

LUCY ELIZABETH – In every book I write, there is a stand out person who makes themselves available to me night and day. For Reign of Chaos – you were that person for me. From BETA reading to brainstorming, you are the reason I was able to see this story through to the end. Thank you for always being there for me, listening to me moan and whinge, and for your continued love and support. You're every author's dream and I feel honoured to have you as both a reader and a friend.

SAM - You have been there for me for as long as I can remember, supporting me and loving my books. Now, not only are you my PA, but also my editor. You make my books better and I can't thank you enough for that.

EMMA - Thank you so much for squeezing me in and making my book look as gorgeous as all the others. I'm so grateful for your love and support!

MR COLE AND MY GORGEOUS CHILDREN - thank you for being so patient with me while I write, and for supporting me in this crazy journey. I get to do what I love most in the world because of your support.

TO MY AMAZING READERS - thank you for loving my books and for devouring my words. You have stuck by this series to the end, and I hope I did it justice for you. You are the reasons I can keep doing what I love, and I'm forever grateful for that. I can't wait for you to see what I have to come!

EAGER FOR MORE CRAZY?

If you haven't read any other series' by me yet, you have to put My Tweedles on your TBR! This deranged retelling of Malice in Wonderlust, twenty years on, is taking on a crazy life of its own, and you do not want to miss out on the fun! Check out the details below. Bye for now my literary lovers.

MY TWEEDLES
Book One from A Wonderlust Adventure
By Maddison Cole

We all know of the fairy-tale,
We thought we knew the end,
But 20 years have come to pass
And Malice's gone around the bend.

Safe inside her padded cell,
Her arms strapped up real tight,
Only the spiders come to call
And ask if she's alright.

Yet through her haze of anti-psychotics
And trauma-induced cackle,
A pair of boys she'd never forgotten
Return to break her shackles.

So if you really want to know the end
Then you'd better come inside,
To learn what happened to the delusional girl
Who wish she could have died.

Trigger Warning: *Unlike the original, all characters in this spin-off retelling are very much adult. Expect steamy scenes, exaggerated episodes, ridiculous rhymes, and apparently, alluring alliteration throughout.*

PRE-ORDER MY TWEEDLE BOYS NOW:
https://amzn.to/3wRIqVd

ABOUT MADDISON

Maddison is a married mum of two, and a serial daydreamer. As a huge fan of all romance tropes herself, it was time to pen the stories which consume her mind most hours of the day.

As a child, Maddison was a jet setter and has lived all over the world, only to return to the south east of England, where she is now happily settled. With a double award in applied arts and art history, Maddison is a creative with a dark passion for feisty females and spicy stories.

If you're a new reader to me – welcome to the mad house! Keep reading for my list of writes, and for up-to-date info, make sure you follow my socials! The reader's group is the best place for reveals, announcements, giveaways and more, and please never hesitate to reach out! I love hearing from readers.

Sign up to my newsletter here:
http://eepurl.com/hx3Zqr

Also, make sure to join my Facebook readers group, Cole's Reading Moles here:
www.facebook.com/colesreadingmoles

facebook.com/maddison.cole.314
instagram.com/maddison_cole_author
amazon.com/author/B086ZQ6SW4
bookbub.com/authors/maddison-cole
tiktok.com/@authormaddisoncole

ALL MY PRETTY PSYCHOS

Paranormal RH with ghosts and demons

Queen of Crazy

https://amzn.to/3O4biQt

Kings of Madness

https://amzn.to/3HzvBCY

Hoax: The Untold Story (novella)

https://amzn.to/3xAJhcA

Reign of Chaos

https://amzn.to/3b95PcI

I LOVE CANDY

Dark Humor RH - Completed

Findin' Candy (novella)

https://amzn.to/3bcueOp

Crushin' Candy

https://amzn.to/3n0TASf

Smashin' Candy

https://amzn.to/3Oniuai

Friggin' Candy

https://amzn.to/3QwlmUb

Candy - The Complete Collection

https://amzn.to/3LvatBu

.

THE WAR AT WAVERSEA

Basketball College MFM Menage - Completed

Perfectly Powerless

https://amzn.to/3OqHTQp

Handsomely Heartless

https://amzn.to/3tMoRfu

Beautifully Boundless

https://amzn.to/3MYiiNG

WILLOWMEAD ACADEMY (CO-WRITTEN WITH EMMA LUNA)

Sexy Student - Teacher Taboo Age Gap Standalone

Life Lessons

https://amzn.to/3tL8eAX

·

A VOODOO'S HAREM

A Halloween Horror Harem

https://amzn.to/3f5xw8F

·

VICES AND HEDONISM SHARED WORLD

A Reverse Harem MMA Romance

A Night of Pleasure and Wrath

https://amzn.to/3Rgg0fC